A LONELY
HEART

Kay Brellend

piatkus

PIATKUS

First published in Great Britain in 2018 by Piatkus
This paperback edition published in 2019 by Piatkus

1 3 5 7 9 10 8 6 4 2

A CIP catalogue record for this book
is available from the British Library.

ISBN 978-0-349-41529-1

Typeset in Palatino by M Rules
Printed and bound in Great Britain by
Clays Ltd, Elcograf S.p.A.

Papers used by Piatkus are from well-managed forests
and other responsible sources.

Piatkus
An imprint of
Little, Brown Book Group
Carmelite House
50 Victoria Embankment
London EC4Y 0DZ

An Hachette UK Company
www.hachette.co.uk

www.littlebrown.co.uk

For Nan and Granddad Kelly: I wish I'd known you.

Also for the men and women who dedicated
themselves to the Voluntary Aid Detachment, serving
at home and abroad during the Great War.

Chapter One

May 1915

The women who'd been on shift at Barratt's sweet factory since eight o'clock in the morning were usually quick off the mark about heading home once the evening bell sounded. But on this particular rainy day in May about a score of them were still loitering by the gate, giving raucous advice to two of their workmates who were rolling about on the wet cobbles intent on battering each other. Word had got round about a catfight after work so the jeering crowd had been ready and waiting outside.

Olivia Bone was one of those who usually sped away to catch the bus home. She lived some distance from the Wood Green factory and liked to get back to Islington for tea with her young brother. But she too had been curious enough to stop and see who was daft enough to brawl over a man.

She bobbed about on the fringes of the group, hoping for a peek at the action, then cursed beneath her breath as she glimpsed straggling, brassy blonde hair gripped in somebody's fist. Then she recognised a voice. Olivia was exasperated, but not surprised. Should have known *she'd* be in on it. With a resigned sigh, she elbowed her way through the onlookers and grabbed at one of the two women rolling about on the cobbles.

'What in God's name d'you think you're playing at?' Olivia yelled at her cousin. By now Ruby Wright had hold of a hank of her opponent's dark hair and was busy delivering a slap to Cath Mason's face.

'I didn't start it! Anyhow, ain't none of your business,' Ruby spat over her shoulder. 'So you can sling yer hook.'

Olivia dragged her away, whacking aside her cousin's hands as she tried to set about Cath again.

'Cath's me friend, you know that,' Olivia bawled, giving Ruby a shake. 'What the hell's this all about?'

'That bitch is after my Trevor,' Cath panted, dragging herself to her knees. Her face was bleeding and striped down one of her cheeks by Ruby's clawed fingernails.

'Got me own bloke – don't need yours, thanks all the same,' Ruby sneered. She swooped on a small fancy hat lying in the gutter and slapped it back on her tangled blonde locks.

'I heard one bloke ain't enough for you, Ruby Wright,' a spectator called, setting the crowd sniggering. ''Specially if he can't pay fer it.'

'Yeah … and I heard that your old man's hanging about down Finsbury Park every payday.' Ruby smirked right back at the woman who'd insulted her. 'Being as it's Friday, you should hurry off home and get his wages before a tart takes 'em instead.'

'Well, you'd know where the tarts hang out, wouldn't yer? Being as you're on the game,' the other woman retaliated, but a moment later she'd slunk off.

Somebody hissed a warning then. 'Miss Wallis is on her way!'

The news that the directors' secretary was coming out of the building caused the rest of the women to scatter. The management wouldn't take lightly the matter of two Barratt's employees making a spectacle of themselves, fighting outside the factory. Mr Barratt was a respectable fellow who set high moral standards and expected them to be upheld by his staff.

'Keep to yer regular clients or you'll have more o' the same,' Cath snarled at Ruby, dragging herself to her feet with Olivia's help. She caught the heel of her boot in the hem of her long serge skirt and cursed as the material ripped.

Ruby tittered on seeing that. She knew she had nothing to fear from Cath's threat. She'd easily been the victor in their scrap; considering she lived in the roughest street in North London, it wasn't surprising she could look after herself. Flicking two fingers at her opponent, she sashayed off while still dusting herself down.

Miss Wallis drew closer to them, the expensive material of her skirt swishing about her polished boots. No rough factory clothing for her. She could have been a society wife in her elegant, fitted suit. Olivia covered up her friend's dishevelment by giving Cath a lengthy goodnight hug. The secretary was a snooty sort. If she could rat on them she would, just to impress on them her senior position. Olivia and Cath chorused a mumbled goodnight to the woman then, once the coast was clear, Cath elbowed herself out of her friend's embrace.

'It's your fault!' she rounded on Olivia.

'I beg your pardon?' Olivia exclaimed in disbelief. 'What's it to do with me?'

'Ruby Wright's your bleedin' family, and you got her a job here. The cow would never have met my Trevor but for that.'

'I did *not* get her a job! She applied for it herself. And even if I did, I still don't see how I'm to blame.'

Following a sullen silence, Cath said, 'Sorry, Livvie.' She sighed. 'Just ... it's all getting on top of me, what with Trevor getting injured and turning funny.' She started to cry softly. 'I know it sounds daft but I wish he'd never got a Blighty one and was still over there fighting alongside his pals.'

Olivia was surprised to hear her friend felt that way. All wounded soldiers wanted a Blighty one – an injury that was severe enough to bring them home to convalesce. Their loved ones usually yearned for them to come home too. But Cath had more to contend with than most. Her fiancé had suffered mental as well as physical injury while battling on the Western Front.

'Now he's home he's just a pain in the backside, and I can't see an end to it neither.' Cath's voice sounded croaky with held-back tears.

Olivia put an arm round her. 'I know it's tough. This bloody war is getting to all of us.'

'Sometimes I wish he wasn't me fiancé. Sometimes I wish another woman *would* take him off me hands 'cos I can't cope with him.' Cath used the cuff of her blouse to wipe her face. 'I know I shouldn't be feeling sorry for meself, considering what you've been through.'

Olivia patted her friend's shoulder to quieten her. She didn't want to talk about *that* or it'd set her off crying too.

Her fiancé had been killed in action in Flanders and at times the memory of losing Joe crowded in on her, making her feel that she was suffocating. There had been

4

mornings when she'd wanted only to burrow back beneath the blankets because the effort of dragging herself off to work seemed too much. But knowing there were so many others who were far worse off than she was had helped her to roll out of bed and get dressed. War widows with broods of children to rear alone had to face each day with a courage that Olivia doubted she'd be capable of finding. Every woman with a loved one fighting the Hun as a private soldier was terrified of receiving a printed form through the post that began, 'We deeply regret to inform you . . . ' and ended 'Lord Kitchener sends his sympathy'. By the time her official notification arrived she already knew Joe had been killed because his commanding officer had paid her a personal visit, bringing back some cherished mementoes.

Lucas Black . . . the officer's name ran through her mind smooth as honey, bringing reminders of his polished manners and raven-haired good looks. Only he hadn't looked quite so dapper the last time she'd seen him. Less than a year ago Lucas had been a director of Barratt's sweet factory, but when he came back from France on an icy day in January to tell her the dreadful news about Joe, she had not at first recognised the gaunt-faced man on her doorstep.

She'd not had a letter from him for a while. She hoped he was keeping as safe and well as could be expected for an army lieutenant serving at Ypres. Shaking off memories of him, she turned her mind to the battles closer to home.

'Did you and Ruby have a fight because she was flirting with Trevor at the dance on Saturday?'

Cath nodded, dabbing her bloodied face with her hanky. 'It was as much him sniffing around her,' she mumbled. 'I don't know what the bloody hell's up with him since he got back.' She sounded frustrated. 'It's as if he's deliberately out to upset me all the time.'

'You *do* know what's up with him, Cath,' Olivia said quietly. 'He's taken a nasty head wound. You can't expect him to be right as ninepence just yet, can you?'

Cath scrunched her hanky into a ball. 'Doctor reckons he's acting weird 'cos he's got shellshock,' she finally said. 'Don't know much about it really 'cos he takes his mother with him when he goes to the hospital, not me. The old cow said I haven't got a clue how to look after him.' She grimaced. 'She did tell me the doctor said we've all got to be patient 'cos it could take a while for his mind to heal … if it ever does heal, that is. Doctor said he couldn't be sure it would.' Cath bit her bottom lip. 'But it bloody well better! How we gonna get married and get our own place otherwise? We can't pay rent if he's too nutty to bring in a wage.'

'Give the bloke a chance,' Olivia said bluntly. 'He's only been home a month. You can't expect miracles to happen.' She thought for a moment and added, 'Why don't you put his mother in her place by doing a bit of swotting up? If you find out more about it all you might be able to help Trevor.' She nudged Cath's arm for encouragement. 'You know what men are like about their health: they won't even take a dose of cod liver oil unless you nag the life out of 'em.'

'Might just do that, y'know.' Cath smiled at her. 'Miss Wallis is arranging another lot of St John Ambulance courses. Perhaps I'll put me name down. And in the meantime I ain't going out to no more dances with him.'

'Probably wisest,' Olivia observed wryly.

A dance had been arranged for the convalescing servicemen at the Wood Green Empire and a party of the women from Barratt's had gone along to show support. Olivia had been saddened to see Trevor, in his hospital blues, acting oddly. He'd always seemed an unassuming man, devoted to Cath. Yet at the dance he'd been loud-mouthed and playing up to Ruby's flirtation even though his fiancée was by his side. Cath had been embarrassed to see him making a fool of himself in front of her work colleagues. As for Ruby ... the more attention she drew, good or bad, the better she liked it.

'Come on, let's get going,' Olivia said as the misty drizzle turned into a proper shower. She pulled up her coat collar, and lowered her head as they set off arm-in-arm.

When they were approaching the bus stop Olivia muttered a curse. Her cousin was already there. Ruby lived just round the corner from her in Islington, in a slum nicknamed 'the Bunk' in recognition of the number of doss houses and villains using boltholes in the road. Olivia had been surprised when Ruby was taken on at Barratt's, given that she lived at such a disreputable address. But standards had been lowered. The factory had been virtually emptied of men of fighting age. Now the management were desperate for staff. Vacancies were being filled by older people and youngsters who looked barely old enough to quit school. Olivia glanced at Cath to judge how she might take bumping into her rival again but it seemed the fight had gone out of her.

'I'm fetching Mum in some groceries so I'll head off down the High Street.' Cath sent a last contemptuous glance Ruby's way. 'I'll see you tomorrow, Livvie.'

'Yeah ... see you in the morning,' Olivia replied. 'Chin up,' she called softly as her friend walked away.

'Don't start on me,' Ruby warned as Olivia joined the queue and stood next to her at the back. 'Ain't my fault that her bloke seems to fancy me.'

'Is that right?' Olivia said sarcastically and left it at that as their bus wheezed up to the kerb. She would have preferred to catch the next one and avoid her cousin's company, but she didn't see why she should make herself any later than she already was. She was hungry and she knew her brother would be too. Alfie would have been back from school some hours ago and there was little in the house for him to eat. She'd need to stop off at the corner shop for a few bits to make something for tea.

'Wouldn't want a bloke like that anyhow.' Ruby began twirling a blonde curl round one finger. 'That Trevor's not right in the brainbox if you ask me.'

Olivia didn't rise to the bait; she knew her cousin was out for a row. She avoided looking at Ruby as the girl plonked herself down beside her on the seat. Instead Olivia gazed out of the window, letting her companion's voice fade into the background.

In the distance she could see Alexandra Palace rising on the skyline. Whenever she passed it she was reminded of the time her boss had asked her out on a Sunday afternoon and taken her for a walk in the grounds. It had been just days after war was declared ... before anybody fully understood what horrors awaited, at home and overseas. Although there had been tension between them, and the sun had turned to drizzle, Olivia remembered it now as a lovely day, one of the best she'd known. It seemed long ago yet only ten months had passed since she'd strolled on those sloping lawns with Lucas Black. And in those months many brave young men who'd never again stroll through an English park on a Sunday afternoon had been buried in foreign soil.

'Are you listening to me? I said we should all thank our

lucky stars we've escaped the worst of it. Those poor blighters on that ship! It sank in just fifteen minutes.'

Ruby's mention of the passenger liner the Germans had torpedoed off the Irish coast cut into Olivia's reflections. Every development in the conflict was discussed over the work benches at Barratt's. But the tragedy surrounding the *Lusitania* had been of particular grisly interest because it had been so unexpected, and so wicked.

'Just a few more miles and they would have made it into port,' Olivia murmured, shocked anew that having travelled all the way from America those civilians had perished when their destination was in sight.

'Walk with you up Campbell Road?' Ruby had stood up as the bus reached their stop.

'Not going that way. Need something from the shop for tea.' Olivia wanted to escape Ruby's company.

'Suit yerself.' She sounded shirty at the rebuff.

The two young women started walking in opposite directions then Ruby came to a halt and trotted back after Olivia.

'Hold up! I forgot to say, there's something you should know ...'

Olivia turned about, frowning.

'They're getting married.'

'Who ... Cath and Trevor? I know they're engaged.'

'Nah, not bothered about them. Me mum told me that her and your dad are getting hitched at the register office next week. She told me not to say nothin'.' Ruby shrugged. 'Don't see why I should do her any favours. She's never done me none. Just thought you should know, and your sisters and brother.'

It took Olivia a moment to digest what Ruby had said. She felt winded yet wasn't sure why she was so upset. She'd known for many months that her father had been unfaithful to her mother with their Aunt Sybil. Agatha Bone had been dead for over eight years, and had gone to her grave without ever realising that her husband and her elder sister had been carrying on behind her back.

Olivia and her siblings had grown up believing Ruby and her younger brother Mickey were their cousins. After so long a deception they still thought of them in that way, despite the fact it had since come to light that Thomas Bone had fathered the lot of them.

But Olivia knew she'd never consider Ruby Wright her sister, and neither would she ever think of Sybil Wright as her stepmother. She didn't really want to admit they were related to her at all.

'Well ... that's a turn up for the books,' Olivia finally commented sourly.

'Take it you won't be going along to throw confetti then?' Ruby smirked. 'Me neither. But if they have a knees-up in the pub after I might put in an appearance.'

'They deserve one another is all I've got to say on the subject.' Olivia set off again.

'See you Monday,' Ruby called after her.

'Yeah ... unfortunately,' Olivia sighed under her breath, and carried on towards the shop.

Chapter Two

'Treated you to some broken biscuits for tea. And I made sure Smithie put in all the Bourbon creams that he had.'

Olivia shook the paper bag by its screwed up top then placed it on the table.

'Bet he tried to palm you off with stale Digestives, didn't he?' Alfie grinned, already diving his hand into the bag.

'Just have one for now. I'm going to make sandwiches for us to eat first.' Olivia took a loaf and a jar of potted meat paste from her bag.

'Is it right that Dad's getting married to that bloody bitch?'

Olivia turned about to see her sister Maggie hovering on the parlour threshold, wiping her hands on a towel. Even had Maggie's words not betrayed her feelings, she would have read these from her sister's pinched expression.

'How did you find out?' Olivia asked flatly.

'Alice Keiver told me – her mum got chinwagging to Ruby down Chapel Street market. Ain't true, is it?'

'Apparently it is,' Olivia said. 'Ruby told me just now on the bus.'

'So everybody else knows!' Maggie stormed. 'Nice of him

to tell *us*, ain't it?' She snorted sarcastically. 'Nancy going to be *bridesmaid*, is she?'

Nancy was their younger sister and still at home with their father and his fancy woman, though she said she couldn't stand living with them and was itching to finish school and get a job so she could leave their household.

'I doubt it'll be a lavish do, if it happens at all.' Olivia wouldn't put it past her father to agree to marry Sybil to keep her sweet but steer clear of any cost or commitment. 'Forget about them,' she added more kindly. She could see the sparkle of tears in Maggie's eyes. 'Let's get tea ready and settle down for the evening.' She eased her aching feet out of her lace-up boots, then padded in stockinged feet into the kitchen. 'How did your day go?' she asked, sawing at the loaf of bread.

'Got an interview on Friday fer another job,' Maggie replied, using her hanky on her eyes.

'You've only been in your present one for a couple of months.' Olivia sounded surprised. Her sister worked in a laundry round the corner in Fonthill Road. But Maggie had always wanted better wages than washing and packing sheets brought in.

'Alice Keiver and her friend are going soldering hand grenades in a new factory that's opening up. She told me they're still taking on, so I'm going to ask fer a job there.' Maggie stuffed her hanky back up her sleeve and gave a little sniff, bucking herself up.

'Fingers crossed you get it, if that's what you want.' Olivia gave her sister a smile.

'You could come too. Don't know why you want to stick at making sweets when the munitions factories are crying out for staff.' Maggie's top lip curled. 'Get you away from *him*, wouldn't it, if you quit Barratt's? Don't know how you can stand even looking at him every day.'

Maggie always referred to their father as 'him' now. Of them all, she was most hurt by the discovery of his adultery. In her opinion her father and her aunt didn't deserve to be happy together. Olivia could only agree with that. Two people who should have respected and cared about Agatha Bone and her children had betrayed them all.

By the time the ghastly skeleton was out of the cupboard Olivia had become involved with Joe Hunter. He had been a man with secrets and past sins of his own, but it hadn't stopped Olivia from loving him. She'd come to a philosophical acceptance of human weakness. Sometimes people did shameful things they regretted, but circumstances – and bonds that couldn't be broken – kept them hurtling on, like poor blinkered horses being spurred towards enemy machine guns by the masters they trusted. But their arrogant, obstinate father had never once apologised or begged forgiveness from his children for the hurt he'd caused to the living or the dead. And that was wrong in her opinion.

'I keep out of Dad's way at work, and he keeps out of mine.' Olivia continued spreading marge on bread.

'Well, on Monday I reckon you *shouldn't* keep out of his way,' Maggie said forcefully. 'You should make a point of telling him what we all think of him and that old cow.'

'He knows without it needing to be spelled out,' Olivia said flatly. 'And I'm not packing in me job 'cos of him. I've got good friends at Barratt's.'

'Cath won't worry about you when she gets married and has kids,' Maggie said succinctly.

'God willing,' Olivia muttered. From what Cath had said about Trevor it seemed they might not be a couple for much longer, let alone have children. Yet they almost had been parents and the baby would have been due about now if Cath hadn't visited an abortionist last autumn.

Olivia's thoughts were interrupted by a bang on the front door. They weren't expecting anybody so she raised her eyebrows in surprise. Indicating her sticky fingers, she said, 'You open up, Maggie.'

It was some minutes later, while cutting the sandwiches into triangles, that Olivia realised her sister hadn't come back and the house seemed to have a sinister quietness mantling it. Wiping her hands on her pinafore, she went to investigate, a weird sensation prickling at the nape of her neck. As she drew closer to the parlour the sound of whispered conversation reached her ears. One voice was her sister's and the other male, but too deep to be Alfie's. Yet there was something familiar about that coarse tone.

It couldn't be, Olivia reassured herself, because she'd heard that Harry Wicks had been reported missing in Flanders. She recalled having hoped without a scrap of guilt that the evil swine had perished.

With a shaking hand she grabbed the door knob and burst into the parlour. At first she didn't see him; but she saw her brother's doubtful expression, and Maggie's defiance, and that was enough to make her heart sink.

Then out he stepped from behind the door she'd flung open, looking dapper in his blue hospital uniform. He'd grown a thick moustache that covered his fleshy top lip and for a moment Olivia struggled to recognise him, but his brown eyes were the same, slithering over her like twin beetles.

'Well . . . nice to see you, Livvie. You're looking good, ain't yer, gel?' Harry Wicks gave her a leering smile.

'What the bloody hell do you want?'

'Don't talk to Harry like that!' Maggie burst out crossly. 'He's come to see me, to let me know he's alive and on convalescence. It's wonderful news!' She beamed at him. 'I was worried that you'd bought it.'

'Nah … you don't get rid of me that easily. Look, good as new.' Harry did a little pivot on the spot, hands spread cockily.

'You'll be wanting to get out of those hospital blues and back into your regular uniform then,' Olivia said acidly. 'And help put an end to this damned war.'

'Can't go back till I'm signed off as A1 by the doc. Need a bit more rest and recreation.' He winked at her.

'I'll treat you to a night at the flicks.' Maggie's soppy smile struck fear into Olivia's heart. She could feel her cheeks growing cold as the blood drained from them. She'd hoped that Maggie had got over her schoolgirl infatuation with Harry Wicks. She had been just fourteen when the dirty swine started touching her up. After Olivia had found out what had been going on between them she'd done her best to force them apart, but like a moth to a savage flame Maggie kept going back to singe her wings some more. And now he was sniffing around again, and Maggie was looking happy about it.

'Is tea ready?' Alfie piped up. He felt awkward beneath the oppressive tension in the room. He remembered Harry Wicks as one of their neighbours back in Wood Green but wasn't too sure why one of his sisters seemed to like him a lot and the other not at all.

'It's set out in the kitchen. Help yourself to sandwiches, Alfie,' Olivia said, keen to get the eight year old out of the way.

As Alfie passed him on his way to the door, Harry ruffled the boy's hair. Olivia had to stop herself springing forward to knock that hand away. She knew it was a false display of affection and that he was deliberately out to aggravate her. Harry Wicks hadn't changed. The war hadn't made him stop and think, as it had others who'd come back humbled by their dreadful experiences.

'You can have tea with us, Harry,' Maggie said. 'It's only sandwiches and biscuits but ... '

'No, he can't,' Olivia butted in.

Maggie reddened and her small mouth pursed into an angry knot. 'Well, in that case, I don't want none either. We'll go out to the caff. I've got me wages as I've just got paid.' She gave her sister a rebellious stare. 'I'll get me coat.'

'Well, before you disappear and spend all your money on him, you can hand over your housekeeping.'

Blushing furiously, Maggie turned her back on them all and dug into her pocket. Having counted out coins she slapped a fistful of them into her sister's waiting palm before sweeping out of the room.

'Didn't need to humiliate her like that, did you?' Harry said, stroking his bushy upper lip while his tongue wet the lower one.

'If she's got money to waste on you, she can pay her way here. Anyway you're a fine one to talk. I remember you "humiliated" her as often as you could at one time. And enjoyed the doing of it.'

'And she loved it, did Maggie.' He gave a dirty laugh. 'Couldn't get rid of her at times, she was hanging around me like a bitch on heat.'

Olivia clenched her fists at her sides; for two pins she would have leaped on him and pummelled him as hard as she could, but she knew he'd only have liked that. Maggie hadn't even had properly formed breasts when Olivia had found him with his hand inside her sister's blouse.

'She asked me to marry her, y'know, before I joined up. Wish I had got married now, and had a nipper. Ain't so much pressure on a family man to fight for King and country, is there?' Harry turned the screws.

'I know you're a bloody coward, you've no need to rub it in,' Olivia said contemptuously.

'This here says I *ain't* a coward.' He waggled his right trouser leg.

Olivia had noticed he moved with a slight limp; that apart, he looked fit as a fiddle. But he'd malinger if he could.

'Reckon your Maggie's still under my spell. She won't want me going back over there, risking me life again.'

'That's 'cos she's never known the half of it where you're concerned,' Olivia replied through her teeth.

'Wonder if she knows the half of what *you're* really like,' he drawled. He looked about the room. 'Nice place you've got here. I heard that Hunter give you his house. Shame he copped a bullet over there and left you all alone. I wouldn't have gone down so easy, knowing you was waiting fer me.'

'Joe died a hero, saving his comrades' lives,' Olivia said in a voice that shook with pride. 'He's got medals and citations from his commanding officers.'

'Fat lot o' use to him dead, ain't they?' Harry circled her, too close for Olivia's liking. 'And it don't change the fact that he was a ponce. Must've done all right at it too if he managed to buy this place. Makes me think *I* should have a go at being a pimp 'cos I sure don't want to go back to living with me parents.' He put his lips close to Olivia's ear. 'You might think you're too good fer me but I don't see how

17

you can be when you settled fer somebody like Hunter. I reckon you should be grateful I'd give a dirty gel like you the time o' day.'

Olivia shoved him away as his lips grazed her skin.

He came in close again, whispering, 'I'd like a place of me own, just like this one. Bet you could do with a man's company, couldn't yer? Expect lots o' little jobs need doing round the house.'

'I can do all the little jobs myself, and if I can't I've already got somebody to help me out.'

'Have yer now?' Harry hadn't been expecting that. He straightened up, smoothing his moustache with thumb and forefinger. 'What's his name then?'

'Jack Keiver ... and if you haven't already heard of the Keivers then think yourself lucky. They live in Campbell Road, and if you make one wrong move Jack'll thump you – or else his wife will.' Olivia chuckled with real amusement. 'If you think I'm joking, ask Maggie about them.'

Harry huffed his contempt for that threat. But he walked away. He'd heard of Campbell Bunk all right and knew that the people living there were all scum or villains of some sort.

'Perhaps if I start me new life as a pimp and get me own place, you'll be all over me then, eh?'

'I wouldn't be all over you if you had a mansion down Tufnell Park. And if you know what's good for you, you'll stay away from Maggie. From all of us.'

'Or what?' he crowed.

'Or I'll tell the police what I know about you and about a nun getting raped. I haven't forgotten a thing.'

Harry sprang away from the fireplace and grabbed her face in one callused hand. 'I haven't forgotten either that you was Joe Hunter's tart. And I ain't scared of your slum pals neither.'

Olivia shoved him away just as her sister came back into the room.

Maggie gave them a suspicious look. 'What's going on?'

'Nothing. You know what I think about him 'cos I've told you enough times. If you're daft enough to give him another chance after the way he treated you, that's your look out.' Olivia paused. She knew that if she tried to ban her sister from seeing him, Maggie would just carry on doing it behind her back, as she had before. She was just fifteen ... still a kid ... but she was old enough to be working, and to marry if she could get her father's consent to it. Olivia shrugged in disgust. 'Go out then if you want, but don't ever bring him back here to my house.' She rounded on Harry. 'And in case that isn't clear enough for you: stay away, you're not welcome.'

As the front door slammed shut behind them Alfie looked up from his tea plate. 'Harry and Maggie sweethearts, are they?' he asked through a mouthful of sandwich.

'I certainly hope not,' Olivia replied, pouring tea with a hand that shook slightly.

'He's too old for her. I thought she liked his brother. Maggie an' Ricky used to be in the same class.'

Olivia sat down opposite Alfie, tipping the Bourbon creams out of the bag and arranging them on a tea plate. 'Have you got homework to do?'

'Done it.'

'Properly?'

'Yeah ... anyway my pal says it's a waste of time learning at school 'cos soon we're all gonna get blown up by a Zeppelin.'

Alfie tucked into his Bourbon creams and Olivia bit into a sandwich but her appetite had gone. She felt queasy. She'd had two shocks in a short space of time. By far the worst was being confronted by Harry Wicks in her own home. She had pushed him right out of her mind, believing him gone from all their lives.

Now he was back, and she knew he had revenge on his mind. He'd use Maggie if he could to get at Olivia, just as he had before. And Maggie, poor fool that she was, seemed bewitched by her first proper boyfriend – even if he had treated her like dirt. She was still childishly flattered to receive the attention of an older man. In a few years' time the six-year age gap between them would be nothing exceptional. Maggie would be considered a young woman rather than a girl not long out of school.

Olivia didn't want Harry Wicks to wheedle himself into a permanent place in her family. Maggie could be a pain but she deserved to settle down with somebody decent. The only hope Olivia had was that Harry's convalescence would soon be over and he'd be shipped off back to his regiment. But no doubt he'd pull the wool over the doctor's eyes for as long as he could.

Chapter Three

Tommy Bone had been working at Barratt's for most of his adult life, barring a hiccup when he'd been sacked for misconduct. But Lucas Black had given him back his job before he went off to fight. By that time the factory was already losing staff to the war effort and the management were glad of Tommy's experience.

Sometimes when father and daughter passed one another at work Tommy would grunt a 'mornin'' or 'evenin'' in response to Olivia's quiet greeting. But she knew that he'd avoid her if he could and that suited her. Her love and loyalty had started to wither even before she'd discovered her brutal father was also an adulterer. Yet a flicker of sadness still stirred in Olivia whenever she thought about their broken family because she knew her mother wouldn't have wanted that.

Alfie's birth had resulted in Tommy losing the wife he'd always claimed to adore, yet for years he had cheated on her with her own sister. Since the truth had emerged Olivia had taken with a pinch of salt all her father's sentimental claptrap. Talk was cheap. But this final act of betrayal in marrying his one-time sister-in-law deserved a comment from his daughter. Olivia was going to give it even though she could read in his face that he believed she'd be too intimidated to say what she might privately be thinking.

'Can I have a word with you, please?'

She had hung about by the factory gates, waiting to catch her father on his way home. They hadn't spoken in ages even though she had been trying to bump into him for the past few days. This evening she'd made a point of slipping out a few minutes before the end of her shift so she wouldn't miss him.

'Eh . . . what's that?' Tommy hung back from the group of work pals he was walking with. He knew why his daughter had been waiting there to intercept him but was pretending he didn't.

'I heard from Ruby that you and Sybil are getting married next week.'

Tommy thrust his hands into his pockets and jutted out his bristly chin. 'Ain't nothing certain yet so she'd no right to be talking out o' turn.'

'Who – Ruby or Sybil?' Olivia asked in the same flat tone. She looked him over. Her father had not bothered with more than basic grooming since his wife died, but had always kept himself clean when she'd lived at home. Today his face looked unwashed and unshaven.

'Don't matter who, 'cos it's none of your business, is it, what I do?' Tommy pursed his lips.

'It's my business that you treated my mum the way you did. And it's my business that you've never said sorry to any of us kids for all the cruelty and deceit we had to put up with from you over the years. I don't expect Sybil to feel bad about the way she's acted. Don't reckon she's got that sort of decency in her, even when she's sober. But before you two tied the knot it would have been nice to have wiped the slate clean. Or at least told us all what you planned to do. But then you're still the same person you always were, aren't you? Doing everything on the sly.'

During her quiet little speech Tommy had been getting redder and redder in the face. 'Don't you talk down to me!' he spat through tobacco-stained teeth, holding one stubby finger close to her cheek.

Olivia didn't flinch or blink, but kept her cool green eyes fixed on her father's florid face.

'If you'd behaved yourself instead of going off with that pimp we'd still be a family and Sybil wouldn't never have moved in,' he snarled at her.

'I'm glad, and proud, of what I did to get Alfie away from you. You led him a dog's life. And that's something you really ought to hang your head about. So good riddance to the pair of you . . . I reckon you're going to need some luck, shackled to her.'

'You finished?' Tommy roared, unable to control his temper. It was out of character for him to draw attention to himself. He seemed oblivious of the heads turning his way. Automatically he started bringing up his fist, as he used to when all his kids were under his roof and he intended to keep them in line.

'Yeah, I'm finished.' Olivia glanced at his quivering hand with disgust gleaming in her eyes. 'That's the only answer you've ever had to put forward, isn't it?' She turned away, saying over her shoulder, 'We don't have to listen to that anymore.'

Tommy watched her walking away from him, her head high and her slender back ramrod-straight. His cheeks, moments ago florid, turned pale beneath the stubble. At one time his eldest girl would never have spoken to him in that tone. Olivia had always had gumption but she'd keep her backchat controlled so as not to rile him too much. Before they'd had an almighty bust up he'd been close to Livvie, who reminded him of her mother in looks and temperament. But for all his wife's courage and intelligence he'd managed to deceive Aggie until the end, because she'd always trusted him to be truthful. Whereas Olivia looked at him with big green eyes that seemed to see down into his black soul.

Yet despite their differences he still secretly adored Olivia. His youngest girl still lived with him but Olivia was the gift his wife had left him and he couldn't stop himself from watching her from shadows, to make sure she was all right. She'd go mad if she knew he spied on her in Islington, to see what she got up to. Even if he spotted the kids all out together, Livvie was the only one of his children who drew his eye. He knew she hadn't got herself another boyfriend since Joe Hunter's death. Tommy was glad the former pimp had copped it; blamed him for the break-up of the Bone family. If Tommy hadn't found out that Olivia had been seeing a man . . . and a villain at that . . . without permission, things might have been different now. His eldest might still have been at home, running the place like clockwork for him, as she used to. Sybil was bone idle and had never meant more to him than a part-time fancy even though their relationship stretched back to when they were kids.

He had no intention of marrying his sister-in-law, even though she'd told him he was the father of her two children. Her husband had run out on her when he'd found out what had been going on. Tommy reckoned he only had Sybil's say-so that *he* was her kids' father and he could hardly ask Ed Wright, even if he knew where to find the man. It was true all six children shared a family resemblance but then their mothers had been sisters so that was no real proof of his guilt.

Sybil might have got her hooks firmly into his house and his wallet but she did nothing other than sit on her backside, boozing, while he was at work. There was no cosy comfort in the place as there had been when his Livvie had been watching over everything. So Tommy stayed out a lot to avoid going back to a dump with an empty larder and cold grate. He'd been nagged at for weeks to book the register office and seemed to remember coming in drunk one night and saying that he would, to shut Sybil up. If she'd booked it herself for next week, she'd be turning up alone to take vows. Over his dead body would Aggie's wedding ring go on her sister's finger.

*

Olivia was late getting home, having stopped off to speak to a neighbour who lived round the corner. She'd got to know the Keiver family even before her father had chucked her out. Tommy and Sybil had done their utmost to keep their families apart in case their dirty little secret leaked out, but Olivia and Ruby had bumped into one another by accident as young women and thereafter met up regularly. Those clandestine meetings had brought Olivia from Wood Green to Islington, and into the sphere of the inhabitants of the notorious Bunk. Campbell Road was a place where a person sought refuge when down and out and desperate for a bed.

At first Olivia had been startled, even intimidated, by

Mrs Keiver's coarse language and aggressive manner. But the older woman had proved to be a good friend to her ever since the night Olivia turned up on her doorstep, battered and bruised following a beating from Tommy. It had been less than a year ago but sometimes it seemed as though half a lifetime had passed since that gloomy autumn evening when she had climbed the rickety stairs to knock on Matilda Keiver's door. Olivia had reasoned that if anybody knew where a cheap room was to be had, Mrs Keiver would as she collected rents in the area.

The Keivers lived in a slum tenement, with five people sharing two first-floor rooms. It had been six of them until their eldest girl left home to work in Essex. But, poor as they were, and without being well acquainted with Olivia, the Keivers had given her bed and breakfast and helped her put a permanent roof over her head in a tiny place just across the road. Olivia had since moved on from there. But Matilda's assistance, at a time when she'd been very low, was something that she'd never forget. Now that she was firmly on her feet she strove to repay the other woman in small ways. She'd babysit Matilda's youngest daughter when nobody was home and treat little Lucy to biscuits and sweets. It was little enough in Olivia's eyes to make up for what she'd been given.

And when in need of a confidante ... as she had been today ... she'd always make a point of stopping by at Matilda's. Unfortunately, a neighbour had already been drinking tea in the front room when Olivia arrived so she had just accepted a quick cuppa and made her way home without chewing the fat about her family woes.

Olivia was still brooding about her confrontation with Tommy earlier when she turned the corner into Playford

Road. Lifting her gaze from the pavement, she had a shock. She hadn't seen her youngest sister for weeks, and hadn't been expecting to either. It didn't bode well that Nancy had shown up out of the blue carrying a carpet bag so Olivia speeded up towards her, fearing that her own run in with their father earlier might be to blame. When feeling guilty he always wanted to take it out on somebody. Perhaps Nancy had got in the way.

'Can I stay with you, Livvie?' the girl burst out as soon as her big sister was within earshot.

'He's hit you.' Olivia sounded despairing and gently touched the red mark on her sister's cheek.

'Weren't Dad,' Nancy sniffed, picking up the bag at her feet. 'Sybil whacked me. She's pie-eyed on gin and went loopy when I got in from school and told her it was her turn to make the grub. I'm sick of being their skivvy. And I'm sick of feeling hungry. There's never anything to eat even though I give up all of me doorstep money to her. Not even got a couple of coppers in me purse after working me fingers to the bone scrubbing steps all day Saturday.'

'Come inside.' Olivia quickly put her key in the lock, having noticed that a neighbour was taking an interest in their conversation.

'Maggie! Alfie!' she called on closing the door.

'Nobody's in. I knocked loads of times but no reply.' Nancy shrugged out of her coat in the hall.

Alfie should have been in by now. Olivia had got him his own key cut so he could let himself in after school. She guessed he was playing out in the neighbourhood with his friends.

'Let's get the kettle on and you can fill me in on it all,' she said.

'You let Maggie and Alfie live with you. Can I stay an' all?' Nancy pleaded.

'If you want. I did ask you before, didn't I? You said you wanted to stay in Wood Green to be with your friends. You'll have to get up early to get to school on time.'

'I'm done with school.' Nancy's lip curled.

'What d'you mean . . . done with school?' Olivia frowned. 'You're not even thirteen until next month.'

'Don't care. One of me friends has already left and got a job as a tea gel in a biscuit factory. *And* she's a month younger'n me.'

Olivia took the kettle off the stove and filled the teapot. She sent Nancy a sideways glance. 'You think you're getting a job as a tea girl?'

'Why not?' She jutted her chin defiantly.

'What's Dad got to say about that?' Olivia recalled that their father had made her and Maggie continue studying until they were fourteen, and they'd had to get their school certificates to a certain grade to satisfy him. But perhaps his kids' education was something else he no longer bothered with . . . like shaving and washing himself.

'Ain't telling him. Just doing it.' Nancy sounded adamant. 'Or Maggie reckons she might be able to get me a job in her munitions factory. They're taking on all the time and they ain't asking for birth certificates.'

Olivia knew that was true. Maggie had started her new job earlier in the week and had been full of how the supervisors were asking everybody to bring along their friends for interviews, to fill all the vacancies. The factories springing up to help the war effort were competing fiercely for staff with other local manufacturers. As more and more men were being drawn away to join the armed forces, women who'd not worked since they got married were being lured from their homes by good wages to form a wartime workforce. Olivia knew that if her twelve-year-old sister couldn't wait to turn thirteen before seeking a job she'd probably get away with it. And even thirteen was too young by yesterday's standards.

Nancy was a tall girl for her age and she had quite a mature way about her; Olivia thought her youngest sister had more sense in her little finger than Maggie had in her whole body. So in all, she wasn't going to make a song and dance about what Nancy was planning to do.

'Got any biscuits?' the girl asked, stirring a spoonful of sugar into her tea.

Olivia got down the tin from the shelf and handed it to her. She sipped tea thoughtfully as Nancy prised the lid off and helped herself to a Bourbon.

'What about Barratt's? Have they got any vacancies?' she asked.

Olivia gave her an old-fashioned look.

'Oh ... yeah ... you're right,' Nancy said. 'Best not put meself in Dad's way, eh?'

'Definitely not. Will he mind that you've left home?'

'Doubt it; he's hardly ever there. He probably won't even notice I've gone. *She* couldn't wait to get rid of me.' Nancy nibbled her biscuit. 'Feel sorry for Mickey though. He's not a bad lad. Reckon him and Alfie would get on all right, yet they've never even met, have they?'

This mention of their brother had reminded Olivia he still wasn't home. It was unusual for Alfie to miss a meal.

'I'd better pop out and see where he's got to before I start on the sandwiches.' She put down her cup. 'You can sort yourself out a bed upstairs, can't you? You'll find sheets in the airing cupboard on the landing. Alfie's got the smallest room but there's a spare divan in Maggie's room at the back that you can use.'

'Right-ho.' Nancy settled down comfortably at the table and plunged her hand into the biscuit tin again.

*

'Was just popping round to see you.' Matilda Keiver bumped into Olivia at the top of Campbell Road. 'Did you want to have a natter? I tried to shift me friend, but she don't take a hint. Can talk the hind leg off a donkey, that one.' Matilda didn't miss a trick and had known Olivia had more than passing the time of day on her mind when she'd turned up earlier.

Olivia shrugged. 'Wasn't much. Just wanted to have a moan about bloody relatives getting on my wick.'

Matilda chuckled and gave a sage nod. 'You come to the right place then. There's not much I don't know about them sort of problems.' She rested her chapped hands on her hips. 'Shall I come round yours? You can make me a cup o' tea to keep me tongue oiled while I let yer know what I do to sort out my bloody relatives ... and one in particular.' She turned her head, staring at a nearby house. It was no secret in the neighbourhood that Matilda Keiver despised her brother-in-law.

'Can't right now ... I'm looking for Alfie.' Olivia grimaced an apology. 'He should've been back hours ago. Have you seen him playing out?'

'He is in the Bunk, but he ain't with any kids. I just saw him with a bloke in hospital blues.' Matilda frowned. 'Didn't like the look of him to be honest but stopped meself butting in, 'case he was a friend of the family.'

'He's not!' Olivia turned pale. 'He's a bloody pig if it's who I think it is. I don't want him hanging around Alfie.'

She started off at a run and her friend hitched up her skirts and started after her. Matilda Keiver might have been in her mid-thirties, but she was a fiery-haired bruiser of a woman with plenty of energy. She was soon jogging by Olivia's side down the road.

'Wrong 'un, is he?' Matilda puffed out.

'He damn' well is! I wish he'd leave us all alone.'

Olivia saw them both then, loitering by the corner of Paddington Street that bisected Campbell Road almost at its centre point. She put on a spurt as she saw what was going on. 'What the hell d'you think you're doing, giving him cigarettes?' She snatched a dog end from her brother's lips and threw it to the ground.

'Calm down, Livvie.' Harry Wicks sounded affable but his shifty eyes told a different story. He'd not seen her coming and hadn't liked being taken by surprise. 'Yer brother just asked me for a little puff of me fag. No harm done, is there?'

'I say there is!' Olivia insisted. 'He's only eight years old.' She turned to Alfie. 'Get yourself home. I've been waiting for you before I start tea.'

Alfie blushed and shuffled his feet uneasily. 'I was only asking Harry about his brother. Ricky's got a better job – he's earning ten bob a week in the grocer's. Wish I was.'

'Ricky's a lot older than you.' Olivia made an effort to control her temper. If this had been a chance meeting, so be it. But Harry Wicks had no need to be in Islington at all. Unless he'd come for Maggie ... or to cause trouble.

'See, nothing to get het up about,' Harry smarmed. 'A

little drag on a fag won't do him no harm. I was always having a crafty smoke at that age.'

'He's nothing like you. Never will be. It was me kid sister you were over here after last week. I've already told you to stay away from all of us.'

'Maggie ain't a kid now, is she? She's all grown up,' Harry purred.

Olivia swung away from him to curb the temptation to lash out. 'Nancy's at home. Go and say hello to her, Alfie. I'll be along in a minute.' She gave her brother's shoulder a little push and he started trotting up the road.

'I've been killing time talking to him while I was waiting for Maggie to show up.' Harry sounded peeved. 'She told me not to stop by yours to meet her 'cos you're a rude cow. She's right about that. But I'm done hanging around so tell her I said toodle-oo ... and not to bother me again.'

Matilda had been quietly observing the scene, arms crossed over her chest and head cocked to one side. Suddenly it seemed as if she could no longer contain herself. She took a step forward and said, 'You're not wanted round here ... so piss off and don't come back.'

Harry gave her a scornful glance that told her to mind her own business. 'Free country, ain't it?'

'Round here?' Matilda guffawed in disbelief. 'I'm Mrs Keiver and this is Campbell Bunk and them that live here are a law unto themselves, take it from me.' She prodded Harry's shoulder with her forefinger while she spoke. 'If you know what's good for you, you'll sling your hook and keep it slung.'

'Harry!'

Olivia turned her head to see Maggie hurrying up from Seven Sisters Road, waving frantically.

'Sorry I'm late. We had to stay and finish an order for horseshoes for the bloody Russian army before they'd let us home.' Maggie came to a breathless halt but her smile and explanation weren't for her sister.

Harry took a glance about, noticing that they were drawing attention. Bystanders had the same idle yet threatening demeanour as Mrs Keiver, he saw. Taking Maggie's arm, he started to yank her back down the road.

Olivia sprinted after them, furious at the way he'd taken control of her sister. 'Get your hands off her.'

Maggie, pulled in two directions, twisted her arm free from Olivia's grip. 'Me 'n' Harry are going for a bite to eat. I want to say goodbye as he's getting shipped out next week.' A sheepish glance accompanied her explanation for choosing to go with him.

'Well, that's good news at least!' Olivia felt a wave of relief pass over her. She warned Maggie: 'If you're home after ten o'clock you'll find the door locked.'

It was pointless trying to stop her sister from going with him. Besides, if he'd told Maggie the truth about returning to his regiment, at least he'd soon be at a distance. And with any luck the evil swine might not come back again.

It made Olivia's blood boil that a man as kind and decent as Joe Hunter had perished when the likes of Harry Wicks had been invalided home with a minor injury. Though not everybody had thought Joe kind or decent. Plenty of people had dubbed him the local villain. Olivia felt sorry that they'd never known him as she had ... just the myth that surrounded him. She knew that the irony of an ex-pimp being lauded as a war hero would make Joe chuckle if he were still around. She'd not cared what prejudiced people had believed about the man she'd loved. She'd faced down her father's wrath and her colleagues' sniggers about her relationship with Joe. And she would gladly do it all again, if only she could turn back the clock. Those months before the war, living at home with her violent father, had seemed hellish at the time. In hindsight she judged them to be the sweetest days she'd known because Joe had been with her, helping her through.

Chapter Four

'I've been thinking about what we talked about and I'm starting St John Ambulance training next week,' Cath said as she accompanied Olivia through the open factory gates on a sunny morning in June. 'I know I won't learn about shellshock, but at least if I'm a voluntary first aider Trevor's mother won't be able to go on at me for being a useless item who knows nothing.'

'Quite right.' Olivia gave her a nod of encouragement.

'Why don't you come along?' Cath suggested. 'They're crying out for volunteers. I can practise bandaging your arm and you can put splints on my leg.'

'I think I will.' Olivia barely paused for thought. As a child she'd dreamed of being a nurse. Memories of her mother dying while giving birth to Alfie would never leave her. She'd been just ten when it happened. Young as she was then, she'd felt guilty that she'd not known what to do to save Aggie.

'Miss Wallis is letting me know when training starts next week,' Cath continued. 'Wonder if *she'd* get down on her hands and knees and give somebody the kiss of life?' Cath gave Olivia a dig in the ribs. 'She would Lucas Black, that's fer sure,' the girl cackled. 'The snotty cow gets on my wick, the way she looks down her nose at us.'

Olivia had been subjected to that haughty stare too so knew what Cath meant.

The company ran regular first aid courses. In a place where open pans of boiling liquid sugar were commonplace, and heavy equipment was used, it was vital to have people on site who could give basic treatment. But most of the men who'd been trained in the past had joined up and any women with nursing experience had been urged to fill hospital vacancies. The hospitals were recruiting because a number of regular nurses had gone with the troops to set up field hospitals in France.

It was generally believed to be only a matter of time before the Germans flew further inland to bomb towns and cities. Women had already started stuffing medicine chests with bandages and antiseptic, just in case the unthinkable happened and their house was hit. More than ever before it seemed sensible to learn the rudiments of first aid.

Olivia and Cath parted company at the factory entrance. Olivia went to the production line while Cath headed to the packing room. In common with her roller-out colleagues, Olivia fastened a piece of sugar sacking around her waist as a makeshift apron to protect her clothes. Ever since she'd started work here the workers had been moaning about management failing to provide staff uniforms. Olivia was no different from the rest of them in feeling it wasn't too much to expect at least a sturdy pinafore and cap to be given to them. Clothing could be ruined by an accidental spillage of syrup and would be expensive to replace. By the end of her shift handling the various sweet mixtures,

Olivia's hands were stiff and gritty with sediment and her hessian-covered lap littered with offcuts. But those on the boiling pans had more to contend with than crusted palms and fingernails. Boiling syrup could spit and burn a hole in a skirt or trouser leg or give a nasty scald to bare skin.

It was a mild summer morning. Added warmth from the huge boilers chugging away in here for hours on end had caused beads of perspiration to form on Olivia's brow even before she'd started rolling out the thick sugar paste. The hand-held roller embedded with moulds resembled a large pastry-rolling pin. It bit into the mixture, leaving the sweets cut and ready to be separated and stacked for wrapping. The factory buildings always felt hot and airless, even in the winter months. A pall of treacle-scented steam hung in the air and the clang and thud of the equipment being worked in the background added to the oppressive atmosphere. Outside the sickly stench could be detected many miles away when the wind was up.

An hour later, with a mountain of confectionery in front of her but her mind miles away, Olivia sensed somebody leaning over and muttering in her ear.

'What?' She was annoyed to have her reminiscences rudely interrupted. Cath's ribald talk of Lucas Black had started Olivia thinking about her old boss and the day she'd found out he'd joined up. She had gone to his office to wish him luck. Months later he'd returned from France to tell her that her fiancé had been killed there in Lucas's own Company. They'd parted sombrely on that icy January evening but he had asked her to write to him while he was serving at Ypres. She'd not had a letter from him in six weeks and very much hoped he was all right.

'Getting a stepmother then, ain't yer? Or so I heard.'

Olivia shrugged and carried on with her work. Nelly Smith was the sort of woman you never knew how to take. She might be friendly one day and gossiping about you behind your back the next. Nelly was her supervisor so Olivia tried to keep things on an even keel between them. They'd fallen out on occasions . . . mostly because her father and Nelly didn't like one another. But Olivia wasn't sure that she liked Tommy Bone either, so she couldn't hold that against the woman, family loyalty notwithstanding.

'Tommy's really getting hitched again then, is he?'

Nelly seemed determined to hover at her shoulder until she got an answer. 'Better ask him that,' Olivia said shortly.

'Well, I would, but I don't reckon he'd give me an answer. Not one that was polite anyhow.' Nelly sniggered. 'I heard from your old neighbour that yer father's carrying on with his sister-in-law. But she's not a friendly type, according to Mrs Cook, so I understand why you had a bust up and moved out. The sister-in-law's got a kid about your brother's age, hasn't she? Mrs Cook reckons the boys are the spit of one another.'

As Nelly took a breather Olivia gave a neutral grunt, hoping she would go away. People might know that Tommy Bone had his wife's sister living under his roof but nobody, other than the family, knew just how close the relationship between them all *really* was. It would make Nelly's day to have that juicy titbit to chew over with her pals.

Less than a month separated the births of Alfie Bone and Mickey Wright. Yet the two boys had no idea of each other's existence. Ruby wasn't known for her discretion but even she became close-lipped when outsiders asked about her family. As Nelly started to nag again for an answer about Tommy's forthcoming wedding, Olivia changed the subject. 'You going on the first aid course that Miss Wallis is arranging?'

Nelly huffed her derision. 'Don't need none o' that! Me mum and me nan taught me all I need to know about dealing with minor complaints and keeping me family chipper. Picked it up over the years and it's all stored up here.' She tapped her temple.

'Right,' Olivia said doubtfully, and turned her attention back to the caramels.

Nelly prodded her shoulder. 'I'll let you have one o' me pearls of wisdom: them lozenges we churn out fer soothing bad throats . . . as much good as nothin', they are. You might as well suck on a . . . '

'Oi – pack it in, Nelly Smith! You got a dirty gob on yer this morning, ain't yer?' One of Nelly's cronies had been eavesdropping on the conversation and butted in. It seemed she'd succeeded in being comical because the women either side of the bench started guffawing.

'Wasn't gonna say nothin' bad,' Nelly chortled, wagging a finger. 'Suck on a lemon . . . or put the juice in hot water with a spoon o' glycerine stirred in it.' The amusement was soon wiped from her face as she spied the immaculate Miss Wallis weaving towards them between the work benches. 'What's *she* bloody want?' Nelly muttered.

Pinning a meek expression on her face, she bustled off to meet the directors' secretary. Within a minute or two she was trotting back towards Olivia. 'She wants to see you in her office.' Nelly cocked her head. 'What's that about then?'

'Your guess is as good as mine.' Olivia stood up, undoing the sacking apron and wiping her sugar-encrusted fingers on the coarse cloth.

'You want to apply for the first aid course, I believe?' Deborah Wallis spoke as soon as Olivia closed the door behind her. 'I saw Miss Mason and she told me.'

'That's right,' Olivia replied, wondering if she should sit down. She'd not been invited to do so. But then this woman didn't like her . . . never had because Lucas Black had shown her favouritism when he'd been running things at Barratt's. There'd been talk then that Miss Wallis and he had been lovers, and that the secretary had started the rumour herself, desperate to hook him. Olivia doubted they'd had an affair because he'd told her himself about his real girlfriend. He'd been aware that his secretary fancied him, but as far as Olivia knew had never taken advantage of Deborah's crush on him.

'I've booked you in on the training, and Catherine Mason as well. It starts on Monday, after work from six till seven o'clock. It will run for a few months and includes attendance on two evenings.'

'Right-ho,' Olivia said. She hesitated, wondering if that was all, and if it was, why the secretary had made a meal out of it when a message could have been sent via her supervisor. She had half-turned to go back to work when Deborah said something that brought her to a halt.

'I saw Lucas Black yesterday evening. I just thought I'd mention he's been back on leave, in case you didn't know. I believe he's spent time with his family but is due to ship out from Dover tomorrow.'

'Did he ask you to let me know?' Olivia blurted after a moment of stunned silence. She had felt sure that if Lucas returned he'd set aside an hour or two to come and see her. But it seemed she'd been wrong. He'd visited his secretary but not the factory girl he'd once asked to be his mistress before he'd found out about Joe Hunter and things had turned tricky between them all.

Suddenly she felt angry. If Lucas had decided he didn't want her as a penfriend he should have told her himself rather than let her fret that he might have come to harm. Glancing at Deborah, she noticed satisfaction glimmering in the secretary's eyes and all became clear. Deborah Wallis had used the first aid training as a ruse to find out if Lucas had called on Olivia. Now that she had her answer the woman was finding it difficult to contain her triumph.

'How is Mr Black?' Olivia kept her voice clear and level.

'He said he is well, but sometimes a face tells the whole story when words do not.' Deborah sounded smug because she held more knowledge than she was prepared to share.

Olivia remembered how battered in body and spirit Lucas had looked when he'd arrived on that freezing winter night, white with mist, to tell her that Joe had been killed in action. 'Well, if you see him again before he leaves for France ... ' She hesitated before adding, 'Please wish him all the best from me, and safe journeys.'

Her conversation with Miss Wallis played on Olivia's mind for the rest of the day, making her feel restless to do something ... although what she didn't know. But she did know she didn't want to pass on any message to Lucas through that stuck up cow. She wanted to speak to him herself – and tear him off a strip for ignoring her. She was relieved when the final bell sounded and she could set off home. On saying goodnight to Cath, who was off shopping in the High Street, Olivia headed towards the bus stop. She noticed her cousin up ahead, strolling along with a few colleagues. Olivia hung back, wanting to avoid Ruby's company.

As the crowds of workers teeming through the gates petered out she found herself loitering alone by the factory and dwelling on reasons why Lucas had cut her off without explanation. Five minutes later she eased her back from the wall and shook herself into action. Plunging her hands into her jacket pockets, she briskly set off. Halfway along Mayes Road a long low whistle came from somewhere but she continued on her way without taking any notice. It wasn't unusual for men to whistle at her. She was a pretty blonde, or so she'd been told. Before she'd started work at Barratt's Olivia had been a waitress at a pie and mash shop catering for navvies; she'd got used to their bawdy compliments and straying hands.

When the sound came again she glanced idly sideways and the sight of a car made her hesitate because it looked familiar. So did the extraordinarily handsome man who was standing by the driver's door with one hand resting on the roof of the Austin.

A spontaneous burst of joy tightened her chest as she stopped and turned towards him. For a moment their eyes remained locked then he broke the spell with a crooked smile, beckoning her. And she didn't hesitate to cross the road and join him.

'Lucas!' She immediately extended her hands to him, squeezing his warm fingers in affectionate welcome. She gazed hungrily at his strong tanned features and sun-bleached dark hair for almost a full minute then shook her head. 'How are you? You look well ... better than I expected.'

'Is that a compliment?' he asked in the wry, cultured tone she remembered so well.

"Course it is,' she said gruffly. 'I wasn't expecting to see you. I believed you were on your way to Dover, to ship out again.'

'Who told you that?' His deep blue eyes glanced towards the factory as though he were answering his own question.

'Miss Wallis said she'd seen you. Did you get my letters? I've been worried about you.'

'I'll give you a lift home and we can have a talk,' he said, opening the car door.

'Oh ... thanks ... if it's no trouble.' Olivia immediately slid onto the passenger seat of the Austin. She felt wonderfully content that he'd spared the time after all to come and see her before rejoining his regiment. The car glided away from the kerb, and she broke the ice with, 'Thought it was a rough sort, whistling at me like that.' She tutted a mock reprimand.

'Perhaps I am a rough sort now.' He slanted her a mischievous look. 'You'll have to blame the company I'm forced to keep over there.'

They fell silent; Olivia knew that their thoughts had turned to Joe Hunter. Undeniably, he had been a *rough sort* ... but they'd both had proof of the decent and courageous man he'd become.

'I've been to see Freddie Weedon today. Do you remember Joe mentioning him?' Lucas asked.

'Oh, I do! Freddie was his best pal in the machine-gun team.' Olivia frowned. 'You told me he was badly injured on the day Joe perished. How is Freddie now?'

'He's making an amazing recovery.' Lucas's voice held a mixture of wonderment and satisfaction. 'His wounds were so bad that I thought he'd never get as far as the clearing station, let alone the hospital ship at Calais. But he's back in England and is now on his feet and convalescing at

43

Southend. He's fired up about returning to the fray as soon as he's fit.' Lucas shook his head. 'There aren't many like him. A lot try to swing the lead and stay put once they get a ticket home.'

'Heroes like Joe and Freddie put the malingerers to shame,' Olivia said passionately.

Lucas glanced at her. 'You sound as though you're referring to somebody in particular.'

'Just a fellow my sister likes. I know he's a coward.' She shrugged, shaking her head to indicate he wasn't worth talking about. And he wasn't. She refused to waste any of her precious time with Lucas even thinking about the likes of Harry Wicks.

'Are your family well?' Lucas lit a cigarette while steering the car into Hornsey Park Road.

'If you're asking after your old sparring partner,' Olivia said ruefully, 'yes ... Dad's much the same as ever.' Even as she spoke she realised this wasn't strictly true. She wasn't sure Tommy Bone *was* the same man he'd been just six months ago. When she'd waylaid him after work that night she'd had the opportunity to notice the changes in him. Even without Nancy telling her they fought like cat and dog, her father's sour-faced, grimy appearance spoke volumes as to how he felt, deep down, about the way things had turned out with Sybil Wright.

Lucas knew her father of old, so he was aware Tommy Bone was an unpleasant man. But he was also a proud one. He'd treated Lucas Black as his rival at the factory. Lucas hadn't been one of the Barratt family and therefore had no right to be a director, in her father's opinion. If anything, Tommy believed *he* had more right to be managing things than that upstart. He'd been with the firm for decades and had gained a reputation as an influential figure amongst the workforce – until Lucas sacked him for misconduct. Tommy had then been reinstated but everybody knew he'd never regain the power he'd once held. Things were changing at the factory ... throughout the land ... since the war had begun: men were disappearing from the workplace and being replaced by women and youngsters. Tommy Bone liked to be top dog in a masculine environment. Being surrounded by women didn't suit him. Nelly Smith in particular didn't suit him because she was a female version of himself.

Olivia knew her father wouldn't want his old boss aware that he'd deteriorated and now turned up at work looking like a vagrant. And whether he deserved her loyalty or not, it didn't occur to Olivia not to give it.

'Deborah Wallis told me you came home to see your family.' She shifted the focus to Lucas. 'How are they? They must miss you and worry dreadfully for your safety.'

'Mmmm ... '

His murmured reply held such an ironic inflection that Olivia tilted her head to read his expression. She knew little about his people because he'd never discussed them with her. The only person he had brought to her attention had been his girlfriend ... because he'd wanted her to know it wasn't a serious relationship and Olivia could easily take the other woman's place. All she had to do was say yes. But she never had. Instead she'd become engaged to Joe Hunter.

'That was an odd reply,' Olivia said lightly. 'Your mum and dad must have been overjoyed to have you back, looking so well.'

'My father died a few weeks ago and there were important matters to sort out and a burial to arrange. I was granted compassionate leave. That's why I'm back.'

'Oh! I had no idea. I'm so sorry!' Olivia's pretty face crumpled in sympathy.

'No need to be,' said Lucas in the same dry tone. 'We didn't get on.'

'Well, I'm sorry about that too then,' she said simply. 'How's your mum taking it all?'

'In the way of women of her generation and station in life ... stoically. Dry hanky ... dry gin,' he said sourly as he turned into Playford Road and drew the car to a halt.

'What d'you mean by that?' Olivia asked, sensing that behind his clipped words and hard profile was more emotion than he wanted to reveal. When he remained silent, she said, 'Sorry if that sounded prying. It's just ... you know quite a lot about my folks. I don't even know if you've got brothers or sisters.'

'A brother.'

'Oh,' Olivia said brightly. 'Older ...younger?'

'Older ... he suffers with his health. D'you fancy going out somewhere this evening? My last night. I travel to Dover in the morning.'

'I wish you were home for longer. Why didn't you come and see me sooner?' she asked. 'When Miss Wallis told me that you'd be leaving tomorrow, I thought you might go back without even saying hello to me.'

'It crossed my mind to do just that.' He shrugged. 'But here I am. No willpower where you're concerned, Olivia. Never did have.'

'Why are you being so peculiar? What have I done?' she demanded, hurt. 'I thought we'd become friends after what you did for Joe.'

'Is that all it was that brought us together? What I did for Joe?' Lucas was watching his fingers drumming a tattoo on the steering wheel. 'I thought we were friends before Joe turned up.' He made a terse gesture. 'Sorry . . . I sound like a bloody kid. I've had a lot on my mind and it's turned me sour. I wanted to come and see you sooner. In fact, there were only two people I really wanted to spend time with while I was home: Freddie Weedon and you.' He gave her a smile. 'Since you're better-looking than him, I saved the best till last. I want your face to be the one on my mind when I get on that blasted troop ship.'

'I'm sorry too. I didn't mean to sound whiney. Just . . . I've missed you and been worried about you. When you didn't write, I feared the worst. Was your brother able to help with the funeral arrangements if he's not well?'

'No, he's not up to anything like that. But it's all over with now. The earth's already settling . . . the wreaths are dying.' Lucas had been to Highgate cemetery that morning and stood looking at the fading roses, wondering why he could make himself feel only pity for the man who'd brought him up in affluence and comfort. 'Shall we go to a supper club this evening?'

Olivia was surprised by his abrupt change of subject but sighed, 'I'd love to, Lucas . . . '

'But?' he prompted with a sardonic edge to his voice.

'But . . . I've still got my younger ones to think of.'

'You're still looking after your brother?' He sounded genuinely surprised.

Olivia nodded. 'He can't go back to Dad's, nor can the others. My two sisters have moved in with me as well.' She hadn't intended to sound so apologetic. 'Dad's got a new woman and she's not very nice. None of us will ever go back there now,' she said firmly. 'I'm able to house them all, thanks to Joe.' She glanced at her late fiancé's gift to her: a terraced house that she loved to come home to every evening. She noticed a group of neighbours had stopped gossiping over the hedge and were watching them.

'Oh, come in, please.' She grimaced wryly, with a glance sideways. 'We're giving that lot a field day.'

'Don't want to put you out, if you've got a houseful ...'

'Come on, you're no trouble. I know you can behave yourself.' She gave him a saucy grin and got out of the car, beckoning him to follow her up the front path.

'Looks like you've been missed.' Lucas started to chuckle.

Olivia glanced at him then at the parlour window. A trio of faces was peeking out from behind one edge of the curtain.

'They usually wait tea until I get in. They're all probably hungry.' Olivia discreetly pulled a face at Maggie to make her drop the net curtain and stop gawping at them.

Chapter Five

'Who's that brought you home?' Maggie hissed, poking her head around the kitchen door. 'I think I recognise him.'

By the time Olivia had let herself into the house her brother and sisters had scampered to their bedrooms, leaving her to show Lucas into an empty parlour. But Maggie, unable to contain her curiosity, had crept back downstairs.

'It's Lucas Black. He was my boss at Barratt's before he joined up. He's staying for tea 'cos he's shipping out again tomorrow. It's the only chance we'll have for a get together.'

'I remember him now.' Maggie gave her sister a knowing look. 'You sucked up to him so Dad could get his job back at Barratt's. Whatever you did worked too, didn't it? Dad *did* get his job back.'

Olivia felt her hackles rise at Maggie's sly tone but she let it pass, not wanting anything to ruin her happiness at seeing Lucas.

'So you're over Joe already, are you, and on the hunt for a new boyfriend?' Maggie cocked her head. 'Didn't take you long to find somebody. He's a good looker and rich too, I'll bet.'

'It's nothing like that!' Olivia hissed, hoping none of her sister's impertinence had travelled as far as the parlour. Maggie had been growing nastier since Harry Wicks had turned up out of the blue and set them against one another. 'Just pipe down or he'll hear you being rude.'

'I don't care. You never mind Harry hearing *you* be rude about him.' Maggie defiantly crossed her arms over her chest.

'I really wish I didn't need to be rude about your boyfriend, Maggie. But you need to hear the truth about Harry. You deserve somebody far better than him, can't you see that?' When her sister continued to look sulky Olivia asked calmly, 'Have you forgotten how he treated you? You were just a kid when he started touching you. What sort of man does that?'

'He said he couldn't help himself ... 'cos he was so attracted to me. I felt the same way. I still do and always will. He was me first-ever boyfriend, so he's special.' Maggie's expression displayed a mixture of pride and bashfulness.

'How would you feel if somebody did to Nancy what Harry did to you?' Olivia continued cutting fruit cake into small slices. She could see she'd touched a nerve with Maggie by bringing their younger sister into it. Maggie wasn't looking so pleased with herself now and Olivia reckoned it might be as well to let her brood on it. She also knew this wasn't the time to finish the conversation, with Lucas just next door. 'Tell the others tea's nearly ready.'

'They won't come down while *he's* here. I told 'em to make themselves scarce.'

'Well, there was no need. Lucas doesn't mind having tea with us all. He's not a snob, you know.'

'Whether he is or he isn't don't matter to me. I don't want none. I'm going out.'

Olivia put down the knife and turned to her sister, feeling disappointed that she'd not managed to reason with Maggie and wipe that sulky expression off her face. 'Oh? Where are you off to?'

'Seeing Harry, if you must know.'

Olivia felt her heart plummet. 'But ... he's gone back to his regiment, hasn't he?'

'No, he hasn't. The wound in his leg opened up again.' Maggie snatched a sandwich from the plate, biting into it, then slid another into her skirt pocket. 'I'm glad he's still at home. He might get killed over there next time.'

'With any luck,' Olivia muttered beneath her breath.

'I'm getting me coat then I'm off.' Maggie picked up a piece of fruit cake and squirrelled that away as well.

'You haven't got any money for the caff this time, have you?' Olivia said.

'Got enough fer a bag of chips.' Maggie sounded defensive.

'For him?' Olivia shook her head on seeing her sister colouring up. 'So on top of everything else, Harry Wicks is a ponce who won't even treat you, or himself, to a bag of chips.'

'You're a fine one to talk!' Maggie snorted. 'Joe Hunter was a *proper* ponce. The worst sort! I've heard people say he was your pimp as well as your boyfriend.'

Olivia slapped her sister's sneering face before she could stop herself. 'You mean Harry said it! And don't you *dare* speak about Joe like that. He was a good man, the best, and you've got a short memory to criticise him. I recall that before Joe went off to fight, he stopped that vile brute trying to rape you.'

Maggie cupped her red cheek, bottom lip quivering. 'Harry would've stopped when I told him to,' she whined. 'Don't know if I *would've* told him to anyways. I liked him

51

kissing me. Besides, weren't none of your business. You and Joe shouldn't have poked yer noses in.'

At the end of her tether by now Olivia lunged to grab her, to shake some sense into her. But Maggie scooted off, almost bumping into Lucas approaching along the hall.

He dodged aside just in time as the girl fled up the stairs, snivelling.

'Thought I'd come to see if you needed a hand. Everything all right?'

'Yes ... just family problems.' Olivia closed her eyes and took a deep breath, wishing he'd not witnessed that embarrassing scene. 'Sorry to take a while with the tea.' She sighed and sat down at the kitchen table. 'Not a very nice atmosphere to invite you into, I'm afraid. I wouldn't have if I'd known what sort of mood Maggie would be in.'

'Do you want me to go?' Lucas asked quietly.

'No! Of course not. I want you to stay, for as long as you can. You might not be home again for ages,' she said huskily.

Their eyes met and she felt the sting of tears in her own. If Lucas was unlucky he might never come home ... never say a proper goodbye. Her last memory of Joe was saying farewell to him in Campbell Road. He'd collected her from work on his cart then dropped her off outside her house. That was the final time they'd touched or spoken. He'd not wanted to do last-minute goodbyes, he'd said. Before Olivia had entered the tenement to climb the stairs to her cramped room she'd blown him kisses, knowing that in the morning he would be on a troop ship taking him overseas. Now he lay where Lucas had buried him: in a corner of a French churchyard behind an aid post. Olivia knew with fierce certainty that one day she *would* go there and tell him all the things she'd never had a chance to say.

And she'd leave him a posy of flowers, as he had done for her, on the table of the house he had bequeathed to her in his will.

Lucas sat down opposite her at the table. 'Bloody relatives, eh?' He gave a wry chuckle and briefly pressed his hand over her clasped fingers.

'Do you get on well with your brother?' Olivia turned her hand, curling her fingers about his palm while looking earnestly at him. She'd like to know about his relationship with his family because through it she'd understand him better. At times he was quite a puzzle still, with his ironic comments and odd sense of humour.

He shook his head, pursing his lips. 'No ... we don't get on.'

Olivia felt saddened and a little shocked that he seemed isolated within his own family. Squabbling relatives wasn't something she would have associated with the well-to-do. 'So you're not close to any of them?'

'Unsurprisingly, really,' Lucas answered. 'None of them are my blood kin.'

'What d'you mean?' Her fingers squeezed his, begging for an answer when he would have broken free and got up from the table.

'I was adopted,' he said after a short pause, and withdrew his hand from hers. 'I expect I spring from rough sorts. That's why I whistled at you. Bad blood ... ' He stood up and raked his hand through his hair as though he regretted having disclosed as much. 'I'd better get going. I've still a few things to do before setting off tomorrow. Your brother's waiting for his tea.' He glanced over her shoulder.

Olivia half-turned to see Alfie hovering on the threshold, Nancy just behind, leaning against the doorjamb.

'Maggie said to come down,' Nancy explained with a hint of apology.

'Yes ... come on ... tuck in.' Olivia got to her feet and put the kettle on the stove to boil. She followed Lucas into the passage as he politely withdrew. She hadn't heard the door being slammed so imagined Maggie was still sulking in her room.

'My sister's got in with a bad sort,' she quietly told Lucas, knowing an explanation for Maggie's earlier behaviour was required. 'And the worst thing is the little fool just won't see through him.'

'How old is she?' Lucas looked at the stairs he'd seen her climb earlier.

'Fifteen – old enough to know better,' Olivia continued in the same quiet tone so the others wouldn't hear. 'God knows he's proved that he's no good.' She looked earnestly at Lucas. 'He's not like Joe ... a man burdened by vice, rather than freely choosing it. Harry Wicks is just an evil swine, but to Maggie I seem like the greatest hypocrite, having a go about her boyfriend when Joe was hardly an angel.' She paused then added, 'I'm sorry you didn't get any tea.'

'Life goes on much as it always has.' He smiled grimly. 'Even over there ... with the shrapnel raining down, I found myself wondering if my mother would turn up drunk at my father's wake.' He grimaced momentarily. 'But I'm glad I was dragged back here. It's been an opportunity to see you, and to catch up with Freddie.'

'And was your mother drunk at your father's wake?'

'No ... but my brother was.'

'And I'm guessing he said something you didn't like.' Olivia cocked her head, waiting for an answer.

'It wouldn't be the first time.'

'You didn't fight your own brother at your father's funeral?' Olivia said, aghast.

'I don't hit cripples,' Lucas replied. 'And he knows it. But that doesn't stop him trying to provoke me into it.' He turned away, indicating he'd said enough.

'Do you still fancy going out later?' Olivia followed him a few paces.

He turned towards her and from one ruefully elevated dark eyebrow she saw that he would indeed like to go out.

'Well, so do I! And you get to choose where we go as it's your last night.'

'I'll take you out, Miss Bone, on one condition,' Lucas said with affected authority. It was the sort of tone he might have used to her when he was her boss.

'And that is, sir?' she answered with a show of politeness.

'We don't talk about our relatives,' he said quietly.

She could see that he meant this so she extended her hand. 'Pact.'

He shook it. 'I'll come back for you in an hour then, shall I?'

Olivia nodded. 'I'll be ready. I'll just make sure the younger kids are settled for the evening.'

Lucas touched her cheek. 'You are unique, you know.'

'You told me that once before,' Olivia said. She knew they were both remembering that walk on the Alexandra Palace lawns when he'd suggested she become his mistress. He'd said she was unique then . . . in an idly patronising way. He wasn't being flippant now. He seemed more puzzled by her close attachment to her siblings.

After Lucas left Olivia got halfway up the stairs when she heard a scurrying sound on the landing. Looking up, she saw Maggie's shoes disappearing from sight, and shot after her. 'Have you been eavesdropping?' Olivia came to a breathless halt in her sister's bedroom doorway.

'What if I have?' Maggie flounced down on to her mattress. 'You're always spying on me and Harry.'

'I thought you were going out.'

'I am.' Maggie got up to peer out of the window. 'Harry said he'd wait for me across the road as you're always so narky.'

Olivia couldn't think of anything to say that might penetrate the hold Harry seemed to have over the girl. Instead she went to her room and drew a brush through her blonde hair, pushing some waves into it. She stopped herself from going over to her bedroom window, to watch her sister strolling off with a man Olivia despised. Today of all days shouldn't be spoiled by thoughts of Harry Wicks – not when she had the company of a man a hundred times his worth. She pulled from her wardrobe her prettiest blouse, with a pristine piecrust collar and embroidered panels on the bodice. She changed her skirt too, for the bottle green one she kept for best. Then she sat on the bed and put on her fancy brown leather boots. They pinched her feet a bit but she was determined to go out with Lucas in the very best clothes she owned.

She heard the toot of a car horn and quickly dabbed lily of the valley scent behind her ears. Grabbing her velvet hat, she deftly pinned it on her crown then told Alfie and Nancy she'd be out for an hour or two before hurrying to join Lucas.

Chapter Six

'Oi, hold up, Livvie!'

Olivia had just paid a call on her cousin in Campbell Road when her name was hollered by Mrs Keiver, who came charging up the street after her.

Weeks ago, Ruby had borrowed five shillings, having come out with a sob story about her boyfriend being injured down the market and unable to stump up his half of their rent. Olivia had been passing the Duke pub the other day and had glimpsed Riley McGoogan through the window. He'd looked to her to be in fine fettle, laughing and joking with an older fellow. She'd realised if she didn't remind Ruby of the debt it would never be repaid. As it was she'd only received half a crown and a sulky look as her cousin reluctantly handed over the coin.

'How are you doing, Matilda?' Olivia asked as the older woman puffed to a halt in front of her.

'Reckon I've been better, luv.' Matilda pulled a face. 'My Jack's driving me bonkers ... going on about joining up.' She shook her head. 'That bombing over Stoke Newington started him off again and he ain't stopped since. I know this bleeding war is dragging on but we just want our men safe at home.'

'Amen to that,' Olivia said in a heartfelt way.

'Sorry ... that was thoughtless.' Matilda grimaced in embarrassment. This poor girl's fiancé would never be safe at home again. 'Who'd've thought we'd see the day? My Alice and your Maggie making grenades and things in factories,' Matilda rattled on to cover her slip. She made to cross the road to the corner shop. 'Oh, I almost forgot what I wanted to speak to you about.' She hesitated at the kerb and pursed her lips. 'Now, I ain't sure how you'll take this but I'll tell you anyway to put you on yer guard. A man's been hanging around asking questions about you. He spoke to me neighbour but Beattie didn't tell him nothin' 'cos she didn't like the look of him. She pointed him out to me just as he was sloping off into Paddington Street.'

'He asked about *me*?' Olivia frowned. 'Who was he, d'you know?'

'He told Beattie his name was Walter Baker, but he was lyin'.' Matilda scowled. 'He can use whatever name he likes but *I* won't ever forget who he *really* is. It's been a long time since he lived here and he looks different now. Perhaps he thought he could sneak back and nobody'd know him. Ain't surprising Beattie never recognised him. He's gone skinny as a rake and taken to wearing a cap, 'cos he's almost bald. He used to be quite a fine figure of a man with thick wavy hair. Thought himself Jack the Lad, he did, and gave his wife such a hard time, knocking her about to keep her quiet while he was off with his women.'

'Who is it?' Olivia butted in, anxious to find out why this stranger might be interested in her.

'Herbie Hunter, that's who. If he's sniffing around then

he must know that you and his son Joe were very close.' Matilda wagged a cautioning finger. 'If he bangs on yer door, you tell him in no uncertain terms to sling his hook. He's bad news, even by Bunk standards.'

Olivia knew that was true; Joe had told her how he hated his father for beating his mother and injuring his baby sister when she wouldn't stop crying. Joe had vowed to kill his father if he ever clapped eyes on him again.

'You let me know if he starts bothering you and I'll get Jack to put him on his backside. Don't want his sort round here.'

With a wave Matilda crossed the road to Smithie's corner shop and Olivia carried on home, deep in thought. If Joe's father *had* turned up out of the blue, looking for her by name, then he'd obviously made it his business to find out about recent events. He would know that Joe had perished on the Western Front and that she was living in his son's house ... that was now hers. Or did Mr Hunter believe he had a claim on Joe's property? Olivia's prickle of uneasiness became a surge of anger. Well, let him come round! She'd soon tell him what she thought of him *and* what his son had thought of him as Joe was no longer able to do it himself.

In fact, when she turned the corner into Playford Road she saw that a weedy, balding fellow, like the one Matilda had just described, was loitering at the far end. There was something vaguely familiar about him and then she recalled where she'd seen him: in the pub with Riley McGoogan earlier in the week. So, it seemed Herbie had been hanging around for days, no doubt trying to find out as much as he could before approaching her.

It was a warm evening and he was fanning himself with the brim of his cap. He'd noticed her approach but was pretending he hadn't. He flipped the cap back onto his bald head then made a show of ferreting in his pocket for a pack of cigarettes. Olivia slowed down, trying to make up her mind whether to dash over and confront him or slip indoors without saying a word.

She was certainly not a coward; she'd done battle at work and at home on occasions when she'd thought a bad situation merited it and her conscience wouldn't let her keep quiet. But she had her brother and sisters to think about. Maggie, Nancy and Alfie were under her roof and she didn't want to stir up any unnecessary unpleasantness that might also envelop them. There was a faint chance that Mr Hunter had just turned up to make the acquaintance of the woman his late son had hoped to marry. Perhaps he was a reformed character who'd repented his sins. Even as she thought it she knew it wasn't true. His shifty stance and furtive peeps from beneath his cap brim told her more than enough about the sort of character Herbert Hunter was.

On impulse she jogged across the road to speak to him because she didn't want him to bother her once she went inside. 'Heard from a friend of mine round in the Bunk that you've been looking for me, Mr Hunter.'

She could see she'd startled him by being so brazen. And he startled her right back. As he brought up his chin and stared at her she saw that his eyes were the same shade as her dear Joe's: a deep tawny colour. But there the similarity between father and son ended. Joe had been a broad-shouldered handsome man with light brown hair. This individual looked as though he might have once been the strapping fellow Matilda had described, but his face and body had shrivelled. His shoulders were stooped and his arms, beneath rolled up shirtsleeves, looked more skin and bone than flesh.

Yet, oddly, his face retained some youthfulness, despite the wrinkles on his jowls and neck, which was partially covered by a colourful knotted scarf. Her own father had just turned fifty but this man looked years younger. Olivia understood Matilda's observation that Herbie thought himself Jack the Lad. He had a conceited way about him, hardly merited by his unattractive appearance.

Having taken a leisurely last drag on his cigarette, Herbie dropped it to the pavement and ground it out with his toe. 'Reckon yer mistaken there, luv,' he said then sniffed. 'Me name's Baker ... Walter Baker, but I'm always happy to make the acquaintance of a pretty young gel.' He gave her a crafty wink.

Olivia ignored his outstretched hand. 'Joe told me that you were a womaniser. He told me lots of things about you. So did my friend Matilda.'

'Is that right?' Herbie decided against continuing with the sham. He'd only intended using an alias with the people in Campbell Road because he'd not wanted the likes of Matilda Keiver recognising him and bringing up things that should stay dead and buried. Thirteen years might have passed but the ruckus he'd created just before he'd been run out of the street by a mob ready to lynch him was unlikely to have been forgotten. He'd spotted Matilda in Campbell Road, but had hoped she'd not recognised him. It seemed the cow had, though, and she'd grassed on him.

'So what is it you're after?' Olivia asked bluntly.

'Just come to see me son's fiancée.' Herbie cocked his head and crossed his thin arms over his chest. 'Was gonna introdooce meself properly in me own time. Thought I'd make it a surprise.'

'It's that all right!' Olivia stated coldly. 'I know Joe hadn't clapped eyes on you in ages. Not that he wanted to.'

'Can tell what my boy saw in a good-looking gel like you.' Herbie ignored the rebuff and continued to act smarmy. 'Bet you must have lots of admirers. Wouldn't blame yer one bit fer moving on now, though.' He shook his head, acting sorrowful. 'Unhappy memories round here for you, I'll bet. And being as Joe's not coming home, you won't even have his grave to visit, will yer?' He slung his arm about her shoulders in what was meant to be a fatherly gesture. 'Going back Wood Green way, are yer, ducks? Be close to yer own folks ...'

'*I'm* here to stay. But I doubt you will be.' Olivia squirmed out of his embrace. 'The people in Campbell Road don't want you around and neither do I.' She felt incensed that he knew so much about her and that he'd had the cheek to act familiar with her. She guessed that Riley McGoogan had been the one with the loose tongue. Olivia resolved to ask Ruby to tell her boyfriend to mind his own business in future.

'That ain't a very nice welcome,' Herbie moaned. 'I'm Joe's next-of-kin ... all he had left, apart from you.' His eyes wandered deliberately towards the house across the road. 'Gonna invite me in fer a cuppa, are you, Olivia? I'll tell you all about Joe as a nipper, if yer like.'

'I don't need you to tell me a thing. Joe told me all about his upbringing,' she said scathingly. 'That's why you should get going and never come back.'

'He bought that place you're living in, didn't he?' Herbie gave up on hints and innuendo and cut to the chase.

'He did, then left it to me in his will.' So she'd been right in suspecting his father had come to see if Joe had died leaving anything of value he could get his hands on.

'Be nice to have a memento of me son's. A watch or something like that.'

Herbie wasn't ready to give up on making a profit from his visit. But his pretence at friendliness had disappeared. His hard eyes and twitching mouth told Olivia he was having difficulty holding in his temper.

'He didn't leave you anything at all, not even a letter. Sorry.' Olivia was on the point of turning to cross the road when she heard running footsteps just behind.

'Who you talking to, Livvie?' Alfie called out.

'Well ... well ... who's this little chap then?' Herbie grinned and bent to hold out a hand for Alfie to shake. He squinted at Olivia. 'Can't be me son's. He looks like *you*, though, Olivia, don't he?'

'I'm her brother Alfie,' he piped up. 'And I'm eight.'

'Are yer now? Well, you need feeding up to make you bigger, don't yer, son? You don't look that old. Pleased to meet yer though.'

'Go home, Alfie,' Olivia said quietly. 'I'll be over in a minute.'

Alfie loped across the road and let himself in.

'So, got a kid brother living with you, have you?'

Something in the man's tone made Olivia's skin crawl. But she said nothing else and crossed the road.

'I'll make meself scarce then, Olivia ... fer now,' Herbie called after her.

Olivia glanced back to see a satisfied smile slanting his mouth. As he sloped off she felt a queasiness in her belly. She quickly opened her gate but couldn't stop herself hesitating by the door to peer after the figure just disappearing around the corner.

*

63

Olivia wasn't the only one to have been watching Herbie Hunter's scruffy back as he swaggered off. Tommy Bone had come out on this Saturday afternoon, as he often did, to catch the bus to Islington in the hope of observing his eldest girl enjoying her weekend. He never approached Olivia, but would trail in her wake to watch her browsing the market stalls or disappearing into Hornsey Baths. Sometimes he stood in the shadows nearby while she chatted with her neighbours. When she was indoors, he'd loiter in the environs of Playford Road, waiting for her to emerge. There was a nook behind a hedge on the corner where he could secrete himself and gain a good view of her house.

Over the months of his vigil he'd witnessed things about his family that he hadn't known before. For example, he'd seen his daughter Maggie knocking about with Harry Wicks.

Tommy had been surprised and indignant to know *they'd* hooked up behind his back when Maggie was so much younger than Harry. When Tommy had first seen his neighbour hanging about dressed in hospital blues, he'd thought Harry must be after Livvie, and that *had* got his goat. His Livvie deserved better than a butcher's apprentice, which was what Harry had been before he joined up. She'd deserved better than a pimp too, or so Tommy had thought, until Sybil had told him, having heard it from Ruby, that Olivia had inherited her fiancé's property. After that Tommy had felt more kindly disposed to Joe Hunter, especially as he was now dead but had left Olivia set up for life.

Another thing Tommy had discovered was that his youngest daughter Nancy was out working in an Islington factory rather than finishing her schooling in Wood Green. Again he felt too apathetic to do anything about that, although not so long ago he would have knocked ten bells out of her for doing it. Livvie was the only one to interest him because she was so similar to her mother, in looks and character. And since his eldest now had a home to call her own he felt more determined than ever to heal the rift between them.

Sybil had taken over in Wood Green to such a degree that Tommy felt like a stranger in his own house. In fact, he was trying to think of a way to ask Livvie to let him move in with her. They'd be a family again ... a proper family ... Aggie's family. He was sure Livvie wouldn't deny her old dad all the home comforts she'd once uncomplainingly provided for him. Now he never had a hot meal on the table or a clean shirt to wear. After he'd made it clear to Sybil he wasn't getting married, she'd stopped doing anything at all for him and turned her back on him in bed every night.

Tommy had felt despondent since the day he'd got home from work to discover that Nancy had packed her bags and left. His youngest daughter had been the last link to his old life in Wood Green with Aggie and their children. He'd read from Sybil's smug expression that she was glad she'd managed to eject every one of her sister's kids from the nest so that the cuckoos could settle in. She and her son Mickey now had the place to themselves. Though Tommy didn't mind Mickey; in fact, he preferred him to Alfie.

When Alfie had been at home it had been hard for him to breathe around his son. If his youngest child had never been born everything would have been right, he believed. His wife would still be at Tommy's side and they and their three daughters would be a contented family. His conveniently skewed nostalgia brushed aside the spectre of his wife's sister and the two illegitimate children Sybil had given birth to, unbeknown to Aggie.

Tommy lit a cigarette then set off up the road, tailing the fellow Livvie had been talking to. He was curious to know this stranger's identity, and where he lived. He was too old and ugly to be an admirer but Tommy had taken against him because it was obvious that Livvie didn't like him. She'd jumped like a scalded cat when he'd got too close and put an arm round her shoulders. Tommy had been on the point of bounding out of his hidey-hole to confront the man but had stopped himself. If he'd done that it'd give the game away that he'd been spying on her.

It wasn't like Livvie to be intimidated by anybody; she was a strong principled young woman and without a doubt Tommy was proud of her, though he'd never admitted as much. So, he was going to warn this skinny runt off in case he came back and bothered her again. Tommy chuckled to himself. Then he'd let Livvie know what he'd done to protect her. She was fair, was Livvie, and might do him a good turn back and agree to him moving in with her and the kids.

*

Herbie Hunter hadn't worked the mean streets of Soho as a young man, dodging other pimps' wrath while on their patches, not to know when he was being stalked. And this fellow, lumbering along like an elephant, wasn't even doing a very good job of it.

He stopped by a lamp post and struck a match, just so he could get a crafty glance at his opponent. Herbie dragged on the cigarette then through an exhalation of smoke saw the man was loitering by a draper's window, pretending to take an interest in ladies' vests. Herbie started off again, wondering if somebody from Campbell Bunk had followed him, and if so, why. Anybody who remembered what had gone on would hate him but they'd not put themselves out to pursue him when he was heading off in the opposite direction.

He'd fled the Bunk following a serious incident that could have got him imprisoned. The coppers hadn't caught up with him because those living in the Bunk preferred to police their own. By the time the law had got involved Herbie had been long gone. He blamed his wife for the trouble that day. She'd gone out and left him in charge of the kids. The youngest wasn't his child. The fact that his wife had slept with a foreigner hadn't bothered him. It had been his job to find her punters and all he was interested in was the colour of their money. From the moment the baby had been born, though, he knew she'd made him a laughing stock – letting *that* happen. The fact that Herbie had introduced the man to her in the line of business in no way altered his view that it was an infernal liberty she'd taken in dropping an immigrant's sprog. So he was hardly to blame for losing his rag with a kid who never stopped crying and wasn't even his.

Unbeknown to Herbie, and the man dogging his footsteps, they had something in common. They'd both laid into children; the only difference was that in Tommy's case Alfie had survived being knocked about.

Tommy put on a sprint as his quarry strolled around the corner. It was clouding over and the dusk was coming down early. He was getting irritated that the bloke hadn't arrived at his destination by now. Tommy was hungry and in need of a pint. Usually he was in the pub at this time. But he'd followed the blighter this far so reckoned he might as well see it through to the bitter end.

He took a left into a narrow lane, tripping over an outstretched leg that sent him sprawling flat on his face.

In a flash Herbie was down on one knee beside him, holding a blade to his throat. 'So ... what you after then?' he growled. Even when he'd been a strong athletic man he'd carried a knife. Years of smoking and drinking too much had prematurely aged his physique and he feared coming off worst in a fair fight. These days he never hesitated to pull out a weapon. He'd been more cautious in the days when his fists could speak for him.

'What yer doing?' Tommy blustered, elongating his neck to avoid the cold steel a hairsbreadth from his Adam's apple. He felt a fool for not having been more careful. He'd walked into that one.

'You been following me. Don't deny it.' The blade nicked Tommy's throat. 'You after robbing me?'

'You don't look like you gotta pot ter piss in, mate,' Tommy spat scornfully.

'What you after then?'

Tommy gave up pretending innocence. 'Just after a chat about summat, so let me up.'

Herbie removed his knee from Tommy's chest and beckoned with the blade for him to get up. He held out the weapon at arm's length ready to defend himself. His stalker looked to be twice his weight and if the bloke rushed him, Herbie would go down like a sack of spuds.

Tommy licked his lips while they circled one another warily in the confined space. 'You've been making a nuisance of yerself with Olivia Bone. Don't bother saying you ain't. I saw yer with me own eyes.'

'You out of the Bunk?'

'What?' It took Tommy a moment to realise the other man was asking if he lived in Campbell Road where Sybil and her kids used to have rooms. 'No, I ain't out of that slum!' he answered indignantly.

'Matilda Keiver ain't sent you after me?' Herbie knew that woman and her husband were quite capable of doing it. He doubted she'd bother though. Matilda was a bruiser who'd battle it out with men or women and stand up for anybody she liked. But this particular battle was long over. Herbie's wife and daughter were both dead now, like Joe.

'Nobody's *sent* me after yer, I'm me own man.' Tommy puffed out his chest. 'You'd better tell me who *you* are. I saw you with me daughter. She don't like you, so you'd better stay away. I'm only warning you the once.' He jutted his chin belligerently but was keeping a close eye on the knife.

'Olivia Bone's your daughter, eh?' Herbie concealed his surprise and disappointment. He'd pumped Riley McGoogan for information about Olivia and had been told that she didn't have a boyfriend or parents on the scene. It had suited Herbie to know that she was on her own. That way he'd be better placed to get what he wanted out of her. 'Well ... seems we was almost related once then. Me son's Joe Hunter.'

That took Tommy back. He narrowed his eyes suspiciously. If Hunter Senior had come sniffing about, looking like he needed a few bob to tide him over, there was only one reason for that in Tommy's mind. Joe Hunter had been a wealthy man, by Bunk standards, owning his own property. 'Well, don't matter who y'are, we don't want you hanging around outside *our* house,' Tommy emphasised.

'Ain't *your* fuckin' house!' Herbie was incensed to think

that a property that should rightfully be his had been taken over by another man.

'Think you'll find it is, mate, all signed and sealed.' Tommy couldn't stop himself boasting. 'Joe Hunter left me daughter that property 'cos she was his intended. She ain't yet of age. *I'm* her father, looking out for her till she is.'

'Yeah, and I'm Joe's *real* next-of-kin. Flesh and blood trumps fancy pieces where I come from. Me son never married your daughter, did he? Maybe he never would've. He was a good-looking man. Easy come, easy go, with women, was Joe. So we'll see about that,' Herbie blustered. He felt rage building in his chest but turned away, sauntering towards the mouth of the lane.

Tommy was no less enraged on hearing the fellow speak about his Livvie as though she were some tart his son had hooked up with. He gave a contemptuous laugh on seeing his adversary retreating, although he hadn't forgotten he'd been tripped up and had a knife held to his throat. Now the knife had disappeared and the weasel had his back to him, so Tommy saw his chance of revenge. He took a silent bound forward and swung a rabbit punch to let Herbie Hunter know he didn't appreciate being ambushed and threatened.

Herbie saw the shadow on the wall looming and instinct more than malice made him spin around and lash out. The knife tore into Tommy's chest and he gave a grunt of surprise rather than pain as he clutched at himself. For a moment he gaped at Herbie then he took his hands off his chest and saw the blood spurting. The shock of it made his knees sag and he wilted quite gracefully to the ground.

'You stupid bastard. What d'you do that for?' Herbie dropped down beside Tommy, leaning over him. Just a quick glance at the blood bubbling between the wounded man's lips was enough to make Herbie fall back onto his posterior. He blinked rapidly, looking left and right, then dug a hand into Tommy's pockets, emptying them of a ten-shilling note and some change. He took Bone's cigarette case too because a quick flick of the clasp had shown it was almost full. Then, springing up, Herbie slipped out of the alley with his head down. Moments later he was sprinting, hell for leather, into the darkness.

Chapter Seven

Herbie wanted to move back into Campbell Road. The area and its inhabitants, with their cunning, secretive ways, suited him. He'd always felt at home there. At present he was renting a basement room in Muswell Hill. That suited him too, even though it was running with damp and no bigger than a coal bunker, which he imagined it had been at one time. The atmosphere smelled sooty and the cold brick floor was covered in black grit.

He never saw the landlord and posted his tanner a week rent through the door of the room above where the landlord's brother lived. Herbie rarely saw him either, being as the poor sod had only one leg and was virtually housebound. Sid Monk paid a neighbour to do his bit of shopping for him. Herbie had a feeling he *was* the landlord, but when Herbie had taken the room a month ago the fellow had hobbled to the door on a crutch and told him he wasn't, he just collected the rent for his brother. Sid had told Herbie not to bother him in future but to put the rent through the door, which was fine by Herbie. He liked to be left alone as well.

He guessed that Sid used such tactics so his tenants didn't take the piss because he was a cripple. Herbie wasn't bothered who really owned the shithole ... but he was bothered about the mess he was in now.

He was sitting on the edge of the flock mattress that served as his bed with its single threadbare blanket. He had dropped his head into his hands as he brooded on what he'd done last night. But it hadn't been his fault. If the stupid git hadn't crept up on him like that they'd both have got home safely.

The coppers wouldn't see it like that, though, and Herbie didn't want them delving into his past and opening a can of worms. He was tempted to creep back to see if Tommy Bone *had* managed to drag himself off. But he knew it was futile.

Herbie stood up and padded to the dirty window that let in a little light from the street. He'd jumped straight into bed last night, in a panic, and had fallen off to sleep surprisingly quickly. He twisted his wrists to and fro examining his crimson-crusted hands, then he brushed down his donkey jacket. The stain on the dark material barely noticed but the blood on his shirt was clearly visible. He cursed. He'd have to burn it and it was the only decent one he had. He pulled out of his pocket the cash he'd stolen and the cigarette case. He'd got five cigarettes left so took one and lit it, turning the case over in his hands. With any luck he might be able to swap that for a new shirt. But not round here. He'd go further afield. In fact, he reckoned he'd use some of Bone's ten shillings to take a train ride and see his sister. Not that the miserable cow was likely to give him much of a welcome in Southend.

*

73

'Shhh! Here she comes ...'

Olivia was used to Nelly and her cronies whispering about her behind her back, so took little notice of the awkward atmosphere as she deposited her bag under the bench. On the bus to work that morning, she'd been remembering Maggie questioning her about continuing to work at Barratt's when munitions vacancies were readily available. That conversation had stuck in Olivia's mind. Her sister saw munitions as a way of making good money and without a doubt Olivia would like a pay rise too. But it was the realisation that she felt guilty for not doing enough to help with the war effort that really made her ready for a change. Always at the back of her mind was Joe, and the sacrifice he'd made to keep the folk at home safe. Apart from that she knew she was outgrowing her first full-time job and was ready to taste new things.

When she'd started at Barratt's it had seemed sophisticated to be working in the big place where her father had always made his living. She'd grown up with the smell of sweets in the air she breathed. Barratt's had dominated the local landscape for many years. Everybody knew somebody who worked at the factory; it had been the hub of the Wood Green community. And still was. But just a couple of years ago the place had been vibrant and exciting, filled with people. Things were different now. The hubbub was still to be heard at dinnertimes when staff took a breather outside to stretch their legs before afternoon shift started. But the sound of lads catcalling the factory girls with lewd suggestions had all but disappeared as, one by one, they went off to fight overseas. Joe and Lucas and those fresh-faced youths had faced up to a new and terrifying test. Olivia knew if she moved job she'd miss Cath . . . and her dad too, oddly enough . . . but it was a small enough sacrifice to make. Her train of thought was interrupted as her colleagues' sibilant whispering increased in volume.

'Poor cow . . . can tell she don't know nothin' about it. First her fiancé and now this.'

Olivia focused on her colleagues, frowning when several pairs of eyes swerved aside rather than meet her gaze.

Briskly, she put on her sacking apron and settled down at the bench to roll aniseed balls. The pungent smell of the aniseed was in her throat as she bent over the sugar paste. But her mind was alert now to those around her. She sensed there could be more to it than just gossip and wondered if she was in trouble of some sort. Her uneasiness increased with Miss Wallis's appearance. The secretary and Nelly put their heads together before both peering at Olivia.

Something in their sombre expressions made Olivia's guts lurch. Immediately she thought of the last time Deborah Wallis had come down to the factory floor to summon her upstairs. She'd wanted to talk about Lucas . . .

Olivia rose from her stool, blood draining from her face, just as Nelly hurried over.

'Miss Wallis wants you to go to her office, love,' Nelly said in the gentlest tone Olivia had ever heard her use. But still the older woman avoided meeting her eyes.

'Is it bad news?' Olivia gazed earnestly at her.

'Just go and speak to her, Livvie,' Nelly sighed, and patted her shoulder.

Olivia walked the length of a bench that seemed interminable, knowing all eyes were on her and that the murmuring following her progress would grow louder the moment she'd quit the room.

On Olivia's entering the office, Deborah Wallis used a similar soft tone while inviting her to take a seat.

Olivia felt her hands shaking and gripped them together. 'I'll stand, thanks,' she said hoarsely. Usually neither woman would have given her a kind word. 'What is it?' she blurted. 'Have you received bad news from France?'

Deborah looked perplexed before enlightenment struck. 'Oh, I don't have any news of Mr Black. I need to speak to you about your father.'

'My dad?' Olivia nearly giggled with relief. She sank down into the chair she'd been invited to use. 'What's he done?'

'It's my sad duty to tell you there's been an accident.'

'Accident?' Olivia parroted. It was Monday morning. The day had only just begun! Surely he couldn't have got into trouble in the short while since starting work. He'd caused uproar at Barratt's before by being stupidly careless, and had been sacked by Lucas because of it. Olivia felt a coldness creep over her. 'Has somebody been injured out in the yard?'

'It's nothing to do with work, my dear.' Deborah rose from behind her desk to come and place a comforting hand on Olivia's shoulder. 'Your father was hurt in an incident in the street. It appears that Tommy was attacked late on Saturday night.'

Olivia swivelled on the seat to gawp at Deborah. 'Attacked?' she echoed. 'A fight, you mean?' She abruptly sprang to her feet, frowning.

'A constable came here briefly this morning and spoke to Mr Barratt. You should take today off and spend it with your family.'

'Is my father in hospital?' An awful suspicion was worming into Olivia's mind that a tragedy had occurred rather than an accident.

'I believe he was taken to hospital.' Deborah chose her words carefully. 'But you should go and see Mrs Wright for the details. The police have informed your aunt about it all. So don't worry about work or anything like that. You'll want to go and see her.'

'He's dead . . . isn't he?' Olivia whispered with a mixture of shock and disbelief.

'I'm so sorry, Olivia.' Deborah shook her head. 'It's hard to believe that Tommy Bone is . . . that something like this has happened to him.'

Like an automaton Olivia said thank you and goodbye before hurrying from the secretary's office.

Before returning to the factory floor to collect her things, she took a breather in the corridor outside, trying to control her thundering heart. She didn't know for sure *what* had happened, she impressed on herself. Deborah hadn't confirmed anything other than that her father was in hospital. There could still be hope that his injuries, however bad, weren't fatal and he might recover. He was strong as an ox . . .

She marched into the workroom, expecting the whispering to start up again. Only stillness and silence accompanied her to her seat. Apart from Nelly, who came shuffling close beside her as though she believed the girl might swoon and need support.

Olivia was on her way out again with her jacket and bag when Sal, who sat beside her at the bench, said in a rousing voice, 'Best of luck, Livvie.' And then others joined in, chorusing, 'Good luck, love.' Just before she went out of the door, Nelly gave her a spontaneous hug. 'Be thinking of you, Livvie, and yer family, too.'

Out on the forecourt Olivia glanced up to see Deborah

Wallis watching her from the office window on the first floor. Deborah raised a hand before dropping her chin to her chest and turning away. Olivia leaned back against the brick pillar, trying to control her shaking. The nicer people were to her, the more upset she became, fearing the worst. Suddenly she pushed away from the brick and began running in the direction of Ranelagh Road and the house where she'd spent her childhood and youth before her father had kicked her out. He'd believed she'd been carrying on with Joe Hunter and got herself pregnant. And she *had* been seeing Joe ... but not in the way her father had meant. Their love had been an innocent affair, unlike his.

Word had spread fast, she realised, as she breathlessly rounded the corner. Neighbours had congregated by the gate and as she approached they parted to let her through, patting her shoulder and murmuring condolences.

'So sorry to hear about it, Olivia. Best wishes to the family from all of us.' Olivia recognised the spokeswoman. Usually Mrs Wicks liked to keep to herself. If she ever found out about her eldest son's disgusting antics she'd probably never show her face outside the house again. But Olivia's good manners prompted her to murmur thanks to Harry's mother while she hurried up the path.

The door had been left on the latch and inside the air smelled musty ... unfamiliar. When Olivia had lived here the house had held the scent of washed cotton and Sunlight soap. She entered the parlour and squinted into the murky environment. There was no sign of her aunt but she could hear muted voices.

The room was littered with odds and ends, and felt cold and damp despite the sunshine outside.

'Where's your mum, Mickey?' As her eyes adjusted to the

dim interior Olivia noticed her young cousin seated at the table. He had that anxious wide-eyed stare children have when unsure how to deal with upset grown ups.

'She's in her bedroom,' he whispered. 'She's been crying. Mrs Cook from next door's with her.'

Olivia crouched down at the side of Mickey's chair, taking his hands in hers and squeezing them. She was sure that if there'd been any hope left, Sybil would have been at Tommy's hospital bedside. Although she herself felt shattered Olivia wanted to comfort Mickey; the poor lad hadn't even known that Tommy Bone was his father. He'd grieve for an uncle, if he grieved at all.

'D'you know what's happened?' she asked him in an unsteady voice.

He nodded vigorously. 'Uncle Tommy's been murdered.'

'Did the police come and tell you that?' Again Olivia had difficulty controlling herself enough to speak.

'They told Mum. She fainted. That's why they asked Mrs Cook to come and sit with her for a while. They said they'd come back later and talk to her again when she'd calmed down.'

Tears had sprung to Olivia's eyes and wet her cheeks. Absently she used the back of her hand on them.

'Where's Ruby? Mum's been asking for her.' Mickey pushed back his chair and stood up, fidgeting on the spot. 'Ruby'll know what to do,' he said plaintively.

Olivia had forgotten all about Ruby, and about her brother and sisters. Tommy Bone had six kids. Somebody would have to break the news to all of them. She imagined that Ruby would get the news from people at work, as Olivia had.

'I'll just go and have a word with your mum.' Olivia

didn't relish the prospect. She and Sybil had never got on, and Olivia knew that would not change now.

The bedroom stank of stale sweat and gin. When Olivia entered Mrs Cook got up from the chair by the bed, relief evident on her face. She hurried over to Olivia, and indicated they should step outside.

'Poor cow's cried herself to sleep, I think,' she whispered once the door was closed. 'I'll be going now you're here. Not much anyone can do, I'm afraid. Terrible business. I'm so sorry, love.'

'D'you know any details of what happened?' Olivia asked, sniffing back fresh tears. She was desperate to understand how big arrogant Tommy Bone could have met such an abrupt and violent end. He'd been an abrasive character, and certainly not everybody had liked him, but she'd never known him to associate with villains or even be in a fight.

"S far as I can make out, your poor father was attacked in an alley. He wasn't found till Sunday morning, so it was too late for anything to be done, the constable said. Wicked people about, there are.' Ethel Cook sorrowfully shook her head. 'Place ain't the same since all them Belgians turned up.' She wagged a finger. 'I said that to the copper but he didn't answer me. That got me thinking ...'

'That you, Rube?' Olivia's aunt called..

'I'll leave you be, Livvie. You'll want to be on your own to talk about things.' Mrs Cook beat a hasty retreat.

Olivia opened the bedroom door and entered the room to see her aunt peering at her from the bed. The curtains were drawn. Olivia imagined they stayed like that most of the time, tragedy or no tragedy.

'Oh, it's only you, is it?' Sybil sank back down against the pillows. 'Your father didn't have a good word to say about you, miss. Same goes fer me, so you might as well clear off.'

'I want to know what happened,' Olivia croaked. 'What did the police tell you?'

'Somebody's murdered yer father, that's what they bleedin' said! And now I'm left not knowing which way to turn,' Sybil whined. She elbowed herself to a seated position on the mattress. 'What're me 'n' Mickey going to do to keep a roof over our heads with no money coming in?' She slapped her palms down hard on the mattress in rage and frustration.

Olivia lowered herself into the chair Ethel Cook had vacated. Her father had been no pushover. She imagined he'd been taken by surprise to have suffered fatal injuries. 'Was it a robbery? Is that why he was set about?'

'Don't know ... might've been.' Sybil seemed irritated by the questions. 'Unlike him not to have a penny on him or his cigarette case,' she mumbled. 'The copper said he'd nothing in his pockets except his pay slip from Barratt's. That's how they knew who he was.' She plucked at the bedclothes. 'They kept asking me if he had any enemies ... well, he didn't. Not that I knew of anyhow. But then, he didn't have no friends neither.'

'Bill Morley at the factory was his friend,' Olivia said quietly. 'Dad had others too, I'm sure.'

'Yeah ... you know everything, don't yer!' Sybil said nastily. Suddenly she flung back the blankets and got up, shuffling to the window to peer out from behind one edge of a curtain. 'Nosy bleeders out there.' She banged on the window. 'Go on! Piss off the lot of yers!'

'D'you want a cup of tea?' Olivia asked as she saw Sybil reach beneath the pillow for a gin bottle then turn her back to take a crafty swig. 'I'll make one.'

'If you can find a bit of tea 'n' milk I'll have one,' Sybil said without a hint of appreciation. 'Put plenty of sugars in it 'cos I need it to steady meself. Nervous wreck, I am.'

Olivia went back to the parlour. She didn't want to run the gauntlet of the neighbours so gave Mickey some coins for the shop and sent him out with a warning not to answer questions. The boy had been born with a deformed foot but it didn't stop him getting about and he quickly loped off.

She was setting out the cups when Ruby rushed through the door.

'Just heard at work about yer dad.' She gave Olivia a hug. 'Bloody hell! So sorry, Livvie. I know we've all had our ups and downs in this family but what a terrible thing to have happened.' She glanced about. 'Where's me mum? At the police station?'

'No ... in her bedroom.' Olivia jerked her head at Sybil's door, her expression speaking for her as to the woman's mood.

'Sober, is she?' Ruby knew her mother of old: Sybil was an alcoholic who used any drama as an excuse to open a bottle. Something like this could keep her out for the count for weeks. Ruby greeted her brother as he came in with his arms full. 'All right, are you, mate?'

Mickey put down the groceries and clasped his arms about his sister's waist, seeking comfort.

'Come on ... pull yerself together now,' Ruby said briskly. 'It'll be fine.' She disengaged herself from his embrace.

Olivia made the tea and then held out a cup and saucer to Mickey. 'Take your mum her tea, will you, there's a good lad?'

As soon as he went off the two young women exchanged morose looks.

'What d'you think your mum'll do now? Will she stay

here?' Olivia knew if she kept her mind on practicalities she'd keep the tears at bay. She'd not always got on with her father, in fact at times she'd believed she'd hated him, but not now.

Now the ache in her chest reminded her that her affection for her father had never completely died. There had been a bond between them that couldn't be broken by anything except this final parting, and she guessed it had been forged, not by either of them, but by their mutual love for Aggie Bone. In her heart Olivia had cherished a belief there'd come a time when they would all be reconciled. Perhaps when the two boys were older and became aware of how they were really related, the removal of that final deceit would take with it any residual bitterness between the Bones and Wrights.

But it was too late for that, or for goodbyes. There was so much Olivia would have liked to get off her chest in a final conversation with her father. She regretted having spoken harshly to him at the factory gate. She could have been kinder . . . less bent on digging up the past. He hadn't married Sybil and Olivia wondered whether her intervention might have caused him to delay. She knew that Sybil would blame her for sticking her oar in, if she ever found out about that meeting. As Tommy's widow, Sybil might have been entitled to a pay out of some sort. Olivia wouldn't have wanted her aunt to miss out financially. The woman had been seriously involved with her father for very many years . . . more years than he had been married to his legitimate wife, if Sybil were to be believed.

'D'you think your mum and Mickey will stay here?' Olivia repeated the question because her cousin seemed to be staring into space.

Ruby shrugged. 'Gawd knows. She'll need to get a job and pay her way. She ain't moving back in with me, that's fer sure.'

'Don't want to neither,' Sybil said from the doorway, narrowing her eyes at her daughter. 'I'm stopping right where I am.' Overhearing Ruby's criticism seemed to have stiffened Sybil's backbone. She now had that familiar belligerent jut to her jaw.

'So who's going to pay the rent?' Ruby asked bluntly.

'Never mind the rent,' Sybil snapped. 'Who's paying fer the bleedin' funeral?' She turned to Olivia. 'You and your sisters are all working so must be pulling in a fair amount between yers. *You* don't have rent to pay, do you? Joe Hunter left you his house, buckshee.'

'I ain't chipping in for no funeral costs,' Ruby declared, sounding adamant. 'Can't make ends meet as it is. Anyway, Tommy never took to me, and I didn't like him.'

'He was yer ... ' Sybil bit back the rest, winding in her neck as she saw her son watching and listening. 'You know who he was!' she hissed, pointing a finger at her daughter. 'It wouldn't hurt you to show willing outta respect.'

Ruby snorted in disgust. 'He must've left summat around the house. Have you checked his pockets? His suit and overcoat and so on?' She started pulling open the drawers in the sideboard, fingers scrabbling this way and that as she searched for something of value.

'I've already checked the usual places,' Sybil said. 'Straight after the constable left I had them drawers out 'cos they said Tommy hadn't got a farthin' on him. Whoever done it must've cleared out his pockets 'cos he ain't left a single coin here that I can find.'

Olivia felt suffocated by the grief squeezing her chest, yet her aunt and cousin were able to search for money before her father was even cold. 'Dad paid into a funeral club,' she burst out, hoping to stop them bickering. 'He paid premiums for us kids too, at one time. He might have stopped those when we all left home though.'

As a child Olivia could remember the insurance man banging on the door once a week to collect their contributions. Her mother had always put the pennies – eight in total – in a jam jar, kept on the shelf by the tea caddy. The breadwinner had been insured for the most. Thrupence a week had gone into the pot for her father. Aggie had been insured for tuppence and the Bone girls had had a penny policy each. The fistful of coins had been handed over as regularly and religiously as the rent. After her mother died her father had drawn on the insurance money to pay for his wife to be decently laid to rest.

After that Tommy had still put the money by in the jar but he'd taken it out again and settled with the insurance man himself. Olivia had wondered why he'd go to the bother of putting the coins in only to empty them back out. She'd guessed that after his wife died he'd deemed the matter of funerals too serious to be left to chance. Rather than risk being tempted to spend the money, he'd kept it out of harm's way until it was time to hand it over.

'Don't know nothin' about any penny policy or funeral club.' Sybil sounded defensive. 'I expect yer father stopped bothering with any of it. He didn't know he was going to get murdered in an alley, did he?'

'He'd never have done that!' Olivia knew he would have kept up his payments rather than risk the shame of a pauper's burial. Tommy had always been proud and would never have burdened those he left behind with the worry of finding the cost of laying him to rest.

'You're his next-of-kin, I suppose, being as you're the eldest.' Sybil glanced slyly at Olivia.

'Mum's right,' Ruby piped up. 'If he had money invested, all well and good, otherwise you'll have to find the cost of it. We're not as well off as you lot.' She crossed her arms over her chest. 'Anyhow, you're his *real* family.'

'When it suits your mother, we are.' Olivia gave Sybil a hard stare. 'I'm going to North Middlesex Hospital,' she said, making for the door. 'That's where Dad is, isn't it? Perhaps they'll be able to tell me a bit more about what happened to him. Then on the way back I'll stop by the Mission Hall. The nuns had something to do with running the funeral club. They might know how I can find out about the policy, if it's still going.'

'Seem to remember now that Tommy *did* let the policies lapse,' Sybil rattled off. 'So won't be no need to go bothering the sisters. When the insurance fellow come to collect last time ... months ago it were ... the jar was empty so I told him not to bother in future, 'cos he wouldn't get paid.'

Olivia exchanged a glance with her cousin. Ruby looked ashamed, as well she might, to discover that her mother had even been raiding the funeral jar.

'Let us know when you've made the arrangements. Any day'll do. We ain't fussy, are we, Rube?' Sybil shuffled off back to her bedroom.

'She's probably glad now they never got married, or she'd be his next-of-kin,' Ruby said sourly. 'I don't know how she'd try and worm out of it then.'

'My dad paid into that club for years in case something like this happened.' Olivia shook her head sadly.

'I'll pop round yours later, Livvie ... have a talk. I'll help out making a few sandwiches for the wake. We'll have it

86

here, I suppose. D'you reckon the neighbours might have a collection for her?' Ruby had brightened up. 'They always do that in the Bunk, y'know. Mrs Keiver goes banging on doors for a pudding basin whip-round for the widow.'

Olivia didn't bother answering. She stood looking round the room. Years ago, she'd spent some happy times in this house with her mother and father and younger sisters. They'd had parties. The Wrights had come as guests, and so had other friends and relatives. She remembered Christmas evenings when they'd had a houseful and had all eaten sausage rolls and sung songs around a piano while the adults got tipsy on brown ales. The instrument was long gone though. Her mother Aggie had been the only one able to tinkle a tune and there'd been no point in keeping it after she'd passed away.

Tommy Bone had always done his duty, if grudgingly. He'd worked hard and paid the rent and clothed and fed his motherless brood. And he would have saved for his funeral, too. If he'd stopped putting money in the jar for the insurance man because he'd discovered Sybil was stealing it then he'd have found somewhere else for it. Somewhere Sybil couldn't find but a person who knew him well might. Olivia had known him better than anybody else. Even better than his wife, it seemed, who'd never discovered that he was cheating on her in all their years of marriage.

When he'd stolen sweets from the factory Olivia had found out that he'd concealed the boxes in the outhouse, where some old gardening tools and paint pots were kept. And where nobody but he ever went.

'I think I'll take a look in the shed. There were some shears out there and I could do with a pair for the hedge at home,' she said.

'Help yerself,' Ruby said, looking rather surprised. 'Me mum won't be doing no gardening, that's fer sure. 'S'pose I'd better get back to work or me pay'll be docked,' she sighed. 'Cath said to tell you she's thinking of you. Given 'em all something to chinwag about, ain't it?'

After Ruby had gone Olivia took the key for the outhouse from the hook on the wall and went out to the backyard. There were two brick-built sheds. From the age of ten until she left home, she'd spent every Monday toiling from morning until evening in the washhouse, moving between the copper and the mangle and the washing line. But she passed that and went to the other building. The boxes of pilfered toffees were long gone but she stood looking around the dim interior that smelled of must and creosote. Tommy had been a methodical man and the shelves held a neat assortment of old tins that had been utilised for nuts and bolts and nails. She took the tins down one by one and looked inside. They were empty but for a few bits of metal rattling around in the bottoms.

She glanced up at the roof, sagging in places where the timber beam had rotted. But one area looked to have recently been nailed back as there was a hanging splinter of clean pale wood. Olivia stretched up, running her fingers along the top of the beam. They met an obstacle that felt quite flat and cold. She dislodged it by curling her fingers around an edge and pulled it towards her. It was an old tobacco tin. She shook it, then with a frown eased off the lid. Within was a couple of folded five-pound notes. She put them back and put the lid on, slipping the tin into her coat pocket. Then she unhooked some shears that were hanging on the wall and laid them on the work bench before going out.

'Tell your mum I'll come back and see her later, Mickey. And I'll take the garden shears another time.'

The boy nodded. He had his chin cupped in his hands and was reading a comic, open in front of him on the table. Olivia realised that he'd be better off at school than at home doing nothing but absorbing his mother's gin fumes and depression.

'Going to school this afternoon?' she asked him, forcing some lightness into her voice.

'If Mum says I can.' He sounded pessimistic, and turned a page of his comic.

Olivia ruffled his hair. 'Your sister's right, Mickey ... it'll all turn out fine in the end.'

'I liked Uncle Tommy. He used to bring me in sweets.'

'He liked you too, Mickey,' Olivia said. And she knew it was true. Her father had preferred his illegitimate son to Alfie. Her poor little brother had paid the price of being born and ending Aggie Bone's life.

*

'Have you a brother? It would be better if I talked to him about this, my dear.'

Olivia was sure the constable didn't mean to sound patronising. He wanted to spare her the ordeal. 'I do have a brother but Alfie's only eight. I'm the eldest of Mr Bone's children, and the one who deals with everything. You can talk to me quite openly, sir.'

When Olivia had arrived at the hospital and enquired after her father, she'd been told to head towards the waiting room because a Constable Ridley was still on the premises. The elderly fellow had been seated and scribbling in his notebook when she arrived. He had gained his feet, approaching her on legs that appeared to be suffering from bad cramps because he extended the limbs carefully in front of him before placing his feet on the floor.

'My aunt told me that my father was stabbed . . . ' Olivia felt her bottom lip begin to tremble and sank her teeth into it.

'He was, my dear, and I am very sorry to have to confirm it.' Constable Ridley squeezed her shoulder sympathetically. 'But the injury was severe enough for him not to have suffered. The wound would quickly have proved fatal.'

'You mean, even if he'd been found sooner . . . ' Olivia's voice broke. She couldn't finish what she'd been about to say about her father's chance of survival.

'I fear the outcome would have been the same, Miss Bone. The doctor who examined him said there would have been little hope of saving him. The post mortem report is awaited, but . . . ' Ridley shrugged, indicating he didn't believe it would bring more to light than he'd already told her.

'Have you any idea who did it?' Olivia asked huskily.

'I'm afraid we do not, Miss Bone. And I won't pretend we're hopeful. We have very little to go on. The fiend got clean away.' The policeman sighed. 'There have been other similar attacks in the area but none quite so severe. Mainly robberies with violence. Bringing the guilty to justice is never easy.' He gave another of his weary shrugs.

'Why is that?' Olivia demanded.

'These refugees seem to be able to disappear into thin air. We had quite a good description the last time of a fellow with a foreign accent spotted near the scene, but with your father we've turned up a blank.' He loosened his collar. 'Your poor father wasn't able to talk to us and tell us anything, you see.'

'But you'll make further enquiries or how can you be sure it was an immigrant?' Olivia said pithily. The more tiresome it all seemed to Constable Ridley, the sharper her tone grew.

'Of course we will,' Ridley said smoothly. 'We'll be questioning people in the neighbourhood and noting anything at all that might give us a lead to work on.'

'But you're not confident of ever arresting anybody, are you?' Olivia said, sounding shocked.

'Unfortunately, Miss Bone, with the war effort depleting our numbers, we haven't the resources we once had for matters such as these.'

'Are we now a lawless society then?' Olivia demanded.

'No, but everything's different in wartime,' Ridley said sadly.

Chapter Eight

'It can't be our dad! It must be a mistake!'

'It isn't a mistake, Maggie. The policeman was still there when I turned up at the hospital. I talked to him and he took me to see Dad. I've identified his body.'

Olivia's mind calmly revisited that shrouded silhouette and white, waxy visage that had been all that was visible of her father in the hospital mortuary. Constable Ridley had asked her if she felt up to seeing the corpse and at first she'd feared the ordeal might be beyond her courage. But although it wasn't the Tommy Bone she knew, once close to him, searching his features for something familiar through her blur of tears, her only thought had been to try to comfort him. She was glad his wounds had been concealed beneath the sheet. Her fingers had curled away just inches from his forehead as the cold coming off his skin alarmed her. Instead, she'd laid her palm on his grey-streaked hair, its coarseness springing against her quivering fingers.

'But ... I only saw him a few weeks ago,' Nancy wailed over the sound of Maggie's whimpering.

Olivia tightened her arms about her sisters' shoulders

as they both snuffled against her chest. Only Alfie hadn't immediately sought her embrace on hearing that their father had been stabbed to death.

'Did he die all alone and in pain?' Nancy used her knuckles to smear the tears from her face.

"Course he did!' Maggie shouted, elbowing free of Olivia. 'He was *murdered*, you *idiot*!'

'Hush ... please stop arguing,' Olivia implored. 'You'll only upset yourselves more.' She was feeling shattered and unequal to refereeing her sisters today. The shocking news had badly affected the girls, as was to be expected. But there was no use in trying to hide the facts from them. They were no longer children to be shielded from life's cruelties, but young women, out at work. Olivia understood their disbelief, though, because she knew she herself still hadn't properly digested the fact that Tommy Bone had gone from their lives in an abrupt and gruesome way.

'Can I see him?' Alfie spoke at last, looking curious rather than emotional.

'I want to as well,' Nancy sniffed.

'I don't know if I want to.' Maggie scrubbed her eyes dry. 'We're orphans. We've got nobody now,' she lamented dramatically.

'We've got each other. We've been doing quite well without Dad's help for a long while.' Olivia strove to sound reasonable although she hated the idea of having no parents as well. 'There's lots to do if we're to give him a good send off.'

'We can't afford much of a do,' Maggie hiccuped.

'Well ... for a start, you can all look out some decent dark clothes to wear and make sure they're clean and pressed and ready for the day. I don't know when the funeral will be but we might as well prepare for it.' Olivia hoped that occupying her sisters' minds with important tasks would make them buck themselves up. 'We should wear armbands from tomorrow. I'll go out in the morning and buy some black crêpe and then you two can start making them.' She pulled open a door in the sideboard and took out a box containing a sewing kit.

'Wish I'd not left home now,' Nancy croaked. 'I would've stayed too, but for that cow smacking my face for no reason.'

"S'pose Dad'll get taken back to our house in Wood Green. If we want to see him we'll have to go back *there*, where *she* is.' Maggie rounded on Olivia. 'If you hadn't got involved with Joe and moved out none of this would've happened.' She jabbed an accusing finger at her sister. 'We'd all still be living together and Dad would be all right.'

'Me leaving home has got nothing to do with him getting set upon at Muswell Hill,' Olivia pointed out in exasperation.

But Maggie's words *had* struck a chord with her. The last time she'd spoken to her father he'd come out with a similar phrase about it being her fault the family had broken up. Olivia didn't have a rose-tinted view of it all; she remembered the reality of being on tenterhooks every day, never knowing what sort of mood their father would be in, or whether he'd be drunk or sober, when he rolled through the door at night. He'd been a difficult, unpleasant man, more often than not. They had all been unhappy even before it came to light that he'd betrayed his wife and children, living a double life with his sister-in-law. But for all that, Olivia felt a niggle of guilt. She could have done more to mend bridges in the months that followed her leaving home. She'd seen her siblings regularly but she'd not attempted to have a heart to heart with Tommy, fearing a rebuff. And now it was too late ever to know if he would have agreed to them clearing the air. But she'd never have returned home. Once she'd tasted freedom and found love with Joe she knew she'd never give it up.

'I'm glad we live here,' Alfie said quietly, slipping his hand into Olivia's. 'I never wanted to go back there with him.'

'Wouldn't put it past Aunt Sybil to keep the funeral a secret,' Nancy said. 'She'll do it all behind our backs to spite us, won't she?'

'She won't get away with it!' Maggie shrilled. 'I'm *going* to the funeral and she can't stop me. We've got more right than her to be there.'

'She calls herself his wife even though he didn't marry her after all,' Nancy said. 'She's not one of us Bones. She's still a Wright.'

'Aunt Sybil wants me to arrange the undertakers,' Olivia interrupted as things grew heated again. Suddenly she felt fatigued and sat down in a fireside chair. She'd been on her feet, hurrying from place to place, since seven o'clock that morning when she'd set off for work. But it was the mental anguish that had sapped her energy. 'The constable told me there's going to be an inquest and a post mortem. Then after that we can lay Dad to rest.' She sighed, knowing that the friction within the family would only increase until then. A full day hadn't passed since she'd found out the shocking news yet already she was wishing the funeral over with.

'Will it cost much to bury him?' Alfie piped up. 'I've got two bob saved from doing odd jobs. You can have that, Livvie.'

'I've got enough to pay for it.' Olivia smiled to show him she appreciated his offer.

'Where d'you get that sort of money?' Maggie sank into the chair opposite. 'Me friend at work lost her mum and, 'cos they didn't have insurance, they couldn't afford nothing but a cheap pine box. They didn't have flowers or family back afterwards.'

'I've got just enough for a modest do, that's all that matters.' Olivia decided not to tell them about their dad's tobacco tin money. Olivia didn't want their aunt getting wind of the fact that Tommy had had some savings after all.

Olivia had only momentarily considered giving Sybil the cash she'd found. She'd realised quite quickly that if she did so her father might still end up in a pauper's grave. She didn't trust Sybil one bit, despite all her aunt's boasts about the sacrifices she'd made for Tommy Bone. And there was another, better reason why Olivia had kept the tin in her own pocket: in her heart she knew that her father would expect her to do this one last thing for him, and lay him to rest. He'd want to be beside his beloved Aggie. And he'd trust Livvie to make sure he was. Sybil might have arranged to have him buried elsewhere, in a plot that would eventually take the two of them.

'Shall I put the kettle on?' Alfie said as a solemn silence descended on the parlour.

'Yes ... make some tea, there's a good lad.' Olivia gave him a smile. 'In a minute when we've all had a breather I'll make us something to eat.'

'I'm going out,' Maggie said. 'I want to see Harry and tell him what's gone on. He always knows what to say to make me feel better.'

Olivia felt frustrated that her sister could talk such drivel. Especially on a day such as today. It proved to her that the girl was still well and truly beneath Harry Wicks's thumb.

'Tell him if you want, but he probably already knows as his mother was one of the women congregated outside

Dad's house.' Olivia paused. 'The neighbours passed on their best wishes to us all.'

'I hope they catch whoever it was and string him up!' Maggie started snivelling again.

'Have they arrested anybody?' Now the initial shock had worn off it occurred to Nancy to enquire about the man who'd done the terrible deed.

'The constable said they were still making enquiries.' Olivia tried to sound optimistic, to give them all a boost. But she imagined the others suspected, as did she and Constable Ridley, that the brute had got clean away.

As Alfie came in carefully balancing the tea tray, Olivia said, 'I'll make us a bite to eat to go with it.'

'Don't feel like eating.' Nancy wrinkled her nose and linked arms with Maggie for their mutual comfort.

'*I'm* hungry,' Alfie said, and smiled.

*

'I was on me way round to see you, love. Just heard the news off your brother.' Matilda's face was creased in sympathy. 'How're you coping, Livvie? I know you and yer dad had yer ups and downs but this must've knocked you fer six. You'd think this bloody war would make even wicked buggers stop and think what they're doing.'

'I keep hoping I'll wake up one morning and find I dreamed it all.' Olivia blinked as her eyes began to fill up. 'I felt like that when I found out about Joe. Kept expecting him to knock on the door.' Rightly or wrongly, she knew that his death had been far harder for her to bear than her father's was. Yet she and Joe had only known one another for a year, and the last months they had spent apart. Sometimes at night, though, she was sure she felt his arms about her and the scent of coal from his cart would drift over her, making her smile in her sleep.

Matilda gave her a comforting hug then tutted in disgust. 'Well, there's somebody you *don't* want knocking on yer door.' She jerked her head at the fellow talking to her brother-in-law. 'Can see why *they* get on. Two peas outta the same rotten pod.'

Olivia glanced around and groaned. She'd hoped she'd seen the last of Herbie Hunter. But he didn't seem interested in her. He and Jimmy Wild were propped against the wall by Paddington Street crossroads, having a natter. It was Saturday afternoon and the doggers out were in evidence – kids who were stationed about here and there keeping an eye peeled for the police while an illegal gaming session was on.

Faintly Olivia could hear the dealer calling out numbers and knew that further around the corner would be a gaggle of men hunched over the pavement watching rolling dice. Others would be lounging against the wall of the doss house with a fan of cards in their hands or encircling an upturned box with a mound of money on it.

Matilda had observed Olivia's reaction to seeing Herbie. 'Did he make a nuisance of himself and upset you last time he was hanging around?' She crossed her arms over her chest. 'If so I'll have it out with him right now.'

'No ... he hasn't done anything.' Olivia didn't want Matilda causing a ruckus. Joe's father had a right to go wherever he pleased. 'I saw him outside our house so I marched up to him. He pretended he'd just stopped by to reminisce. Really he wanted to know if his son had left him anything. So I made it clear he hadn't.'

'Joe wouldn't have left him the shit off his shoe,' Matilda snorted.

'Joe hated him all right,' Olivia said flatly. Noticing Matilda still glowering in Herbie's direction, she decided to get going before the woman made good on her promise to pick a fight. 'I'd best get down the market before it starts packing up. Alfie needs a smart pair of trousers for the funeral.'

'Has the date been set?'

'It's next Friday.' Olivia felt a lump form in her throat. 'The post mortem's done and the inquest didn't tell us much we didn't already know.' She paused. 'Dad was robbed and stabbed and left to bleed to death.'

Matilda drew Olivia into her arms and rocked her as though she were a child. 'Chin up, Livvie, there's a good gel.'

Olivia scrubbed at her wet eyes with a hanky.

'Now, if you need any help at the wake, you've only to ask and me 'n' Alice'll show up and make sandwiches. I promise to be on me best behaviour with yer aunt Sybil.' Matilda pulled a comical face.

'We'll manage between us. But thanks anyway.'

'Very welcome, love.' Matilda turned homewards.

Olivia set off up the road, heading for the market. She made to pass by the gambling school at a safe distance from Joe's father, but as she drew closer he pushed himself away from the doss house wall and stepped into her path.

'Sorry to hear you've had such bad luck, love.' Herbie gave her one of his wonky smiles, fag drooping from his lower lip. 'Me friend Jimmy Wild just told me all about what's happened to yer dad.'

Olivia tried to swerve around him with a murmur of thanks.

'Terrible thing to have happened.' Herbie whistled through his teeth. 'Police'll catch up with him, you wait 'n' see.' He shook his head as though greatly disturbed by the tragedy. Which he was, but not for any reasons he wanted her to know. 'What a thing! Got any leads, have they, Olivia?'

'Still making enquiries,' she answered hoarsely then muttered she had to get on and moved determinedly past him.

Herbie watched her, continuing to swing his head dolefully so as to impress on any observers how dreadful he thought it all. He'd noticed a few people glancing sympathetically Olivia's way. News travelled fast and he had pondered long and hard about showing his face around here again. Then he'd realised that if he didn't, it might arouse more suspicion than if he did. He'd heard from Sid Monk, who'd made a rare trip to the door to talk to him when he dropped his rent through the letterbox, that the police had been going house to house in the neighbourhood, asking questions about a murder. Herbie had been relieved he'd been out and missed them.

He'd disposed of all the evidence: had burned his shirt in the grate in the cellar and had chucked the murder weapon in the sea at Southend when he went to visit his miserable cow of a sister. She'd made it clear he could stay just the one night. Herbie had thought of throwing away the pewter cigarette case too. In the end he'd not the heart to miss out on getting what he could for it so had taken it to a pawnbroker's on the seafront and exchanged it for a tanner and a frayed shirt. As far as he was concerned he was home and dry. Over a week had passed and he'd not had a visit from the police. He didn't have a criminal record for anything more than living off immoral earnings and petty theft. That had all been a long time ago. He was a reformed character now, so he told everyone who recognised him from the old days. There was nothing to link him with the murder. And in any case, it hadn't been a murder. It had been an accident, and more Tommy Bone's fault than his.

*

'There ... you can have them fer just a shilling, love. Can tell you're having a bad time of it.' The stall holder crossed himself, nodding at the black armband on Olivia's sleeve.

She gave him a grateful smile, accepting the discount. The trousers were Alfie's size, but at three bob had been a bit steep for second hand. They were of good quality and just needed a press. She held them up to examine again. At a shilling they were indeed a bargain.

'Come out of a posh house Hampstead way, they did,' the trader said. 'Little Lord Fauntleroy probably grew out of 'em before he'd had 'em on twice. Good as new and a quality wool superfine.' He tested the material between thumb and forefinger.

Quickly Olivia handed over the silver before he talked himself into wanting his three bob for the trousers after all. Walking away, she peered in her purse. She had enough left to buy some black net to sew onto her best blue velvet hat to make it right for mourning. Maggie and Nancy had already chosen their outfits, but their hats would benefit from a trim too.

She wondered if having Maggie on her mind had made her imagine hearing her sister's voice. Glancing about she spotted the familiar light brown hair and thin figure up ahead. The girl was examining second-hand costumes hanging up on an awning. Olivia speeded up, weaving in and out of the crowd to join her, thinking they could choose the hat netting together. Then she saw Maggie wasn't alone. Olivia's pace faltered and she cursed below her breath.

Harry Wicks was chatting with a chap who appeared to be lighting his cigarette for him. Unfortunately Harry spotted her before she could slip back into the throng. He raised a hand and sauntered over, puffing out smoke. Maggie noticed her sister too and trotted at her boyfriend's side to meet her.

'What've you got there?' Maggie asked.

'New trousers for Alfie.'

'Very sorry to hear about all of your troubles,' Harry announced, cigarette jammed in the corner of his mouth.

Olivia acknowledged his condolences with a small movement of her head, while quashing an urge to snap that he'd yet to offer an apology for the trouble *he'd* caused in the past.

'We was just off to the caff.' Maggie dragged on Harry's hand. She didn't like the way he always stared at Olivia. It annoyed her that *she* was the one who liked Harry yet he seemed to show more interest in her elder sister.

'Fancy coming to the Greengage Caff for a bite to eat?' Harry tempted Olivia. 'My treat.'

That made Maggie's hackles rise further. He rarely treated her to a cup of tea let alone a bite to eat. Harry always made a point of saying he was stony broke and wished he was still in a proper job instead of taking the King's measly shilling and risking his life to boot.

'I'm off home . . . thanks anyway.' Though Olivia despised Harry she was becoming resigned to the fact that her sister wasn't going to give him up. So she realised she ought to try to tolerate him or eventually she'd fall out with Maggie. She loved her infuriating sister too much ever to want that to happen. At times she forced herself to feel optimistic that

Maggie's good influence on Harry might make him change for the better. Joe had led a very misspent youth but he had turned over a new leaf for her sake.

'Dad had one just like that, Harry.' The comment drifted back to Olivia before she'd taken more than a few steps away from the couple. Curiosity made her glance over a shoulder as they strolled off arm-in-arm. She saw a flash of grey metal in Harry's hand and then the box disappeared into his pocket and he lit a new cigarette from the stub of the old one.

Olivia digested what she'd seen and heard for a moment.

'You've got a pewter cigarette case like my dad's,' she burst out, having tapped Harry's shoulder.

'Maggie reckons it's similar.' Harry looked surprised but pleased that Olivia had rejoined them. He pulled the cigarette case from his pocket to display it.

'It's not *similar* ... it *is* Dad's,' Olivia whispered in shock.

'Can't be,' Maggie snorted. 'That was stolen when he was ... ' Her voice tailed off. 'It just looks the same, that's all!' She sounded angry and alarmed.

'It *is* Dad's. I should know, I bought it for him the last Christmas we were all together at home.' Olivia snatched the case from him, turning it over. 'There's a scratch on the bottom shaped like a crescent.'

Harry turned pale. 'There is 'n' all. The bloke that sold it to me let me have a copper off 'cos it was marked.'

'What bloke? Who sold it to you?' Olivia demanded.

'Army pal o' mine. We was brought home on the same hospital ship from France. Met up with him for a drink last night to say toodle-oo. He's hoping to go back to his regiment if he gets signed off fit.'

Olivia believed Harry was telling the truth about how

he'd acquired it. He'd looked appalled to know it might be the one stolen from her late father.

'Here ... take it. I don't want it. Only give ninepence fer it. If it belonged to yer dad you're welcome to it.' Harry thrust the pewter case at Olivia. The significance of what he had in his possession wasn't lost on him.

'Your pal must've done it.' Maggie slapped a hand over her gaping mouth.

'Nah ... wouldn't be Freddie. He's all right, is Freddie. Decent bloke.' Harry licked his lips. He didn't want to get dragged into any police enquiry. There were things in his past that didn't bear scrutiny. He wished now he'd never bought the poxy thing. He'd thought it'd look flash to have that in his pocket instead of a battered carton of Weights.

'Freddie?' Olivia recalled Lucas telling her he'd been to visit Freddie Weedon who was convalescing and hoping to get signed off fit. But Freddie was a common enough name. And not all wounded soldiers wanted to shirk if they could.

'Freddie Weedon. Know him, do you?' Harry had noticed Olivia's expression change.

'He was Joe's best pal. They were both machine-gunners. I knew he'd been injured.' Olivia felt astonished. Joe had been nobody's fool. He had told her he liked Freddie. Lucas had said the same thing. Yet how could nice Freddie Weedon have got hold of her father's cigarette case?

'He's probably still about somewhere. I was just talking to him when I spotted you.' Harry craned his neck for a glimpse of his pal.

'He was the fellow you were standing with a short while ago?'

Harry nodded. 'I'll keep an eye out fer 'im. And if I see him, I've got a few questions need answering.'

Maggie looked on the point of blubbing. 'Shall we go 'n' find a policeman?'

'Shut up, you daft cow!' Harry took her face in his hand and gave it a squeeze that wasn't as playful as he'd have liked it to appear.

'Leave her alone,' Olivia snapped, pulling him away.

Harry let his hand drop. He moved off with a last glare for Maggie. 'You don't go involving police fer no reason. You give my pal a chance to explain first. Who's to say he didn't find it? Could be, whoever attacked yer dad chucked it away.'

'If Freddie's got nothing to hide then he won't mind answering questions at the police station, will he?' Olivia reasoned. But she was also reluctant to get Freddie involved with the police if he was innocent. One thing she had quickly learned, having lived in the worst street in North London, was that you never voluntarily had truck with coppers if you could sort things out for yourself. Much as it surprised Olivia, she agreed with Harry. The culprit might have regretted taking the case as it could be traced, and so had got rid of it. Freddie had been praised as a good sort by two men she trusted.

'I'm off home . . . coming?' Olivia looked at her sister, but although she could see the imprint of Harry's cruel fingers still on Maggie's chin, her sister shook her head.

Olivia walked back through the market alone, peering left and right to try and catch sight of a slightly built fellow with wavy brown hair. It was all she could recall of the man who'd been with Harry. She'd not taken much notice of him but recalled he'd been dressed in hospital blues. But Freddie Weedon wanted to get signed off as fit and go back to France to fight. She needed to catch up with him before he did.

Chapter Nine

Barely had Olivia dropped into a chair in the parlour to ponder on the cigarette case mysteriously turning up when there was a bang on the door. She'd risen to answer it, hoping it wasn't Constable Ridley. He'd taken her address at the hospital and had said he'd let her know of any developments. Something *had* come to light and she was now in a quandary as what to do about it. As she reached the hall Alfie dashed down the stairs, beating her to the door. He was disappointed to find it wasn't a chum asking him to play out.

'A man's here to see you, Livvie.'

Olivia peered past Alfie, amazed to see the very person who'd been on her mind.

Freddie Weedon extended a hand, introduced himself, then added, 'Hope you don't mind me calling out of the blue. I just wanted to stop by and tell you that Joe Hunter was the best pal I ever had. He was a real good soldier too. The best . . . ' Freddie's voice faded as he noticed Joe's fiancée was looking dazed.

'Sorry . . . shouldn't have come,' he said. 'Bet you don't

need any reminders of Joe's army days, do you? I'll be off.'
He turned on the step.

'Oh, don't go! It's not that.' Olivia had forced herself out
of her state of shock, giving Freddie a smile. 'It's good to see
you, and to hear about Joe. He wrote to me and said you
were his best friend so I'm very pleased to meet you.'

The compliment was so well received that Freddie
blushed. But he continued fidgeting uncertainly.

'Do come in. I'd like to have a chat about Joe.' Olivia
closed the door after he'd stepped over the threshold.
'Actually ... I'm glad you've come. I saw you in the market
earlier with Harry Wicks, and he told me who you were so
I knew you were in the neighbourhood.'

'Oh ... yeah ... I know Harry.'

Olivia discerned a hint of derision in Freddie's voice and
warmed to him. He didn't like Harry so they already had
something in common. 'Joe often mentioned you in his letters. He was glad he'd met you on the troop ship over. He
thought it was smashing that you managed to get posted
together.'

'He mentioned you too ... oh, nothing too personal,'
Freddie quickly corrected himself. 'You was something
precious that Joe kept all to himself. But he was always
saying he missed you and he was over the moon to get your
letters. He read them every night.' Freddie looked her over,
with admiration in his eyes rather than lechery. 'Yeah ... Joe
was a very lucky man. He knew it too and couldn't wait to
make you his wife.'

Olivia smiled although raw emotion was making her
throat ache. Every time she heard a little bit more about Joe's
last months she felt both proud and sorrowful.

She turned to Alfie, quietly watching as he tended to do

when he sensed something might be amiss. 'Would you put the kettle on?' she said lightly, letting her brother know the visitor was a friend. She turned to Freddie. 'You'll stop for a cup of tea, won't you?'

'If it's no trouble.' He clasped his hands behind his back in an endearingly humble way.

'Oh, sit down, please.' Olivia opened the parlour door and indicated a chair. She sat down as well then took the pewter case from her pocket, placing it on the table to watch his reaction.

'I had one just like that,' Freddie immediately announced. 'That's strange ... I sold it to Harry Wicks, and you just said you know him.' He frowned. 'Is it the same one? Did he give it to you?'

'It is the same one. It belonged to my late father.'

Freddie gawped in disbelief.

'My dad was robbed of his cigarette case,' Olivia explained. 'I'm pretty sure this is it.'

Freddie took a deep breath then gave a low whistle. 'That's a rum coincidence, all right.'

'How did you get it, if you don't mind my asking?'

'A pal left it to me. He didn't have it long. He come back with it one day and when I asked where he got it he tapped his nose, like it was a secret. Poor old Dickie ... he wasn't the full ticket, if you get my drift. Anyhow he left it to me ... don't know why 'cos we weren't old pals. But I did like him, and was sorry for him.'

'Left it to you?'

'Yeah.' Freddie rubbed the bridge of his nose as though trying to decide whether to continue. 'Not a nice subject to bring up but the poor sod did himself in. We was convalescing together in a nursing home in Southend. The trenches

108

sent poor Dickie crackers.' Freddie tapped his skull. 'That's why I say he wasn't quite the ticket. Anyhow, he went out walking one day. When he come back that evening he had that on him.' Freddie pointed at the case. 'I commented on it, said I liked it ... more to make conversation than anything. To be honest, I don't bother with cigarette cases. I don't keep fags long enough to move 'em around. If I've got 'em, I smoke 'em.' He coughed again and wiped his mouth. 'The doc's always going on at me about cutting it out since Fritz put a dent in me chest.' He smiled wryly. 'Thing is ... I reckon it's a bit too late to worry about damaging me lungs.'

'Harry said you were going to rejoin your regiment.'

'I know they won't let me back on the frontline. I'd be a hindrance, not a help. But I want to do what I can, even if it's just driving a truck or an ambulance. But got to sweet talk the doc into signing me off, first.'

Olivia felt full of admiration for Freddie's selfless bravery. 'Lieutenant Black said you were courageous. He said you were lucky to survive your wounds.'

'I remember that Joe mentioned our commanding officer was your boss before the war.' In fact Freddie would never forget the day that Private Joe Hunter and Lieutenant Lucas Black had fought over this woman in a trench while their comrades covered their backs. He guessed Olivia knew nothing about that, and he wasn't going to be the one to tell her.

Just as she was about to turn the conversation back to the cigarette case Alfie came in bearing the tea tray. He placed it down on the sideboard.

'That's a good lad you've got there,' Freddie said. 'Can see the family likeness. Brother, is he?'

'Yes, he is. Sorry, should have introduced you two earlier.'

She drew Alfie closer. 'This is Mr Weedon, one of Joe's army pals, Alfie.'

'Freddie to me friends.' He extended his hand to give Alfie's a single pump. 'Pleased to meet you, lad.'

'Can I go upstairs to read me comics?' The boy took his cup off the tray and hovered by the door.

'Yes ... off you go.' Olivia was relieved that her brother had taken himself upstairs. She didn't want him hearing about the cigarette case turning up. First she wanted to think things through and decide whether or not the police should be informed. If Alfie told his pals all about it accusations would be made against Freddie. Olivia didn't want that because she believed every word Joe's friend had said.

'So you inherited the case from your fellow patient at the nursing home.' She picked up the thread of their conversation once Alfie was out of the way.

'Poor blighter used to say he was suffering a living death. Then he decided to do something about that so he threw himself off Southend pier.' Freddie shook his head. 'The cigarette case was in his room with the rest of his stuff. The matron give it to me 'cos he'd left a note saying I could have it as I'd liked it.' Freddie picked up the pewter case and turned it over. 'It is the same one I sold to Harry. I was glad to be rid of it in a way. Seemed to me to be cursed. From what you've said about your dad ... I reckon I'm right an' all.'

Olivia regretted having bought it as a Christmas present for her dad because it did seem to bring bad luck. But it *had* been Tommy's and *was* a memento. For those reasons she was glad to have it back.

'So, was your dad in Southend when he lost it?'

'No ... he was robbed and stabbed to death in Muswell Hill.'

Freddie whistled in shock, crossing himself. 'Best get rid o' that.' He pointed at the case. 'I ain't superstitious but that seems like more'n coincidence. If I'd known, I'd've chucked it in the sea after poor old Dickie.'

'I'm not superstitious either. I *was* thinking of burying it with Dad on Friday, but I don't think I will after what you've told me. Just in case. I want him to rest easy with my mum.'

'Lost both of them, eh?' Freddie looked sympathetic. 'Me too. Only got me sister Hilda left now. But we're good friends. I'm off over Walthamstow to see her. She's older 'n me and never married.' He looked proud when he added, 'She used to be a nursing sister but now she's a top secretary in Whitehall.'

'Will you go back to Southend after seeing her?'

'I was gonna stop with Hilda and let her feed me up. I need to persuade the doc that I'm fit as a fiddle.' He gave a wry chuckle. 'No chance of getting signed off, I reckon. That does get me a bit depressed at times. I don't want to be stuck here reading about the war in the papers and wondering what's *really* going on.' He waved his hands in exasperation. 'I want to do *something* to help the lads over there. I'm bored stiff down in Southend.' He looked thoughtful. 'But it's puzzling me how Dickie got hold of the cigarette case when it was stolen round here, I do admit. Perhaps I'll turn me hand to a bit of detective work. It'll give me something to do.'

'Would Dickie have got it from an army pal?' Olivia suggested.

'I'll ask around about the blasted thing.' Freddie gave it a considering look.

'I do appreciate this.' Olivia patted his arm gratefully. 'It could lead to my dad's murderer being caught.'

'Should swing fer it, the bast—' Freddie coughed and looked apologetic.

'My friend Matilda lives in the Bunk round the corner, and uses worse language,' Olivia said gamely.

'Heard about that place, I have.' Freddie hissed a caution through his teeth. 'If they like you, yer all right. If they don't ...'

'If they don't, you're in big trouble.' Olivia chuckled.

Freddie joined in her laughter and that made him cough again until he was red in the face. 'Sorry,' he croaked. 'Lungs are playing me up something rotten.' He felt ashamed to have accidentally spat phlegm onto his trousers. Discreetly he removed it with his handkerchief.

'You've made a wonderful recovery though,' Olivia said gently, smoothing over his embarrassment.

'Everybody thought I was a goner ... me included.' He put his handkerchief away. 'Well, I'd better be off now.'

'Thanks for coming to see me.' Olivia looked earnestly at him. 'Do let me know about any clues you may find, won't you?'

'I will, I promise. Thanks for the tea and say goodbye to your brother for me.'

Noiselessly, Alfie jumped up from his crouching position at the top of the stairs and crept to his bedroom. He'd known that if he stayed in the parlour with them they wouldn't talk about anything important. He'd been expecting to hear about how Livvie's fiancé had died. Alfie knew Joe had been a hero and had got medals for bravery. The boy had got on with Joe and had wanted him as a brother-in-law. He wondered if Freddie might be his brother-in-law instead because he seemed nice as well and Livvie seemed to like him. But what was really on his mind as he quietly shut his bedroom door was the unexpected news about the pewter cigarette case. It had turned up and Freddie was going to turn detective to try to solve the mystery of how it got to Southend. Alfie liked the sound of that and wished he was older so he could turn detective as well. It'd be more fun than school.

*

'You did 'im proud, love!' Ethel Cook whispered in Olivia's ear. 'I know you didn't get much help neither.' She slid a scornful glance at Sybil, busy topping up her tea with gin then concealing the bottle in her bag. The grieving 'widow''s son and daughter sat either side of her at the parlour table, staring glumly into space. 'Yer dad'll rest easy now he's sleeping by his Aggie's side,' Ethel added in an undertone.

'There were some lovely flowers,' another neighbour piped up. 'The big display must've set somebody back a few bob.'

'Mr Barratt sent them, from the factory.' Olivia had been glad to see the impressive display from the directors, yet disappointed that not one of them had attended the funeral. Their vase of wax lilies under a glass dome had been the first tribute to arrive that morning and in her opinion her father deserved such recognition. Tommy Bone had spent the majority of his working life at Barratt's sweet factory. She knew that if Lucas had been around he would have come and shown his support even though he and her father had clashed on numerous occasions.

Her father's friend had arranged for a whip round and had turned up at the graveside with a modest wreath from Tommy's work colleagues. She knew that he would have been pleased to see so many signatures on the accompanying card, remembering him and wishing him peace. Not everybody had got along with Tommy Bone, and with good reason, but there had been shock and sadness at his sudden, violent passing. Bill Morley had accepted Olivia's invitation to come back to the house for the wake. He'd stayed long enough to have a cup of tea and a sandwich before excusing himself to return to the factory for the afternoon shift. Olivia realised that with the war giving the Grim Reaper overtime, people were becoming hardened to frequent reports of deaths and funerals.

The coffin hadn't spent any time in Sybil's parlour after all. She'd not wanted it giving her the creeps, or cluttering the place up. So Tommy's body had remained at the undertaker's until the day of his final journey. Olivia was glad that none of her siblings had again mentioned wanting to see their dead father. She was old enough to accept that the Tommy Bone she'd seen in the mortuary was no longer the dad they'd known. But it would have upset the younger ones to visit him in a cold, forbidding atmosphere and gaze upon his death mask.

When the horse-drawn hearse had arrived at their old house in Ranelagh Road Olivia and her sisters had placed some scented blooms, cut from the rose bush in the back garden, along the top of the coffin. As for Sybil, she'd contributed nothing ... not even making any effort to prepare the spread for the wake. But Ruby had helped her half-sisters make some sandwiches and cut slices of Madeira and fruit cake that had been covered with a clean white cloth Olivia had fetched from home. Even Alfie and Mickey had pitched in, setting cups and saucers and stacking up tea plates to be used later on when they got back from the churchyard.

Tommy Bone's funeral had brought his two boys together at last. They'd seemed to get on well, and to be oblivious to the curious eyes that lingered on them while they talked together. Neighbours' whispers about their likeness to Tommy, and to each other, soon tailed off when a member of the family was close by.

Then, at the appointed hour, Sybil had insisted on sitting beside the driver. Although there'd been room for Olivia on the vehicle too she'd chosen to walk with the rest of the mourners behind the hearse. And so they had set off on the short journey to St Michael's Church. Neighbouring houses, lining the route out of Ranelagh Road, had had their curtains drawn as a mark of respect and people stood solemnly by their gates, heads bowed. Tommy Bone had lived in the street for a long while and those folk knew him and his harsh ways. But nobody believed he'd deserved to go in the way he had. In particular, Olivia had drawn sympathetic glances. Nobody had a bad word to say about the girl who'd reared her brother and sisters and kept house for their drunken father from the moment his wife had died all those long years ago.

'Here, love, have a sandwich.' Ethel held out the plate to Olivia. 'Might as well use 'em up now most people have left. Only go stale, they will.' Ethel took one herself and bit into it.

'Not feeling very hungry, thanks.' Olivia went to join her sisters seated on hard chairs while Ethel handed round the plates of food. The two girls were staring morosely into the empty fire grate.

'Come on, buck up,' Olivia whispered. 'Dad wouldn't want you being upset because of him.' She'd come out with the only thing she could think of to cheer them up, although she too felt herself on the point of blubbing. Soon they would clear everything away and go home to Islington and the Bone family's life at this place would be a closed book. She still wasn't aware of what Sybil intended to do: stay put or find somewhere cheaper to live. She wasn't really interested in finding out either. But Mickey's future was another matter. She knew her half-brother would suffer, living alone with his alcoholic mother. She glanced at her aunt and noticed the woman's spiteful gaze already on her.

'I'd better go and speak to Sybil before we start clearing up. After that we'll head home,' she muttered to her sisters.

'So ... what's the damage fer it all?' Sybil demanded nastily. 'Must've cost a pretty penny. I was expecting a pine box not that fancy affair with brass handles. And them horses didn't need plumes. That must've set yer back extra ... '

'It doesn't matter,' Olivia interrupted. 'It's all done and paid for.' She raised a hand to wave to the remaining neighbours as they took their leave in subdued voices, patting the shoulders of family members as they went.

'Tommy leave you something, did he?' Sybil wasn't to be put off sniffing out the cost of his send off. 'Get a letter off a solicitor, did you? 'Cos if so, whatever he had should be mine.'

'I've not heard from anybody like that,' Olivia replied truthfully. 'We'll wash up then get going back to Islington.'

'Good riddance,' Sybil rumbled under her breath as Olivia moved away.

'Back in work Monday?' Ruby started helping Olivia to collect crockery. 'Cath's been worried about you and sends her best wishes.'

'I know, she sent me a note.' Olivia had been grateful to

receive Cath's heartfelt condolences. But between the lines she'd read that her friend was still feeling unhappy herself because of problems with Trevor. When Olivia had read the letter she'd reflected on the fellow Freddie Weedon had told her about who'd drowned in the sea rather than endure a *living death*, as he'd called his mental anguish. That had led her to wonder whether Freddie had made any headway in his detective work in Southend. But this wasn't the day to ponder a murder but rather for them all to console and support each other as a family. Tomorrow it would be back to normal.

'How's your mum coping on her own?' Olivia began washing the plates in tepid water but glanced over her shoulder at Sybil, ferreting in her bag again for the gin.

'Moaning all the bloody time. But that ain't unusual.' Ruby rolled her eyes. 'She reckons she's staying here and taking in a lodger to help pay the rent.'

'She's not looking for a job then?'

'Not sure she's capable of holding down a job.' Ruby made a scornful noise. 'Look at the state of her.'

'What about Mickey?'

'I said he could come and live with me 'n' Riley. Mum won't have it though. She dotes on him and reckons we're all scum in the Bunk.' Ruby smirked. 'Perhaps she's forgot she lived there herself for nigh on six years.' The girl turned serious. 'I think Mickey would be better off away from her. Dote on him or not, she'll have his errand money off him so he's not got a penny to call his own. Then in a year or two she'll have him out working full-time.'

'He's not nine yet!' Olivia protested.

'Don't matter to her,' Ruby said. 'Mum'd keep him home from school now if she thought she could get away with it. She tries it, though, I'll make sure the school board man pays her a visit.'

Olivia gave her cousin an admiring glance. 'Good for you.'

'Wish I'd paid more attention to lessons, instead of just biding time until I could leave. I wanted to be a secretary, y'know, when I was little. But once Dad up and left us, I had no chance. The day I turned thirteen she had me out working, doing whatever came along.'

'I wanted to be a nurse,' Olivia said. 'I'm doing the St John Ambulance course with Cath and I don't mind the training at all.'

Ruby wrinkled her nose. 'I didn't fancy it. Mind you, living in the Bunk, I should really know how to patch somebody up. Riley's always getting into scraps.'

As Mickey limped past them, bringing more dirty plates to be washed, Olivia wondered how the lad would fare out in the world with his crippled foot. It was hard enough for the able-bodied to earn a living.

Maggie and Ruby took cloths to dry the washed crockery, stacking the clean plates neatly on the sideboard.

'So ... your friend Cath's set the date at last,' Ruby said.

Olivia flicked water off her fingers, looking surprised. 'News to me.'

'Trevor said they're getting married in the autumn.'

'I thought you were staying away from him.' Olivia frowned.

Ruby gave an insolent smile. 'Can't help it if the bloke keeps pestering me, can I?'

She sauntered off with Olivia's narrowed gaze following her. It had become clearer why Cath was still worried about her fiancé.

'Right then ... that's us done.' Olivia neatly hung up the

wet teacloths on the cooking range. Her sisters and brother came to join her, buttoning up their coats.

'We'll be off now,' Olivia said to Sybil. 'Only one thing I want to take with me ... oh, two actually. There's some garden shears in the shed that'd come in handy, and I'd like this.' She pulled open the drawer in the sideboard and took out the framed picture of her parents on their wedding day.

'Take the shears, I don't want 'em. And the photograph as well, if yer like. But leave the frame. Could be worth a few bob.'

'That belonged to my mum!' Olivia protested.

'Well, now it's mine,' Sybil spat back. But she didn't get up or even turn around.

Ordinarily, Olivia would have made a fight of it. It wasn't right that her aunt Sybil got to keep the frame that Mum had bought for her own home. But Olivia knew this wasn't the time for such a squabble. She removed the photograph and put it in her bag, leaving the silver frame in the drawer.

'And if any solicitor gets in touch about your father's affairs, let me know. 'Cos if you don't, I'll be over after you when I find out he's left money after all,' stood in for a fond farewell from Sybil.

Chapter Ten

'Hope you don't mind me coming here. Joe told me you worked at Barratt's factory so I took a chance on catching you on your way home. Can you spare a minute for a chat?'

''Course I can! It's good to see you again.'

Olivia had immediately recognised the wiry, dark-haired individual standing on the opposite pavement when she came hurrying through the open factory gates in a crowd of fellow workers. Having introduced him to her friend, she added, 'Freddie was Joe's army pal. He's convalescing in Southend.'

'Just malingering really. Should be back over there by now giving Fritz what for,' Freddie joked, suppressing a cough. 'Anyway, pleased to meet you.'

'Likewise, I'm sure,' Cath replied, shaking hands. 'Well, I expect you two have some catching up to do so I'll say ta-ta. I'm ready for home,' she announced. 'Trevor's on convalescence too. We're going to the flicks later to see Charlie Chaplin.' She squinted through the sunlight into Freddie's smiling face. 'You look brighter than my fiancé does, you lucky thing. He's still not well in himself even though his scars are fading.' Cath's upside-down smile said it all really.

'Shame about that,' Freddie said with real feeling.

'We've set the date though. So got something to look forward to ... apart from the cost of it all!' She tutted. 'Well, see you in the morning, Livvie.' Her friend started off along the road.

'Sorry to show up out of the blue,' Freddie said the moment they were alone. 'I've only got a day pass and have to get to Aldgate by eight o'clock to catch me train to Essex. If I miss it I'll be in hot water.'

'You journeyed all the way from Essex to see me?' Olivia sounded surprised. She hadn't expected to see him again so soon. Just over a week had passed since they'd last spoken and she'd imagined he'd write if he discovered anything. She liked Freddie but they barely knew one another. She hoped she hadn't acted too familiarly with him and given him the wrong idea.

'I've killed two birds with one stone by coming to London. It was me sister's birthday so I took Hilda out for lunch earlier and got her some flowers.' Freddie dabbed a hanky to his mouth. 'I made sure I had some time spare to come and see you as well. I wanted to let you know what I've found out about the pewter case.'

'Is it enough for the police to go on?' Olivia asked excitedly.

Freddie wrinkled his nose, shaking his head. 'I've only turned up how poor old Dickie got his hands on it, and it's not a nice tale.'

Olivia tried to hide her disappointment. However minor the discovery, it was good of him to come and let her know about it. 'If you're not too pushed for time, would you like to have a bit of tea with us at home before setting off for the station?'

'Reckon I would ... yes ... if it's not putting you out.'

Olivia gave him a smile, threading her hand under his arm in an amicable fashion. 'Well, come on then, Private Weedon. As you're in a rush, and I'm peckish, let's catch the bus and we can talk on the way.'

They did chat on the busy bus, but only about incidentals as they both felt that to be wisest. Discussing the details of a murder seemed best done behind closed doors.

Olivia put the key in the lock while hoping to herself that she'd bought enough ham for them all to get a slice in a sandwich. She'd not counted on another mouth to feed, but didn't regret inviting Freddie back on the spur of the moment. She hoped too that Maggie would be in a better mood than she had been when Lucas came for tea.

She'd not thought of him for a while, even though she'd received a letter from France earlier in the week. With all the commotion here she'd not had a chance to read it properly or reply yet, but now the funeral was over she'd be able to deal with the matters that had been set aside. If anybody understood the trials of dealing with battling relatives following a bereavement, Lucas did. It had not sounded as though he'd had a pleasant time with his lot after his father passed away.

'Take a pew in the front room.' Olivia pushed open the parlour door to gesture Freddie in. 'I'll put the kettle on.'

'Is that Mr Weedon?' Alfie came haring down the stairs. 'I was looking out of me window and saw you come in.'

'Freddie's staying for tea,' Olivia said. 'Where's Nancy and Maggie?'

'Ain't seen 'em,' Alfie replied. "'Spect they've met up and gone to the caff as there was nothing much in the larder when they looked this morning.'

'Well, there's something now.' Olivia lifted the bag she was carrying and took out a loaf and a quarter of ham together with a slab of walnut cake that she'd bought during her dinner break stroll to the shops with Cath.

'I'll spread the bread,' Alfie offered, opening the drawer for a knife. He was hungry but he was also itching to find out if Freddie had done his detective work and knew who'd killed their father. He'd decided to use the same tactics as before. He'd make out he was going to his room then eavesdrop from a spot on the stairs.

When Olivia entered the parlour Freddie jumped up from his chair and politely took the tea tray from her. Once they'd settled down at the table and she'd handed round the plates of food, Freddie took a bite of his sandwich.

'Cor, this is a tasty bit of ham,' he said.

Olivia smiled. It was nice to have her efforts appreciated. The kids never thanked her for queuing in the shops for their benefit. Even Alfie was starting to take liberties as he got older and more confident. It was time they did a bit more for themselves, Olivia realised.

'Got it in the butcher's in Wood Green High Street.' She didn't mind entering that shop since Harry Wicks no longer worked there. Before he'd joined up she'd always avoided the place. 'Maggie and Nancy have missed out not coming back for tea today. Anyhow, I think you deserve that baked gammon more'n they do, Freddie. Thanks for making time for me on your sister's birthday.' Olivia proffered the sandwich plate again. 'Eat up.'

'I want to help if I can,' he said, selecting another dainty triangle. 'Does your friend Cath know about how I fit into all this business with your dad?'

'I think it's best we keep things quiet for now.' Olivia had let the tea brew for a while and now poured out a strong cup and gave it to him. She remembered that Joe had liked his tea strong enough to stand a spoon up in.

'You've not told the police about me having the case?'

Olivia shook her head. 'I wouldn't want you to be dragged in,' she said flatly. 'The constable told me they're understaffed because of the war. He hinted that he thought a Belgian might be responsible but he'd little to go on.'

'Appreciate you keeping me out of it,' Freddie said gruffly. 'I didn't fancy getting collared for questioning. I didn't want old Dickie's name sullied either. Although he doesn't come out of it very well.'

'Oh?' Olivia put down her tea, anticipating hearing something significant.

'Dickie *did* steal the case. Not from your father,' Freddie hastened to say, then seemed to be in two minds whether to carry on. 'The blasted idiot pinched it from a pawn shop on Southend seafront.'

'A pawn shop?' Olivia echoed in surprise.

'Whoever attacked your father must've disposed of it there. Apparently Dickie saw it in the window and took a fancy to it. He went in, saying he wanted to inspect it. When the pawnbroker's back was turned, the daft sod ran off with it.' Freddie sorrowfully shook his head. 'Poor old Dickie ... I told you he wasn't the full ticket. He was a likeable chap, but he did peculiar things.'

'Did the pawnbroker tell you how he got it in the first place?' Olivia leaned forward, eager to have her question answered.

'That's where we come unstuck,' Freddie sighed. 'He never met the fellow because his son did the deal originally. Now his lad's enlisted in the navy. The pawnbroker didn't think the cigarette case was worth the tanner and shirt that were given for it in exchange.' Freddie looked apologetic. 'No sentimental value to him, you see.'

'Dead end then, for the moment.' She sounded disappointed.

'I'll go back again and find out a bit more when the son's home on leave. I didn't want to arouse the bloke's suspicion so acted nice and casual about it. I'll be keeping a watchful eye on the place, though, until I get signed off as fit.' Here Freddie's expression turned rueful. 'I explained about Dickie and me being at the nursing home. I said my friend had had problems that finished him off.' Freddie paused. 'The pawnbroker was shocked my pal had done himself in. Said he'd let the matter drop as it could be his boy next coming back damaged in the brainbox. And he's right about that.'

'Yes, he is,' Olivia said solemnly. 'My friend Cath would agree with that too.' She pushed the cake plate toward Freddie. 'Help yourself,' she urged. 'The least I can do is feed you after you've put yourself out for me.'

Freddie took a slice of walnut sponge. 'I know we aren't well acquainted. But I owe Joe me life, so I'll do whatever I can to help you. It's what he would have wanted.' Freddie clucked his tongue. 'It's what he would have *expected*,' he corrected himself, glancing heavenwards and giving Joe a jokey wink. 'Ain't that right, mate?'

'I know Joe was brave on that final day – Lieutenant Black told me,' Olivia said simply.

'Understatement to say he were *brave*. No words're good

enough for what he done, holding our position like that.' Freddie cleared his throat and discreetly smeared a tear from his eyes with a swipe of his thumb. 'Weren't just me he protected, it were all of us left in the platoon. He gave us a chance to scarper before the line broke. He kept firing the machine gun till he was out of ammo then he really set about the Hun. Your Joe could fight like a demon ...' Freddie suddenly squeezed shut his eyes as an image of monstrous carnage flashed in front of his eyes. 'I went back for him ... so did Lieutenant Black. We couldn't leave him there. Reinforcements arrived just after I got hit in the chest ...' His voice grew hoarser until it faded away. He cleared his throat abruptly. 'Sorry ... you don't want to hear this.'

'Oh, but I do,' Olivia assured him. 'The least I can do is listen to what you all suffered over there.'

'I keep thinking that but for Joe's courage, I might've been buried beside him in that churchyard at the back of the aid post.' Freddie put down his empty plate. 'Anyhow, that's enough about the trenches. I might be back in 'em soon enough. And I don't mind. Never win this war, will we, unless we all do our bit?'

He fell quiet then and Olivia did too, sensing he needed time to compose himself. Her whole being seemed to throb with sorrow following that harrowing report, yet she felt an underlying tingle of warmth and pride that the man she'd hoped to spend the rest of her life with had been held in such high esteem by his comrades. Joe might have had a dreadful start in life, with a prostitute for a mother and a brief, bleak childhood marked by cruelty. From when he'd been Alfie's age he'd tried to keep his mother safe from violent punters and his brutal pimp of a father. But despite it all Joe Hunter had turned into a good man. The best she'd known.

'Joe wouldn't have let this business about your dad's killer rest, y'know.' Freddie had been pondering on what to do next, to track down the murderer. 'Joe would've found him. Don't know what he'd've done to him when he did, but it wouldn't have been nice.' Freddie's eyes bulged at the thought.

'Lucas told me it makes brutes of men ... being over there. Joe had a bad reputation. But he was only ever kind and generous to me.'

'He could be a soft-hearted bugger.' Freddie gave a wan smile. 'He wanted to rescue a lad fallen on no-man's-land. He knew it were against the rules but he went anyway to get him.'

'I didn't know that.' Olivia sounded amazed.

'The boy was too far gone to save. Thing is, Joe didn't know that so he felt he had to go and make sure. I tried to stop him, but over the top he went, risking his own life and a court martial. In the end all he could do was comfort the lad.' Freddie glanced up, noticing silent tears squeezing between Olivia's lashes. He sighed regretfully. 'Sorry! Stupid to tell you that. Enough now about the damn' war.'

'I honestly don't mind talking about it. And I'd rather hear the truth than some make-believe story. And even though *he* didn't make it home, I'm glad *you* did.' She scrubbed her hanky over her eyes and briskly stood up, collecting their plates.

'Without the angels I'd never have set foot in Blighty again. I'd never have met you and come to tea and talked about Joe.'

'Angels?' Olivia wondered if he meant he'd prayed for his recovery. But Freddie Weedon didn't look the religious type.

'The gels in the hospitals.'

'Oh ... you mean the nurses who tended you.'

'Not the *real* nurses ... they can be dragons.' He pulled a comical face to show they'd terrified him. 'But the other ones, the volunteers who clean you up and make sure you eat yer dinner and take yer medicine and have a shave ... ' Freddie gave a reverent shake of his head. 'Wonderful, they are, bless 'em each and every one. The patients call 'em Poppy Angels 'cos in the summer they brighten up the wards with loads of vases of pretty red flowers picked from the fields. Gives the hospital a home touch, that does. It's just what you need while you're waiting for the doc to sign you off with a Blighty pass.'

'You wounded heroes deserve to be treated well.'

'Some of the poor souls really are a gruesome sight. I looked a mess but there were many far worse. Made you wonder how they was still drawing breath, some of 'em. But those sisters, they'd chat to 'em about this and that, like it was normal to see a bloke with just his eyes and mouth showing through his bandages. It ain't a job fer the faint-hearted, that's fer sure.'

'Fighting in the trenches isn't for the faint-hearted,' Olivia pointed out. 'Thank the Lord that the men and women who're up to the job come forward, when they're needed, whatever the cost to themselves.'

'Amen to that.' Freddie sounded satisfied with her home-spun philosophy. His mind returned to the theft. 'I've not spoken to Harry Wicks since I sold him the case. Has he asked you how I might have got hold of it?'

'I've not seen him. I don't get on with Harry and he knows

it,' Olivia admitted bluntly. 'If he brings the subject up I'll tell him you bought it in Southend. But I doubt he will. He won't relish answering police questions so probably wants to forget he ever had it in his possession.'

'I'm glad you feel the same way as I do about him.' Freddie's top lip curled. 'He isn't well liked. You didn't get this from me, but rumour is he injured his own leg to get a Blighty pass.'

It didn't surprise Olivia that the man Maggie seemed besotted with would sink so low. 'Those Poppy Angels you spoke of must hate having to deal with the likes of him.'

'They'll look after anybody ... even the enemy. I had a shot-up German in the bed next to me once and they treated him nice.' A faraway look misted Freddie's eyes. 'We was short of rations over Christmas 'cos the supplies never turned up. The sisters went without to make sure all the patients got a roast dinner. Yvonne brought us round a little present each. Notebook and pencil it were, and a pair of socks.' Freddie whistled through his teeth. 'Had chilblains like conkers on me big toes so the socks wasn't 'alf handy.' He chuckled softly. 'Almost worthwhile having half me chest caved in to meet Yvonne.'

'You fell for her, didn't you?' Olivia said softly. 'That's why you want to go back and drive an ambulance, isn't it? To be close to Yvonne.'

'She's got a fiancé. Lucky blighter, he is.' Freddie looked bashful at having let slip his feelings for the nurse. 'He's a sergeant in the RAMC. She joined the Voluntary Aid Detachment so she could follow him out there.' He cocked his head. 'She's like you ... fair and pretty. And a real strong character.' Freddie paused. 'Me sister said she'd be willing to join the VAD being as she's got nursing training and no ties. Nobody to miss her, she said. *I'd* miss her. She called me a daft ha'porth when I told her. But if the worst happened, I don't reckon I could go on without my Hilda. She's all I've got.'

'You could keep an eye on her over there when you go back.' Olivia realised that for all his chirpiness Freddie *was* a bit down in the dumps. And little wonder with what he'd been through.

'*She'll* keep an eye on *me* more like!' Freddie guffawed and set himself off coughing. He pulled out his pocket watch. 'Crikey!' he wheezed. 'Is that the time? I'd better get a move on. Thanks very much for tea. I'm stuffed to the gills now, what with having shepherd's pie earlier with Hilda.' He patted his belly. 'I'd best waddle off to the station 'cos I don't want to miss me train.'

Olivia accompanied him to the door. 'Let me know if you find out anything else, won't you?'

Freddie tapped his nose in a conspiratorial way. 'I'll keep an eye on the pawn shop.'

After he had gone Olivia was washing up the plates when she spotted Alfie hovering in the kitchen doorway.

'Where's Dad's cigarette case, Livvie?' he asked her.

'In a drawer in my room,' she replied over her shoulder. 'Why d'you want to know?'

'You should get rid of it,' the boy said seriously. 'It's cursed. Don't want it in the house.'

'I didn't know you were superstitious,' she said with a smile.

'You'll be sorry if it brings us more bad luck,' Alfie muttered, and slid his used crockery into the washing up bowl.

'I know it seems unlucky. But it's something of Dad's, to remember him by. Anyway, I'll look after you, don't worry.'

Olivia ruffled his hair, then handed her brother a tea towel. 'Your turn to dry up.'

Earlier she'd thought it was time the kids made more of an effort to help out around the house. There was no time like the present to make a start.

She glanced at her brother as he wiped his plate. She was glad that he'd left her and Freddie to talk privately. Alfie seemed to be a different boy since they'd moved to Islington. Without his father's oppressive presence he was becoming more outgoing. Perhaps too outgoing, she thought wryly, remembering some of the scraps he'd been in with school pals. She'd not seen him shed a tear for his father, at home or at the funeral. And he'd not asked for a rose to place on Tommy Bone's coffin either. Sometimes it was hard to recall the sensitive little boy who'd once jumped at his own shadow.

Chapter Eleven

'I reckernise you. You're the brother of the lass me son was gonna marry. Alfie, ain't it?'

Alfie stuck his hands in his pockets and squinted up at the thin-faced man giving him a brown-toothed grin.

'Don't remember me, son? Me 'n' yer sister was having a bit of a natter a while back.'

'Yeah . . . I remember. You was outside our house.' Alfie grimaced as he saw his pals start to drift away because he'd been collared by a grown up. He didn't have that many friends and had been enjoying his game of football in Campbell Road before this bloke butted in.

'Herbie Hunter's me name. I'm Joe's dad, did you know that?'

Alfie shook his fair head. He didn't think this man looked anything like Joe. His sister's boyfriend had been a beefy, well-groomed man. This fellow looked like a scrawny tramp. But Alfie had liked Joe so he supposed he should be polite to his father.

'Heard you and yer family's had some real bad luck lately.' Herbie made a sympathetic noise. 'Was having a chat with Mrs Keiver and she told me you lost yer pa. What a bad business.' In fact Matilda hadn't told him. She never spoke to him, just scowled in a threatening way if she spotted him. But Herbie wanted to gain the boy's trust and he knew that Matilda Keiver and Livvie Bone were friends. As soon as he'd noticed Alfie playing football he'd seen a chance to find out if the police had turned up anything. He was hoping to get an indication that Tommy Bone's case was going nowhere. No more coppers had been round Muswell Hill asking questions. 'Bet you miss yer dad, don't you?' Herbie crooned.

Alfie didn't miss his dad at all; he'd hated the brute. But he nodded because he knew that was what was expected of him.

'Tell yer what ... I'll buy you a bag o' sweets from Smithie's. My way of letting you know I wish it hadn't happened and I feel sorry for yer.' That was the truth too. Herbie *did* regret it because he hated constantly being on his guard. On the other hand, now he'd got Bone Senior out of the way, he knew he might have a better chance of getting his foot in the door of Joe's old house. But he'd have to bide his time and play it right or he'd get nowhere.

Herbie put his hand on Alfie's shoulder, guiding him towards the shop while keeping a weather eye out. He knew if Livvie Bone spotted them together she'd poke her oar in and drag the boy off.

'Got on with my Joe then, did yer?' Herbie asked, handing over a bag of liquorice.

'Yeah ... he took me out to the flicks once. Saw *Ivanhoe*. It was great.' Alfie remembered the evening well; they'd seen a film then had supper in a Corner House on the way back. But of course his father had had to go and spoil it. He'd seen them all coming home in the dark and had tried to pick on Joe and Livvie for letting his son stay out late. Then his father had fallen down drunk in the street and Joe had had to carry him to bed.

'My Joe gave you treats, did he? He was generous. Took after me, y'see.' Herbie rammed home his point by nodding at the bag of liquorice Alfie was diving into.

'Oh, thanks,' he said, remembering his manners. He was thawing towards Joe's dad. He seemed all right on the whole, just a bit smelly and scruffy.

Alfie sank down to lounge on the kerb outside the shop and finish his sweets. His big sister hadn't seemed to like Joe's dad so Alfie wasn't planning on taking his liquorice home and getting into trouble. He didn't want to lie to Livvie about where he'd got it. She was the only person in the world he really loved. She'd always looked after him, protected him from his father, even when that meant she'd suffered instead.

Herbie hunkered down by Alfie's side. 'Funeral all done and dusted now, ain't it?'

Alfie nodded, winding a black bootlace into his mouth.

''Spect you've got some good memories of your old man, ain't yer?'

Alfie didn't have any, so instead said, 'Hadn't seen him in months before he got murdered.'

'I see . . . so you live with yer big sister but hadn't seen yer dad for a while,' Herbie muttered to himself.

'Got a nice photo of him and me mum when they got married though.' Alfie tipped out the final piece of liquorice onto his palm. 'She wouldn't let us have the frame so the picture's just stuck in a drawer.'

'Wouldn't let you have the frame? That's a bit mean of

yer sister.' Herbie sounded all indignant on Alfie's behalf.

'Nah, weren't Livvie. Aunt Sybil lived with me dad in Wood Green and she wanted to keep the silver frame in case it was worth a few bob.' Alfie could remember Sybil's exact words that day. He'd thought her mean as well. In fact, he hadn't taken to her at all. His cousin Mickey had seemed all right though. In fact, Alfie hoped to see him again. Mickey had said he was good at playing football even though he had a gammy foot.

Again Herbie digested a nugget of information. Tommy Bone had made it sound as though he lived with his daughter in Joe's old place. 'Our' house he'd called it, but perhaps that had just been wishful thinking on his part. 'I'll get you a frame, Alfie, from a totter I know. Then you can stand the pitcher up again and look at it properly.' Herbie gave the boy a wink.

'Ain't got no money to pay fer it.' Alfie sounded disappointed. He really wanted to stand the photo up. He liked studying the pretty lady he'd never known. He understood she was his mother, but Aggie Bone was just a beautiful stranger to him even though she was the image of Livvie.

A crafty light gleamed at the back of Alfie's eyes then. He'd thought of a way of getting his frame even though he knew Herbie Hunter wouldn't lay out a penny on his behalf. If Joe's dad agreed to his suggestion he'd manage to kill two birds with one stone. 'If you get me a picture frame, I'll swap you a cigarette case for it. Used to belong to me dad, but he don't need it now, of course.'

Herbie had rolled himself a cigarette while they'd been talking and was in the process of lighting it. He choked on a lungful of smoke, turning his head aside so Alfie couldn't see his startled expression. 'Cigarette case, eh?'

he spluttered, and nodded repeatedly, playing for time to calm himself down. The kid's announcement had knocked him for six. Herbie wondered if Tommy Bone had owned two similar items because he couldn't fathom out how the cigarette case he'd pawned in Southend had made its way home. 'You sure you got that case, son? I heard yer dad was robbed . . .'

'It *was* stolen from me dad.' Alfie glanced up at the man, frowning. 'Me sister's got it back now though.' Alfie just wanted to get rid of the thing. Freddie Weedon had called it jinxed. Alfie reckoned it was, too, being as the man who'd stolen it from a pawnbroker had jumped off the pier and drowned himself. Alfie had overheard Freddie saying he'd wished he'd chucked it in the sea to break the curse. Alfie was glad he hadn't. If the cigarette case could be swapped for something useful, Livvie was sure to be pleased, and thank him.

'Well, that sounds an interestin' offer,' Herbie said. 'Tell me a bit more about this case then.'

'I'll go and get it if you like and show yer . . .'

'No!' Herbie pulled the boy back down to the pavement as he jumped up. 'No need for that, son,' he blustered. He'd hoped never to see the damned thing again. He certainly didn't want Livvie Bone finding out he'd asked about it. 'I believe you if you say it's a good 'un. Just wonderin' how yer sister managed to get it back if it was stolen.' He narrowed his eyes. 'Clever gel to do that, ain't she?'

'Mr Weedon got hold of it down Southend way.' Alfie watched Herbie dragging repeatedly on his cigarette. He could tell the man wasn't that keen on doing a deal. Alfie knew Livvie couldn't afford to buy a photo frame because he needed new school trousers. He'd slid on the playground in a game of British Bulldog and torn the knees out of his. To persuade Joe's dad into agreeing to the swap he said, 'Keep a secret?'

'Who, me?' Herbie chuckled, but licked his lips nervously and glanced about. "Course I can. Tell you what ... if you tell a secret then I will too. How's that?'

Alfie nodded vigorously.

'You go first then, son.'

'Mr Weedon's found out how the cigarette case turned up in Southend and soon he'll know who done me dad in. He's investigating the murder for Livvie,' Alfie whispered, eyes popping in excitement.

'That *is* a secret.' Herbie's complexion was whitening beneath the greyish stubble on his face. 'This Mr Weedon seems a clever sort 'n' all then. Is he yer sister's new boyfriend?'

'Don't think so. They ain't lovey-dovey. Freddie's one of Joe's army pals. He got shot up over there and reckons Joe saved his life.' Alfie's voice thrummed with pride. The more he heard about how brave Joe had been, the more he wished he'd had him as his brother-in-law. Joe's dad would be just as proud of him. Alfie stared at Mr Hunter, expecting to hear the fellow say as much. Herbie seemed more intent on rolling himself another cigarette and Alfie noticed that he seemed all fingers and thumbs.

'So ... me son's pal's involved in it all, is he?' Herbie muttered. 'Ain't that a turn up?'

'Freddie's nice although he's not well,' Alfie said. 'He's always coughing his lungs up. That's why he's staying in a nursing home in Southend and doing his detective work while he's getting better. He come up to London 'specially to tell Livvie what he'd found out.'

'Well, I never,' Herbie croaked from behind the roll-up wagging between his lips. 'That's a rum tale. Wonder if the coppers know what he's up to?' His narrowed eyes were fixed on Alfie's face as he waited for an answer.

'Freddie and Livvie ain't gonna tell 'em yet. First Freddie's getting more clues. He knows where to go too. It's a pawn-broker's on the seafront at Southend.'

'So they brought you in on all o' this, did they?' Herbie squinted through smoke at his young companion.

Alfie blushed.

'Ah.' Herbie gave him a slow wink. 'That's why it's a secret, is it? You've been doing a bit of earwigging at keyholes.'

'Not really . . . ' Alfie started to protest, but his voice was drowned out by a shout.

Herbie whipped about nervously on hearing his name bawled out. His pal Jimmy Wild was beckoning him.

'That's me mate, over there. Just off down the Duke with 'im.' Herbie patted Alfie's shoulder. 'So . . . we'll keep all this secret and just between us, eh, Alfie? Or no deal.'

Alfie nodded. 'You was gonna tell me a secret.'

'Next time. I'll catch up with you another day. First I'll do a bit of duckin' 'n' divin' to get me hands on a nice pitcher frame. So you keep schtum about all of this.'

'Ain't telling nobody. It's our secret.' Alfie sounded solemn.

'Good lad,' Herbie said, and hurried away.

*

'Didn't take long for her to return to her old ways, did it?' Olivia said.

'Nelly's only got one way . . . and that's her way.' Sal, who sat next to Olivia on the production line, scowled at their supervisor, who was standing on top of the work bench and agitating for a strike.

It wasn't the first time since the war started that Nelly Smith had decided the labour shortage was a useful bargaining tool when dealing with Barratt's management. She'd tried before to get a pay rise by threatening a mass walkout. The munitions factories springing up were luring workers with better rates. Some of the factories were open round the clock to meet the demands of the military. Night work was especially lucrative and more and more women were willing to suffer the unsociable hours to reap the rewards on offer.

Olivia got on well with most of her colleagues. They agreed with her that using the war to put money in your pocket was pretty despicable when husbands and fathers and sons were being slaughtered abroad. Nelly was a two-faced hypocrite. She'd suck up to Deborah Wallis in the hope her name would be remembered in the boardroom and stab her fellow workers in the back to feather her own nest. But Nelly had her own little band of cronies who lapped up everything she said in the belief she'd see them all right.

Tommy Bone had been a similar character to Nelly in his heyday. Just like her, he hadn't known when to shut up and be grateful for what he had. After Tommy had been murdered the shock of it seemed to mellow Nelly for a while. She and Tommy had never got on but she had recognised in him a kindred spirit.

Now, though, things were getting back to normal at the factory. People no longer stopped Olivia to commiserate on her family's awful loss. Regularly, women turned up at work red-eyed from weeping about their own tragedies. Nobody said much ... just mumbled their sympathy. They knew that another form had been received by a wife or mother, dreading its news. Tommy Bone had at least died in his own country and seen a score more years than those lads over there, people would say as they became accustomed to living with fear and anxiety that it might soon be their turn to wear black armbands. Worse still was suffering the torture of wondering what had happened to their strong young men who'd been reported missing.

'So you with us then, Livvie Bone?' Nelly shouted, interrupting Olivia's thoughts.

'Reckon you already know the answer to that, Nelly. So I don't know why you even asked.' Olivia dusted herself down. They'd been bagging up sherbet that afternoon and dust had settled thickly on the bench, and over the floor, and even the large wooden clock on the wall. The women were covered too, from head to toe, in fine white powder that they banged from their clothes and sucked from their fingers. Satisfied that she was as presentable as possible for the journey home, Olivia untied her sacking apron then gathered her things from under the bench, ready to set off.

'Wish she'd give it a bloody rest,' Sal said, shrugging into her coat.

'Nelly'll never change,' Olivia replied in a resigned voice.

Outside, she met Cath coming out of an adjacent building that led to the packing department.

'Nelly Smith's doing her usual ... causing trouble,' Sal said by way of greeting.

'So's she!' Cath jerked her chin at Ruby Wright, who came sauntering along. A fellow who looked old enough to know better bumped into her and whispered something that made her preen. He tried to grab her for a crafty cuddle but got pushed away.

'You'll need yer wallet fer a crack at that one,' one of the other men called, starting off guffaws among the crew loading the carts.

'Better make sure it's full 'n' all,' Ruby whipped back, tossing her bleached-blonde head.

The fellow cradled his crotch. 'Oh, it's full all right, love. Don't need to worry about that.'

'Full of hot air more like,' Sal muttered, spying her married brother-in-law making a prat of himself.

'Seen any more of that Freddie Weedon?' Cath asked when Sal had said goodbye and was out of earshot.

'Not for a week or so. He's back in Southend. I hope the sea air's helping him get better. He's got a rotten cough on him.'

'He seemed nice . . . ' Cath arched an eyebrow.

'He's mooning over a VAD serving in France,' Olivia said to dampen down Cath's grin.

She'd been thinking a lot about Freddie's unrequited love. He'd said Yvonne was like her, and from the way he'd described the young woman Olivia reckoned they did have things in common. If circumstances were different she'd be willing to volunteer and go and help the wounded troops in any way she could, even if it amounted to just brewing up pots of tea. Olivia greatly admired the plucky women risking their lives on the Western Front. The feeling that she should be doing more than make toffees was strengthening in her all the time. She'd found herself taking more notice lately of women in uniform when they passed her in the street. They always seemed purposeful and energetic as they went about their business.

Olivia knew she would like to feel that way too. She was

young and strong and fit. She'd been washing and cooking and cleaning since she was ten years old and wasn't scared, or incapable, of hard graft. She was sure she could be of help in the war effort.

As they walked out through the open gates Olivia glanced back at the factory buildings. Now that her father had gone and her cousin Ruby had arrived, she felt differently about Barratt's. Working at the factory had always been her father's job, not hers. With his death it seemed her own close tie with the place had been severed. She was hungry for change, she realised. Sweet-making was no longer enough for her. Yet she wasn't sure that moving to another factory was the answer either.

'You're looking thoughtful,' Cath remarked as they set off in the direction of Hornsey Park Road.

'I'm trying to decide whether to apply for a job in the munitions factory where Maggie works,' Olivia announced. 'At least then I'd be doing *something* to help put an end to the fighting.'

'I'll come,' Cath said immediately. 'I've had enough of this place too.' She glanced over at Ruby, showing off to her admirers, and her lip curled. 'Sooner I move on from this dump, the better I'll like it.'

Chapter Twelve

'What d'you think yer doing?' Maggie hissed.

Nancy glowered at her sister, mouthing at her to shut up as she slipped the Yardley lipstick into her bag then sauntered away from the make-up counter in Gamages and started examining a silk scarf.

Maggie felt her heart thudding under her bodice. She knew that store detectives worked in Gamages because while she was at school one of her friend's mums had been caught shoplifting there and had ended up in court. Linking arms with Nancy, she started dragging her sister towards the exit in as unobtrusive a way as possible because she'd just spotted a fellow in a dark suit and he didn't look like he was buying anything. Once they were outside she shoved her younger sister away from her.

'What the hell you playing at?' she burst out. 'You could've got us arrested.' Maggie jabbed a nod at the store detective, stationed by the door with his arms crossed over his burly chest.

'Don't be daft,' Nancy said dismissively. 'If you're clever you can do it without anybody seeing. I had me eye on him from the moment we went in. He didn't see nothin', I made sure of it.' She narrowed her eyes at Maggie. 'Don't go blabbin' to Livvie about this.' Nancy could see she'd shocked her sister by taking the lipstick. It was as well Maggie didn't know what else she'd had from the stores in the West End or she would probably go mad. Once Nancy had gone into Selfridges without a hat and come out wearing a nice velvet job. She'd explained away her luck by telling her sisters one of the women at work had let her have it for a florin because it didn't suit her. Nancy had imagined Maggie would secretly admire her for having the guts to do it ... that's why she'd given her a nudge and allowed her to see the lipstick disappearing into her sister's bag.

'It's all right fer you,' Nancy snapped. 'You earn good wages doing nights at the munitions factory. I can't even afford to go to the flicks with me friends more'n a couple of times a week, after I've handed over me housekeeping money. I'm sick of being a tea gel and want a proper job.'

'You ain't even old enough to be working!' Maggie retorted. 'You should think yerself lucky you've got a job at all. Dad made me stick at school until I was gone fourteen ...'

'What's this all about then?' Harry Wicks had been browsing a gentlemen's outfitters when he'd spotted his girlfriend arguing with her sister on the pavement outside Gamages. He'd crossed the road and, so het up had the two of them been, they'd not noticed his approach.

'Oh ... hello,' Maggie burbled, trying to cover her confusion at him showing up out of the blue like this.

Harry gave Nancy a smirk. She was better-looking than Maggie and getting older and shapelier all the time ... But she always looked at him as their elder sister did: with a hint of contempt.

Maggie had intercepted Harry's glance at Nancy and it reminded her of when Livvie had asked how she'd feel if an older man showed an interest in their youngest sister. Nancy had turned thirteen now and had a small bust and her waist was starting to show ... but Maggie was sure Harry was just being friendly, smiling at her like that. Maggie reckoned it wouldn't hurt, in any case, to take his eyes off Nancy by telling him what she'd done. He was sure to be disgusted. 'She's just been a bloody idiot and nicked make-up in there.'

Harry threw back his head and guffawed. 'Gel after me own heart.' He looked at Nancy with renewed interest and gave her a sly wink.

Nancy turned her back on them both. She was furious that Maggie had blabbed that out to him of all people. She thought Maggie was the idiot for having anything to do with Harry Wicks. 'Going home,' she muttered, and marched off.

'Wish I'd not come out with her now,' Maggie complained. 'She said she just wanted to do a bit of window shopping before teatime.' Maggie was feeling awkward. She was wishing she'd kept her mouth shut. Harry was looking like the cat who'd got the cream, staring after Nancy. And that rankled with Maggie. Sometimes she wondered if Livvie was right about him and he was just stringing her along while playing around with other girls. He always told her she was his one and only, though. In any case, it was too late to back out of getting serious with him. Things *were* serious. She had something important to tell him. But she was frightened of how he'd take the news he was going to become a father.

'You could get in big trouble if it gets out you've been thievin', y'know,' Harry drawled.

'Weren't me!' Maggie blustered; she didn't like his tone of voice.

'Nobody'll believe that, what with you being the eldest. Coppers'd think you was the ringleader, Mags.' He chuckled softly. 'Come on then, you naughty gel. Let's get you home.' Harry tucked her hand through the crook of his arm and set off towards the bus stop, whistling.

*

'What're you looking so down in the dumps about?' Olivia asked as she hoisted two bags of shopping on to the parlour table. She'd been to the market and her feet were aching. She eased off her leather boots by prising the heel off one with the toe of the other. Usually she'd carefully undo the buttons as they were good boots but she felt too fagged to bend down and do it properly.

Maggie didn't answer but stormed off upstairs, ignoring the cup of tea Nancy was holding out to her.

'She's sulking because Harry's on light duties, shipping off to France next week to join the catering corps till his leg's healed,' Nancy explained. When Maggie had got home Nancy had been relieved to find that she had more on her mind than their argument. Maggie had forgotten about the shoplifting because she'd been full of Harry having just told her he was going back to war.

Olivia's spirits lifted on hearing that finally some distance would be put between Harry and Maggie. But she didn't like to see her sister upset so went upstairs to speak to her.

'Coming down for tea?'

'Not hungry.' Maggie was sitting on her mattress, picking listlessly at her nails. She'd not found the courage after all to tell Harry she was pregnant. He'd kept going on about the shoplifting spree and it didn't seem to matter how many times she told him she was innocent, he seemed gleefully amused about it, as though he admired what Nancy had done. He'd walked her to her door then dropped the bombshell about going back abroad before rushing off to catch his bus home.

Olivia sat beside Maggie on the bed. From her sister's gruff voice and red-rimmed eyes it was obvious she had been crying. 'Come on ... cheer up.' Olivia put an arm round her.

Maggie tilted her head to rest it on her sister's shoulder. 'Alfie reckons we're jinxed and I do too. That bloody cigarette case you bought Dad is cursed and now it's turned up again it'll bring us more bad luck.' She wiped her wet nose with her hanky. 'Alfie said somebody else has died 'cos of owning it. Now Harry'll get killed as well, I know it. And I need him badly.'

'You're talking daft. Freddie had the case first and he's fine. Harry will be too.' Olivia was annoyed with herself for not having realised sooner that Alfie had been spying on her meetings with Freddie. Such crafty behaviour made her see her brother in a new and worrying light.

'Nancy told me Harry's going into the catering corps. He'll avoid the trenches for a while at least.'

'What d'you care? You don't like him.' Maggie shrugged her sister's arm off her shoulders and jumped up. She started to brush her mousy hair. 'You don't know how much I need him. And I love him.' Maggie tossed her brush onto the bed. 'You don't understand! I want Harry to marry me 'fore he goes.'

Olivia had heard her sister's passionate declarations about Harry Wicks before so ignored this outburst. Maggie was only fifteen and Olivia hoped in time she'd see Harry for what he was and settle down with somebody nice.

'I know *I* don't like Harry. But I like *you*,' Olivia reasoned. 'And I don't want to see you upset.' In an attempt to cheer Maggie up she added, 'I'm proud of you for working in that place in Isledon Road. Any vacancies that you know of there? I want to make munitions instead of sweets.'

'You can have my job if you want,' Maggie replied quietly.

Olivia stood up, frowning. 'Why? Are you leaving?'

'Might be . . .'

'Why? Thought you liked it there, working with Alice Keiver.' The hairs on the nape of her neck prickled as Olivia sensed something was wrong. 'Have you got something better to go to?'

'You don't understand. You *never* understand that we can't all be perfect like you.' Maggie looked flustered and began edging towards the door.

Suddenly she pushed Olivia out of the way and rushed from the room, then straight down the stairs. Before Olivia could give chase to try and comfort her and find out what was going on, she heard the front door being slammed shut.

Chapter Thirteen

The last thing Herbie had wanted was the expense of another trip to Southend when he couldn't afford to pay the rent on the dump he lived in. Ever since young Alfie had told him about Joe's pal turning amateur detective, Herbie had been fretting that a trail could lead back to him. So, rather than drive himself crazy wondering what Freddie Weedon had dug up about the cigarette case, he'd decided to go and find out.

His greatest fear was that the merchant on Southend seafront might give Weedon a description of the person who'd pawned the case. Herbie knew he was noteworthy because of his spindly build and balding head. Then he'd have a problem. Tommy's daughter knew him and would quickly put two and two together once Weedon reported what he'd found out. According to Alfie *he'd* not seen his old man in months. But Herbie couldn't be sure that his big sister hadn't either. Chances were *she* had been with Tommy that afternoon. With a noose dangling over his head, Herbie wasn't taking any chances. She might remember that her dad and Herbie Hunter had been in Playford Road on the day Tommy met his end and start to wonder if they'd come face to face.

It was late summer but an overcast day. A blustery wind was coming off the choppy sea. It took Herbie's cap clean off his head, making him swear and sprint along the promenade after it. Swooping down, he slapped it back on his shiny pate, pulling the brim low to shield his features. Feeling out of breath, he ambled more slowly along the deserted seafront, brooding on his unfortunate predicament. He had no idea what his quarry looked like. In hindsight, he wished he'd questioned Alfie a bit more about Weedon but he'd not wanted to arouse the lad's suspicion. His son's friend could be his downfall and that was a bitter pill for Herbie to swallow. It was almost as though Joe were still able to get at him, even from the grave.

He couldn't say he blamed his only child for hating him. But in Herbie's book you were loyal to your parents and gave them obedience, no matter what. His own father had been a brutal drunkard but Herbie had been too terrified to reject him. Now he regretted having been too soft on Joe. He should have knocked more respect into him before he'd got big enough to hit back.

Herbie blamed his wife for their son cutting him out of his life, and his will too. That *really* rankled. He was a man with nothing, yet he was Joe's next-of-kin and could've been sitting pretty now in his son's property.

Maisie had turned Joe against him, blaming Herbie for their problems when the truth was she'd been a boozy brass before he'd even met her. But Joe had stuck by his mother. And his half-sister, although the kid had been a half-wit. And Herbie wasn't taking the blame for that either. Mixed blood was the reason for the girl's poor health, in his opinion, not his own rough handling of her.

Herbie glanced across the road from under his cap brim then sank down onto a bench opposite the pawnbroker's. He was facing the sea with his back to the shop, but by slouching forward, and planting his elbows on his knees, he could peep over one shoulder and keep it at the corner of his eye. The sight of somebody new behind the counter gave Herbie a modicum of relief. The older bloke wouldn't be able to give a description of him because they'd never met. Still, he sighed despondently. The younger fellow might be back tomorrow, then he'd be in trouble. Herbie knew it was a long shot to hope that a man in hospital blues might turn up and go inside today.

And if he did … Herbie hadn't decided what he'd do about it then. At the moment there was nothing to link Herbie Hunter to Tommy Bone. Nobody knew they'd ever met. Herbie glanced again at the shop and quickly averted his face, hunching into his coat collar.

A dark-haired fellow in hospital blues appeared to be loitering aimlessly by a teashop next door to the pawnbroker's. With an expression of joyous amazement on his face, Herbie discreetly watched the fellow pull out a handkerchief and cough into it. He could see the poor sod turning red in the face with the effort of controlling his lungs. When he did finally stuff his handkerchief back in his pocket, Freddie Weedon sauntered past the pawnbroker's, glancing in casually, in a way Herbie knew he might have done himself while carrying out a recce.

Herbie smiled as he got up to follow Weedon. The fellow hadn't gone into the shop, and that was a shame. If asking questions about the cigarette case were Weedon's game, he wouldn't have received any answers that would incriminate Herbie today.

He was pleased that he'd found his man with no trouble at all. Now he had to decide what he was going to do about the problem of Weedon. And he'd have to do it quickly because he wanted to catch the train home that evening. His miserable cow of a sister had made it clear the last time he'd begged a bed at hers that he'd not be welcomed back any time soon.

*

'Cough it up, son ... might be a gold watch,' Herbie said in a jokey tone, clapping Freddie on the shoulder.

He had been following his son's friend along the esplanade for some time. He'd noticed the fellow's pace faltering as though he was fagged out. Herbie had slowed down in turn to keep a fair distance between them. Then Freddie had stopped and propped one arm on a wall to start barking out a series of coughs. Herbie had decided this was as good an opportunity as he was likely to get to strike up a conversation, so he'd approached him.

'Brave feller, ain't yer, to be out 'n' about after what you've been through with them Hun.' Herbie doffed his cap in a show of respect. 'Sounds like you should be tucked up in bed still, soldier.' He pumped an unsuspecting Freddie by the hand. 'Like to say a thank you to all of you young men who've been doing yer bit over there.'

'Nurses tell us the sea air's good fer us,' Freddie replied, inhaling deeply and glancing about at the dull, sunless vista. 'Have to say, being here beats waking up in a Flanders field full of yeller mud 'n' green gas. I'd go back in a shot,

152

though, if I could get meself signed off.' Recovered from his coughing fit, he blinked the tears from his eyes and took a proper look at the tramp who'd accosted him, wondering if he was about to beg a penny for a cup of tea.

While meandering in Freddie's wake Herbie had been mulling over how to turn the conversation to the cigarette case. He'd thought if he could mention Joe's name and make out it was a fluke meeting his son's friend like this then that might lead to something. He decided to start talking and play it by ear.

'Me son was at Ypres, y'know. Got killed, God rest 'im.' Herbie crossed himself. 'He was a machine-gunner.'

'Me 'n' all!' Freddie exclaimed with a grin. 'I was handling a Vickers at Ypres.'

'My Joe was too!' Herbie didn't know for sure which weapon Joe had used but guessed it would've been the same as his oppo. 'Well ... that's a turn up,' Herbie said, all innocence. 'Joe Hunter was me boy's name, and I'm his dad Herbert.'

Freddie shouted a wondering laugh that caused him to start wheezing again. 'I *knew* Joe. He was me best pal. I'm Freddie Weedon. Spoke of me, did he?'

'Reckon that name do ring a bell, y'know. I'll shake yer hand again in that case, son.' Herbie grabbed Freddie's fingers. 'My Joe was set to marry a lovely lass.' He pressed on as it seemed to be going so well. ''Spect he told you all about Livvie. She's missing him. Breaking her heart is the poor duck ... '

'I *know* Livvie Bone. I saw her not so long ago when I was in London.'

Freddie sounded delighted to be talking to him so Herbie burbled on, 'Yeah, Islington way, ain't it, where she lives?' He slapped his thigh and chortled. 'Well, I never! Small world!'

'Yeah.' Freddie shook his head in disbelief. Slowly, he looked up, frowning. 'So ... what you doing in Southend, Mr Hunter?' The initial excitement of the meeting having worn off, Freddie was reflecting on conversations that he'd had with Joe about their respective families. His friend had told him his parents were dead, though Freddie had guessed that was a lie. This man *was* Joe's father and Freddie reckoned he knew why Joe had not wanted to acknowledge him. Hunter Senior had a sly way about him and he'd clearly come to Southend for a reason. Freddie imagined that *he* was that reason. But he couldn't fathom why Herbert Hunter wanted to see him so desperately, or why he'd pretend this was a chance encounter.

'Me sister lives this way,' Herbie said bluntly. He wanted to turn the conversation back to the real issue, not get side-tracked into answering questions about himself. 'So, if you saw me son's fiancée recently, you'll know poor Livvie's had terrible bad luck. Ain't only lost Joe, has she, but her dad too.' He clucked his tongue.

'The girl's had it from all directions, all right,' Freddie agreed while inwardly still mulling things over. Joe had never mentioned an aunt living in Southend. In fact, he'd seemed to have few living relatives. But here Herbert Hunter was, large as life.

'Terrible business, that murder.' Herbie tried to get more of a reaction from Freddie.

'Oh, indeed it were,' he agreed and pursed his lips.

'Got robbed *and* murdered,' Herbie persevered, hoping Freddie would mention the pawnbroker's he'd just been loitering by.

'Livvie told me the bastard took her father's cigarette case and money then left him to bleed to death.' Freddie played the game, guessing he'd said the right thing when he saw Hunter nervously lick his lips.

'Yeah ... weren't no point to it,' he sneered in a show of disgust. 'Pewter ain't worth much.'

'Didn't say it were pewter. How d'you know that?'

Herbie ferreted in his pocket for his tobacco tin, fumbling to prise off the lid. 'Must've been Livvie told me. Or else I read it in the paper. It were reported in the *Gazette*, I expect,' he blustered. 'Smoke?' He offered the tin to Freddie.

'Not for me, thanks. Trying to cut it out with me chest being the way it is. Never get back to me platoon otherwise.' He stuck out his hand. 'Pleased to meet you, Mr Hunter, but I've got to be on me way. Me pal's expecting me in the pub fer a pint dinnertime.'

'Right-ho. Nice to see you, Freddie. You take care o' yourself, son, and get better soon.' Following his cheery farewell, Herbie kept half an eye on Freddie while rolling himself a cigarette. He knew he'd made a mess of that encounter. Weedon was no mug and had seemed suspicious.

Herbie saw the younger man stroll across the road to a big old building with pillars out the front. A board stuck on the lawn proclaimed it to be Seaview Court. Herbie guessed that was the nursing home where he was staying. Covertly he observed the invalid go up the path to the entrance. Herbie knew Weedon would glance back before disappearing so made a show of looking carefree, marching off purposefully in the opposite direction, puffing on his newly lit fag.

Blaspheming beneath his breath, he took a circuitous route back to the nursing home, keeping himself out of sight.

He knew he would have to stake out the place to see what Freddie Weedon did next. With a self-pitying sigh, Herbie wondered if he'd manage to get back to London that night, or would need to spend it sleeping rough under the pier.

A preoccupied Freddie went upstairs, returning a mumbled greeting to his room mate. He lifted the net curtain and scoured the promenade for a sight of Hunter. He seemed to have disappeared. Freddie inwardly scoffed at himself for being so daft, thinking there was something sinister about the old boy. Nevertheless, he took another peek outside then sat down on the bed and found his writing things. He dashed off his letter to Olivia, telling her that Joe's father had been snooping around in Southend, asking questions about Tommy Bone's murder. He also wrote a letter to his sister Hilda, begging her to forget about joining the VAD because he wanted her to keep safe. He also wrote about how much he liked Olivia Bone. He urged Hilda to get in touch with the young woman and make friends as Olivia was feeling lonely. He put down his pen and pulled from a drawer the difficult letter he wanted to finish. It was to Yvonne, telling her how he felt about her. But he knew he wasn't in the frame of mind to compose a love letter so settled back on the bed and went to sleep.

Many hours later Freddie woke to the sound of rain spattering against the window pane, and the savoury aroma of stew wafting on the air. He was alone now and Freddie guessed his room mate had gone down early to the refectory. He swung his legs off the bed and stood up, collecting the letters that he wanted to post before the gong sounded. He strode out of the Seaview into foul weather. He thought about retreating into the warm and dry, leaving the letters until tomorrow. But something made him determined to get them into the box before he settled down for his dinner. He scowled up at the grey heavens then jammed his hat down on his head, pulling the brim low. Without further hesitation, he set off at a brisk pace into the premature dusk.

Herbie had been sheltering in an abandoned kiosk that proclaimed it sold souvenirs and seaside rock. He had been waiting and fretting all the while, guessing what Freddie Weedon intended to do. As he followed him, he saw the man slip some envelopes into his overcoat pocket to keep them dry while splashing on through puddles. Herbie knew he had no option but to stop him posting the cursed things. If Olivia Bone heard from Weedon about their meeting, Herbie would be in Queer Street. He'd killed and robbed her father and would swing for it if it were ever discovered.

Self-pitying tears stung his eyes, mingling with the rain on his lashes as Herbie hurried along. He'd thought that Freddie seemed quite a pleasant young man on the whole and didn't want to hurt him. Nevertheless he began fondling the blade in his pocket. The first lightning strike divided the leaden sky then a rumble of thunder sounded, bringing a dense gloom to settle over the heaving sea. Herbie kept striding on, making sure his face was averted from those few people hurrying past, seeking shelter from the storm.

Freddie started to jog, his chin down, nestling in the warmth of his upturned coat collar. Herbie speeded up too. He wasn't fit but he was gaining on the fellow in front, who was struggling to keep up the pace. Within a few seconds Herbie was marching alongside his exhausted quarry.

Freddie caught sight of him from the corner of one eye and instinctively veered away, sensing danger. But Herbie put on a sprint and dashed in front of him, bumping him backwards. Freddie regained his footing and quickly did a right turn, heading onto the pier. He could feel his heart pumping as fast as his battered lungs as he sprinted along the wooden boards, finding them slippery beneath his feet. Although incapacitated, he was younger than his pursuer. A glance over his shoulder told him he was putting some distance between himself and Hunter. Freddie darted glances to left and right, looking for something to use as a weapon. All he needed was a lump of wood ... driftwood would do, or failing that another person he could call on to help him. But the pier was dark and deserted and Freddie was tingling with dread. He had seen murder in Hunter's eyes for the brief moment they'd met this evening. All had become clear to Freddie at that moment. He *had* to tell Olivia he knew who'd killed her father and warn her about the danger Joe's dad presented to her and her family.

So intent was he on squinting into the rain to find a soul to help him that he missed the uneven boarding just in front of him. He turned an ankle, crashing down on the wet planks. Freddie bashed his forehead on the boards and through misty eyes saw between the cracks the black sea beckoning him.

With a painful effort he turned onto his back as Hunter loomed over him, gasping and holding his sides. Herbie dropped to one knee, avoiding meeting Freddie's eyes. They both knew what came next.

'Didn't need to do that. Didn't need to tell on me ... ' he whined as his fingers rifled Freddie's pockets for the letters and his cash. Old habits died hard with Herbie.

He pulled out a snotty handkerchief and some silver. He threw the handkerchief away and the wind took it up and over the rails of the pier.

Herbie watched the white flag land in the sea then looked at the man crippled with fatigue. Freddie was barely able to speak by now, let alone fight him off.

'Sorry, son,' said Herbie as he caught hold of the young man under the armpits.

For one relieved moment Freddie thought he meant it.

*

The weather was in his favour, Herbie realised as the rain lightened to a fine veil. He felt the weight of the blade in his pocket and was glad he'd not had to use it. As he passed the pawnbroker's, heading for the station and his ride back to London, he noticed the shutters had been pulled down.

Chapter Fourteen

'You're going to sit down and we're going to have a talk. So you might as well have this tea while it's hot.' Olivia banged the cup and saucer on the table and pulled out a chair for Maggie to use.

'I'm meeting me friends!' the girl snapped. 'Anyhow, don't need no nagging off you.'

Olivia gestured to the chair. 'Sit down, Maggie. The others are out, so let's clear the air. I know something's wrong. You've been moody for days.' Olivia had been trying to ambush her sister to speak to her. But Maggie had taken pains to avoid her, only coming home when she judged the younger ones would be indoors. Maggie had correctly banked on her elder sister not wanting to have a heart to heart in front of Nancy and Alfie.

Maggie knew if she was ever to get her sister off her back she'd have to tell her something. And it certainly wasn't going to be that she was pregnant. Olivia would just think her more of a fool than she did already for continuing to knock around with Harry. The worst of it was that nowadays Maggie was inclined to think her big sister was right about him. She'd plucked up the courage to go and see him the other day, to tell him she was pregnant, but before she'd even said hello he'd closed the door in her face, saying he was going out with pals.

'It's Nancy, if you must know,' Maggie blurted. 'I'm worried about her.'

That took Olivia by surprise. She sat down, frowning. 'Why? What's up with Nancy?' she asked anxiously.

'She's been shoplifting,' Maggie told her, feeling just a twinge of guilt for having grassed her younger sister up. 'I ain't going shopping with her no more. We'll get our collars felt. I've got enough on me mind with what happened to Dad and don't need to be worrying over that too.' She sprang to her feet. She reckoned she'd done enough to get herself out of trouble for now.

Olivia enclosed Maggie in a hug. 'It's good of you to keep an eye on her, Mags. I had a suspicion something wasn't right when she came in with that flash hat. D'you remember she said she'd bought it off a workmate?' Olivia shook her head. 'I was going to question her over it but didn't want to make it seem I didn't trust her to tell the truth.'

Maggie gave a quick nod. She was feeling guiltier still now for having dropped Nancy in it.

Olivia thrust her fingers through her hair to sweep it back off her face. 'What shall we do? I take it you've already told her she's brewing up bad trouble?'

'I did, but she thinks she's so clever she can get away with it. She was moaning about not having enough spending money.'

Olivia knew Nancy was sharp ... but she was only young and likely to cut herself doing something as bad as stealing.

'I reckon she got the message.' Maggie tried to sound

positive, to lift her sister's frown. 'She went off in a huff 'cos I called her an idiot. I'll enquire at the factory about a job for her. If she earns a bit more, she might not feel so hard done by. But as she's not fourteen, I can't promise she'll get taken on.'

'You're a good girl, Mags.' Again Olivia hugged her, planting a kiss on her brow. 'Nancy's lucky she's got you around, looking out for her. And I'm lucky too 'cos I'm not sure I can cope with it all on me own. Now I've got you to help, though ... '

'Alfie's probably forgotten his key again.' Maggie sounded relieved as a knock on the door interrupted their conversation. Her conscience was really bothering her now Olivia had praised her so highly. If her big sister knew the whole truth of it, though, things would be very different. Nancy might have got off scot-free with pinching stuff ... getting away with being knocked up wasn't so easy.

On the way to the front door Olivia was brooding on the notion that just lately fate was dealing the Bone family a very bad hand. But she hoped Nancy would take heed of her sisters telling her off. 'Hello, can I help you?' she asked the stranger standing on the step.

'Sorry to turn up out of the blue,' the visitor blurted out. 'Are you Livvie Bone?'

'I am ... yes.'

'I've come to see you about my brother. Freddie Weedon's his name and I believe you were acquainted.'

Olivia frowned as it became apparent that her visitor was upset. 'You must be Hilda.' She noticed the similarity between brother and sister. Both had dark wavy hair and brown eyes. But the dimple in the chin really gave the game away. 'Is Freddie all right?' Olivia felt a chill stealing over her as the young woman pressed together her quivering lips.

Hilda shook her head and the tears that had been glistening in her eyes spilled onto her cheeks.

'Come in ... please.' Olivia ushered her visitor towards the parlour.

'I'll make some tea,' Maggie offered quietly after Olivia had introduced her to Freddie's weeping sister.

Olivia helped Hilda to a chair then crouched by its side, taking her visitor's hands in hers to chafe them until she quietened down. 'Has Freddie had a relapse? I know he's had a bad cough on him ...'

'He's dead,' Hilda whispered. 'Drowned.'

In a daze, Olivia slowly rose to her feet. She staggered towards the other armchair and sank down into it, having used her hands to guide her backwards. 'Dead?' she echoed hoarsely. 'Drowned? Was it a boating accident of some sort?'

Hilda vigorously shook her head but seemed unable or unwilling to explain straight away. 'Freddie spoke highly of you. I know he would have wanted me to come and see you. He said you and his friend Joe Hunter were fine people.' Hilda blotted her eyes and made an effort to compose herself. 'I can't believe he's done this to me,' she said with a hint of bitterness. 'He told me not to volunteer for the Aid Detachment. Said he didn't want to risk losing *me*. Now see what *he's* done.' She scrunched up her hanky. 'Selfish! Selfish thing to do. Why would he do it? It's not like Freddie to be that way.'

Olivia quickly kneeled at Hilda's side again as the poor woman's body shook with silent sobs. 'What exactly has he done?' She feared she already knew but wouldn't accept it until she actually heard the words. And she felt as unable as Freddie's sister to find any rhyme or reason in it.

'He told me he thought Dickie was crackers for jumping off the pier. When the police came and broke the news, I didn't believe it. Until they told me more. It seems he probably did intend to do it. Only *he* knows the truth of that, though.'

Once more Olivia felt herself descend deep into shock. Her parched tongue seemed to be welded to the roof of her mouth. Eventually she roused herself enough to say, 'Freddie committed suicide, like Dickie did?'

'The police think so,' Hilda croaked. 'His body was washed up at about the same spot where they found his friend's.'

'But ... ' Olivia rubbed the heel of her palm against her forehead, frowning in furious concentration. 'But the last time I saw Freddie, he seemed happy. He was worried about his lungs but hoped to go back over to France as an ambulance driver.' She gestured. 'Why would he say that if ... ' Her voice tailed away and she began scouring her memory for something that could indicate Freddie had been more depressed than he'd let on. He'd said he couldn't go on without Hilda if she volunteered and met her end in France. But anybody might make such a comment if feeling afraid for a loved one's safety.

Outside the door Maggie stood hovering, listening to the two of them talking. It didn't take long for her to get the gist of this awful news. She carefully backed into the room carrying a tray. She whipped an apprehensive glance between the two white-faced women then put down the tea things and left the room with barely a murmur.

Olivia poured the tea like an automaton, still turning over in her head Freddie's throwaway remarks about his state of mind. Had there been an indication he *was* more than simply down in the dumps? Something else occurred to her: the cigarette case. She wouldn't say anything about it to Hilda. Bringing up something as trivial as a piece of pewter being cursed would seem like an insult at such a time. But Olivia had seen in Maggie's frightened eyes that she believed the jinx was still at work. Thank the Lord she hadn't hysterically blurted that out in front of Freddie's grieving sister!

Olivia spooned sugar into one cup and handed Hilda her sweetened tea, urging her to drink it. 'You said the police came to see you.' She gently probed for more information. 'Are they quite sure of what happened? Could it have been an accident rather than suicide?'

'The evidence they have indicates my brother killed himself.' Hilda sounded more composed by now. 'They took a statement from Freddie's room mate. He told them Freddie had been down after Dickie's death. The two of them got on well, whereas none of the other patients at the home took to Dickie. On the day my brother died he came in at about lunchtime, seeming agitated. Apparently he kept looking out of the window.' Hilda frowned. 'His room mate thought Freddie was staring at the pier but couldn't be certain. Freddie wrote letters during the afternoon then fell asleep until it was almost dark. The room mate was on his way to wake my brother for their evening meal when he saw him going out again with the letters in his hand. He thought it was queer Freddie was off to post them when it was growing dark and blowing a storm, especially as he was never usually late for his dinner.'

'What happened to the letters?' Olivia quickly asked, wondering if Freddie had written to her. Had he been agitated because of something other than his inner demons?

Perhaps he'd wanted to inform her about something he'd found out ...

'The police believe he wrote suicide notes. They said if he'd left them on the pier they would have been blown away. They found nothing in his pockets but said everything could have been washed out into the sea. They found his handkerchief on the shore. It had his initials on it. I bought him that set for Christmas.' Hilda wiped her eyes. 'We won't ever know what was in those notes. But there was a half-finished letter in his room. The police believe it showed how low Freddie was feeling.' Hilda took a shuddering breath. 'There was a girl in France he fell in love with. But she was engaged to somebody else.'

'Yvonne ... yes, he told me about her,' Olivia murmured.

Hilda nodded. 'Yes, Yvonne. He'd written to her about his feelings, begging her to break her engagement and give him a chance even though he couldn't promise he'd ever fully recover.' Hilda sighed. 'Sometimes he seemed so positive about getting back to normal. Then at other times it troubled him that he might never be fit enough to support a wife and family.'

'Poor Freddie.' Olivia was numb with shock and could think of nothing else to say.

'You will come to the funeral, won't you? I'd like to ask his commanding officer too but I expect Lieutenant Black is still in France.' Hilda hesitated. 'Perhaps Freddie wouldn't want him to know how he ended up anyway. He spoke highly of the lieutenant and was pleased he'd taken time to visit Southend.'

'Lucas Black is a good man. He wouldn't judge,' Olivia said quietly. 'But he'll be very sad when he hears about this. He was happy that Freddie was recovering so well.' She paused then added, 'I have to write a letter to him in any case. Would you like me to mention what's happened to Freddie?'

Hilda thought for a moment then nodded. 'If you would. It'll all come out in the end anyway.' She put down her half-full cup. 'After the inquest I want to bring my brother home to Walthamstow. I know he'd want his resting place to be with Mum and Dad. I've been told the Church can be funny about suicides. I hope they'll be kind to him.'

'I'm sure they will,' Olivia said although she'd little knowledge of the Church of England's ruling on such matters.

'Freddie would want you to come along and say goodbye. The church is just round the corner from where I live.' Hilda wrote down her address and handed it over. 'I'll let you know of the arrangements.'

'Of course I'll come. Just drop me a line.'

Hilda stood up. 'I should get along now. I'm sorry to come and bother you with such depressing news. Freddie told me that your family has had a rough time of it, what with you losing your fiancé and your dad.'

'I'm so glad you came. It's hard to take it in.'

'I didn't mean to frighten off your sister, or upset her.'

'Maggie's fine,' Olivia said. Their conversation about Nancy's light fingers had already paled into insignificance after what she'd learned about Freddie. At the back of her mind, though, she knew she had to speak to Nancy and tear her off a strip.

She saw Hilda out, embracing her on the step before parting from her with a few encouraging murmurs.

If the police were right and Freddie had killed himself over unrequited love then she had to agree with Hilda that it was a selfish thing to do. And Freddie hadn't seemed like that to her, or to his sister.

Chapter Fifteen

'I thought I told you to stay away from me. I've got important things to do before I ship out, so clear off home.'

'I need to tell you something, urgent,' Maggie hissed. She stared past Harry at the chubby young woman leaning on the wall leading into the alley. She recognised her as the girl who'd had a job in the confectionery shop in the High Street, close to Harry's old workplace. Maggie had been a packer in the laundry opposite the butcher's shop. On her dinner breaks she'd meet up with Harry and often the girl would come out of the confectioner's to watch them. Maggie had smacked her in the face once for making eyes at him.

Harry had said he wasn't interested in her because she was fat from eating all the sweets she stole. Maggie reckoned he'd got interested in the cow now, though.

'What's *she* want?' Maggie narrowed her eyes while her rival sauntered off up the road.

'Nothing. Anyhow, ain't none of your business if I talk to her.'

'Didn't look like nothing to me,' Maggie stormed. 'And it *is* me business if you're flirting. You've got me pregnant,' she blurted in a whisper. 'So in my book that means you're my boyfriend.'

Harry spitefully grabbed her chin, giving it a shake. 'What? You havin' me on?' He raked her thin figure cold-eyed.

Maggie shook her head, wincing from the pain in her face and his angry reaction to her news. But something in his manner told her it hadn't come as a complete surprise. He'd already guessed why she'd kept coming over wanting to speak to him.

'Well, whether you are or you aren't, don't think you've got me wrapped round yer finger, 'cos you ain't,' he snarled, shoving her away. 'If you're sure, you'd better sort things out.' He jerked his head at her abdomen then glanced furtively about as though worried somebody might guess what they were talking about. Harry would never have treated Maggie in such a way if her father had still been around. Tommy Bone might have neglected his kids but Harry knew he'd have got thumped for bullying one of the man's daughters in the street, in full view of everyone.

But Tommy Bone was gone, and so was Maggie's big sister. Although Harry couldn't stop himself thinking about her. If he had Livvie as his girlfriend, he'd never look at another woman.

'What you're talking about costs money,' Maggie hissed.

Harry jabbed a finger close to her cheek. 'If you've come to me fer a hand out, you can piss off.' With that he strode up to his front door and let himself in.

Maggie felt tears of humiliation and anger smart in her eyes. She hadn't come to ask him for a penny. She'd come to ask him to marry her so the baby wouldn't be born a bastard, and to warn him that the cursed cigarette case had claimed another victim. But why should she care about Harry when he clearly didn't give a monkey's about her? She should have listened to Livvie. She'd warned her time and again that he was no good. Her rival was watching from the top of the road with a gaggle of friends. Maggie knew they were laughing at her. She just hoped they'd not guessed she was up the duff or else her name would be mud before she'd had a chance to decide what to do about Harry's bastard.

'Ain't seen you in a while.'

Maggie twisted about, her eyes red and puffy from holding back tears. Harry's younger brother was standing, hands in pockets, smiling at her.

'Don't come over this way much now I'm working in Islington.' Maggie cuffed at her eyes. She'd always known that Ricky fancied her. They'd been in the same class at school and had left at the same time. Ricky had started work as a delivery boy but had since been promoted to a shop assistant in a grocer's store. Maggie had always thought boys her own age boring, and had had a yen for the older Wicks brother, thinking him sophisticated. Harry had been swaggering about smoking cigarettes while Ricky was still in short trousers, kicking a football about with Alfie. When Harry had started flirting with her Maggie had been full of herself. But now she knew she'd just been another one of his fancies. And he wasn't sophisticated, he was a coward. Now he'd got her into trouble he wanted to run and hide. He couldn't even stand still and have a reasonable conversation about it. Like a kid, he'd scarpered home to his mum, without a backward look.

'He's seeing other girls behind me back, ain't he?' she said.

'He's never stuck with anyone fer long,' Ricky answered evasively.

'He is seeing her though.' Maggie jabbed a finger at the fat girl up the road.

Ricky gave a single nod that made Maggie stifle a sob.

'He ain't worth getting upset over,' Ricky said kindly. 'He's only let that wound on his leg heal up to get sent back, away from you and the trouble you're in.'

'He guessed I was up the duff, didn't he? Can't believe he told you, though.' Maggie's voice trailed off and she coloured up.

'He don't need to tell me. I've always been able to read him like a book. Shame me mum can't or she'd boot him out.' Ricky looked Maggie over. 'Ain't the first time he's got a girl knocked up. Last one had a knitting needle job, if you know what I mean. Don't think her old man ever found out. If he had, he'd have killed Harry, I reckon. So what you gonna do then, now Tommy ain't around to go after him?'

'Dunno ... ' Maggie mumbled, wondering what a knitting needle job was.

'I'll marry you if yer like,' Ricky said bashfully. 'Don't make no difference to me.'

Maggie snorted in disbelief. 'Don't make no difference to you who you marry?' she mimicked.

He shook his head, feigning indifference. 'I'm sixteen now and joining up soon. Me pal working down the railway yard's already started his training over Clapham Common and he's a month younger 'n' me. Way this war's going, could be you'll be a widow by the time the nipper's born. But at least it'll have a name, and I'll have had a wife.'

Maggie stared at Ricky and fought back tears. She suddenly realised that she'd been wrong about him. Although younger, he was far more mature than his brother. She believed Ricky had meant what he'd said about marrying her and that made her feel at the same time happy and sad. 'No ta,' she said quietly. 'Appreciate the offer but I'll sort something out.'

As she started off up the road to catch the bus home she saw her cousin Ruby coming out of their old house. Maggie would never think of Ruby as her stepsister. Or Sybil as her stepmother for that matter. Thankfully, as her father had never married the old witch, she wouldn't have to.

'What you doin' round here?' Ruby asked her.

'Just come to see me boyfriend. He's getting sent back over there.'

'Oh ... Harry Wicks, you mean?' Ruby smirked. Harry would always try to chat her up if they bumped into one another. She'd told him how much once and that'd sent him packing. Now he just made lewd gestures if he caught sight of her.

'How's yer mum?' Maggie asked, just for something to say. She couldn't give a toss how Sybil Wright was.

'She's on the warpath 'cos Mickey's gone out and she don't know where. Poor kid don't need her constantly keeping tabs on him.' Ruby craned her neck to look up the road. 'Ain't seen him, have you?' she asked.

Maggie shook her head. 'I'm off to catch me bus home.'

'Walk with you then,' Ruby said. 'I'm on me way back to Islington 'n' all. Riley's promised to take me down the market later and buy me a dress.'

'Lucky you,' Maggie said with a hint of bitterness, thinking that in all the time she'd been with Harry he'd not treated her to so much as a pair of stockings. She'd been faithful to him, yet her cousin got decent presents off her boyfriend even though she messed around with other men.

In a sudden show of camaraderie Maggie linked arms

with Ruby. It had just occurred to her that if anybody knew what a knitting needle job was, her slag of a cousin would. Maggie knew now she had no choice in the matter but to get rid of her baby.

*

It was Saturday afternoon and Mickey had decided to pocket his errand money instead of handing it over. He'd been cutting hedges and lawns and fetching in shopping for old dears in the neighbourhood since eight o'clock that morning. He reckoned he deserved to enjoy what was left of the day. If he'd gone home his mother would've had all his earnings off him and he wouldn't even have had the cost of a ticket for the matinee at the flicks. He would've ended up bored, lying on his bed with only the tattered comics he knew off by heart for company.

Mickey missed his Islington pals and so he'd caught the bus to his old stamping ground, hoping to meet up with a few of them for a game of football. But he'd just spotted somebody even better to hang about with.

Alfie Bone was coming out of Smithie's shop. Having recognised his cousin from the funeral, Mickey immediately loped over to say hello.

'Who d'you support then?' Alfie asked, offering his bag of chews with a grin.

'Who d'you think?' Mickey gave him a playful shove before diving a hand into the bag of sweets.

'The Tottenham lot?' Alfie ribbed him.

'Only one team to support round here!' Mickey punched a fist in the air. 'Up the Arse ... a ... naal,' he sang. His smile soon faded. He'd spotted his sister heading in his direction.

She looked as though she had something to spit out. And he reckoned he knew what it was.

'You're in trouble. You'd better get yerself home,' Ruby shouted.

'Ain't going home. Only just got here.' Mickey sounded belligerent.

'Don't say I didn't warn you then.' Without a backward glance, Ruby carried on up the road to meet Riley and take a trip to Chapel Street to choose her new dress.

Mickey and Alfie gazed at one another, jaws moving rhythmically as they enjoyed their chews.

'Got a ball?' Mickey asked, picking bits of sweet off his teeth with a fingernail.

Alfie nodded. 'Back home though. Have to go and get it.' He held out his bag of chews again and Mickey helped himself. 'Ain't you allowed over here then?' Alfie asked as they strolled side by side.

'Me mum reckons it's a dump.' Mickey wrinkled his nose. 'She ain't wrong. But she ain't telling me what to do now I'm nearly nine,' he added cockily.

'We don't live in the Bunk. We live round the corner in a nice place,' Alfie said proudly. 'It belonged to Joe Hunter once. He was me sister's boyfriend, but he's dead now so Livvie's got it . . . ' He broke off, grumbling, 'Not *him* again.'

'Who's that?' Mickey had spotted the old fellow bowling down the road in their direction, a crooked smile behind his drooping fag.

'Joe's dad.' Alfie wondered if Mr Hunter had come to tell him he'd found a frame for his photo. He didn't really want to talk about that right now. He was more interested in having a game of football with his cousin.

'You two brothers, are yer?' Herbie said by way of greeting as he came to a halt by the two fair-haired lads.

'He's me cousin, Mickey Wright, over from Wood Green.'

'Crikey Moses! The pair of yers could be twins.' Herbie ran a levelling palm over the top of their blond heads trying to distinguish who was the taller.

'All us cousins got fair hair.' Alfie repeated what he'd heard his sisters say when people commented on how alike the Bone and Wright kids were. The girls hated being associated with Sybil and her lot and would've denied being related to them at all, if they could.

'Well, pleased to meet yer, son.' Herbie had seen the boy limping along and nudged Mickey's arm in a jokey fashion. 'You got that gammy foot fighting in the trenches, did yer?'

'Yeah ... just waiting fer me medals to turn up,' Mickey said sourly. He'd had many such comments – mainly off his pals – since the war started so now had a few ready rejoinders to fire back.

Herbie chuckled, although he wasn't feeling at all lighthearted. It was still eating at him that he'd had to do away with Freddie. He'd stopped feeling guilty on the way home on the train that day, justifying to himself what had happened as regrettable but necessary. But he was fretting that the police would unearth a thread that led back to Livvie Bone. The fact that her father had also recently met his end might seem an odd coincidence, worthy of further investigation. So Herbie had come looking for his go-between to find out if anything had filtered through from Southend yet. He knew he had to keep one step ahead of the lot of them or he'd get his neck stretched.

Alfie seemed quite relaxed so Herbie breathed out too. He guessed news hadn't yet reached the Bone family that the amateur detective wouldn't be reporting back. Herbie turned his attention to the crippled lad. Something about him was niggling at the back of his mind, then Alfie helped him remember what it was.

'We've gotta go.' Alfie edged away. 'Ain't got long. Mickey's expected home to help his mum now me dad ain't around.' Alfie was aware of his cousin scowling for being made to seem like a mummy's boy.

"Course, you lived with your uncle Tommy, didn't yer, Mickey? That's a good lad, keepin' yer mum company.' Herbie patted his shoulder.

'She don't mind me staying out.' Mickey sounded narked. 'We're getting a lodger soon, to help pay the rent. So she won't need me around at all then.'

'Getting a lodger, eh?' Herbie turned thoughtful. 'Well . . . I'll be off now to see me pal and let you boys have a kick about.' In fact, he walked straight past Jimmy Wild's place and carried on up the road, whistling tunelessly.

Women on their own always interested Herbie. They often wanted a man about the house. He knew he could do with getting his boots under a table in a different neighbourhood. He wanted to distance himself from Muswell Hill, just in case the coppers did come back nosing around about Tommy Bone's murder. Then there was always the chance that Sibyl Wright could set him up in business again if she had a half-decent face and figure on her.

*

'Yes? Help yer, can I?'

'Reckon you might be able to, love.' Herbie gave the woman a wink but she didn't appear flattered by his lazy

176

charm. In his turn, he was having trouble disguising his disappointment. Sybil Wright had a face that could sour milk. He knew that any idea of putting her to work was a non-starter. Even the dockside whores kept themselves in better shape than this ragbag staring him out.

'Thought I'd come to introdooce meself – say how sorry I was to hear about old Tommy's passing.' Herbie adopted a mournful smile.

'Oh, yeah?' Sybil said dubiously. 'And how's my Tommy know you, may I ask?'

Herbie doffed his cap, but quickly put it back on to cover his bald patch. He was no longer a fine specimen of manhood but – he cast another jaundiced glance at Sybil Wright's sluttish appearance – he might still be in with a chance with this one,. He guessed she wasn't getting many offers.

'I'm Joe Hunter's dad – Herbie's me name.' He gave her another sympathetic smile. 'I know what it is to lose some-one dear to me 'eart.'

'Joe Hunter's dad, are you? I heard the boy couldn't stand the sight of you. Neither could yer wife Maisie.' Sybil crossed her arms over her chest. 'I knew 'em both.'

'I ain't had an easy life, it's true,' Herbie sighed. He was beginning to think he was wasting his time. If the miserable cow wasn't even going to ask him in for a cup of tea and a bit of reminiscing, he might as well get going. 'Well . . . just thought I'd stop by and say I was sorry to hear off Livvie about her dad. Must've been a blow for you too.'

'Spoken to *her*, have you?'

Herbie picked up on the note of acrimony in Sybil's voice. 'Yeah. Bit of a madam, ain't she? Not the sort I would have chosen fer me son. But there y'are . . .'

'She's a madam all right,' Sybil snorted, still guarding the doorway. But her narrowed eyes were less hostile.

'Looking to move back round this way meself.' Herbie thought it was worth a last-ditch attempt to befriend her and put forward his credentials as a lodger. He glanced about. 'Prefer this neck o' the woods to Islington, if I'm honest.'

'And are yer honest?'

'As the day is long.' He gave her another mischievous wink. 'Know of any cheap rooms going?' he asked innocently.

'Might do . . .'

'I'm just off down the pub to wet me whistle. I'll call back on me way home, shall I? You could have a think about any places yer know of in the neighbourhood and let me know. I'll take a look at 'em while I'm this way.'

'I'll come with you if you're paying?' Sybil barked out. The prospect of a drink was always welcome, especially a free one. Usually she drank alone, and indoors, but as he wanted a room and she wanted a lodger, having a natter in a pub would let her sound him out before speaking up. She was getting desperate. She was in arrears with the rent and the landlord had told her he'd evict her if she didn't come up with the necessary soon. Sybil owed her daughter over a pound for rent money loaned to her. Ruby had made it clear she wasn't shelling out any more. Without a man's wages to live off, and with her son still at school and only earning odd job money, Sybil knew she'd have to find work. Unless this bloke proved useful.

'Always treat a lady to a drink, me,' Herbie eventually said through gritted teeth. He hadn't been expecting her to invite herself along. He'd banked on her asking him in for a cup of tea. Now he was wondering if he had enough in his pocket for them to have a drink each.

Herbie earned a bit doing casual work for his one-legged landlord and from helping sweep up down at the market, but was always short of spending cash. And he'd had enough of it. He should be in Joe's old house, taking in lodgers himself, not begging a room in somebody else's poxy place.

'I'll just fetch me coat then and be with you,' Sybil said, and shut the door in his face.

Herbie loitered on the step, rolling a cigarette. By the time he'd got it lit and she'd reappeared he'd worked out that one way or another he was going to have to persuade Sybil Wright to accept him as her lodger. And one way or another he was going to have to get her off her backside and working so that between them they could pay the rent.

Chapter Sixteen

'I've just had a set to with my Alice.' Having made her announcement, Matilda steered Olivia to a quiet spot away from flapping ears in the busy street.

It was a humid Indian summer evening in Campbell Bunk; the sort of September that refused to accept autumn was round the corner. As the glaring sun was setting on the horizon the off licence was doing a roaring trade in pop and bottled ale. People were sitting, swigging, on doorsteps and handcarts to cool off, and barefoot scamps wearing just grimy pants and vests darted about, dodging cuffs after begging their parents for farthings for sweets.

'Alice had been acting secretive, you see,' Matilda continued. 'She didn't want to grass on yer sister but eventually spilled the beans rather than get her neck wrung. Reckon you'll get landed with sorting this out, so you'll need fair warning. These things won't wait ... '

Olivia finally guessed what Matilda was getting at and her enlightenment must have shown in her face.

'Ah ... I see you *do* know about it.' Matilda sounded relieved. 'In that case I'll mind me own business and get on.'

'I'd rather you didn't, actually ... mind your own business, that is.' Olivia tipped back her head to frown at the clear sky before fixing the older woman with a plaintive look. 'I could do with some advice. I know I have to speak to her about it, but she'll deny it then I'll have to call her a liar. Just don't know what to do, Matilda,' she admitted bluntly.

'Apart from flay her alive, you mean?' the older woman dryly replied.

'That's about the size of it,' Olivia ruefully agreed.

'When I got wind that Alice had been asking around about abortionists, I thought it was me daughter up the spout,' Matilda whispered. 'Ashamed to say, when I found out it was for Maggie instead, I breathed a sigh of relief.'

Olivia gasped and turned white. She'd thought Matilda was hinting that she'd heard about Nancy shoplifting in Gamages.

'Oh ... I see you didn't know after all.' Matilda grimaced her apology for having come straight out with it. The poor girl looked as though she might faint.

'I thought you were talking about Nancy,' Olivia hissed.

'She up the spout an' all?' Matilda's eyes popped.

'No! Neither of them is ... as far as I know.'

'Hope I haven't got me wires crossed, then,' Matilda said. 'It's not like Alice to make things up, though.' She pursed her lips. 'Reckon me and her need another conversation. If she's hidin' something ... I was sure she'd have more sense after her sister ... ' Matilda broke off and frowned. As she'd been talking her eyes had focussed on a bizarre sight for the Bunk. 'There's a posh army officer across the road. I'd like to think it's me he's staring at. Reckon I'd be kidding meself, though.'

Matilda was glad of the distraction. Usually she kept

family skeletons under lock and key but had almost let one slip out. Her eldest girl, Sophy, had got herself in the family way. In the end the problem had taken care of itself but not before a great deal of heartache had been caused for the people involved. Sophy was now working on a farm in Essex with her sweetheart, her bad time behind her. If Alice had brought that sort of trouble back to her door, Matilda'd knock seven bells out of her ... then send Jack after Geoff Lovat.

Olivia's eyes had landed on a dark, distinguished-looking fellow dressed in smart khaki, idly swinging his cap by the brim. Her sombre expression was immediately transformed by a radiant smile.

'Take it you know him.' Matilda was itching to find Alice but curious enough about the stranger's identity to loiter a moment.

'He's my old boss from the sweet factory.'

'Well, he's put a sparkle in yer eyes, so you'd better go and speak to him then before yer cousin does.' Matilda jerked her chin at Ruby, leaning on a doorjamb and fanning her face, while eyeing the handsome stranger. 'Go on, love, and sorry for worrying you about your sisters. I'm off to find Alice,' she said ominously.

With a wave to let Lucas know she was on her way, Olivia said goodbye to Matilda then dashed up the street. Overjoyed though she was to see him, at the back of her mind lurked the unpalatable information Matilda had just given her. She knew she needed to speak to Maggie as quickly as she could, to put her own mind at rest. Then after that she'd give Nancy a talking to.

'You look like a fish out of water round here,' she burst out, launching herself at Lucas to give him a hug. She felt the roughness of his uniform scratching her cheek and the solid muscle of his body beneath it. He exuded an air of being born to a different class that was heightened by his seedy surroundings. 'You're lucky I've come to protect you, y'know. Campbell Bunk's not exactly welcoming to toffs,' she told him.

'Is that how you see me?' he asked, sounding mildly offended.

'No ... of course not. Sorry, it was a stupid thing to say. You're much more than a toff to me.' Olivia felt awkward.

'I meant, do you think I can't take care of myself?' he ribbed her, trying not to laugh.

Olivia gave his arm a smack, covering her confusion by changing the subject. 'How did you know where I was?'

'Your brother told me you'd gone to the shop round the corner,' Lucas said, feeling bereft when she uncurled her arms from around his waist. Having been reared to curb shows of emotion nothing endeared her more to him than her unaffected happiness to see him. Even a naked mistress's embrace held less appeal for Lucas than a spontaneous cuddle from Livvie Bone. Once he had wanted her in his bed and been tempted to flex his muscles to get her there. But not now. He adored her too much to contemplate coercion. Although she always stirred more than just his heart.

He stroked her cheek and gazed into her big green eyes, noting the sadness behind her welcoming smile. She understood why he'd come and was waiting for the first mention of it. 'I wangled some leave as soon as I heard about your father. It's taken a while but I'm here now. I'm so sorry, Olivia.'

'Somebody told you?'

'Deborah Wallis sent me a letter. Were you going to write and tell me?'

'I have just written to you, not only about what happened to Dad but about some other terrible news. You wouldn't have received that yet.' She threaded her arm through his, urging him up the street. She didn't intend to talk out in the open. She wanted to sit down with him and enjoy his company, if not the bleak topic of their conversation. The news about Freddie would hit him particularly hard. She could understand how those men, living and dying together, became as close as kin.

'You look very well, Lucas. You should have sent word you were coming, I'd have got something nice in for tea.' She glanced up at him. He didn't appear as battle weary as when she'd last seen him. He was more his usual suave self, quite bronzed from the French sun in fact. Or perhaps her own problems, constantly on her mind and reflected in her wan appearance in the mirror, just made him seem the brighter of the two of them.

'I don't know what to say to comfort you. "Sorry" seems pathetically inadequate. Tommy and I had our differences but I never imagined hearing such awful news about his passing. I will miss him, strange as it may seem ...' Lucas tailed into silence with a small apologetic gesture of the hand.

She nodded to let him know she understood his confusion.

He put a finger under her chin, tilting her face up to his. 'You look as though you're bearing up.' He gave her a half smile. 'You could do with some colour in your cheeks. But you're a marvel. You always manage to cope, don't you, Olivia?'

'No ... not always,' she said simply, remembering how she'd just asked Matilda for advice on how to deal with her sister's misbehaviour. Sometimes she felt overwhelmed with responsibility for others, as though she were sinking beneath the weight of it. He was watching her changing expressions so she gave him a bright smile. He was home on leave and deserved to cherish every minute of it, not hear her complaints. 'It's you lot I feel sorry for, waking up every morning to dodge bombs and bullets. We've nothing much to moan about, in the great scheme of things.' She opened her front door and they entered the hallway.

'I wondered why you'd not written,' Lucas said, following her towards the kitchen. 'Self-centred wretch that I am, I had started feeling sorry for myself, thinking you might have grown bored of writing to me.'

'How could I possibly grow bored of my handsome boss?' she teased him. 'Anyway ... absence makes the heart grow fonder, Lucas, didn't you know?' Olivia filled the kettle. A smile was curving her full lips.

'Yes, I do know,' he said huskily. 'I've missed you a lot.'

'Likewise,' she said, turning to meet his steady deep blue gaze.

'Is your brother upstairs?'

'Probably ... reading his comics. The girls are out, I expect. It's too quiet for them to be indoors. They never stop squabbling.' Olivia took the tea canister from the shelf. 'Don't see so much of the kids these days. They're getting older and like to be with their friends. It suits me to have a breather from them.'

'Livvie ...' Alfie had quietly appeared in the doorway and was shuffling from foot to foot.

'What's up?' Olivia stopped scooping tea leaves and frowned at him.

'Maggie's in her room. She told me to come down and get you 'cos she don't feel well.' Alfie sniffed. 'She don't look well neither.'

Olivia dropped the teaspoon. By the time she'd reached the foot of the stairs she was straining her ears to hear what was going on but it was eerily quiet up there. With a surge of panic she raced up and found Maggie on her back, holding her knees to her chest and rocking from side to side on the mattress.

'What is it?' Olivia bent over her sister but she feared she might already know, following her talk with Matilda.

'Dunno, me belly aches something terrible,' Maggie panted.

Olivia turned to see Alfie, standing white-faced by the door. 'It's all right. I'll see to Maggie.' As the boy hovered, shocked by Maggie's guttural moans, she ordered, 'Go and make some tea for Mr Black and ask him to sit in the parlour until I come down.'

She turned to her sister then. 'Are you pregnant?' Olivia held her breath, waiting for the answer. Maggie gave a slight nod then turned her head aside as though she was ashamed. 'Why didn't you say?' Olivia squeaked. She felt her heart drumming madly. She wasn't sure whether she wanted to shake her sister or comfort her with a hug.

''Cos I knew what *you'd* say,' Maggie cried accusingly, then bit her lip against another pain.

Olivia controlled her panic enough to ask calmly, 'Have you done something to yourself?' Her sister's pallor was replaced by a faint blush. 'Have you tried to get rid of the baby? You have to tell me!' Olivia held her breath as she twitched aside Maggie's skirt and saw a large patch of scarlet staining the sheet.

Olivia wasn't a hypocrite so had made it clear that she disliked Harry and was glad he'd finally gone back overseas. In turn she'd let Maggie know she felt exasperated by the girl trailing after him when it was plain he was no good. Now Olivia felt frightened and close to weeping; she should have shown Maggie more understanding. Then her sister might have confided in her about being pregnant and what she intended to do about it.

'Have you been to an abortionist?' Olivia whispered, aghast. Maggie could have risked dreadful injury. The idea that her younger sister might have faced that ordeal alone made her drop to her knees by the bed. She gripped Maggie's cold hands, chafing them. 'Did Alice tell you where to go?' Matilda had gone looking for her daughter, thinking *she* was in the family way. But all Alice had done was try to help Maggie. Because Maggie didn't trust her big sister enough to ask her. Olivia felt guilty tears burn her eyes.

'Alice did say she knew a place but I didn't go there. I had to do something though ... he said so,' Maggie moaned. 'Harry told me to get rid of it.'

Olivia felt futile rage bubbling within. But she forced steadiness into her voice. 'What've you done then? Taken pills?'

'Ruby give me some stuff to douche meself. She said it was easy and wouldn't hurt.'

Olivia sank back onto her heels, stunned. Maggie had gone to Ruby, of all people. Surely Maggie didn't think her own sister such a dragon that Ruby would make a better friend? 'Well, Ruby was wrong, wasn't she?' Olivia finally croaked, getting to her feet. She felt hurt but inwardly was fuming at Ruby. Her cousin should have let her know what was going on rather than interfere. For two pins she would have raced round to the Bunk and thumped her. But she knew having it out with Ruby would have to wait. She wiped sweat from her sister's brow with her handkerchief as Maggie bit her lip against a cramp. When she had quietened Olivia murmured she'd fetch something to clean her up and quit the room. She stopped by the head of the stairs, pacing on the landing to try and compose herself before going down.

Alfie was in the kitchen setting out cups while Lucas upended the steaming kettle into the teapot.

'Problem?'

Her heart flipped over in gratitude for his intensely sympathetic gaze and single, gruff word. In his quiet way he was offering her any help she needed that he was able to give.

'I'm afraid so,' she said hoarsely. 'Alfie, would you go and ask Mrs Keiver to come round? Say I need her quickly for Maggie.'

She waited until her brother had scampered off before bursting out, 'I'm sorry, Lucas. Every time you visit you find us in some sort of commotion.'

'Is this the other horrible news you said you had to tell me?'

She swung her head in agitation. 'No ... this is just ... us,' she answered bleakly. 'Please don't ask me to explain anything right now.'

'I won't. And don't worry or feel embarrassed,' he soothed her. 'It's not your fault that I turn up at bad times.' He shrugged. 'Families can be a pain in the backside. I know.' He took her hands, cradling them in his. 'Can I do something to help? Or do you want me to go?'

'I don't want you to go. I've been longing to see you.' She stared at him and his warm gaze prompted her to go back on her decision to keep it all secret from him. 'My sister's upstairs having a miscarriage,' she rattled off with barely a blush. 'She's brought it on herself. I've sent Alfie to fetch my friend from Campbell Road.' Olivia moved away from him and peered into the hall, anticipating a sound heralding Matilda's arrival. 'My neighbour will know what to do. I don't want to send for a doctor 'cos then word'll spread. Heaven help us, it's not something to broadcast.' She sighed. 'Now you know all that, I'll understand if you want to go.'

'I don't want to go. I'll keep out of the way in the front room. I have some first aid knowledge if you think it might be of use.'

'I'm doing the St John Ambulance course at Barratt's. But dealing with things like this isn't something they teach you.' Olivia took a deep breath. 'Well, moaning won't help,' she chided herself. 'If I can calm down, I expect I can manage to patch her up . . . before wringing her neck.' Olivia heaved out a long sigh. 'Go and sit down then, Lucas. I'll come and find you if I need you. And thanks . . . for everything.'

'Any time.'

He turned away to make himself a cup of tea just as she heard Matilda's none-too-dulcet tones in the hallway. Quickly Olivia went to meet her then led the woman up the stairs. Over her shoulder she gave her friend a censored version of what had gone on because Alfie was trailing in their wake.

'Just as well I never caught up with my Alice or I'd be eating humble pie,' Matilda said pithily.

'Sorry ... I didn't know about this and I should've,' Olivia replied awkwardly.

'Mums are always the last to know, love. And you've been landed with the job of being mother and sister to these kids, whether you wanted it or not.' Matilda stopped outside the bedroom door and gave her a forgiving smile. 'Ain't your fault, Livvie. You're doin' a grand job and I hope your lot realise it, and are grateful for it. So chin up.' She yanked on the door handle. 'What've you done to yerself then, Maggie?' she greeted the girl gruffly as she shut the bedroom door in Alfie's face.

A moment later she was rolling up her sleeves. Having made a cursory inspection of Maggie's nether regions, she announced, 'Lou Porter knows more about this than me. But I'd say she's well on the way to miscarrying, so there's gonna be a mess to clear up.' She frowned at the spreading stain on the bedding as a spasm made Maggie squirm. 'Could do with old newspapers and rags, if you've got some. Better get pots of water heating up too. She'll want a good wash at some point.' Matilda tapped her nose. 'When you've enough kids to feed and a husband with a constant glint in his eye, you get to know a bit about this. Did she take a hot bath to bring this on?'

'Not sure. She might've ... bloody Ruby gave her something to use as a douche.'

Matilda looked grim. 'Right. Well, you start on collecting rags and papers and I'll find Lou and fetch her back with me.'

The two women parted at the bottom of the stairs, hurrying off in opposite directions. Olivia opened the parlour door and peered in. Lucas hadn't left; he was rotating his army cap between his hands, staring at his shoes. He looked up as he heard her enter.

'There is something you can do, Lucas. If you don't mind, that is.'

He got to his feet.

'Would you boil up some water on the stove and fill up a pail with it, while I see to Maggie?'

''Course.'

'What's going on here?' Nancy was suddenly standing on the threshold, swinging a glance between Olivia and the handsome stranger. Her sharp tone indicated she'd picked up on the fact there was a problem. Just now Mrs Keiver had barely acknowledged her before dashing off up the road.

'Maggie's not well.' Inwardly Olivia cursed the fact that Nancy had turned up at the wrong moment. She'd been trying to catch her youngest sister to speak to her about the shoplifting but Nancy had been avoiding her company. She had been equally as fearful of being bawled out as Maggie had been.

'I'll go up and see her . . . ' Nancy turned towards the stairs.

'You can't! Not right now.' Olivia could tell Nancy didn't have a clue what was wrong with their sister. The time wasn't right for difficult explanations so she dug in her pocket and produced some coins. 'Be a help and take Alfie down the caff, would you? And don't come back for a while. I'll tell you all about it later, all right?'

Nancy shrugged, taking the coins, then shouted up the stairs for her brother. Olivia breathed a sigh of relief when the front door closed behind them.

'Fine day's leave this has been for you.' She glanced apologetically at Lucas.

'It's always a fine day when I see you, Livvie Bone.' He'd adopted a jokey tone, making light of a bad situation. 'It's been no different since the day you walked into Barratt's and asked for a job.' He shrugged. 'But I must admit, I was going to Southend to see Freddie today and it might have been better if I had. What is it?' He'd noticed the change in her expression.

'Tell you later about Freddie … I'd better look in on Maggie,' Olivia said hoarsely, turning away.

She wearily climbed the stairs, her mind in turmoil. As anxious as she felt about Maggie, she was furious with her too. Her sister had taken a bad risk, going all the way with Harry. Maggie knew as well as anyone did that unmarried mothers were more likely to receive abuse than pity. And a disgraced girl's family shared in her shame. The last thing Olivia wanted was Alfie being bullied about this at school. She hadn't wanted her brother to remain the timid mouse he'd been while under Tommy Bone's roof, but neither did she want him getting into fights. Nancy was already going off the rails and Olivia didn't want her following Maggie's bad lead with boys. Both girls were risking their futures and Olivia was at a loss as to how to discipline them if they wouldn't listen to reason. They weren't fools and both knew right from wrong.

She'd looked after them all since her mother had passed away when Olivia was just ten years old. She'd often felt stifled by them being in one another's pockets. Her sisters were now of an age to see to themselves. But if they couldn't do so properly then she'd feel she'd failed them. Matilda was right: she *was* struggling to be a parent and also a sister and wasn't sure how much longer she could cope with the task. She was still young and wanted some time to be herself and have a life of her own. Though raw from losing Joe, she hoped to have a husband and a family of her own when the time was right.

'Oh, Maggie,' Olivia sighed, closing the door behind her. 'Why did you let him go all the way? Did you think he'd stick by you?'

'He said he'd marry me,' Maggie mumbled.

'I'm not sure I'd trust that wretch to look after a dog properly, let alone me sister and her baby, so perhaps it's for the best he didn't propose,' Olivia said.

She sat down on the edge of the bed and pushed Maggie's tangled hair off her brow, her mind returning to the time she'd accompanied Cath to a backstreet abortionist. Vi Smith was Nelly Smith's sister-in-law. Whether Nelly had any idea what Vi got up to was anybody's guess. None of the factory girls wanted to bring up the subject with Nelly in case they were asked how they knew so much about it.

Olivia understood what led desperate women to go to such places. At least Cath had had a good man by her side, ready to marry her if she'd chosen to keep her baby. Maggie's prospects would've been no decent husband and no job, and a kid round her ankles at just sixteen years old.

Maggie had been watching Olivia's frowning face. She regretted not having trusted her big sister to sort things out for her. By going to Ruby she'd made more of a mess of things. She felt like death warmed up. Olivia had taken the shocking news better than Maggie had anticipated. When they'd all been at home with their father, Livvie had always been the one they'd turn to when things went wrong. But after their big sister had been kicked out because of Joe Hunter they'd had to make do without her for a while. 'Am I gonna be all right, Livvie?' Maggie asked plaintively.

"Course you are!' Olivia gave her an encouraging smile but she got up and went to the window to look for any sign of Lou Porter and Matilda.

In many ways Maggie was still a child, Olivia realised, glancing over her shoulder at her sister's thin profile and ironing board figure. Maggie had their father's build. In his prime Tommy Bone had been a wiry, attractive man with light brown hair. Then his wife had died and he'd let bitterness and booze take over his life and spoil his character and his looks.

'Have you told anyone else, apart from Ruby and Alice?' Olivia knew the fewer people who were aware of Maggie's condition, the better.

'No ... just them. I can trust Alice,' Maggie said. 'She heard me bringing me guts up in the toilet out the back of the factory. She guessed what was wrong with me. She give me her hanky to use in case I threw up again at the bench. The smell of soldering fumes was making me heave ...' Maggie suddenly let out a mewling cry of pain and hugged her knees to her aching belly.

'Just hold on ... won't be long now.' Olivia rushed to the bed to soothe her sister. 'Matilda and Lou Porter have just crossed the road. You'll be feeling right as ninepence soon.' Olivia's voice was firm. She'd quelled the fear that had been roiling in her own stomach. She wasn't going to let anything happen to Maggie. In anticipation of what was to come she started spreading out newspaper around the base of the bed and stuffed some between the sheet and the mattress, trying not to disturb her sister too much. She heard two pairs of footsteps on the stairs and rolled up her sleeves.

Chapter Seventeen

'Told you it'd all come out in the wash, didn't I, love?' Matilda winked at her. 'Maggie'll be up 'n' about again in the morning and wondering what all the fuss was about.' She grimaced. 'You'll be the one counting the cost of it all.'

Olivia glanced across the pub at Lou Porter. The woman had seen to Maggie – almost hysterical with pain by the time she'd examined her – in an unflappable manner. When they'd been changing the soiled sheets, Lou had said whoever had given Maggie the Eusol to use as a douche needed stringing up. Being young and inexperienced, Maggie had used too strong a mixture and blistered her privates. Lou had handed over some soothing ointment for her to use. Once she had been cleaned up Maggie had promptly fallen asleep. The two older women had rolled down their sleeves and declared it was time for a well-earned snifter.

As Nancy and Alfie hadn't returned from the caff, Olivia had agreed to join them in the Duke for just the one. She knew she could do with something to settle her nerves and she owed Lucas some light relief after such a dismal welcome home. Wasting an evening boiling up pails of water wasn't what any soldier would choose to do on leave. She'd imagined that drinking with folk from the worst street in North London wouldn't appeal to him either, but he'd readily agreed to go to the Duke.

'How much should I pay Lou?' Olivia asked her friend, sipping her port and lemon. She'd not a clue what the woman charged and didn't want to insult her by offering too little.

'Reckon Old Lou'll be happy with a couple of rums, love,' Matilda advised. 'This is my poison.' She waggled her glass of Irish whiskey. 'Lou's old man used to be a merchant seaman and she got a taste fer navy rum. Likes it a bit too much. Same as me with this stuff.' Matilda nodded at the fellow talking to her husband. 'Bet your old boss is more of a Champagne man, ain't he, Livvie?'

Having overheard his wife's comment, Jack Keiver lifted a tankard with a smirk on his chops. 'There y'are, squire.' He handed Lucas his beer.

The men struck up an amicable conversation about the Saturday match at the Arsenal although they seemed at odds about the likely outcome.

'That's a turn-up,' Matilda said. 'Ain't seen Jack so comfortable with a nob before.'

'He's not stuck up. He's all right, is Mr Black.'

'Yeah . . . and I can see he thinks you're all right too, love.' Matilda chuckled. 'So you take care. Don't want Lou back round yours with more ointment any time soon, do we?' Matilda waved away Olivia's protest. 'Good-looking gel like you?' she scoffed. 'I've seen the way he looks at you.'

Olivia decided not to argue. Matilda was well on the way to being under the influence. They'd not been in the pub long but already the woman had downed three whiskeys before Olivia had emptied half her glass. She wondered how on earth Matilda could afford to drink so heavily, then realised that she couldn't ... but did anyway. Just as Olivia's aunt Sybil did, and Tommy had.

Matilda gave her another wink and Olivia returned a rueful smile. Her neighbour wasn't criticising Lucas, she was cautioning her young friend against men in general and the havoc they could wreak on young women they fancied but had no intention of marrying. Matilda was a good friend. And wise.

Lucas was a good friend too. He'd helped Olivia out of difficult situations and protected her and her family from harm when her father had jeopardised his livelihood. But friend or not, Lucas *had* wanted to sleep with her. Joe Hunter, the man she'd fallen in love with, had wanted to marry her. But her charismatic boss had always been there, in the background, watching her with those deep blue eyes, a sarcastic slant to his mouth. The war had humbled him, though, as it had so many men who now knew hell to be a place in Flanders.

Olivia raised her glass in salute as Lou caught her eye. The woman was seated with a group of people at a corner table but they both knew they had unfinished business. Sympathetic women in the Bunk might give you their last ha'penny but they'd want it returned. They had to make ends meet like everybody else. Lou would expect to be paid, as well as thanked for what she'd done. She had said she'd seen women in a worse state from trying to get rid of a baby. In Olivia's opinion that alone was worth the handful of silver she now pushed across the bar with an instruction to the barman to keep filling Lou's glass with rum until the cash ran out.

A female voice she recognised drifted into Olivia's hearing above the din. She turned about, putting down her drink then weaving determinedly through the revellers towards Ruby.

'Want to speak to you,' she uttered coldly. 'Step outside a minute?'

Guessing what this was about, Ruby turned her back and continued cosying up to her boyfriend.

Incensed, Olivia grabbed her cousin's elbow and tugged her away from Riley McGoogan towards the door.

'Who d'you think y'are, manhandling me?' Ruby snarled when Olivia let the pub door swing closed behind them.

'I'll tell you who I am,' Olivia stormed. 'I'm Maggie's sister and the person who looks after her.'

'Ain't doin' a very good job then, are yer?' Ruby taunted, brushing down her sleeves.

Olivia winced. She'd walked into that one. She *had* let Maggie down.

Sensing her advantage Ruby went on the attack. 'Maggie's a little tart and I did her a favour helping her out. *And* she owes me fer that Eusol. Don't come cheap that stuff so she can cough up. Or you can.'

Olivia felt her fists tightening at her sides but she controlled herself. 'Maggie's got bad blisters. She didn't have a clue how to use it.'

'Well, she'll know next time, won't she?' Ruby returned with a nasty laugh. 'You should be thanking me for teaching her a lesson about keeping her drawers on.'

'You stay away from all of us ... ' Olivia started back towards the pub, fearing the rage swelling in her chest might erupt. She was angry at herself, though, because there was no denying Ruby's jibes held some unpalatable truths.

'Got you thinking, ain't I?' the other girl jeered. 'Well, think about this: better Maggie gets a few blisters on her fanny than sticks a knitting needle up it, 'cos that's what she was asking me about. How to do a job on herself to get rid of Harry Wicks's baby.'

The blood drained from Olivia's face, leaving it cold and pale. 'I don't want Maggie learning any of your dirty tricks,' she sent over her shoulder. She was wishing she'd waited until another time to have it out with Ruby. She'd visions of her cousin continuing this argument inside the pub.

Ruby gripped her elbow and swung her back round, slapping her face and making Olivia gasp.

'You think you're so high 'n' mighty, don't yer? Miss Goody Two Shoes who never puts a foot wrong,' Ruby scoffed. 'If you weren't such a frigid bitch then perhaps you might have known how to help Maggie yerself. Then she wouldn't have needed to come to me. Or perhaps she didn't want you looking down on her, like you do me,' Ruby finished bitterly. 'After all, I ain't her *real* sister, am I? I'm just Tommy Bone's bastard.'

'No ... you're not a sister to us and now you never will be,' Olivia said quietly. 'And I wouldn't ever look down on Maggie.' Her face was stinging from her cousin's blow but she wasn't going to give Ruby the satisfaction of seeing her rub her cheek. Although she was itching to retaliate she wouldn't brawl in the street, allowing the cow to bring her down to her own level. Lucas was just yards away and Olivia had already felt embarrassed once today in front of him. She turned away but Ruby bumped her into the road, having different ideas about calling it quits.

'Bet Joe Hunter had to find himself a ma'm'selle over in France, didn't he? Give him anything to remember you by before he went off to get killed, did yer? A little *kiss*, was it?' Ruby snorted. 'Should've sent him round mine. He *was* mine until you sank yer claws in him, you bitch. I'd've sent him off satisfied. I'd done it before and Joe loved it ... couldn't get enough of me ...'

Olivia flew at her cousin, pummelling Ruby's face and arms with her fists. 'You shut your mouth about Joe,' she panted. 'He was my fiancé. He *loved* me.'

As Ruby raised her fists to strike back she was dragged away and shoved along the pavement.

'Get going,' Lucas told her coldly.

'Fuck off!' Ruby sneered, wiping blood from her cheek where Olivia's nails had caught her. 'If you're back on leave hoping for a good time, you're with the wrong girl. Cast-iron drawers that one.' She lewdly gave him the once over. 'I'd let you into mine, soldier boy ... for the right price.' Having spotted Riley watching her from the pub doorway, she gave a toss of her bright blonde head then flounced off, hips swinging.

Olivia's hands were shaking so much she had a job straightening her clothes and pushing her straggling fair hair back into its pins. She avoided looking at Lucas but was aware that he was watching her.

'Are you all right?'

She nodded vigorously. 'I can handle her. She's just me black sheep cousin, showing off, as usual.'

'I see ...'

'Do you?' Olivia's shoulders slumped but she gave Lucas a challenging look. 'Do you *really* see what we're like? Or d'you think all us Bones are quaint and amusing? It's not funny. We're not circus acts, just a disgraceful lot. But you already know that, don't you?' His face was half in shadow so she couldn't read his expression. But he knew how to keep his feelings concealed, in any case. 'You knew my father was thieving from Barratt's. You've just met my tart of a cousin. You're aware that my fifteen-year-old sister got herself knocked up. The proud father had no intention of marrying her. He's so revolting, that's actually a good thing. Then there's Nancy, not yet fourteen and shoplifting lipsticks, so I'm told. And how about me? You've always known the company I keep. I fell in love with a pimp. And now he's dead, I miss him dreadfully.'

Olivia took a breath after rattling that lot off. She blinked back tears that were the result of exasperation at his silence as much as anything. The Duke's patrons had started warbling a rendition of 'Roll out the Barrel'. 'Those are my friends singing too.' Olivia pointed to the pub. 'Salt-of-the-earth folk who knew Joe when he was growing up . . . knew what he went through with his rotten parents. Not so long ago I thought I was better than people like the Keivers. The first time I walked through Campbell Road I felt scared stiff. I wouldn't be without them now, though.'

'You'd be without me, though, would you?' Lucas said quietly. 'Is that what you're saying?'

'No . . . but you're different from us.' She gazed at him. 'What I'm saying is, I'd sooner you went away and didn't come back than be here and despise me. And you will. Eventually.'

He took a single stride to reach her. 'Don't say that.'

'Why not? It's true.'

'It's not and never will be.' He gestured brusquely. 'I've always known who you are . . . what you come from . . . but I keep coming back, don't I? Why would I if I look down on you? If you're after something to dwell on, think about that.' He swore beneath his breath and strode off a few paces before swinging round to face her. 'What was that fight all about? You didn't think your cousin was going to get my attention, did you?'

'Still as conceited as ever, I see, Lucas,' Olivia chided him, a smile softening her expression. 'Oh, Ruby meant what she said about taking you home with her and emptying your wallet. But I wasn't defending your honour, or having a catfight over you. I was warning her to stay away from my sister.' She walked away from the pub and into the shadows. Although the racket within the pub had increased now the piano was being pounded, she wasn't taking any chances on being overheard. 'Ruby gave Maggie the stuff to make her miscarry. I wouldn't have minded so much if she'd done it for the right reason. But she just poked her nose in to get at me and make matters worse.'

Olivia abruptly clammed up then. Enough had been said about Maggie ... about *all* of her family. 'I *am* very sorry to have ruined your evening, Lucas. I know you men treat every hour on leave as precious. There was so much I wanted to say to you, y'know.' Freddie was on her mind and the difficult explanation she still had to make. 'Would you come back and see me in the morning so we can have a proper talk about things?'

'I'll call in a day or two. We need some time apart to cool off. Anyway, I'm going to Southend tomorrow to see Freddie. You look all in. Though you seemed to have your cousin on the ropes just now. Who taught you to scrap like that – Joe Hunter?'

'He'd've been a good teacher,' Olivia said proudly. Joe's astonishing skill and bravery, fighting hand-to-hand in the trenches, had earned him widespread respect and praise. Olivia was immensely pleased that people now remembered him for that rather than for his ill-spent youth. 'Joe'd be cross to know I'd lowered meself to Ruby's level, though. He thought me a lady,' she added wryly.

'And so you are, Princess.' Lucas's voice was droll. 'Come on then, I'll walk you home.' He took her hand, threading it under his arm.

'Come back in the morning, please. I'll be in a better mood, promise. There's something I need to tell you about Freddie and why you won't be able to see him, so there's no point in going to Southend.' Olivia slid a glance up at him as they strolled along.

Lucas frowned. 'Has he taken a turn for the worse?'

'Sort of ... please don't ask me to go into it now.' She knew the news about Freddie would come as a bombshell to him and was overdue. But informing somebody that a friend had committed suicide wasn't something you could just drop into a conversation without a long and fraught debate following. She didn't feel up to it now. She wanted to go home and check on Maggie and the others. Then she wanted to sleep ... and sleep, because she was utterly exhausted by the day's events.

'It's Sunday tomorrow. Fancy a walk in the park if it's a fine day?' she tempted him.

He murmured agreement. When they reached her gate he kissed her lightly on the cheek then got into his car and drove off with only a fleeting glance back.

Olivia sighed, watching the rear lights until he'd turned the corner. She knew he was annoyed that she wouldn't open up to him right now. In many ways he was still her arrogant boss, expecting obedience and showing displeasure when it wasn't instantly given. She pushed it all from her mind and went indoors.

Maggie was up and sitting in the kitchen, eating toast and dripping for supper.

'Wasn't expecting you to be awake, let alone up. You look brighter.' Olivia felt a wave of relief pass over her.

Maggie's grimace was sheepish. 'Stayed up to speak to you. Where've you been?'

'Just round in the Duke with my old boss Lucas and the Keivers. I made sure I thanked Matilda and Lou for what they did for you.'

'Sorry to cause so much trouble, Livvie,' Maggie mumbled.

'Well, I'm not going to say that you didn't,' Olivia replied bluntly. 'But ... I'm sorry too, that you didn't feel you could come to me instead of Ruby. Promise you'll talk to me if you've got any other worries or troubles?'

'I will next time.'

Olivia pulled a wry face that drew a bashful giggle from Maggie.

'Won't be no more of *them* next times. I'm finished with Harry fer good.'

Olivia had heard that before so just grunted and sank down into a chair to ease off her shoes. But she felt a sense of peace descend on her. Maggie was no longer pregnant and she'd suffered no real harm, according to Lou. That was all that mattered to Olivia. The outcome could have been so much worse.

'I mean it about Harry.' Maggie gingerly got to her feet. 'He's been messing about behind me back with that fat cow from the confectioner's. Ricky said it's been going on for a while.' She sniffed. 'Never speaking to the cheating swine again.'

'Do you really mean it this time?'

Maggie gave an emphatic nod.

'Well, that's our silver lining.' Olivia got up and hugged her.

'You were right about him all along. Wish I'd listened,' Maggie snuffled against her sister's shoulder.

'Are your blisters sore?' Olivia comforted her by plonking a kiss on her forehead.

'A bit ... serves me right.'

'Stay away from Ruby,' Olivia warned. 'I've just had a set to with her. She told me you asked about knitting needle jobs.'

'Wouldn't have done it ... honest.' Maggie's eyes popped. 'Not after she told me what it involved. Made me feel sick.' She glanced at the fading red patch on her sister's cheek. 'Did Ruby whack you?'

Olivia nodded. 'I hit her back, don't worry.' She helped herself to the last piece of toast and dripping off the plate, and took a bite. 'I'm turning in,' she said between chews. 'I take it the other two are in bed?' She'd just recalled sending Nancy and Alfie off to the caff hours ago.

'Yeah ... they're both asleep.'

'I'd better speak to Nancy tomorrow about her shoplifting. She could have got you both in dreadful trouble. Gamages has store detectives, you know.'

'Yeah, I know. But about that ... ' Maggie started.

'What?' Olivia had picked up on the note of persuasion in Maggie's voice. 'Don't you *want* me to tear her off a strip?'

'If you do she'll know it was me grassed her up,' Maggie reasoned. 'I've already had a go at her and she promised me she won't do it no more.' Maggie felt guilty for having dropped Nancy in it just to deflect interest from herself. 'Just leave it, can we, Livvie? No harm done, was there? She knows she's been daft and regrets it.'

'You'll keep an eye on her then, and let me know straightaway if any more new stuff turns up?' Olivia sighed. 'This is her last chance though.'

Maggie nodded.

'Reckon you'll be fit for work Monday?' Olivia put a match to the candle on the table in readiness to light their way upstairs.

'I'll be clocking on as usual.' Maggie sounded adamant. 'Ain't losing a day's wages over *him*. I'm saving up to better meself,' she added. 'Alice has got an interview at Turner's in Blackstock Road, 'cos they pay better rates. I said I'd go with her. Alice reckons us younger munitions workers can wangle nights at Turner's and earn some *real* money.' She paused then added, 'The best news is that if I do get taken on, me supervisor's promised that Nancy can have my job. It's a lot more pay. So then she won't need to pinch stuff.'

'Have you told her the good news?'

'Not yet. But I'll get me new job one way or the other and help us all out. I owe it to you.'

Olivia gave Maggie a smile. For the first time she felt she was sharing some of the burden of the younger ones with her sister, and it was a good feeling. She picked up the candlestick with a contented smile. 'Right. Bedtime.'

On the landing Maggie whispered, 'G'night, Livvie. Sweet dreams,' before they went into their separate rooms.

Olivia undressed and lay in bed watching the shadows dancing on the ceiling, hoping that Maggie would be true to her word about staying away from Harry Wicks. For over a year now he had been a thorn in her family's side. If Maggie really had seen through him at last then Olivia knew she could finally breathe a huge sigh of relief.

She turned onto her side and squinted at the shimmering

moon through a chink in the curtains. Her lashes fell over weary eyes as she pictured a man's handsome face. She wondered how she could bear to tell Lucas that Freddie hadn't made it after all. Lucas was looking forward to seeing his old pal. The last time he'd been home on leave he'd been delighted to tell her that Freddie Weedon was making a remarkable recovery when nobody had expected him to survive at all.

Perhaps Freddie had recovered from his physical injuries, but it seemed his mental scars had passed unnoticed and been allowed to fester. In the end they, rather than the battlefield bullet wound that had caved in his chest, had proved fatal.

Chapter Eighteen

'You're an early riser.' Olivia gave Lucas a welcoming smile.

'Not too early, I hope. I wasn't sure what time to turn up.'

'You're just on time. Kettle's boiled. We usually have a late breakfast on Sunday.' Olivia led the way down the hall, the atmosphere thick with the smoky aroma of kippers. 'You're welcome to have breakfast with us. I've got enough in.'

Lucas sat down at the table opposite Alfie, wolfing down his breakfast of vinegary kippers and brown bread spread thickly with marge.

The two girls blushed and smiled shyly at the handsome man their sister introduced to them. It was an unnecessary formality as they knew very well who he was. Lucas took a seat at the crowded parlour table, politely accepting a plate of kippers and a cup of tea.

Maggie was first to put down her knife and fork and excuse herself. Nancy sloped off a short while after, Alfie hot on her heels, leaving Olivia and Lucas to finish their breakfast in private.

Upstairs in the bedroom they shared Maggie began brushing her younger sister's hair. Separating long strands, she began winding them about her fingers to put into pin curls. 'D'you reckon Livvie'll marry that Mr Black?' she asked whimsically.

'I remember when he took her out to Ally Pally. Long while ago that was when we all lived in Wood Green.' Nancy studied her reflection in the spotted mirror as her sister continued doing her hair for her.

'Dad expected Livvie to persuade Mr Black to give him back his job at Barratt's. That's why she went out with him that Sunday afternoon,' Maggie mumbled through the pins clamped in her lips.

'Yeah ... poor Dad,' Nancy sighed. Her father had been violent and unpredictable but he'd been the only parent she'd ever really known. Her mother had passed away when she'd been just a toddler. Now Tommy had gone, she felt bereft. 'D'you reckon they'll catch whoever killed him?'

Maggie shook her head, anchoring another curl in place. 'People at work reckon it was a Belgian. All of them men are thieves and murderers, tramping from place to place. They was treated terrible by the Germans before they fled over here. It's sent them nutty.' She shuddered. 'If half of what I've heard's true, it ain't surprising they go around stabbing people for a few shillings.'

'Don't make it right, though, whatever happened to them.' Nancy sounded angry.

'I know,' Maggie snapped back. She had once felt as mournful as Nancy did about their father's passing. The fright of getting pregnant had taken over, pushing everything else out of her mind. Now she felt guilty for having barely given their murdered father a thought in weeks.

As the girls fell into a moody quiet Alfie had his say. 'That bloke Lucas is too posh to marry Livvie,' he piped up from the bedroom doorway. He'd been kneeling on the landing, playing with an old train set Livvie had got him from Billy the totter in Campbell Road. It had been an unexpectedly lovely gift for his eighth birthday. Livvie had said it would occupy him while he waited for her to get home from the factory. The set *had* proved useful. His sisters never took any notice of him laying out the track outside their bedroom door. But it gave him an opportunity to listen to what they said while they carried out their Sunday morning ritual of titivating themselves.

He knew they kept him in the dark from kindness because they didn't want to upset him with their worries. But he wasn't nervous now he didn't have his father's fists to dodge. He wasn't too young to know things either. He'd turned nine, like his cousin Mickey. He intended visiting Mickey in Wood Green later. He liked his cousin.

'Mr Black can't be that posh.' Maggie pushed in a hairgrip a bit too forcefully, making Nancy yelp and smack her hand. 'Livvie told me he was round in the Duke having a drink with her last night.'

At that moment Olivia called up the stairs that she was off out, and the trio chorused a goodbye.

Maggie went to the window and lifted the net to watch Livvie and Lucas stroll up the road arm-in-arm. They looked a handsome pair, she wistfully realised. Him dark and handsome and her fair and pretty. She realised that her big sister would be twenty soon. It was time she settled down with a man.

It seemed Nancy was thinking along the same lines. 'If Livvie don't find a husband soon she'll be left on the shelf. Girl at work's only sixteen and she's getting married before her sweetheart goes off to war, in case he don't come back.'

Maggie reflected on the proposal she'd received that would have let her keep her baby. A pang of regret tightened her chest. Too late now. She stopped dwelling on Harry's brother and craned her neck to see Livvie and Lucas turn the corner.

'Livvie should find somebody like Joe,' Alfie insisted. 'Freddie Weedon's Joe's pal . . . '

'She can't marry *him*,' Maggie snorted, turning about. 'Didn't you know? He's croaked. His sister come over and told Livvie all about it.' Maggie let the curtain fall into place, unaware that her brother had turned as white as the net.

Alfie's jaw sagged and he formed an astonished 'Oh' with his mouth but no sound emerged. 'Must be the curse . . . ' he eventually whispered.

Maggie shot him a look, feeling a shiver pass over her as she always did when the subject of their father's cigarette case cropped up. 'I went to see Harry to warn him about that bloody thing. He had it in his pocket for a while.' Maggie pursed her lips. 'Ain't bothered about him now though. He can get killed for all I care.'

'Livvie *should* chuck it in the dustbin though or a bomb'll drop on our house,' Nancy said, glancing at her sister from beneath her lashes. She'd heard Maggie say before that she hated Harry but she always ran after him in the end. Maggie had owned up to what the commotion had been about yesterday then threatened Nancy to keep her mouth shut about Harry getting her up the duff. Nancy hadn't needed telling. She wasn't going to broadcast having a slag for a sister. Besides, Maggie had done her a favour, keeping quiet about her pinching stuff in Gamages.

Alfie was having trouble rousing himself from the shock of hearing about Freddie Weedon. Suddenly he burst out, 'He only had a bad cough. That can't've done fer 'im!'

'He jumped off the pier, like his friend did.' Maggie sounded matter-of fact. 'That's what his sister told Livvie.' She put down the brush, having finished Nancy's hair. The girls swapped places and Nancy picked up the pins and started on Maggie's curls.

'I know Livvie bought that cigarette case for Dad and she's sentimental over it but it gives me the creeps. I'm gonna throw it in the dustbin.'

Alfie said nothing. They'd have a job finding the thing because he'd already taken it out of the drawer and hidden it in his room, in readiness to swap for a picture frame. He knew that after what he'd just heard he'd have to do it quickly now. Being as his sisters – especially Livvie – were always looking out for *him*, he reckoned it was his turn to be brave and keep *them* safe from the curse. So when he went out to see Mickey over Wood Green later he'd take the thing with him just in case he bumped into Mr Hunter, hanging about in the Bunk with his pal. He still wanted the frame in exchange if he could get it . . . but if not he'd let Joe's dad have the cigarette case and the bad luck that went with it.

Chapter Nineteen

'I'm sorry to be giving you such depressing news.' Olivia gave Lucas's long fingers a comforting squeeze. 'Though I am glad to be able to tell you about Freddie and my father face to face. It was hard to write it all in a letter. When I'd finished, I dithered over sending it. It seemed wrong to bother you when you should be concentrating on keeping safe.' She paused. 'But I knew you'd want to know. And *I* should have been the one to tell you about my dad, not Miss Wallis. At least when you do read the letter it won't all come as a shock.'

They were sitting on a park bench, Lucas with his head bowed towards his clasped hands. Olivia had moments ago relayed everything she knew about her father's and Freddie's last hours.

Slowly Lucas moved his head from side to side in denial, pursing his lips. 'I don't believe it. Freddie wouldn't have done that. I got to know him well. He wasn't the sort.'

'I thought the same thing,' Olivia agreed. 'But from what the police told his sister, it seems he did.' She paused. 'Did you meet Yvonne ... the girl Freddie fell for?'

'I saw her once or twice when I visited him in the hospital at Étaples.' Lucas straightened, resting his spine against the seat's wooden slats. 'They did seem close. She told me he was her favourite patient. But that's how the sisters are. They're wonderful . . . treat all the wounded boys as though they're special.'

'Freddie took what Yvonne said to heart, perhaps,' Olivia suggested.

'I still don't believe that he would have killed himself over an ill-starred romance, however deeply he felt about her.' A terse gesture reinforced this conviction. 'He wasn't a fool. He would've known she'd find out and blame herself. He didn't have a spiteful bone in him and wouldn't have hurt her like that just because she was with another man. Not Freddie.'

'We could go and visit Hilda Weedon if you want, and see if she's found out anything new from the inquest,' Olivia suggested. She recognised the sense in his argument. Freddie hadn't seemed a maudlin or vindictive character to her either. 'Hilda wanted you to know about her brother's passing but she was worried you'd think badly of him.' Olivia patted his arm. 'I assured her that you weren't like that.'

'Oh, I damn' well am!' Lucas abruptly sprang to his feet and paced to and fro. 'If I believed he'd topped himself after all I did to keep him alive and get him back home, I'd think badly of him all right! I'd blame myself for not throttling him when I had the chance.' He jerked back his head to glare at the heavens. 'Your fiancé would've sold his soul to have the chance Freddie had. All Joe wanted was to get back to Islington and to you. Every soldier over there feels the same way about home. The promise of Blighty keeps them going, even when they're so far gone they've little chance of making it alive as far as the aid post.' Lucas pulled out a pack of Player's and lit one, dragging on it ferociously. 'Something doesn't add up here.' The glowing tip of the cigarette was waved to reinforce his point. 'It's more likely the whole thing was an accident and the half-finished letter to Yvonne is being given too much weight. Freddie went out in the dark during a bad storm. He could've just slipped in the wet and fallen into the sea. Just because the other poor sod did himself in, it doesn't mean Freddie went the same way.'

'I don't want to believe it either,' Olivia soothed. She'd never seen Lucas so het up. 'Nor does his sister. She was as angry as you at the idea of him deliberately ending his life. Hilda's asked me to the funeral. If you like, we could use that as an excuse and go over to Walthamstow later to find out if a date's been arranged yet. It'd give you a chance to talk to her.'

'I would like to speak to her, if only to pay my condolences,' Lucas replied.

As he continued to pace restlessly Olivia got up, realising it would be as well to let him stew on it and talk later when they went to Hilda's. Briskly they started back towards the park gates, each lost in their own thoughts.

'Shall I call for you about six o'clock this evening?'

Olivia murmured agreement.

'Well, I'm hoping that *was* the other horrible news you had to tell me about. I don't think I could stand hearing more,' Lucas said mordantly.

'It was,' Olivia quietly confirmed, deciding not to apologise yet again for ruining his leave with tales of misery. 'Are you spending time with your family this afternoon?' She injected a lighter note into her voice.

'I'll visit my mother at some point before I head back to France. Probably not today though.'

The remoteness in his voice was hard to ignore. Olivia felt rather rude not to have enquired earlier about his family. He certainly knew all the ins and outs about her lot. Whether he wanted to or not! 'Will you see your brother as well as your mum?' she persevered.

'Not if I can help it. But as he's always with my mother he'll be hard to avoid.'

'Aren't you staying with them while you're home?'

'No!' Lucas said in mock horror. 'I've my own house, thank the Lord.'

'Where's that?'

'Hampstead. Want to see it?'

Olivia glanced at him. 'Might do. It's not where your girlfriend lives, is it?' She'd thought he might laugh and deny it. But he didn't. She'd always known he had a woman in his life. He'd told her so himself. But he seemed reticent today about answering her. When he did, it came as a curt headshake and he kept his narrowed eyes on the horizon.

This wasn't enough for Olivia. She felt they'd grown close enough now, despite their differences in class, to discuss such things. He'd never been shy about asking about Joe, after all. 'Are you still seeing her?'

'I told you before I left for France last year that I didn't expect her to wait for me.'

'Still haven't answered me,' Olivia returned in her pert way.

'Don't intend to either.' He smiled but there was a warning glint in his eyes.

'Do you know much about your real parents?'

'I know some of it, and before you enquire, I've no interest in finding out more.'

Olivia glanced at him, feeling she'd been roundly told to mind her own business. So, with a shrug, she did.

*

Alfie had decided to save the bus fare and walk to his old house in Wood Green to see Mickey. Just as he was descending the hill towards Turnpike Lane he spotted his cousin hobbling in his direction.

'Was on me way to see you,' Alfie called, grinning. 'Fancy a game?' He indicated the football beneath his arm.

'I was coming over yours,' Mickey yelled back.

Now he'd made the journey Alfie didn't fancy trekking back to Islington just yet. 'We can have a kick about in Ranelagh Road. I used to play out there with me pals. They'll give us a match.'

'I'm off to the Bunk to ask me sister if I can move in with her,' Mickey bawled. 'We've got a lodger and it's bleedin' murder at home. I've had enough.' He came to a halt in front of his cousin, resting his bad foot on top of the good one. 'It's all your fault, telling him we was cousins. Me mum told him to sling his hook. But he won't and just gives her a thump or buys her gin to shut her up. *And* he's got me old bed. I have to kip on a mattress on the floor in her room.'

'What?' Alfie's features crinkled as he tried to decipher his cousin's garbled complaint. 'What bloke? You don't mean Joe Hunter's dad, do you?'

'Yeah, I do,' Mickey snarled. 'Wish you'd never mentioned us to him then he'd've left us alone, I reckon.'

'*I* never told him you needed a lodger. *You* let *that* out,' Alfie reminded him, sounding equally narked.

Having done a quick bit of thinking, Alfie carried on

towards Wood Green and his old home. He'd looked for Mr Hunter round in the Bunk. Now he knew why he'd not found him. Joe's dad was living in the Bones' old house, which meant he could easily take the picture frame out of the sideboard drawer. Alfie realised that finally he'd be rid of the jinxed pewter case and in exchange could get back the silver frame that had belonged to his mum. The swap made perfect sense to Alfie so he speeded up with Mickey trailing in his wake, moaning, but making a valiant effort to keep up.

*

Lucas inhaled the noxious air, top lip curling as he gazed up at the Barratt's buildings with an odd mixture of boredom and nostalgia. The suffocating smell of boiled sugar hung in the atmosphere even when the factory machinery was idle on the Sabbath. He'd never thought he'd feel sentimental about the old place. But it seemed he did or he wouldn't have stopped by to stare at it. And it wasn't just Olivia on his mind. The sound of her father's loud voice and coarse laughter seemed to haunt the empty courtyard just beyond the iron gates. Tommy Bone had influenced the factory and the people in it with his unorthodox militancy. On the one hand he'd try to undermine his seniors, on the other he'd suck up to Mr Barratt in the hope of a promotion. But Livvie's father had never grovelled to Lucas. Tommy had realised early on that he'd no need to because his daughter had the persuasive power where the managing director was concerned. Tommy Bone wouldn't be forgotten in a hurry, that was for sure. Even the fact that Lucas was standing here now, brooding about his old adversary, would make the man chuckle ... wherever he was. Tommy would have wanted to leave his mark on the world. Would have believed it his right to do so.

Lucas walked back towards his car, leaning against the bonnet. His eyes were half-closed and his mind started to meander like the cigarette smoke drifting between his lips. He contemplated the violent argument he'd had with his own father when he'd discovered arrangements had been made for him to take a directorship in a sweet factory. It had been a wealthy man's attempt to curb his heir's playboy ways. And, with the benefit of having attended an Ypres finishing school, Lucas could concede now that he had needed reining in. He'd been too dissolute in his ways. Yet he'd resented his father for interfering in his life at the time. Until the day a girl had turned up at the factory gate with Tommy Bone's packed lunch. She'd knocked Lucas back when he'd tried to sweet talk her but he'd never forgotten the impression she'd made on him and he had changed after that even though he hadn't realised it at the time. So his father couldn't take the credit for civilising him and neither could Ypres. The fucking war might have beaten the arrogance out of him but it had knocked aggression in. He felt he was spoiling for a fight most of the time. And longing for Livvie Bone. That never went away.

He dropped the cigarette stub, about to get in his car and drive away when he spotted a blond boy haring past at the top of the road with another fair-haired lad limping along at a fair crack behind.

Lucas frowned. He recognised the kid leading the way, which wasn't surprising as he'd sat opposite him at a breakfast table that morning. Intrigued as to what Alfie was up to, he left his car parked at the kerb and followed them.

*

Alfie howled. He hadn't been clumped by an adult for ages and it came as a surprise and a shock to him. He cupped his ringing ear and gave Herbie Hunter a reproachful look. 'Wot's that for?'

Herbie ignored him and gestured to Mickey. 'You'd better get inside. Yer mother's been lookin' for you.'

Mickey backed away. Then, rocking from his uneven gait, he fled up the street. As far as he was concerned he was off to live with Ruby and wasn't ever going inside that house again. He knew that it wouldn't be long before Mr Hunter turned his temper on him instead of his mother or cousin.

Herbie shot a look over his shoulder in case Sybil was in earshot. The last thing he wanted was her hearing about Tommy Bone's cigarette case turning up on her doorstep. She'd be down the police station with a tale for them and then they'd be rounding up the family, asking awkward questions.

On the first day Herbie had met Sybil he'd discovered that she couldn't stand any of Tommy's kids, but Olivia in particular was resented by her aunt. That suited him. Sybil keeping her distance from the Bones' theories about their father's murder was exactly what he wanted. He was furious that this little tyke had come too close for comfort. Herbie was just about settled in his new abode and had got Sybil where he wanted her: under his thumb.

Grabbing Alfie by the collar, he hauled him towards the alley, shoving him a little way into it. 'Don't you ever come back round here lookin' fer me.' He stabbed his forefinger against Alfie's snub nose. 'And don't ever ask me about that thing again.' He slapped away the lad's hand, proffering the cigarette case.

'You said you'd exchange it for a picture frame. I know of one that won't cost yer nothin'. Can I have it? It's in the drawer in there.' Alfie tipped his head towards his old house.

Alfie's pleas were cut off as a hand was clamped around his jaw. Herbie licked his lips nervously. He was jittery about the way that bloody pewter case was following him around. Yet he knew it might be sensible to take it and bury it rather than let Alfie Bone keep flaunting it around. In a way he was glad to be able to have this quiet talk with the lad. He'd been brooding on the consequences of his last trip to Southend.

'So how's me son's old pal doing with his detective work?' he muttered. 'Heard from him, have yer?'

Alfie blinked above the hand painfully gripping his face then jerked himself free of it. 'Freddie's done himself in. Ain't 'cos of the cigarette case being bad luck though,' he quickly fibbed. He didn't want to turn Herbie off taking the thing. 'It's 'cos he fell in love and she didn't want him so he jumped off the pier.'

'Blimey ... poor sod.' A phlegmy chuckle rumbled in Herbie's chest and seemed to go on for ever.

Alfie gave up waiting for him to stop laughing and piped up, 'It ain't got me dad's initials engraved so you could put yours on it.' He still desperately wanted his mum's picture frame.

'Give it here then.' Herbie stretched out a hand, still smirking. It seemed the cigarette case had been his guardian angel. Either that or he was a better assassin than he knew.

'I've got a better offer for you, Alfie.'

Herbie tottered around and gawped in comical disbelief at an imposing-looking army officer leaning against the wall by the mouth of the alley. 'Who the fuck are you?' he spluttered.

'He's Mr Black, me sister's friend,' Alfie interjected, equally startled by Lucas's appearance. He grew even more nervous when the newcomer strolled up and took the cigarette case from his trembling fingers to examine it.

Without needing it confirmed Lucas knew he was holding Tommy Bone's property. Just that morning Olivia had told him a cigarette case had been stolen from her father the night he was murdered. Then it had turned up again via Freddie Weedon, trailing another corpse in its wake. Lucas had been poleaxed from hearing about Freddie's suicide so at the time had barely registered her regrets over buying her father that particular gift. But he was thinking about it now. And about what he'd just overheard.

Herbie licked his lips, darting glances to and fro. From not wanting the blasted case, he was now temped to snatch it and stuff it in his pocket out of sight. He decided to act breezy. 'Do me a favour, mate. If you know the family, take the kid home and make sure he don't pester me no more. Ain't buying no tat off him. Already told him once.'

'He said he'd swap it,' Alfie protested to Lucas. 'Anyhow, that picture frame is ours. Livvie wants it back 'cos it belonged to me mum.' He thought mentioning his big sister might work. And it did.

'Better take it home for her then.' Lucas fixed his hard blue gaze on the older man.

Herbie's teeth ground. He'd already noticed that square of silver in the drawer and had put stuff on top of it, hoping Sybil might not realise when it disappeared. He was

222

surprised she hadn't beaten him to pawning it. But her loss had been his gain. Until now.

'Go and get it.' Lucas dismissed Hunter with a slight elevation of his chin.

A few stained teeth were displayed in a bitter smile as Herbie pushed past Lucas. His guts were writhing with resentment but he felt he had to obey. There was something about Mr Black, and nobs like him, that flummoxed Herbie into submission. He reckoned it must have been all those years spent sucking up to them to lure them as punters for his wife. In her prime, Maisie had been a smashing looker with high-roller clients who'd kept them both in clover.

'You'll regret crossing me, son,' Herbie spat through clenched teeth, thrusting the frame at Alfie then slamming the door in his face.

Alfie didn't care about empty threats. He'd got what he wanted so he stuck two fingers up then trotted after Lucas who'd started off up the road. He'd never had a ride in a car and this one looked so smart that he hopped nervously from foot to foot, scared of getting in it.

With a mutter Lucas came round to open the door for his young passenger. After re-seating himself in the Austin he said, 'This belonged to your dad, didn't it?' Lucas took the case from his pocket and put it on the dashboard. Then he glanced at the boy as he drove away from the kerb.

Alfie nodded, eyes swivelling nervously. Livvie would go mad if her friend ended up with the curse on him. So he stretched out a hand to take the thing back.

'Leave it.'

Alfie did as he was told, fidgeting on the leather seat.

'Does Olivia know you've got it?'

Alfie shook his head.

'How *did* you get it?'

He didn't want to admit to taking it without permission so beat about the bush. 'Freddie Weedon got it from his pal in Southend then he sold it to Maggie's boyfriend. Harry Wicks give it to us 'cos he didn't want the curse either.'

Lucas steered to the side of the road. 'What?' He turned to face Alfie, half-smiling. 'You think the cigarette case is to blame for what's happened to your father and Freddie?'

'We all do!' Alfie's eyes were round with conviction. 'Even Livvie ain't sure about it. She was ready to put it in me dad's coffin until she heard how Freddie got left it by his dead pal, who'd jumped off the pier. She changed her mind in case Dad didn't go to heaven. She just keeps it hidden in a drawer now.'

Lucas picked up the case, giving Alfie a quizzical look, before returning it to the dashboard.

Alfie began pulling at his lower lip.

'You've helped yourself to it without your sister's knowledge,' Lucas guessed.

'I'm doing us all a favour, getting rid of it,' he replied defensively. 'Me sister Nancy reckons a bomb'll drop on us if we keep it in the house. And me other sister Maggie reckons her boyfriend Harry'll get shot up over in France 'cos he owned it once.' Alfie glared at the pewter on the dashboard. It looked harmless enough, shimmering in the sunbeams streaming through the windscreen. But he reckoned it was a demonic thing. He jumped to attention as Lucas made to pocket it, grabbing his sleeve. 'You'd better give us it back. Livvie'll go nuts if she finds out you might get jinxed. She likes you.'

'Does she?' A slow smile quirked Lucas's lips.

'You gonna ask her to marry you?' Alfie demanded. He

didn't want his big sister to marry anyone. He wanted to keep Livvie to himself. But he had to admit that Mr Black seemed all right. Without his help, Alfie knew he wouldn't have the picture frame on his lap.

'What would she say if I did?' Lucas kept his thoughtful gaze eyes front.

'Dunno. She hasn't got a boyfriend, so she might say yes. You'd better give us that back or you'll die and she'll be a widder.'

'I'm not superstitious, Alfie. Curses won't work on me.' Lucas fished a coin from his pocket and handed it over. 'Now I've bought it off you fair and square. You're rid of it. You'll hand that to your sister, will you?' He put the case in his pocket.

Alfie nodded, gawping at the half-crown. He'd never had so much money in one go. Yet he was still uneasy. He couldn't give Livvie the coin or she'd go mad at him for taking the thing without asking and for putting Mr Black in danger by selling it to him.

'Almost let *him* have it. Wish I had,' Alfie muttered to himself, rubbing his boxed ear. He didn't care about Mr Hunter having the bad luck. If Livvie noticed the case was missing he'd say he'd swapped it for the picture frame. It was almost the truth. She would surely understand and approve of his intentions. As for the half-crown ... he'd buy his own school trousers off the second-hand stall down the market and give his big sister the benefit of the money that way.

'That fellow said he'd already told you once he didn't want the cigarette case. When was that?' Lucas set the car in motion again.

'A while ago. He used to hang about in Campbell

Road but he found out me aunt needed a lodger. Cousin Mickey said his mum's had enough of the old so and so already though.'

'So you've been talking to him about your dad. Who mentioned the cigarette case?'

'Me. I thought he was all right 'cos he's Joe's dad. Joe was nice.'

'*He's* Joe Hunter's father?' Lucas's surprised glance at his passenger made it necessary for him to correct his steering to avoid the kerb. Olivia hadn't mentioned Hunter Senior arriving on the scene.

Alfie's fair hair flopped into his eyes as he nodded vigorously. 'He bought me some sweets and offered to get me a picture frame off a totter as me aunt wouldn't let us have this.' Alfie stroked the silver frame. 'I can put me mum 'n' dad's wedding picture back in it now. I said I'd have to swap the case for it as I'm skint.'

'He changed his mind, though, about having it?'

'Yeah.' Alfie sighed. 'I told him a secret 'n' all to persuade him. He never told me one back and he said he would.'

Lucas stopped the car at the top of Playford Road rather than outside Alfie's house. He'd sooner this meeting was kept private until he'd got everything straight in his mind. 'Did you tell him something that you weren't supposed to know?'

Alfie pulled at his lip before saying, 'Mr Hunter wanted to know how the cigarette case had turned up out of the blue. I told him Joe's pal was investigating. As soon as Freddie got a good lead from the pawnbroker in Southend, Livvie was going to tell the police about it so they could catch me dad's murderer.'

Lucas took the case from his pocket again and stared at it.

'That's why he just asked you about Freddie.' Lucas hadn't overheard all of it but he'd caught Hunter laughing and calling Freddie a poor sod.

'Yeah. Now Freddie's gone we'll never know who did it. I reckon you should chuck that at a German. It'll be another dead 'un.' Alfie solemnly squinted a wordless warning of the dangers of owning the thing.

'Freddie's not the only one who can ask questions, Alfie,' Lucas said. 'I'll see what I can do. In the meantime you stay away from Mr Hunter, understand?'

Alfie beamed and nodded. This fellow was an army officer and just by talking to him Alfie could tell he was clever. He reckoned Mr Black would be more help than Freddie had been in digging up clues. 'He said I shouldn't have crossed him, but I ain't scared of that old tramp,' Alfie said cockily.

Lucas shot out a hand, grabbing the boy's arm. 'You listen to me. You stay clear of that house and him. Understand?'

Alfie squirmed in his unrelenting grip and nodded his head in agreement.

'Go on then. Your sister will be waiting for you.'

Alfie got out, clutching his precious silver frame. He hesitated. 'You won't tell Livvie you've got the cigarette case?'

'I won't lie to her.'

'But if she don't ask?' Alfie wheedled, sticking his head back into the car.

'I'll tell her. When the time's right,' Lucas said, and put the car in gear, prompting Alfie to slam the door quickly and trot off home.

Chapter Twenty

'It's lovely to see you again, Olivia.' Hilda Weedon beamed a sincere welcome. 'As for you, sir, I've heard so much about you that it's good to put a face to a name.' She inwardly marvelled at what a face it was too. Lieutenant Black was one of the handsomest men she'd ever clapped eyes on. But of course her brother wouldn't have thought to mention that when speaking of his commanding officer.

Hilda had immediately dashed off to make tea when they'd arrived and now poured out and handed round filled cups. 'Freddie spoke highly of you, sir. And of Joe. He thought his friend Joe was the best and wished he could have known him longer.'

'Amen to that,' Lucas murmured.

'After what Freddie went through you'd think he'd never mention the war ever again. But he talked about his army pals all the time.' Hilda placed a plate of Bourbons and custard creams on the table between her guests' armchairs. 'It was his dearest wish to be well enough to return to the frontline even though he'd had the stuffing knocked out of him once. Pining for Yvonne was probably a big part of it . . . ' Her voice tailed off.

'Freddie was well respected by all who knew him,' Lucas said tactfully. 'His old comrades will be sad to know he's passed away.'

'I'd sooner you didn't mention what happened to him . . . ' Hilda began.

'I won't, I promise. But eventually news will filter through and people will get to know,' Lucas gently pointed out. Despite his calm exterior he felt enraged that Freddie would be branded a coward once details emerged. Lucas was almost sure his friend hadn't committed suicide. But he couldn't air his suspicions when he'd no proof as yet to back them up.

'Sorry to turn up uninvited,' Olivia interjected. Hilda's face had dropped and Olivia didn't want their visit to be upsetting. Lucas was right, though: eventually the grapevine would supply the details of Private Weedon's death. She hoped that such a fine man would be remembered with kindness and not condemnation. 'We just dropped by to see if the funeral had been arranged yet. Hope you don't mind.'

Hilda put down her cup and saucer and stood up. 'Actually, your visit is well timed. I'm writing out cards.' She took a black-edged funeral notification from a handful on the sideboard. 'It'll be a quiet affair . . . just a few people.' She held it out to Olivia. 'There, you might as well take yours with you and save me a stamp.' She turned to Lucas. 'Of course, you're very welcome to attend too, Lieutenant Black. I know Freddie would have wanted you to be there.'

Lucas had glanced at the date before Olivia slipped the card into her bag. 'I'd like to attend, but I'd be in trouble if

I did. I'm due to ship out in a day or two. I was lucky to be granted this extra leave as it is.'

Hilda smiled her understanding and sat down again.

'Did the inquest turn up anything new about Freddie's death?' Olivia asked.

'I didn't expect it to, and unfortunately I wasn't proved wrong.' Hilda took a gulp of tea before continuing. 'The coroner recorded a verdict of suicide. I won't challenge it; I can't let it upset me as I've made my own plans.' She inhaled deeply. 'Freddie wouldn't want a fuss made anyway. He'd just be happy that I brought him home to Mum and Dad.'

'He's back in Walthamstow now?'

'At the undertaker's in town. They thought it best for me not to have him here at the house, given the circumstances. I agreed; I don't want ghoulish neighbours barging in to pay their respects. He was in a rough sea for a while and got a bit battered, but I kissed him farewell in the funeral parlour. He was still my dear Freddie.' Hilda smoothed the lap of her black skirt, composing herself. 'The vicar here has been a boon to me. So helpful and kind.' She paused. 'He's an understanding man but there's only so much he can do. There won't be a full funeral service and Freddie must be buried outside the churchyard in unconsecrated ground.' Her voice wobbled into silence briefly. 'So now you know, if you'd sooner not come along ...'

'Try and stop me!' Olivia said, loudly and clearly.

'Hearing that has made me even sorrier I won't be able to attend,' Lucas said. He strode to the window, averting his wrathful features from the two young women.

Olivia sipped tea, glancing at him from time to time with a frown. She hoped he wasn't about to erupt as he had earlier when she'd told him the news about Freddie.

'My parents are buried close to the churchyard wall. The vicar has kindly arranged a plot just the other side so they will all be together as far as is possible. How's your family doing?' Hilda changed the subject.

'Driving me mad, as usual,' Olivia replied. She too was glad to talk about something else. 'I'll be relieved to get back to work tomorrow for a rest. Although I'm thinking of changing jobs.'

Hilda looked interested to know more so Olivia carried on. 'My sister Maggie's a munitions worker. I feel I should be doing more than just making sweets at Barratt's. I want to do something for the war effort. I'm young and strong and know I can help in a better way than knitting socks and scarves. I'd try *anything* rather than feel so useless . . . '

'You do an admirable job, coping with your family the way you do,' Lucas interjected. Having controlled his temper, he walked back and rejoined the conversation. 'Munitions factories aren't pleasant or safe places to work.'

'Neither's a sweet factory,' Olivia shot back .

'Touché,' he said dryly.

'I've joined the VAD,' Hilda announced. 'I've some nursing training from when I was younger. Then I turned my hand to secretarial work because it paid better. I was a bit rusty after a few years out of it but I've been on a refresher course. I started that even before Freddie had his accident . . . Anyway, I applied and have been accepted as a nurse. I'm off to Boulogne before the end of the month, once I've kitted myself out. The woman who interviewed me said that they're crying out for volunteers.'

'I've seen the posters around saying volunteer nurses are urgently needed. Freddie would be proud of you.' So was she proud of Hilda, Olivia realised. And envious.

'Yes, I believe he would.' Hilda sounded convinced of it. 'Though if he'd been here he would have moaned his head off.'

Lucas had been drinking tea, listening to them talking. 'You'll be welcomed with open arms, Miss Weedon.' He put down his empty cup. 'The hospitals are constantly understaffed when their medics are redeployed elsewhere. Every forward push puts the clearing stations and the field hospitals under immense pressure. The sisters constantly struggle to do the work of their absent colleagues. But do it indeed they do. God knows how.'

Hilda stood up with a satisfied smile. 'I will make a difference then. That's all I want to do, and ease the men's suffering a bit. More tea anyone?'

'Thanks but no,' Olivia said, collecting her bag and getting to her feet. 'I should head home. I'm up early for work and I've got to patch Alfie's school trousers before I turn in. He's in my bad books for ripping the knees out of a fairly new pair.'

'Boys!' Hilda gave a wry cluck of the tongue.

At the door Olivia turned to Hilda and gave her a hug while Lucas waited by the car. 'I do admire you, y'know, Hilda, volunteering like that. I'd like to volunteer now the kids are older. Alfie's still at school but Maggie's doing well at work and is old enough to look after him. And Nancy's just got a better-paid job so could help.'

'Well ... why not then?' Hilda challenged.

'I'd never get taken on. I've no proper medical training. Just a St John Ambulance certificate from the first aid course I did at Barratt's.'

'Well, that's a start. All sorts of volunteers are needed. What training's necessary to wash bandages and sheets?

Or comfort a wounded man with a drink of water?' Hilda touched Olivia's cheek fondly. 'Not *proper* nursing, perhaps some uppity sorts would say, but a patient won't care who fetches his meal, or reads aloud his letter from home.' She paused. 'Would you go abroad?'

'That's what I want.'

'Are you twenty-three?'

'Do I need to be?'

Hilda nodded. 'For service abroad.'

'I'm twenty-three then.'

Hilda gave her a wink. 'That's the ticket. If one good thing has come out of what's happened to Freddie, it's making your acquaintance, Livvie. And that of Lieutenant Black.' She sent him an admiring glance. 'He's a bit of a dreamboat, isn't he? And he likes you.'

'I like him too. He's been a true friend. He used to be my boss at Barratt's, before he joined up.'

'Let's hope ... God willing ... that at some time he will be again when this war's finished with and we all get back to normal.'

Olivia remained quiet, reflecting on what 'normal' was. In her heart she knew that things would never again be as they had before the war. Life had changed and with an odd thrill that both alarmed and invigorated her, she realised that for her the greatest changes of all might be yet to come.

'Freddie urged me to make friends with you,' Hilda said. 'I cherished a silly hope that you two might become close. I wanted my brother to forget about the nurse in France and settle down and be safe here.' She paused and considered this. 'That was selfish of me and no better than his wish to keep me at home, safe and idle. I understand why he wanted to get the job done over there. I do too. We must all pitch in or it won't ever be done. Or not to our liking.'

'I feel the same way,' Olivia said simply. She patted her bag in which was the funeral invitation. 'I'll come to the house, shall I, on the day and walk with you to the church?' She guessed Hilda would like some support with all eyes on her. The neighbourhood gossips had been given a lot to chew on.

'Thanks ... I'd appreciate it.' Hilda glanced at Lucas, strolling to and fro while smoking and contemplating the purplish evening horizon. 'He's waiting for you. Go on.' She briefly embraced Olivia then turned and went back inside the house.

*

Lucas had knocked for Olivia at six o'clock on the dot. He'd displayed no sign of the disbelief and frustration that had consumed him on first learning about Freddie's suicide that morning. On the drive over to Walthamstow he'd talked calmly of things he remembered about Joe and Freddie and how they were both missed in his platoon. In fact, several times, she had found herself staring at him because he seemed to be in an unfathomable mood. She did so again now as they drove away from Hilda's. He still seemed preoccupied and she guessed that hearing about Freddie's restricted burial rights had started him brooding.

'Did you mean what you said about quitting Barratt's?' Lucas asked.

'Yes, I do. It's not the same there anymore. You've gone, Dad's gone and my friend Cath Mason wants to leave too.' Olivia sank back into the seat, watching the first emerging stars in the sky. 'Nelly Smith is still up to her old tricks, using the war to her own money-grabbing ends.' She puffed a sigh. 'You're not missing anything not being there, y'know.'

'I stopped by the old place earlier today. Still looks and smells the same.' He paused before adding, 'I saw your brother while I was in Wood Green.'

Olivia groaned. 'Was he up to mischief?'

'Nothing to worry about. We had a little chat. He was with a lad who's the image of him and has a crippled foot. Alfie called him his cousin. Tommy set up home with your aunt then?'

'We're a scandalous lot.' Olivia gave a short laugh. 'As you already know.'

'You didn't approve of them living together, I suppose.'

'Aunt Sybil is my mum's sister, and she's a cow. What d'you expect?' She made a gesture of exasperation. 'If Sybil'd made Dad happy it would've been something. But she didn't.' Olivia's eyes stung as she reflected on the last time she'd spoken to her father. 'You didn't see my dad in the months before he died. He was a shadow of his former self. Oh, he'd still swagger about, but his heart wasn't in it. He seemed empty inside. He was no longer the Tommy Bone you knew. Or I knew.'

'He had regrets, I expect.'

'Oh, yes, he did,' Olivia strongly agreed.

'Apparently your aunt also has regrets. Your brother told me she let Joe's father lodge with her. But she wants him out.'

'*What?*' Olivia goggled at him in disbelief. 'I didn't know they were even acquainted. I knew she wanted a lodger though.'

'You didn't tell me Joe's father had turned up.'

Olivia wrinkled her nose in disgust. 'Herbie's not the sort you'd make conversation about. Joe hated him, and Mrs Keiver told me how horrible he was too. He ambushed me in the street to find out if Joe had left him anything in his will.'

'His house?' Lucas suggested after a pause.

'Herbie'd like to get his hands on it, I'm sure. I told him Joe gave it to me. And I made it clear I didn't want him visiting me. He's always hanging about, but he's not spoken to me again about the house.'

'What was Tommy doing in Muswell Hill on the night he was attacked?'

Olivia slowly shook her head and sighed. 'I don't know. The constable said they'd checked all the local pubs. None of the landlords remembered my dad being in that night. That was unusual for him. He drank every night.'

'Perhaps he was changing his ways.'

'Perhaps. It certainly wasn't like Dad to just go out for a walk.' She shrugged. 'But then, as I said, he wasn't the man I knew anymore.'

'He was found almost midway between your home and his. Perhaps he was on his way to visit you.'

'He never visited.' Olivia sounded sad. 'I only saw him when I bumped into him at work. Even then he never spoke to me unless I spoke first.' She felt her throat aching with emotion but struggled on. 'From the day I moved out he turned his back on me and I really wish it hadn't been like that.'

Lucas took her hand, brushing his thumb against her palm. Olivia curled her fingers about his quite naturally.

'He was too proud and stubborn to back down. Or admit he was wrong, or apologise.' She sniffed back tears. She'd thought she was slowly coming to terms with her father's death but talking about him had resurrected the raw grief she'd felt when Deborah Wallis had broken the news. 'Dad didn't seem interested in any of us kids anymore.'

'Maybe that was just how it seemed.' Lucas circled his thumb on her palm in a caress. 'I'd bet that Tommy Bone thought about you, and cared about you, more than you knew. Most men would die for their children.' He paused, steering one-handed round a corner. When they were on the straight again he continued, 'I've emptied the pockets of more fallen men than I want to count. The photographs are always kept in the breast pocket, close to the heart. Most are of wives with small children surrounding their feet ... five or six sometimes, with a woman who looks no older than you. And the boy I've to bury is often a similar age. And I ask myself, why would they leave them when they don't have to? Family men aren't expected to volunteer. They still have a choice. Or so I, in my ignorance, think. But those young fathers ... they don't see it that way. They're like lions engaging rivals away from their lairs, so that their mate and her young ... their young ... will survive. And they make me feel ashamed.'

'Why?' Olivia had listened to him speak with her eyes half-closed but she now swung in her seat to face him. 'You're as brave as them. You volunteered and you've fought alongside those men, risking your own life countless times.' She put her hand on his arm. 'Don't feel guilty because you survived and they didn't,' she said firmly.

'It's not that. I didn't volunteer for noble reasons. I wanted to put distance between us because I was driving myself mad wanting you.' He pulled up abruptly outside her house. 'What are you going to do?' he abruptly changed the subject.

'About what?' Olivia had been startled by the passion in his tone just then. Earlier that day he'd not denied still seeing his girlfriend. Yet Olivia had felt sure he'd been on the point of kissing her a moment ago.

'You're thinking of volunteering in some capacity, aren't you?'

'I am ... yes.'

'Serve on the Home Front then. I don't want you to go to France with Hilda.'

'You said to her they're crying out for help over there,' Olivia replied, bristling at his authoritative tone. 'Anyway, I'm too young for France.'

'Hilda seems a good woman but I don't care about her in the same way that I care about you. You may not be old enough, but I know you're not easily put off once you set your mind to something. Stay safe at home.'

'I expect my dad thought he was safe at home,' she pointed out. Again she was conscious of his eyes travelling over her face in a way that felt like a caress.

'You're needed here, by your family, Olivia,' Lucas said. 'Your dad ... well, that was just something unforeseen by all of us. But you and the kids will be fine, I promise.'

'You can't protect us against the Zeppelins,' Olivia reasoned. 'I do appreciate you worrying about us. But I'm determined to help even though I'm not sure what use I can be. I'll need to speak to the kids before I make any decision. I couldn't just up and leave them.'

'You don't know what you're letting yourself in for. I couldn't bear it if anything happened to you, you know.' Lucas closed his eyes, wiping a hand over his face.

'I don't think I could bear it if anything happened to you,' Olivia returned solemnly. 'Not after Dad and Joe and Freddie.'

'I'm tough as old boots, no need to worry about me.'

'Coming in for a cuppa?' Olivia made an effort to sound cheery. She wanted them to part in good spirits. 'Can't offer you a proper nightcap 'cos I haven't got any alcohol in. We could have a quick one in the Duke if you like.'

'Thought you had sewing to do,' he reminded her.

'I do ... but I don't mind burning a bit of midnight oil for your sake.'

'I'm journeying back to Dover tomorrow on the night train.' Lucas stroked her cheek with his knuckles on hearing her instinctive gasp of disappointment. 'I'd love to stay longer but I have to make a move now. Got things to do. Write to me, please?'

'Wish you'd another day at home. Of course I'll write.' Olivia gazed at him ... waiting. He'd never kissed her properly on the lips. Just pecks on the cheek. And she realised she wanted a kiss from him. Again she felt sure that he wanted to pull her into his arms but was controlling himself. Her eyes locked with his in the gloom, making her very aware of his masculine beauty. Hilda was right, he was a dreamboat, and Olivia supposed she was no different from any other woman in fancying him rotten. She knew Joe wouldn't mind if they kissed. In his last precious letter ... the one Lucas had brought her with the keepsakes from Joe's pockets ... her dear, brave fiancé had written that he knew Lucas still wanted her and that she should marry him.

Joe had misread her boss's intentions towards her. But Lucas did desire her and it had been a long time since she'd

239

felt a man's lips move on hers. She hadn't realised she'd been staring hungrily at him until she heard his challenging, 'Go on then.'

Olivia planted her lips on a mouth that was hard and cool and unlike the memory she had of Joe's. She was about to draw back when Lucas's hand slid to the back of her head, keeping her still while he returned her kiss with relentless sensuality. Feeling startled, Olivia made to draw back but he wouldn't allow her to. His mouth became sweetly seductive as though he was aware of what she needed and was prepared to deny himself to give it to her. Olivia melted against him. Even had she wanted to resist further she wasn't sure she'd have been able to.

'I've waited a long time for that, Olivia.' Lucas's voice sounded wry as he eventually held her away from him.

'I hope it was worth it,' she teased, hoping to disperse the electricity in the air. Something sweet between them had just been shattered and she wasn't sure if she regretted what she'd done. A flirtation wasn't what either of them needed. She felt guilty too because he pointedly hadn't denied still seeing his girlfriend when she'd asked him earlier.

He was spoken for and she'd just crossed a barrier she shouldn't have. She disliked women like her cousin Ruby who went after other girls' men.

'It'll do for now,' he said sardonically. 'Go on, Livvie, off you go . . . can't do goodbyes, especially not now.'

'Joe said that about goodbyes, the very last time I saw him. Wish you hadn't said that, Lucas.' Olivia felt a pang of uneasiness.

He turned back to her, pulling her across the seat and cupping her face between his hands. 'I'm not superstitious, and don't believe in jinxes. Neither do you need to. There's always another explanation. Say goodbye to Alfie and your sisters for me. I'll be back, soon as I can get leave.' He swept his lips over her temple, returning to do it again and again. 'There are things I want to say to you ... but not right now in the middle of this damn' war. There's no point in making promises or plans just yet.'

He abruptly got out of the car and came round to open the door for her. Olivia threw her arms about his waist, giving him a farewell hug. 'I'll write to you. Promise to take good care of yourself, Lucas.'

Quite roughly, he disengaged himself and got back in the Austin then drove off with the briefest of waves.

Once round the corner Lucas gave vent to his frustration and punched the steering wheel. He too regretted that kiss. He'd tasted her now and she'd been sweeter than nectar. But she'd be in his head, worse than ever, driving him mad with longing, even though he still had Caroline to turn to.

Chapter Twenty-One

Herbie hadn't made any friends in Wood Green. But he'd made enemies. The person who hated him most was the woman he lodged with.

They were sitting in the parlour to either side of the unlit fire, avoiding one another's eyes. Herbie knew Sybil was brooding on the fat lip he'd given her earlier. She'd noticed that the silver frame had gone missing from the drawer and had let rip. He'd quietened her down with his fist when she'd tried again to evict him. He was going nowhere other than to the pub. And if she locked him out as she had before she'd get another smack for good measure.

For her part Sybil was biding her time, waiting for him to make a move. As soon as he went out . . . so was she. She was following Mickey to Islington. She knew her son had gone to Ruby's. He'd threatened to move in with his sister before when she and Herbie had been going at it hammer and tongs. And Sybil was never coming back. He could have the house for as long as he could find the rent on it. The only consolation she had was knowing soon he'd be out on his ear. The Jewish landlord was hard as nails. He'd send his heavies round to evict Herbie as soon as the rent was short.

Sybil was seething at losing the home she'd shared with Tommy. With hindsight she realised she'd had the life of Riley when he'd been alive, and she hoped the scumbag who'd murdered him would rot in hell. She'd rented out a room to make things easier for herself, not harder. Since he'd moved in Herbie had given her just five bob for rent and now had her taking in washing to keep a roof over their heads. She flexed her red-raw fingers on her lap. She'd sooner that, though, than he'd acted on the hints he'd dropped about finding her *other* work, as he had Maisie. Everybody knew his late wife had been an old brass almost up to the time she'd passed away.

Sybil couldn't believe she'd been idiotic enough to let Hunter through the door. She'd heard reports of what he was like. How he'd treated his family. Nobody had a good word for him. But his promises of housekeeping cash, and doing odd jobs for her, had been too tempting for her to turn down. Then there was the gin he'd bought her. At first. Now she was lucky if he treated her to a brown ale once a week.

Herbie was done with sitting in silence with the sullen cow. He yanked his coat off the peg on the wall and grunted that he was going out. If he heard the snarled 'Good riddance' that followed him, he didn't show it. He moseyed off down the street, brooding on what had happened with Alfie earlier. He felt uneasy about Olivia Bone having that army officer as a friend. Herbie reckoned the man was the influential sort and could spell trouble. Livvie Bone was too sharp and outspoken for her own good. Herbie remembered the way she'd tackled him outside Joe's house that first day they'd met. She wasn't going to be easily put in her place, with or without her posh army pal backing her up. She was the sort of girl who might never rest easy until she got to the bottom of her father's death. The boy might believe in gremlins being to blame, but she didn't seem so fanciful.

At a quarter to eleven Herbie emerged from the pub to wander home. He'd spent so long finishing his last pint that he'd been the only customer left and the landlord had turfed him out. He didn't fancy going back yet even though he knew Sybil would have turned in and he wouldn't have to look at her ugly mug. He passed the house without noticing that, unusually, it was in complete darkness. Even when she went to bed Sybil left a candle burning in case she got up in the night to use the po. Herbie carried on mooching along, hoping to tire himself out with the exercise and the flask of whisky he had tucked inside his jacket. He took a swig, wondering if Olivia Bone was going to prove to be too much of a problem, and would need dealing with. Pondering on killing somebody no longer made his guts squirm. He supposed that was because he'd grown used to it ... and good at it, leaving no trail. Alfie believed the cigarette case to be the root of all evil, so if an accident happened to his big sister, the boy would know where to lay the blame.

Herbie smirked then started to whistle in short bursts as he hunched into his coat. It was a cool September night so he took the whisky out again to warm himself up. By the time he'd reached Tottenham the flask was empty. He sniffed the air. Up ahead he could smell the Carbuncle Ditch. He knew he'd walked further than he'd intended so slowed his pace. It was time to turn around and head for home. Had Herbie not been so deep in thought he might have noticed that a vehicle had been tailing him for some time, at a distance.

Like an animal sensing danger his head snapped up as a car door clicked shut.

'What you after, squire?' Herbie had hesitantly crossed the road, uneasiness loosening his guts. The single gas lamp was yards away and gave scant light. But Herbie recognised him just from his height and breadth and the way he held himself. It seemed weird that the fellow occupying his mind should suddenly materialise in the street silhouetted against the autumn mist.

'Alfie told me you owed him something else. I've come to get it.'

Herbie snorted. 'Don't owe the lyin' little tyke nothin'.'

'You promised to tell him a secret. After he told you one. So let's hear it. Or shall I take a guess at it?' Lucas noticed Herbie's face was twitching nervously. 'I knew Tommy Bone and Freddie Weedon. I knew your son Joe as well. He and Freddie were in my platoon. They were good men.'

'Dare say they were. But ain't got time fer no reminiscing right now.' Herbie made to hurry away but a grip on his arm swung him back, making him stumble into the hedgerow.

'I say you have. Because I've got time to call in at the police station with Tommy Bone's stolen cigarette case and tell a tale about who pawned it in Southend.'

'Dunno what you're on about, guv, or how it ties in with me,' Herbie blustered while with agitated fingers he began rubbing his bristly chin.

'It all ties in with you, Hunter.' Lucas stepped into his path as Herbie tried to get past. 'The only mystery is how a man as brave and decent as Joe sprang from you.'

'You couldn't have known him like you say then, if that's

what you think of him,' Herbie spat. 'He pimped his mother out fer a living, and other whores.'

'You might have made him in your image but he broke free of your taint eventually. And if he was still alive, he'd be here now, not me.'

Herbie shrugged, smiling insolently and tapping his head as though he believed Lucas to be off his rocker. But his other hand was slithering into his pocket to find the hilt of his knife. He'd been too hasty, relaxing and believing the murders had gone unsolved.

'Old times' sake, fer me boy, I'll have a chinwag, if you like, squire. But I ain't stopping here long.'

'Did Tommy Bone find out you'd been pestering his daughter about Joe's house and come after you? Pushing and shoving you, was he? He could be a belligerent, aggravating bastard, I know.'

'You're barking up the wrong tree, mate.' Herbie relaxed. Black was fishing, which meant he didn't have it *all* worked out. Still, he was dangerous and Herbie cursed him for poking his nose in. A bloke like him, from money, wasn't so easily dealt with as the likes of an orphaned factory girl. But if Black simply disappeared somewhere he'd never be found ... Herbie squinted past his opponent to the fetid water he could smell but not see in Carbuncle Ditch.

'I know what you've done, Hunter,' Lucas said with soft menace. 'And I've written it all in a letter, lodged with my solicitor. Now, I'm off to France tomorrow but he's got instructions to take a close and special interest in Olivia and her family in my absence. If anything were to happen to any one of them, then my instructions in that letter will be acted upon, even if I'm killed. D'you understand what

I'm saying? I know you murdered Tommy Bone and Freddie Weedon. And you're going to pay for it.'

Herbie licked his lips. He wished now he hadn't taken so many nips of whisky while walking along. His brain was befuddled and he couldn't think as quickly as he needed to. But the silky steel in his pocket was a great comfort. 'Yeah ... I understand. You're pissing in the wind, son,' he jeered. 'If you had proof of anything you'd've already had me arrested.' He rubbed the bridge of his nose then tipped back his cap on his head. 'Weedon's a suicide ... young Alfie told me so. As for Tommy Bone ... ' He gave an exaggerated shrug. 'Well, I never met him in me life. Ask Livvie, she'll tell yer. Her old man 'n' me, we never even got introdooced. Shame about that 'cos we might have shared grandkids if things had turned out different.'

There was too much truth in the man's bluster for Lucas's liking and it was making his back teeth grind. Herbie was darting furtive glances to and fro and Lucas was certain he was right about him. 'Why d'you kill Freddie? Getting too close, was he? Did he talk to the pawnbroker you sold this to?' Lucas took out the case, flipping it over in his hand before slipping it back inside his breast pocket. For all his insouciance he clenched his fists to prevent them going for Hunter's throat. 'You smeared his name, you evil bastard. Freddie deserved a good long convalescence, but he was prepared to go back to Ypres and fight a stinking war for the likes of you. Now he'll be whispered about and branded as deranged, or a coward.'

'You're breakin' me 'eart,' Herbie scoffed. He knew Black was frustrated by his lack of evidence. It pleased him to think that he'd got one over on a nob. Herbie had bowed and scraped most of his life to this sort. He'd been looked down on and despised by those men who'd fucked his wife and laughed as he'd scrabbled on the floor for the money they flung at him on their way down the stairs.

So he turned the screws. 'You're right ... me son's pal deserved a good long rest and I gave it 'im. After he'd had a swim. There's me, twice his age, but I could outrun him when it counted.' Herbie sounded proud of his confession to being instrumental in Freddie's death.

'Twice his lungs, that's why,' Lucas snarled. 'Brave man, aren't you, picking on an invalid?'

'Tommy Bone were a big bloke ... looked strong and fit. But when it came to it, he weren't no match for me either.' Herbie hadn't liked being reminded he'd beaten a cripple. 'Clever, see.' He tapped his head. 'Not a scratch on me either time.'

Lucas felt a peculiar sense of relief hearing Hunter admit to what he'd done. He'd been driving himself insane, turning things over and over in his mind, wondering if his imagination were running riot. 'The pawnbroker will remember who he got this from.' Lucas tapped his breast pocket. 'So what're you going to do about that? Kill him too? All of my suspicions about you, and what you've done, or might do, are written in the letter lodged with my solicitor. Be bad for you, don't you think, if it all came to pass?' Lucas sensed rather than saw Hunter was rattled and rammed home his advantage. 'It's just a matter of time before you feel that noose tighten around your neck.' He gave his breast pocket another provocative pat before turning towards his car. Lucas knew it wouldn't matter to such an evil bastard if he was strung up for two murders or ten. And he wanted Olivia safe. Nothing else in the world mattered. He wasn't going back to France until he knew she was. Even if that meant going AWOL.

On night patrol in Ypres every sense was heightened. Every sound was assessed for danger; even the breath of a comrade in line behind was felt. And because of it, accidents happened. Lucas had known a jumpy rifleman bayonet his pal in the gut because he'd startled him by getting too close. He swung about, dodging aside as Herbie's blade caught him on the sleeve. They circled one another in silence but for their rasping exhalations.

Herbie lunged and the knife ripped into his opponent's coat, slicing flesh. Lucas held his side, dodging back and out of reach.

'Know what done for 'em both?' Herbie panted as he feinted then scored another hit with the blade, not as deep this time. 'Couldn't mind their own business. Had to poke their noses in. Just like you.' He snorted with triumph as he caught Lucas's shoulder, making his opponent grunt in pain. 'When I'm done with you, I'm going after that Livvie Bone. Time she disappeared. That's my son's house she's sitting in and now he's gone it should be mine. *Mine!* And I'm fucking having it.'

Herbie stumbled as the kick aimed at his knee jolted against bone. He had to finish this. Black was young and athletic and even unarmed and wounded could have his feet from under him. Herbie knew that once he was down, he was finished. Snarling, he ran at Lucas's chest, the blade penetrating clothing then hitting home.

Lucas felt the thud and spontaneously swung his fist before Hunter had time to retreat. Herbie's teeth clacked shut on his tongue, making him yelp. The weapon fell with a clatter to the ground and he spiralled down beside it, semi-conscious.

Lucas heaved in his breath, dragging Herbie upright

and slamming a fist into his face again and again. Once he was sure he'd knocked the man out cold, Lucas hoisted the body up onto his shoulder. He pivoted on the spot, wondering what the hell he was going to do with him. What he did know for sure was that he'd never leave Olivia at Hunter's mercy. The evil swine might think he was bluffing about the letter. Lucas wasn't, but he couldn't afford to take any chances.

In the still silence he became aware of the noxious smell of sewage. He stumbled through some overgrown weeds and peered down into an expanse of oily-looking dark water. Shifting position, he lowered Herbie into it, with barely a splash, watching him sink. Then Lucas collected the knife from the ground and lobbed that in too. He stood there, smoking and using his handkerchief to stem the blood seeping from the wounds on his torso. He could feel gaping flesh and guessed the deepest cuts needed stitches but he'd patch them up himself when he got home. He waited a few more minutes until the silver gleam on the water stopped rocking and he could see the reflection of the moon.

He got in his car and fished for a pack of Player's in his greatcoat breast pocket. His searching fingers encountered the metal cigarette case and he pulled it out, rubbing his thumb over the indentation where Hunter's knife had struck close to his heart.

'Well, Alfie, this might not have done the other fellows any good, but perhaps it's my lucky talisman,' he murmured, then with a slight smile he put the case back in its place and started the car.

Chapter Twenty-Two

Olivia heard an ominous rumble of noise even before she'd rounded the corner into Mayes Road and spotted a crowd surrounding the factory gate. Although she was still some distance away it was evident to her a fight had broken out and instinctively she knew that her cousin would again be behind the trouble. Gripping her skirts in her fists, she sprinted along the pavement. Arriving out of breath, she elbowed a path through the onlookers and reached the front. It seemed Ruby hadn't come off best this time. They were on the ground and Cath was astride her opponent, using a fistful of Ruby's hair to bash her head up and down on the cobbles.

'I had a go at pulling Cath off your cousin, but, bleedin' hell, she's got a paddy on her! She won't let go. You'd better talk some sense into the pair of 'em, Livvie,' Sal gabbled. 'They'll be out on their ears else.'

'Stand and stare, why don't you?' Olivia's sarcasm emerged in a furious hiss and was directed at the few men in the group. They could easily have separated the fighting women if they'd wanted to. But they were relishing the entertainment too much. As were Nelly Smith and her little gang.

Olivia hooked her hands under Cath's armpits and yanked her away so forcefully that they both fell backwards, landing in a heap. Hoots went up at the spectacle of the two young women with their long drill skirts up around their thighs and their drawers on display. Then a whisper went round that had the crowd breaking up and hurrying towards the factory buildings.

'Time your cousin packed up messing about with other women's men, ain't it?' Nelly Smith prodded Olivia's arm. 'Likes of her ain't welcome around decent folk.'

Cath had manoeuvred herself onto her posterior and Nelly bent to pat her on the back before following the others inside.

'What the hell's going on, Cath?' Olivia scrambled to her feet, brushing herself down. 'You after getting yourself sacked?' she stormed. Ruby was in the process of clambering to her knees a few yards away. Her cousin looked to be in worse shape than Cath was. Her blonde hair was a mess of coarse tangles and she had scratches on her cheeks. The way Cath had been hammering Ruby's head against the cobbles, Olivia felt thankful her cousin hadn't been knocked out cold. She glanced up and groaned a warning. Now she knew why everyone had skedaddled. They had spotted Deborah Wallis standing, hands on hips, at her office window. No doubt the secretary had witnessed the whole disgraceful scene.

'Well, we're for it this time,' Olivia announced bleakly, helping Cath up. 'Miss Wallis is on her way.'

'Don't give a toss,' Cath said flatly, watching her rival getting unsteadily to her feet.

Olivia had seen that hate-filled glance and sighed. 'Me cousin's been flirting with Trevor again, I take it.'

'It's more than that,' Cath said forcefully. 'He's broken off our engagement and moved in with her. We're not getting married. It's all finished.'

'What?' Olivia's jaw sagged and she goggled in amazement at her friend.

'They've rented your dad's old house in Ranelagh Road,' Cath said. 'The cow found out it was empty and they've moved in.' She pressed together her trembling lips. 'That bastard has thrown me over for the likes of that slag. He's made me a laughing stock. *And* I stuck by him when he was convalescing and even did that bloody St John Ambulance course to try and help nurse him. Me dad said if Trevor was properly right in the brainbox he'd kill him. But he's just a pathetic specimen.' Cath pursed her lips. 'I feel sorry for *me*, not *him*.'

Olivia was itching to find out more about it all but questions would have to wait. Cath had worked herself into a paddy and looked as though she might launch herself at Ruby again. Olivia slung an arm round her friend's shoulders in the hope of restraining as well as comforting her.

Matilda Keiver had told her that Sybil had moved back in with her daughter, much to Ruby's disgust. It was no surprise to Olivia that her aunt had thrown in the towel on living with Herbie Hunter. Lucas had already told her that they weren't getting along. The only thing up for debate was why Sybil had ever allowed such an unpleasant individual into her home in the first place. Olivia had assumed that Herbie had remained in the house after Sybil left. But perhaps he'd not been able to afford the rent either. She hoped she'd never see him again.

Meanwhile the secretary had emerged from the factory entrance and was sweeping regally towards them.

'Ruby's not worth losing your job over, Cath,' Olivia warned in a whisper as her friend gestured an obscenity at her rival. If Cath wasn't careful there'd be no doubt in Miss Wallis's mind as to who was responsible for this rumpus. Olivia reckoned it wouldn't be right if her scheming, selfish cousin got away with it scot-free.

'Can't believe I've wasted eight years of me life on him, Livvie. We was sweethearts at fifteen, y'know.' Cath set her shoulders and jerked up her chin. 'Well, good riddance, I say.' She smeared away her tears. 'They deserve one another.'

Olivia could only agree. It had always been Cath and Trevor from the moment she'd started at Barratt's. Cath Mason had been her supervisor in packing before Olivia moved to the production line. They'd been friends from the start. Cath had shown her the ropes, sticking by her when some of the others took against her simply for being that troublemaker Tommy Bone's daughter.

If Cath's fiancé hadn't suffered shellshock he might still have been the loyal, loving fellow she had fallen for. But once people had been to war they were changed. Even those men who believed themselves survivors often were not. Like Freddie Weedon who now lay in unconsecrated ground, separated by the churchyard wall from his parents.

'All of you. In my office. Now,' Deborah Wallis ordered crisply. Her eyes flitted over the trio of young women in an encompassing, contemptuous glance.

'I ain't done nothin'!' Ruby protested. 'Go ask the others. That mad cow just come runnin' at me and knocked me over then started bashing me. Ask the others. Go on.'

Deborah turned a stony stare on Cath, elevating pencilled eyebrows.

'It's true.' Cath sounded defiant. 'And before you tell me I'm sacked, I'll tell you that you can take yer job and stick it up yer bony arse!' She stabbed a finger at Ruby. 'The day that bitch started work here was the day I should've left. If the likes of her are welcome then this place ain't good enough for me.'

Olivia watched the secretary's superior expression wilt. If Deborah had been expecting meek humility from her rowdy factory girls then she'd just had a surprise.

With a smirk Ruby headed towards the factory entrance, obviously thinking Cath's confession put her in the clear.

'You can wait.' Olivia bounded forward and dragged Ruby around. 'Don't act the innocent! You might not have started the fight this time but you're the *real* culprit.'

'Well, that's family loyalty, ain't it?' Ruby said nastily. 'And us so *closely* related 'n' all.' She wrestled her arm free, giving Olivia a significant stare.

Olivia knew why Ruby looked so smug. Her cousin was threatening to expose the real relationship between the Bone and Wright kids. But Olivia no longer cared if the truth were revealed. If Ruby had confided in Trevor, a fellow who acted so oddly that he'd ditch his fiancée for this tart, then the secret might already be out in any case.

'Livvie Bone had nothing to do with this,' Cath declared loyally. 'She just pulled me off that slag. Livvie ain't put a foot wrong.'

'I shall decide the rights and wrongs, thank you,' Deborah snapped. 'We'll discuss the rest of this sordid incident inside my office.'

'Can we just have a couple of minutes to talk first?' Olivia needed to persuade her friend to calm down and apologise for being rude or else she'd lose her job before she had the chance to sort out another to go to. With or without a wedding to pay for, Olivia doubted Cath could do without her wages.

'Five minutes only. Then, if this commotion isn't satisfactorily explained, none of you will be welcome back on the premises.'

''Bye then,' Cath jeered at the secretary's ramrod-straight back.

Olivia saw the woman stiffen but she carried on towards the factory entrance, her neat buttoned boots clacking on the cobbles.

'Bitch,' Cath said, scrubbing at her face with her hanky. She sniffed and gave Olivia a teary smile. 'Go on. You get inside or you'll lose your job.'

'So will you.'

'I don't care. I don't want the poxy job. I'm finished with Barratt's.'

'So am I,' Olivia said, and realised she meant it. She'd come to work this morning on the bus, ruminating on giving in her notice to volunteer at the St John Ambulance Headquarters. Well, she'd done dithering over it. If she got turned down to be a VAD then she'd apply at the munitions factory. But she'd need a reference for that and she didn't want Miss Wallis to think it was anything personal. So she would go inside and tell the secretary, politely, what her plans were. She could tell that Cath wasn't going to back down. With a hopeless shrug, Olivia followed her cousin into the building, keeping a distance between them. She felt ashamed of Ruby. She'd ruined Cath's life yet didn't seem to care less. And she'd probably suffer no more than a ticking off. Olivia hoped that Ruby's colleagues in packing cold-shouldered her. She deserved it.

Ten minutes later Olivia had given her two weeks' notice, Cath had been sacked and the pair of them were walking arm-in-arm along Wood Green High Street. Olivia had asked Miss Wallis if she could just do an afternoon shift that day. Surprisingly, the woman had agreed. The secretary had seemed quite flustered by the catfight. Olivia understood why. Cath had flabbergasted Olivia as well by being so rude and reckless. But it was done now, and there was no going back. They were about to turn over new leaves.

'Well, our bridges are well and truly burned,' Olivia announced. 'I'll have to dip into me savings now until I sort out what I'm gonna do next.'

'What're you planning on doing?' Cath frowned. 'I thought you'd decided on getting a job at Maggie's factory.'

'Changed me mind. I'm applying at the St John Ambulance to join the Voluntary Aid Detachment. Freddie's sister's already done it. She's off to France soon, as a VAD nurse.'

'Well, you kept that quiet.' Cath regarded her friend with wide-eyed wonder. 'What happened to poor old Freddie decided that for you, did it?'

'Yes, it did ... amongst other things.' Olivia sighed. 'If it hadn't been for the nurses in France, Freddie said he would never have made it home at all. They make such a difference to all those young soldiers.'

She was also remembering what Lucas had said about the dedication and care the nurses gave to the wounded servicemen. He'd sounded full of admiration for them. Olivia wanted to hear him praise her in such a way. Oh, she was woman enough to feel flattered that he desired her. She was also woman enough to feel piqued that he wouldn't tell her more about the girl who could be her rival. Now that they'd kissed ... properly kissed ... she wanted more answers from him. He knew her well enough to realise she'd never be his bit on the side, so what did he intend to do? Whatever happened between them, Olivia wanted him to be properly proud of her and for a better reason than that she was his pretty factory girl with a heart of gold. She knew it pleased and surprised him that she was capable of rearing her younger siblings, but she wanted more from him than his good opinion on how well she could keep house. She was proud of him for being strong and courageous and she wanted them to be alike, if not in their stations in life then in their characters. If she wasn't his equal in some way, there'd be no real future for them as a couple. And she couldn't bear to contemplate that now she knew she was falling in love again.

'Want any company when you go for an interview at the St John?' Cath burst out.

'You want to volunteer as well?' Olivia sounded surprised.

'Why not? No reason to stop around here, have I?' She laughed bitterly. 'In fact, the further away I am from this place, the better I'll like it.'

'You're twenty-three – old enough to go overseas, if you want. It's what I want. And as we're the same age ... ' Olivia gave her friend a wink.

Cath winked back. 'You've been thinking this through, haven't you?'

'I have. And now I'm straight in my mind about things, I want to get started.' Olivia gave a firm nod. 'How about you, Cath? What if Trevor realises he's acted like a blasted idiot?'

Her friend shook her head. 'I love him but it ain't enough

if I can't trust him. I thought at first I should be loyal and stick by him.' She sighed. 'After the abortion, I wouldn't risk getting knocked up again. I told him I wasn't going all the way.' She tapped her head. 'I thought his problem up here might have affected him down there.' She smiled wryly. 'It had, but not the way I hoped! He was always trying to get into me drawers but I wouldn't let him. I know what he sees in your cousin. Ruby Wright wouldn't keep him … or any man … out of *her* drawers.' Cath's face was mournful when she added, 'Anyhow, we could have gone our separate ways without him making a complete fool of me with that slag.'

Olivia hugged her friend to comfort her. 'Well, so long as you're really sure you want to turn your back on it all.'

'I do. So what's next in the way of volunteering?' Cath asked brightly.

'Now *that* I'm not sure about. But I know somebody who might be able to give us some tips. Fancy a trip to Walthamstow?'

*

Olivia hadn't seen Hilda since Freddie's funeral. It had been a glum, overcast day in keeping with the mood of the occasion. Olivia had been sad and disappointed to see how few people had turned up. Brick that she was, Hilda had remained composed throughout and had spoken proudly about her brother at the shortened service, only weeping later at the graveside beyond the wall when throwing flowers onto the coffin. Olivia had become tearful then too. Although she'd not known Freddie for long, she had come to like him very much.

Hilda whooped with delight on opening the door to her

unexpected visitors. 'You've come to wish me well on my travels, have you?'

'Looks like we're just in time too. When are you off?' Olivia had noticed the packing cases in the hall.

'First thing in the morning. From Charing Cross Station with a contingent of other VADs.' Hilda shook her head in wonderment. 'It's really happening at last. I can't wait for the adventure to start.'

Olivia felt inspired by such excitement. But she needed to keep a cool head if she was to find out all she needed to know. 'We've decided to pitch in as volunteers as well. Oh, this is me friend Cath Mason.' Cath shyly nodded her head to Hilda. 'We've packed in our jobs and are prepared to do whatever's needed to help out. We've both got our first aid certificates. Would you point us in the right direction, Hilda?'

'I'll do my best.' She led them through into the sitting room. 'You'll probably be considered for general service without more in the way of medical training. The regular nurses aren't welcoming even to outsiders like me who've a bit more to recommend them for the job.' She chuckled. 'I'm just a "Kitchener" nurse, viewed as not quite the thing by those who believe *they* are. But Kitchener's army is making a fist of it, and I reckon his volunteer nurses can prove their worth too.'

'We're factory girls. We're used to holding our own,' Olivia said, with a hint of defiance that drew a giggle from Hilda.

'I know you'd take no nonsense off anybody. And quite right too.' She smiled at them both. 'Fancy a cuppa?'

'We won't stop, thanks. Can see you're up to your ears and I've only got the morning free. Got to clock on this afternoon.'

'I'll come with you and introduce you to Miss Deakin, if you like,' Hilda offered. 'I can't promise anything other than it'll cost you to join but Miss Deakin's a down-to-earth type who'll give you a fair hearing. She can't be that fussy if she took me on! Actually, she asked me then if I knew of any single friends who'd be interested in signing up.' Hilda explained, 'She's very competitive. Her opposite number in the Red Cross had attracted more volunteers than the St John lot. She was determined to up her quota.'

'Are you sure you've got time today for a trip to town with us?' Olivia looked at the open packing cases. 'You look awfully busy.'

"Course I've got time!' Hilda patted Olivia's arm. 'You found time to support me through Freddie's funeral, didn't you?' She frowned then, as though something had occurred to her. 'When I said it'll cost you, I didn't mean just your jobs. You do know you'll be expected to kit yourself out with everything you'll need as a volunteer in a camp hospital?'

'Everything?' Cath echoed in alarm. 'What sort of kit? Expensive, is it?'

'Well, I've got myself a camp bed and camp chair. A ground sheet and sleeping bag. Bowls and a lantern. It's very important to have a lantern. Then clothes, of course, to suit the winter.' Hilda carried on with her catalogue of requirements. 'Can't do without a mackintosh and wellingtons. Warm stockings and walking shoes and so on. Miss Deakin'll give you a useful list.'

'That's me out then,' Cath said flatly.

Hilda gave a rueful smile. 'That's why a lot of VADs are well-to-do young ladies.' She pointed her nose towards the ceiling. '*That* sort have an allowance from Daddy to dip into.'

'That's a blow,' Olivia said. 'I've not got enough put by for the outlay.'

'I'd've had some savings, too,' said Cath, sounding frustrated, 'if I'd not spent 'em paying out for the bloody wedding. Doubt I'll get the deposits back now.'

'Cath's just broken up with her fiancé,' Olivia explained, discreetly rolling her eyes to dissuade Hilda from voicing any curiosity. 'There's got to be a way we can be of use, though.' She wasn't ready to give up yet. She was trying to work out how far her modest kitty would stretch.

'I borrowed money from the bank when I knew I was giving up my job,' Hilda volunteered. 'They took the deeds to this place as security. The house passed to me and Freddie when Mum and Dad died.' She pulled a face. 'Now it's just mine. I know Freddie would approve of what I've done.'

Olivia blinked, digesting that. 'The bank loaned you money because you own a house?' A wondrous look of joy spread across her lovely face. She elbowed Cath in the ribs. 'Buck up. All might not yet be lost. I might have a way to raise some money so we can get the stuff we need.'

"S'long as it's not by joining your cousin's part-time profession, then I'm game,' Cath returned drolly.

'Daft cow!' Olivia chided. She adopted a haughty pose. 'Let's go with Hilda and see if we can persuade Miss Deakin what a jolly fine addition to her team we'd make.'

*

The St John Ambulance Headquarters was a hive of activity with army personnel and civilians constantly toing and froing. The sound of typewriters being pounded issued from several offices as the girls passed along a dingy brown-painted corridor.

Once Olivia and Cath had been introduced to Miss Deakin, Hilda excused herself. She explained she needed to go and finish her packing and get a good night's rest before turning up at Charing Cross Station at the crack of dawn next day.

'Well, you look like a couple of healthy gels,' the middle-aged woman who'd greeted them announced, wagging a finger at two chairs to indicate they should sit down. 'How old are you, Miss Mason, and what can you offer me in the way of skills?'

'Twenty-three and a first aid certificate,' Cath promptly replied.

'And you, Miss Bone?'

'Twenty-three,' Olivia lied, sitting forward on the hard chair. 'And I've a first aid certificate too. I've worked in a pie and mash shop so I know me way around a kitchen. I've done me family's laundry since I was ten years old, so I know me way around a copper and mangle as well.'

Miss Deakin sat back in her chair. 'Quite an all-rounder then ... for someone of your tender years.'

She raised an eyebrow as she studied Olivia. In her opinion, young working-class girls were better suited to the rigours of voluntary work than the posh types. The upper classes might be willing to help and have the money to support themselves and buy fancy kit, but most had never done anything arduous in their lives.

Olivia blushed, knowing the woman was dubious about her claim to be twenty-three.

'And what family ties have you?'

'I'm single,' Cath said with emphasis. 'Living with me

263

mum and dad. They're fit enough to do without me though.'

'I'm single,' Olivia confirmed. 'My brother and two sisters live with me but the girls are out working. Maggie's fifteen and will be head of the household till I come home.'

'You believe she'll cope?' Miss Deakin asked, tapping her pen on the desk.

'She'll have to,' Olivia returned.

'I'm all for young people being stood on their own two feet.' Miss Deakin discarded her pen on the blotter. 'Doesn't do to mollycoddle 'em or you make a rod for your own back. Right, let's get you some forms to fill in.'

Chapter Twenty-Three

'You're really going to leave us on our own?' Nancy exploded angrily.

Olivia had been late getting in. Feeling peckish, her youngest sister had started making some sandwiches for the family's tea. A knife loaded with jam hovered mid-air while she clutched it, listening with increasing incredulity to her big sister's news. Now she threw it down in a temper and stalked off.

'If I get accepted as a VAD, as I very much hope I do, then of course I will be leaving home.' Olivia knew she sounded callous but was determined not to be swayed by any tears or tantrums.

She'd understood the sense and the truth in Miss Deakin's warning about mollycoddling young people. Olivia loved her siblings and wanted them to be happy. But she'd already taken too much responsibility for their well-being and it had backfired on her. If Maggie hadn't always taken for granted that her big sister would be there to sort out her problems, she might not have slid into bad ways in the first place. From Nancy's reaction it seemed she was also reluctant to embrace maturity; yet she enjoyed acting like a grown up with her work pals on nights out. As for Alfie, the soft spot Olivia had for him needed to harden. He regularly came in with scraped knuckles, having been in a punch up, with no proper excuse other than 'they started it'. He was learning to stick up for himself.

'What's a VAD anyway? And what are you going to be doing exactly?' Nancy demanded, ramming her hip against the kitchen table.

'VAD stands for Voluntary Aid Detachment. People can volunteer at St John Ambulance or the Red Cross. Haven't you seen Kitchener's recruitment posters? We must all help our boys over at the Front in any way we can.' Olivia took the hissing kettle off the hob and filled the teapot that Nancy had abandoned. 'I'm not really sure yet what I'll be asked to do. It'll be something menial, I expect. Cooking, cleaning, laundry ... along those lines. I expect there's a ton of dirty linen to be got through every day in the hospitals. Sheets and bandages and medical gowns and so on.' She paused, stirring the brew before settling the cosy over the brown china pot. 'Miss Deakin who interviewed me said some of the nursing sisters have to do the washing themselves when they're short-staffed. That's not right. The nurses should concentrate on saving patients' lives.'

'Will you have a rifle?' Alfie piped up while Maggie and Nancy brooded on their eldest sister's shocking announcement that she really was going off to work as a skivvy for no pay. And, worse, was leaving them to fend for themselves.

'I doubt it!' Olivia said with a grin. 'I don't think laundresses are issued with guns.'

'You might get given 'em to clean though,' Alfie said with some logic.

He'd surprised Olivia by appearing the least affected by her news.

Maggie had so far not commented. She'd been trying to make up her mind if she was pleased or angry about taking over from Livvie as head of the household. She couldn't quite believe that their positions were about to be reversed. Maggie had always envied her elder sister for being luckier with her looks and brains and everything else besides. But Livvie was giving up a good job in a factory to go to a foreign land and be up to her armpits in dirty bandages. Maggie didn't envy her one bit now. In fact, she thought her sister was nuts. Maggie had left her laundress days behind her and had no intention of ever going back. 'So ... I'll be in charge while you're gone,' she said finally.

'You and Nancy can do things between you. You're all growing up now. It'll do you good to be independent.' Olivia gave them a reassuring smile. 'I won't be going straight away. There's a lot to be sorted out yet so you've got time to get used to the idea of me not being around. You can start by sharing out the chores.'

She could see that she'd knocked them for six. But there were other people now who needed her more than these three did. Nancy and Maggie earned fair wages and Alfie had his errand money to buy himself a few treats. They lived rent-free in a comfy house. By pooling money, and being economical, they had the means to keep themselves warm and well fed through the coming winter months. And if they messed up and got cold and hungry, they'd know to spend the kitty more wisely in future. They were luckier than most and definitely more fortunate than those boys – some no older than Maggie – who were existing on army rations, or hospital food, wondering if they'd ever see home again.

Olivia had not come straight home after finishing her afternoon shift. She had dashed along the High Street and into Barclay's to see the manager before the bank closed for the day. With his help she'd opened her first bank account. Previously her money had always either been kept in her pocket or in a savings jar. To her surprise he'd seemed neither disapproving nor very surprised when she'd told him what she intended to do. In fact, she'd noted a glint of respect in his kind old eyes and had blossomed beneath it. He'd said he'd write to the solicitor who'd dealt with Joe's will. Then once all was in order the bank would forward her seventy pounds as a mortgage loan ... and perhaps more later, if she needed it. Olivia had shaken his hand then breezed out of the bank in a dream. It had all sounded too easy when Hilda had told her how she'd got a loan. But as Olivia walked home it had sunk in just what it meant to be a woman of property.

Joe's bittersweet legacy to her had bestowed on her riches and privileges that her parents could only have dreamed of, paying rent and scraping by all their lives as they had. The reality of the security and freedom Joe had given her made her more determined than ever to visit his resting place and thank him. Many months ago, when bringing the news of her fiancé's death, Lucas had promised her that he would one day show her where he had buried Joe. God forbid anything happened to Lucas or she might never know where that churchyard in Flanders was.

'I will do my best to look after those two and the house.' Maggie broke the quiet in the parlour. First Alfie then Nancy had left the room, leaving their elder sisters alone. 'But I'm not sure I feel *that* grown up, you know, Livvie,' she confessed.

Olivia gave her a spontaneous hug. Maggie looked almost to be on the verge of tears. 'I don't suppose Ricky Wicks felt that grown up when he went along to enlist and lied about his age either,' Olivia told her, and remembered that she herself had lied about being twenty-three that very afternoon for the same reason: to be braver than she felt. But she'd make good on her boasts, just as Ricky would, and all the others who'd left behind everything familiar to sail into the unknown and do their patriotic duty.

'You know I'm not that much of a cook, and who'll do the mending? I can't sew in a straight line.'

'Neither could I, at first. But you'll learn, and teach Nancy and Alfie as you go.' Olivia grabbed Maggie's hands, holding them up before her. 'You've got six hands between you. Don't let those two idle around. It's only human to be a bit scared when you don't know what's round the corner. I'm petrified of even setting foot on the boat, let alone getting off at the other side.'

'You'll be all right, Livvie,' Maggie said simply. 'You always are.'

'Aunt Sybil's turned up.' Nancy had just poked her head round the parlour door to announce their visitor. 'She's got a face on her,' she warned in a hiss.

'What the bloody hell does she want?' Olivia muttered, but obviously not quietly enough.

'I'll tell you what I want,' said Sybil, barging in. 'I want to know where me daughter's got to. Being as you work with her, I thought you should know. I went over to Barratt's earlier to catch her after work but there's no sign of her and the rent's overdue. Ruby ain't been home in days.'

Olivia nibbled her lip, wondering whether to grass her cousin up. She'd guessed Ruby had no intention of living with her mum for long. Now it seemed her cousin had set up house with Trevor on the sly. The last place Sybil would think of looking for her daughter was the house she herself had just scarpered from. Unless she already knew Herbie had gone missing and left the place vacant.

'Well, you going to answer me?' Sybil barked.

Was she? Olivia wondered. She owed neither her aunt nor her cousin loyalty. They'd certainly never shown her family any. 'Why don't you ask Riley where she is?' In the end, Olivia's conscience wouldn't let her drop Ruby in it. She covered up the fact that she already knew Ruby had another man.

'Done that!' Sybil scoffed. 'He's not seen her either, and says he don't want to. She's been cheating on him.' Their aunt snorted. 'Ain't sure why that surprised him. She don't hide what she is.' She fidgeted restlessly. Her daughter might be a part-time tart but usually Sybil never so much as hinted that she knew as much. 'Now Riley's moved out too, I'm short by a lot,' she hastened on. 'Got Matilda Keiver on me ear for her guv'nor's rent.' She gave Olivia a sly look. "Course, you're pally with her. You could put in a word for your auntie, couldn't yer, Livvie?'

'Matilda won't listen to me where money's concerned,' Olivia cut across her.

'Well, if you could help me out with a quid, I'd be grateful, dear. I know yer dad would want you to. Tommy'd be breaking his heart if he knew the state he'd left me in.'

'Sorry ... I'm short meself,' Olivia replied briskly. It was Ruby's place to look after Sybil, not hers. Although she felt sorry for Mickey, she knew if she went down that route her aunt would never stop scrounging. Then, when Olivia had gone overseas, the woman would be pestering her sisters to pay her rent. 'Matilda always knows of people wanting chars, you know,' Olivia said pointedly. 'You could enquire about a job.'

'Yeah . . . and when I need your advice, I'll ask for it,' Sybil snarled and stomped out.

'Good riddance,' Olivia breathed as the door slammed after her aunt's departing figure. She glanced at Maggie who'd kept quiet during this visit. 'If she comes back begging, tell her no.'

'I ain't lendin' her a single penny.' Maggie sounded adamant. 'Nor am I givin' up me savings to keep this place going. So Nancy and Mickey had better stick to the rules.'

Already Maggie sounded more sensible and that heartened Olivia. 'Right then. Let's finish those sandwiches and get the tea poured before it stews.' She went to the parlour door to call up the stairs: 'Nancy! Alfie! If you want to eat you'd better come down and lend a hand otherwise you'll go hungry.'

'From today it'll be your job to share out chores, Maggie,' she told her sister. 'You can start by telling Alfie the parlour grate needs sweeping out.' Olivia did up the buttons on her cardigan. 'Reckon we'll need that fire lit later too. It's turning cold in the evenings now.'

*

'Come and dance, Livvie.' Maggie grabbed hold of her sister's elbow, tugging her towards a gap between the heaving bodies.

'I can't!' Olivia groaned, freeing her arm. 'Me feet are killing me.' She'd only just finished doing the Lambeth Walk, jigging about in Matilda's front room, when Maggie urged her to start again. Jack had struck up a new tune on the piano and Matilda and her sister Fran were doing their own version of the can-can while shrieking with laughter.

271

Over in the corner Cath Mason was sipping sherry and looking happier than Olivia had seen her in a while.

Matilda caught her eye and called, 'Come on, Livvie! This is your party, y'know. Shake a leg, gel.'

'Make the most of it, luv,' Fran added her encouragement to Matilda's. 'You won't be doing no knees-ups around them hospital beds.'

'Dunno so much,' Jack called with a wink. 'Cheer them poor bleeders up no end that would. Put 'em back on their feet quicker than a dose o' salts, seein' our Livvie dancin' ragtime.'

'Pack it in. You're making her blush,' Matilda reprimanded.

'I'd pay good money to see Livvie dancing round my bed.' Jimmy Wild gave a dirty grin that terminated in him licking his lips.

Matilda glared at him. As did his wife.

'Gonna get a breath of air.' Olivia had noticed that Fran and her husband had started bickering. She didn't want to be the cause of any row between the couple. Before Joe had gone off to fight he'd warned her about Jimmy Wild. He was a known lecher and had a fancy woman as well as a wife.

When she got downstairs Olivia noticed the bonfire was still alight. It wasn't Guy Fawkes Night for two months but they had set off fireworks and roasted chestnuts around the blaze. It had seemed as though every one of Matilda's neighbours had put in an appearance at the party she'd arranged in Olivia's honour. Matilda had told her she couldn't leave without a good send off. The Keivers needed little excuse for a shindig. Nevertheless Olivia was grateful to them for the gesture. She leaned against the iron railings fronting the house and gazed at the stars, knowing that in a short while she'd be watching the night sky from a foreign land. But that no longer worried or even excited her. She felt accepting of whatever might lie ahead.

'We're off now, Livvie.' Cath had come out to say good-bye while her future husband hung back a bit in the dingy hallway of the tenement, letting the girls say their private farewells.

Olivia gave her friend's hands a squeeze.

'You're not angry with me, are you?' Cath asked timidly.

"Course I'm not!' Olivia hugged her. 'I'm pleased ... about everything. And you take care of yourself and Trevor, and this little one too.' She smoothed a discreet palm over her friend's flat belly. Cath had just found out she was pregnant again.

'Couldn't go through another abortion.' Cath swallowed a sob. 'Just couldn't. And I never was as sure as you about going abroad, what with the cost of it. I know you said you'd stump up for my kit, but I didn't want you to, Livvie.'

'I know. You've done the right thing.'

Cath gave a weak smile, urging her friend to walk up the road with her a little way. 'I've made a mess of things, Livvie. Don't really know what to do,' she whispered.

"Course you do! Trevor's come to his senses and you're getting married.' She cupped Cath's face in her hands. 'If you think I reckon you're a fool taking him back, then you're wrong. I don't!'

'Perhaps he's the fool, for wanting me back,' Cath said and darted a look back at her fiancé. 'Ain't his baby, Livvie,' she confessed, then bit her lip. 'I slept with another man. I'd had a few drinks and thought: what was good for the gander, was good for the goose. It was only the once. But I got meself knocked up again.'

'Who was it?' Olivia finally asked, having found her voice.

'Friend of Trevor's from the railway yard come round and

273

said he was sorry to hear about Trevor throwing me over. I knew he liked me. Always giving me the eye, he was. But he's married himself. Anyway Mum and Dad were out and we had a few drinks and one thing led to another . . . '

'Will he tell Trevor?' Olivia asked.

Cath shook her head. 'He won't want his wife finding out what we did. Ain't seen nothing of him since.'

'Trevor thinks it's his baby, though?' Olivia slid a glance past Cath to the man in hospital blues, leaning against the splintered doorjamb, smoking a cigarette.

Cath nodded. 'Soon as I was late, I knew. Regular as clockwork, me. I just went round Trevor's and told him I'd done me thinking and would marry him if he still wanted me. We stayed in a hotel together that night . . . celebrating our engagement being on again.' Cath spun the small diamond on her finger. 'Crafty cow I am, see. Then, when I told him I was pregnant, he was over the moon.' She rubbed her forehead. 'What a way to start off being husband and wife . . . with such a lie.'

'You're doing the right thing for the baby.'

'Dunno what's got into me or him. Never thought either of us would behave so deceitful.'

'The world's gone mad, Cath.' Olivia remembered Lucas saying that on the day he'd brought her Joe's things. He'd told her about boys who should still have been in school, fighting in the trenches. 'Perhaps it's not surprising we're all acting a bit crazy. If anybody had told me even a year ago that I'd be off to France to work as a ward maid in a military hospital, I'd've had hysterics.'

Cath's watery eyes begged for further reassurance from her.

'Listen, what Trevor don't know won't hurt him. He took a risk by cheating on you with Ruby. Now it's your turn. You'll

274

have a family, Cath. I haven't a clue what's ahead of me. So, way I see it, might as well grab your bit of happiness while you can and cross those other bridges when you come to 'em.' Olivia plonked a kiss on the side of her friend's head. 'Don't forget to write to me and send me a wedding snap. And if I'm not back in time, I want a Christening picture sent over an' all.'

'You'd better be back. You're godmother,' Cath choked. 'Take care of yerself, Livvie, won't you?'

'And you.' Olivia hugged her tightly. 'Go on, get off with you, before you make me bawl me eyes out.'

'Right then. Time for home.' Cath beckoned Trevor while wiping away her tears.

Olivia waved to the couple as they set off arm-in-arm in the direction of Seven Sisters Road to catch the bus to Wood Green.

'Everything all right, Livvie?' Matilda had swayed down the stairs and emerged unsteadily from the sour-smelling tenement. 'You don't want to let me brother-in-law bother you. Jimmy's just a useless git.' She waved the beer bottle she held for emphasis.

'I'm fine,' Olivia said, on a sigh. 'Just saying 'bye to me friend. She's getting married in a couple of weeks.' Olivia stood watching the couple turn the corner.

'Gonna miss you when you're gone, Livvie.'

'Miss you too.' Olivia suddenly felt in need of a maternal cuddle and held out her arms.

Matilda gave it to her, rocking her while breathing beery breath against her cheek.

'Come on, out with it. You're having second thoughts, ain't yer? Nobody'd blame you if you changed yer mind. Huge, brave thing you're doing, Livvie. But ain't no shame in staying here after all, to care for your family.'

'I'm just having a wobble. Had too many port and lemons. Talking to Cath didn't help.' Olivia put her finger to her lips to indicate a secret was coming. 'She's up the spout.'

'That Trevor of hers is well on the mend then,' Matilda guffawed. 'Good luck to 'em.'

'And so say all of us ... and so say all of us ...' Livvie chanted, suddenly feeling quite tipsy. 'Wish you and me mum had known one another, Mrs K. She would've liked you.'

'She would've warned you off me and my lot,' Matilda snorted. 'And with good reason. We ain't the sort even *I'd* want me kids to hang around with. But reckon the Bunk's where I'll stay.'

'And me ... when I come home again.'

'Don't reckon you will, love, or not for long anyhow. You're better than this. Always have been. Anyhow, just make sure you keep yer head down over there. I'll get my Alice to write you some letters. I'm no scholar, y'see.'

Olivia was surprised that Matilda couldn't write but said nothing as the other woman looked bashful for having admitted to it.

'Alice gets on well with Geoff Lovat,' said Olivia to change the subject. The young couple were strolling up the road arm-in-arm, also taking a breather. They'd been waltzing about together upstairs earlier.

'Geoff's a good lad. I hope they'll have a future together one day. But right now, I don't reckon it's a good time for making plans.' Matilda upended the bottle into her mouth. 'How's Maggie doing now after all that other business?'

'She seems to have pulled herself round.' Olivia sighed. 'I wish she'd come to me to sort it out instead of her cousin.' She frowned then, remembering what Maggie had said about her big sister being unapproachable ... too critical.

Ruby had more or less said the same thing, with knobs on. 'Do I act above meself, Matilda?'

'We'd all like to be a bit more like you, that's fer sure,' she replied tactfully. 'Some people are leaders, some followers, and them that won't do either ... well, they just resent everybody. So don't go listening to nothin' Ruby Wright's got to say. She's just jealous of you. And Maggie's finding her feet. She's the leader now and I reckon she'll cope with the others by following your example, so no reason she shouldn't be all right. Let's hope Nancy don't come home and give her the sort of fright she gave you. That'll learn her quick as yer like about the drawbacks of bein' the guv'nor.'

Olivia smiled and rolled her eyes at Matilda's homespun philosophy. She always felt better after talking to her. 'It's Alfie worrying me now.' Olivia leaned back against the tenement wall. 'He's always getting into fights.'

'And I know why,' Matilda said, waggling the empty beer bottle then standing it on the doorstep. 'Your brother's been looking out fer his cousin. Mickey gets teased a lot 'cos of his limp. I know Sybil wanted to move away from here to stop him getting bullied. But kids can be mean bleeders wherever you live.'

'Alfie never said he was fighting *Mickey's* corner.' Olivia frowned. There seemed to be a lot her brother kept to himself. Not so long ago he would've told her everything.

'Stickin' up fer family is what we do round here, so I take me hat off to him. Those two lads could be brothers.'

'Who told you about that? The Wrights?' Olivia straightened up sharply. 'I knew one of 'em would blab.'

'Ain't sure what yer on about ... Oh, it's all right, I've just woken up,' Matilda said dryly. 'Nobody's blabbed but this makes it a lot clearer why Sybil hightailed it to Wood Green and your dad took her in.' She cocked her head. "Course, there's a likeness between you and Ruby, too.'

Olivia could have kicked herself. Port had loosened her tongue and she'd jumped the gun. But she trusted Matilda not to spread the story any further. As a particularly raucous rendition of 'Pack up Your Troubles' streamed out of the open first-floor window, Olivia put her hands over her ears and grimaced.

'Coming up fer a nightcap?' Matilda asked.

'Just one more then. After that, I think it's time me and Maggie was on our way home.'

'Talk of the devil,' said Matilda, nodding her head towards a figure further down the street. By the light of the bonfire she had spotted Sybil Wright padding along in their direction.

'Bleedin' racket going on in yours, ain't there?' Sybil sniffed her disapproval, drawing level with the Keivers' house.

'Just people enjoyin' themselves,' Matilda retorted. 'And I'll be round for that rent you owe tomorrow, now you've had yer first pay packet.'

'That tight-fisted so and so you got me in with don't pay on time,' Sybil snapped back. She'd taken a job helping a friend of Matilda's sell washing soda and soap, door to door, off a handcart.

'Matilda's thrown me a leaving party,' Olivia said to defuse things. 'Fancy a drink?'

That made Sybil stop and consider. 'Might do, I suppose. Should drink to me niece's health as you're off soon. Just the one though.'

Olivia hadn't formally invited her aunt to the party in case Ruby turned up as well. She hadn't wanted Cath and Ruby in the same room in case punches were thrown.

According to Sybil, who now knew where her daughter was living, Riley had taken Trevor's place, moving in to the house in Wood Green with his cheating girlfriend. Olivia wondered what Mrs Cook felt about having that pair as next-door neighbours.

'Need a bleedin' shoe horn to get them all in, I reckon,' Matilda muttered as Beattie Evans, swinging a brace of pale ales like skittles, crossed the road and headed up the stairs with Sybil hot on her heels. Matilda loved it really when the place was heaving with people all having a good time.

'Coming up?' she asked over one shoulder when Olivia didn't immediately follow her.

'Yeah ... in a minute,' she replied. She'd come outside in the first place hoping for a quiet moment to herself, but hadn't yet got it. She warmed her hands by the bonfire. Powdery ash was swirling upwards in the light breeze. She closed her eyes against it while wondering what Lucas was doing at this moment and whether he was missing her as she was missing him.

She'd dreamed of him last night, she knew, although she couldn't remember the dream exactly, only the sense that he had figured in it. She longed to see him but hadn't written yet to tell him she was on her way overseas as a VAD. She didn't want to worry him. He'd be cross with her, she knew. He hadn't wanted her to go to the Front but she hoped, if they were lucky enough to meet up there, he'd be as pleased to see her as she'd be to see him. And perhaps, if they found a quiet moment to talk, she'd find out more about how he really felt about her ... about how he felt about his family too. In many ways she'd fallen in love with a stranger, she realised, and that wouldn't do.

Chapter Twenty-Four

'You'd better come quick! Looks like Alfie's broken something.'

'What?' Olivia had been packing her clothes when Maggie whipped into her bedroom, garbled out her message then dashed back downstairs. Olivia dropped into the open trunk the underwear she'd been folding then sped after her sister. Nancy was already in the parlour with Mr Keiver and Alfie. Jack had hold of their brother, keeping him upright. The boy was grimacing in pain.

'You've been fighting!' Olivia burst out, seeing straight away that Alfie sported the beginnings of a black eye. But it was the way he was holding his right foot off the ground that put fear in her heart.

'Ain't broken,' Alfie said quickly. 'Look. Can stand on it.' He put his boot gingerly to the floor. 'Just turned it over on the kerb. Be all right tomorrow, Livvie, honest.'

'Why can't you bloody well behave?' Olivia shouted in frustration. Alfie's accident couldn't have happened at a worse time.

'Bigger lad was pickin' on him,' Jack explained soothingly.

'Alfie was trying to scarper and took a tumble. Could be it is just a sprain.' He renewed his grip on the invalid, helping Alfie to hobble towards an armchair.

Olivia turned to her sisters, watching white-faced. They all knew she was leaving for France tomorrow. From the girls' appalled expressions it was clear they'd no stomach for being landed with nursing an invalid.

'Should've picked on somebody his own size,' Jack said. 'That kid's at least fourteen. I saw him off, anyway. Don't reckon he'll be back for more. I'll be on me way then.' Their neighbour doffed his cap and withdrew from the room with Olivia's heartfelt thanks following him. She'd always liked Jack from the first day she'd met him, when he'd offered to escort her into the Bunk to search for Ruby. It had been Olivia's first introduction to the worst street in North London and she had felt wary of the people and the place. Now she considered Campbell Road her second home.

Her brother regretted causing her trouble at such an important time, Olivia could see that. He was sitting with his hands clasped, head bowed towards them as though unable to meet her eyes.

Olivia curbed her temper. 'What've you got to say for yourself?' she asked him.

'Weren't my fault. He was pushing and shoving us,' Alfie mumbled. 'Mickey tried to have a go back at him fer calling his sister names, but he can't do it. He loses his balance and falls on his arse.'

'I know you mean well, Alfie,' Olivia sighed. 'But Mr Keiver won't always be around to rescue you.'

'Well, I *am* gonna stick up for Mickey ... 'cos he's me brother.' Alfie jumped up, thoughtlessly putting weight on his injured foot and subsiding again with a grimace of pain.

The girls exchanged startled glances that had little to do with Alfie's yelp of pain. When it had first come to light that Tommy Bone had fathered them all, it had been decided to leave the two boys in blissful ignorance of the truth. Though Alfie was probably now ready to know about it, Olivia had not so far plucked up the courage to tackle the subject with him.

'Who said that Mickey's your brother?' she asked calmly.

'The lad that beat me up called Ruby a tart and said their mum was one 'n' all 'cos Mickey's me bastard brother. Aunt Sybil ain't *my* real mum, is she, Livvie?' Mickey sounded distraught at the idea of it.

Olivia sighed and shook her head. So that secret *was* out, no doubt courtesy of Ruby Wright. It hadn't occurred to Olivia when making a list of loose ends to tie up before leaving for France that this important conversation with Alfie should be amongst them. But her brother didn't seem to want to talk about it anymore. He'd gone white as a sheet.

'Ow ... me foot's killing me,' he groaned.

'I knew it'd all go wrong!' Nancy shrilled. 'You're being bloody selfish, Livvie, leaving us to look after him when all he does is get into trouble. Just 'cos I'm the youngest out of me and Maggie, and earn less than her, don't go thinking I'm packin' in me job to keep house. 'Cos I ain't! I like me new job makin' munitions and I'm hanging on to it.'

'Neither am I packin' up work!' Maggie snapped. 'Thanks for clearing off just as we're about to get shown up. Everybody'll laugh at us when they hear Ruby Wright's our bloody sister.' Maggie yanked on Alfie's arm. 'Go on! Clear off up the road to yer stepmother. Now you know all about it, she can look after you.'

'Get off me!' he groaned, wriggling free.

'For pity's sake!' Olivia slapped Maggie's hands off Alfie. 'This is my house and I say he's staying here.'

'It's that bloody cigarette case causing all this trouble,' Maggie sniped. 'There's been nothing but bad luck since we got it. When I've enough saved, I'm finding me own place far away from all of you.'

She slammed out of the room then with Nancy marching after her.

Olivia sat down and sighed. Perhaps the girls were right and she was being too selfish. She'd learned lately that she didn't get everything right and should listen more to what others had to say. Perhaps her posting should have been delayed to give them more time to adjust to doing without her. But would that day ever come? She caught Alfie watching her from beneath his brows. 'Are you still fretting about curses as well?'

He shook his head and quickly averted his eyes.

'Reckon you are. I'll take it with me and throw it overboard, if that'll make you feel better.' Olivia got up and crouched by his chair, holding a palm to his forehead. His skin felt clammy. 'Let's take a look at your leg then.' She touched his swollen ankle gently and carefully eased off his boot. But it didn't seem as though any bones were broken. 'You need to keep your foot up. I'll put a cold compress on it and see how that helps.' She fetched the footstool and propped his grimy heel on it. 'Time you had a bath, y'know.'

When she returned with a bowl of cold water and a cloth he had a little colour back in his cheeks.

'Thanks, Livvie,' Alfie said as she gently bathed his painful, puffy ankle. 'I don't mind you going and helping the wounded soldiers. It's *them* being selfish, not you.' He jerked his head towards the door his two other sisters had left by.

'You'll make a good nurse,' he said sweetly. 'Look . . . better already.' He wriggled his toes to prove it.

'Well, I'm going to do me level best over there,' she said. 'But you really must start to act more sensibly or I'm not sure I'll be able to go at all. Maggie and Nancy have enough on their plates, working to keep this place going. They don't need you adding to their problems and making them worry about jinxes.'

'I'll be good, promise. Anyhow, the curse weren't to blame for me getting hurt. I got rid of it.'

Olivia half-smiled at him. 'You got rid of the curse?'

'No, I got rid of the case. Mr Black bought it off me. He said he'd take it, 'cos he ain't superstitious.'

Olivia dropped the flannel into the water and sank back on her heels, staring at her brother. A chill started to creep over her. 'You sold Lucas Dad's cigarette case?'

Alfie nodded. 'I didn't waste the money he give me. I bought new trousers with it.'

He had indeed surprised Olivia by coming in with trousers that he'd paid for himself. At the time he'd mumbled about having saved up.

She felt an odd compulsion to check upstairs in her drawer even though she believed what Alfie had told her. Lucas had the pewter case in his pocket and she felt terrified even though she was sure she didn't really believe in jinxes any more than he did. 'I wish you hadn't done that, Alfie.'

A bang on the door brought Olivia to her feet. She gave her visitor a wan smile.

'Jack told me Alfie's in the wars. Can I lend a hand?' Matilda asked. 'You must be up to your ears in stuff to do.'

'Thanks for coming round. I don't think he's broken his

ankle. Best get him into bed, though, before he causes more mischief.'

'What can I do to help?'

'Prop up the other side of him and help me get him up the stairs, if you will.'

They ignored Alfie's protests that he was fine where he was and got him into bed.

'You've starting nursing earlier than expected then,' Matilda joked as Olivia closed the bedroom door. 'You're off tomorrow, ain't yer, love?'

'I am.' Just a moment ago she'd been considering postponing her trip abroad. But not now. She'd decided that her family had to start doing without her.

Telling herself she was acting daft hadn't worked. The worm in her mind was burrowing deeper, tormenting her with visions of calamity looming for Lucas. She would try to find him and take that lump of pewter and bury it. If she did not, and he were killed, she'd always wonder . . . and blame herself.

Chapter Twenty-Five

'Oh, Gawd! I feel sick. I don't want to throw up ...' Olivia gasped and pressed a hand to her sealed lips.

'Keep looking at the horizon, ducks, it'll help you feel better.'

Olivia had squeezed shut her eyes and was reluctant to open them but she'd try anything to calm her queasiness. Her eyelids flickered and she did as she was told, watching a spot where slate-grey sea met an equally sullen-looking sky. Drawing in long, measured breaths through her nose, she sensed the monstrous rolling in her guts finally begin to abate.

The bewhiskered, middle-aged fellow who'd given her the good advice sent her a paternal smile as they leaned on the ship's rail side by side. Olivia was clutching it with white-knuckled hands whereas her companion seemed quite relaxed. He was dressed in smart civvies, a Homburg tucked beneath his arm. Of all the perils Olivia had anticipated encountering when embarking at the port, sea-sickness hadn't once crossed her mind. Yet it was proving to be a horrible ordeal.

'If that little beauty lures one of Fritz's submarines in close you'll soon forget about your jelly belly, ducks.' The fellow pointed to the hulking warship cruising alongside then began scanning the waves for any sign of torpedoes. His greying hair was flapping and tangling in the strong breeze as he turned his head to and fro. A lone bottle webbed in fronds was on a collision course with them. 'I hope that's all we're up against,' he commented then cupped one ear. 'Hear that?'

Indeed Olivia had been aware of a rumbling sound that ebbed and flowed. She knew now it wasn't distant thunder but guns, a sure sign they were close to the French coast.

'Our lot giving 'em what for, I hope.' The sound of Allied guns prompted the gentleman to renew his scrutiny of the sea.

Olivia shifted her vision from the comforting horizon to take in the destroyer escorting them. His warning about the ever-present peril from enemy craft felt shockingly real, yet still she couldn't block out the awful thought that she might vomit in front of him.

She inhaled sharp, salty air and stared straight ahead. 'Thank you for that tip. I think me collywobbles have steadied a bit now.' After a few moments of feeling reasonably well, she turned to rest her spine against the rail. She reasoned that if she could keep her mind occupied then the deck undulating beneath her feet might seem less obvious. Glancing about, she wondered where the other passengers were destined for, and which of them she'd see again after today.

Civilians, mufti-clad servicemen and VADs were milling about up on deck. There were about sixty members of the British Red Cross Society and St John Ambulance Brigade travelling in her party. Some volunteers seemed already to be acquainted with one another. Olivia felt a bit left out watching the uniformed women chatting together, but it wasn't that they were a standoffish bunch. She'd chosen to keep her distance from them rather than embarrass herself by bringing up her breakfast on their toes.

Besides, there would be time to get to know people once they were back on dry, if foreign, land. Olivia had never studied French and hadn't fully grasped the names of the towns Miss Deakin had pronounced in an immaculate accent. But a place called Étaples had stuck in her mind because she'd been told a large St John Ambulance hospital had opened there recently. There were many such hospital compounds, Miss Deakin had explained, some housed in requisitioned buildings, others in wooden huts or marquees, which had sounded quite impractical to Olivia. When they reached northern France, her interviewer had informed her, the group of VADs would be split up and sent wherever they were needed along the Opal Coast. The pretty name made the region sound exotic. But Miss Deakin had bluntly told her it was quite the opposite since large areas of it had been turned over to military training camps and infirmaries.

Making friends too soon would be fruitless as only a few of those volunteers who'd boarded the train with Olivia at Charing Cross would be with her by journey's end. But she had noticed another young woman in the party who seemed, like her, to be slightly left out of things. She hoped she might have a chance to get to know this girl better.

They had gravitated towards one another on the railway platform and managed to exchange a brief hello. Olivia had gleaned from their short conversation that the girl was of similar working-class stock to her. It hadn't just been her dropped aitches that had given the game away. Like Livvie she only had basic luggage, and not much of it. VADs with cut-glass accents tended to possess towers of leather cases, and handfuls of coins to distribute to porters to deal with it. Unfortunately, in the confusion of stowing trunks and producing documents, Olivia and her fledgling friend had become separated and ended up in different carriages. Olivia hadn't bumped into her again.

Spots of rain were descending from the heavy clouds. Instead of making for the cabins, as some were doing, Olivia lifted her face to the sky, welcoming the refreshing sensation. Her thoughts turned to home. Her family hadn't seen her off from Charing Cross. The girls had work to go to on a weekday morning and Alfie had school. Besides, last-minute goodbyes would have been too upsetting for all of them. There had been a strained atmosphere in the final hours before they settled down for bed last night. Her sisters would engage in little conversation with her, though she had done her best to reassure them that she trusted them to cope with running things while she was away.

But that morning they had all been up early to hug and kiss her one last time while the Hackney driver loaded up her stuff. Finally she had boarded the cab and, with a last wave, set off. On the short journey to Charing Cross Olivia had clutched her hanky, believing she would cry. Yet she'd arrived at the railway station dry-eyed, with her heart beating dizzyingly fast. There'd been no regret or sorrow, just amazement that she, Olivia Bone, factory worker, was now a VAD on her way to France. And there was no going back, she thought wryly, as she listened to the waves slapping the ship's sides.

289

'D'you suffer from seasickness?' she asked the man still peering suspiciously at the waves.

'Used to,' he said. 'This is the fifth trip I've made to the Western Front. I've earned my sea legs, I suppose.' He rested an elbow on the rail. 'I should introduce myself. I'm Bertie Spencer, a journalist for the *London Evening Chronicle*.' He ran his eyes over her smart dark uniform and the arm brassard with its embroidered insignia of the Maltese Cross. 'I'm guessing you're a very new recruit on your first sortie abroad.'

'I am. Olivia Bone's my name, and I'm pleased to meet you.' She shook his outstretched hand.

'Have you volunteered as a nurse?'

'Yes ... well, after a fashion,' Olivia said wryly. Work as a ward maid was mainly cleaning, not nursing, although she intended to learn as much as she could of that while busy mopping floors. Then, when the war was over, perhaps a new career might open up for her. She didn't think she'd ever return to Barratt's.

'If you've got a useful pair of hands, you'll be more than welcome,' Bertie told her.

'Where are you heading, Mr Spencer?' she asked.

'Straight to hell, ducks.' He grimaced. 'I'm meeting a photographer close to the frontline. Between us we'll file a report about life for the lads in the trenches ... and try not to depress the folk back home too much. It's all about keeping up morale, you see. If mothers really knew what their brave boys were up against they'd be marching on Whitehall ... ' He broke off and frowned. 'What's that commotion?'

A group of well-dressed people had appeared on deck and the ship's stewards were dancing attendance upon them, holding up umbrellas to keep the faint drizzle at bay.

'I heard a rumour that one of the upper crust might be on board,' Bertie whispered. 'Perhaps it's true.' He sounded excited and whipped a notebook from an inner pocket. 'Toodle-oo, ducks ... duty calls.' He gave her a wink before scooting off.

'Didn't like to barge in. Is he a friend of yours?'

'Oh ... hello again.' The young woman Olivia had spoken to at Charing Cross had materialised by her side. 'He's a war reporter. He was kind enough to tell me how to settle me stomach by staring at the horizon. Nobody warned me about seasickness. I didn't get a vaccination for that,' she quipped. 'His name's Bertie Spencer and he's rushed off to get a scoop. The Quality's on board by all accounts. That's what all the fuss is about.' She nodded at the group of people being fawned over. Bertie was bobbing about on the fringes, trying to avoid having his eye poked out by an umbrella.

Olivia returned her attention to her new friend. She was a pretty brunette and looked as bright and chipper as she had on dry land. 'Take it seasickness doesn't affect you, you lucky thing?'

The girl shook her head. 'Come from a family of dock-workers from Poplar. Me dad used to take us out on the river quite a lot so me and me brothers got used to boating and fishing and swimming.'

'That's handy. You can hold me up then if we hit a mine and sink. I haven't got the foggiest how to stay afloat.' Olivia tried to make light of it, though it was a real concern. She wished now that she had learned to swim. The closest she'd come to the water was taking a boat out on Finsbury Park lake with a few school friends when she'd been about thirteen.

'Better tell you my name. I'm Olivia Bone. Livvie, me friends call me. I'm pleased to meet you. Have you joined up as a nurse?'

'I'm Rose Drew.' She shook hands. 'And no ... I'm not a nurse. But I can drive, y'see. That's why they took me on. I saw the recruiting posters for ambulance drivers so offered me services.'

'Wish I could drive,' Olivia said.

'I'll teach you, if you like,' Rose offered at once. 'Me dad taught me. He used to drive a truck down the docks and sometimes he'd bring it home with him. I was always badgering him to show me how to use the gears, even before I was big enough for me feet to reach the pedals. Dad was going to get his own haulage business going with me brother, but nothing come of it. Mum went mad when he joined up. He's forty-five but said he was thirty-nine to the recruiting sergeant.' Rose looked momentarily misty-eyed. 'Anyhow, I told Mum I'd come out and keep an eye on them both.' She raised her eyebrows quizzically. 'How about you? Got family serving over here?'

'Mum and Dad's passed on. Got younger sisters and a brother though. Alfie's still at school. But I've got a good friend serving at Ypres and I really want to find him.' Olivia thought about Lucas, wondering where he was and whether those guns that were now a constant thump in the background were anywhere near his position. She prayed he'd left that pewter case behind in England but feared he had it still in his uniform pocket ... as a reminder of her. She'd given Joe her silver locket as a good luck charm. But it hadn't saved him.

'Boyfriend, is he?' Rose asked archly, having read the faraway look in Olivia's eyes.

'Ummm ... I suppose something like that ...' Olivia wasn't sure how to answer. She would have liked to say yes, but it was far too soon.

'Ah-ha! Like *that*, is it?' Rose teased her.

'Me fiancé was killed at Ypres late last year,' Olivia explained. 'Not sure how I really feel about there being someone else. Besides, this one might be spoken for already.'

'Oh! Sorry about your fiancé.' Rose blushed. 'Me and my big mouth.'

'But the fellow I told you about is special ...'

'Yeah, I understand. It's just too soon to tell.' Rose took out some cigarettes and offered the pack to Olivia.

'Don't smoke, thanks.'

'Reckon you will soon,' Rose said dryly and lit up, taking a long, savouring drag. 'Best not start right now, though, if you're feeling queasy.' She turned her head, blowing smoke down wind so as not to make Olivia suffer.

An eerie whine followed by an explosion made the two girls duck down and a few shrieks were heard from startled female passengers. Their ship hadn't been hit. In fact, the crew on deck seemed relatively unperturbed and Olivia realised that the German shell had come down a safe distance away.

'Bleedin' hell! That's woke me up,' Rose spluttered, pitching her dog end into the sea.

Olivia pointed ahead as she saw land. 'Looks like we'll be docking soon.'

As the pilot navigated the ship into harbour Olivia heard the raucous shouts separate into unintelligible foreign words that mingled with the squawks of seabirds swooping low for pickings. 'Stick close together, eh?' She winked at Rose although she was still feeling jittery after that first proper taste of warfare. 'Be nice to end up posted to the same place, if we can swing it.'

Rose nodded. 'It certainly would. Don't fancy getting billeted with them snooty sorts.'

'Calling me common, are you?' Olivia affected an air of indignation that drew a giggle from Rose. But Olivia knew they were both feeling nervous. The fluttering in her guts had started up again and this time it had little to do with seasickness.

*

'Étaples?' the woman barked. 'Who told you you'd be sent there?'

'Nobody. I just remember that name from my interview in London,' Olivia replied. 'I imagined I might end up there as it had been mentioned. But I didn't say I *wanted* to go there.'

The matron tutted. 'You certainly would not if you had the least idea what you were talking about. I have served there and can tell you – Étaples is a dirty, unpleasant sort of place.'

Olivia bit her lip to quell a smile. Having lived in a slum notorious for being the worst street in North London, dirty, unpleasant places would hold few surprises for her.

The matron had greeted her – if that was the right word – in the night duty room of the hospital. Within the space of a minute Olivia's relief at having finally arrived at her destination had been dampened. She longed to be back in the Papillon guest house, drinking bitter French coffee with Rose. But that had been yesterday, although it seemed so much longer since they'd reluctantly parted company.

Having disembarked together at Boulogne, they and the rest of the VADs had overnighted at various hotels, which were in fact little more than houses whose truculent owners let out a few rooms and provided a meagre breakfast in the morning. Olivia and Rose had been lucky enough to share a spartan chamber at the Papillon and a plain supper of bread, cheese and hot black coffee. Nevertheless it had been very welcome. Breakfast that morning had been a similar meal, and nothing had passed Olivia's lips since. Now it was eleven o'clock at night, and she was dog tired and ravenous.

Sadly Rose had been allocated a posting that had sent her in a different direction. Olivia had said a fond goodbye and good luck to her new friend as Rose boarded the train. Later on she'd discovered her own destination. She and two other volunteers had clambered aboard a train heading to St Omer. As they'd rattled along, they'd chatted politely and waved to the trooping Tommies they'd passed, who'd cheerfully saluted them. The men all looked fit and healthy and it had lifted Olivia's spirits. Perhaps this meant that things were going well for the Allies. But then one of her companions had noted these were new recruits and probably had no idea what awaited them in the trenches. Olivia had recognised the sense in that remark but had felt none of the affinity to these sensible, self-confident women that she'd had with Rose. She'd listened to her fellow VADs talk about having obtained hygiene certificates and attended college lectures and hospital visits. She would have liked to have had the time to study and achieve further qualifications, but that would have taken months when Olivia wanted to be helping others now.

On reaching St Omer, her travelling companions, much to their dismay, were redirected to another platform and a train to Wimereux. Apparently a clerical error had occurred, and that was where they should have gone. Olivia had travelled on alone to her allocated hospital, in the back of a Red Cross ambulance that had been sent to the station to collect her.

Matron had been studying Olivia's file and now closed the Manilla cover. 'I think you might fit in here, Miss Bone,' she concluded. 'We are in urgent need of extra staff as we've lost some recently to the casualty clearing stations down the line.' She sighed. 'Of course ... you have no qualifications to recommend you for more than cleaning and pot washing.'

'I have a first aid certificate,' Olivia pointed out. 'Miss Deakin saw no reason why I shouldn't eventually gain the experience to be a nursing auxiliary.'

The matron tutted. 'It is all very well for those sitting in comfortable offices in Blighty to spout their pearls of wisdom to gullible girls. What we need here are nursing sisters with gumption and proper hospital training.'

'I can strip a soiled bed and make it up again. I can give a patient a glass of water and wash his face. I can do all that without having anybody train me. It's common sense.'

'But would you want to wash his face if his nose was hanging from it? You could risk damaging him further.' The matron spoke in clipped, quiet tones.

Olivia swallowed, feeling she'd just been put in her place effortlessly. She knew that nursing men with dreadful injuries must be both a delicate and a stomach-churning business. So be it. If she were squeamish at first, she'd combat it ... just as those brave lads had to summon up their nerve every time they dashed onto no-man's-land.

Olivia remembered Hilda Weedon warning her that some of the regular nurses believed they were a cut above Kitchener recruits. This woman certainly did. But Olivia didn't resent her attitude. A war zone was no place in which to suffer fools gladly. And being eager to help wasn't the same as being able to. The last thing she wanted was to be a hindrance.

'I'll watch and listen and learn, and when I'm thought ready to do more, then I will. I won't let you down.'

Olivia gave a bright smile even though she was finding it hard to keep her eyes open. All she really wanted to do now was sleep, and perhaps eat too, if anything was available. Even a curled up sandwich would be like manna from heaven to her grumbling belly. Then tomorrow the work, whatever it was, would start.

'You'll share a hut with some other VADs. There's a bunk ready for you there. Then when your own things turn up you can make yourself more at home. I asked one of the others to leave you a plate of sandwiches in the common room, in case you were hungry when you arrived. But if you're ready I'll show you straight away where the sleeping quarters are.'

'I am hungry,' Olivia said quickly. 'Best keep me strength up.'

The matron smiled at her for the first time. 'That's the proper attitude, Bone. You might just surprise me.'

Olivia hesitated at the door then turned back to face her superior. She stuck out her hands, roughened from years of family laundry and frequent washing to remove sticky sugar residue. Even before that, when she'd worked in the eel and pie shop, she'd scrubbed her hands frequently to get the fishy smell off them, sometimes till blood was close to being spilled. Her hands with their short, neat nails looked older than she did, Olivia reckoned.

'They might not be pretty but they're another pair. I won't believe anyone who says they're not needed.'

'You're a healthy young woman, that's obvious.' Matron tapped her own brow. 'But you'll need to be strong here too. Some of the sights on the wards are enough to make even me want to weep. And I've been here from the start.'

'I understand,' Olivia said quietly. 'But I've coped with many bad things that I'd rather not have seen.' She took a deep breath as a memory that she usually kept locked away was allowed to surface. 'When I was ten my mother bled to death while giving birth to my brother. I was alone with her. Even now I can remember feeling useless because I didn't know what to do to stop Mum from dying.' She caught her wobbling lower lip with her teeth, to steady it. 'Afterwards I just carried on doing what she would have done. I looked after my dad and the younger ones. You have to, don't you?' She looked at the older woman, not expecting sympathy or admiration. She hadn't told that story to elicit soft words or to impress her. She just wanted Matron to know it wouldn't be the first time she'd cleaned up a lot of blood, or watched somebody dying.

'It must have been hard to witness such a thing,' her senior commented.

'It was very hard. I know that while I'm here there'll be days when I'll wish I hadn't come. But I reckon you have those too. I expect everybody here in France wants to go home. But I'll surprise you.' Olivia put up her chin. 'Once I've had a kip.'

Gladys Bennett suppressed a chuckle. 'Very well ... the gauntlet is down. Now go and have your supper then get some rest. You do look quite white in the face, Miss Bone.' She paused before enquiring, 'So how long is it since your mother passed away?'

'About ten years,' Olivia said thoughtlessly.

'You're not twenty-three then.'

Olivia looked sheepish.

'I won't rat on you. You really are determined to help, aren't you, my dear?'

Olivia nodded, keen to get away before she incriminated herself further. But there was something on her mind. 'Before I go and leave you in peace, I wondered if you might know of a friend of mine. I asked the Red Cross clerks at Boulogne but nobody there could help me with her whereabouts. Hilda Weedon's her name. She came out as a VAD a while ago. She was a proper qualified nurse. I'd like to keep in touch with her, that's all.'

'I have met your friend,' Matron said in mild surprise. 'Now she *did* end up at Étaples. I was there at the same time as Hilda. You could write to her at that address. If she's moved on, they'll redirect her post.'

Olivia knew it would've been a fluke to have ended up working alongside Hilda. Still she felt disappointed that Freddie's sister wasn't in the neighbourhood. 'Oh, sorry, just one last thing. There is somebody else I'd like to track down. I only know her name's Yvonne and she's engaged to a sergeant in the RAMC.' Olivia could see from her companion's startled expression that she knew immediately who was meant.

'Hilda also enquired about Yvonne Fairley. Her brother became fond of her, I believe, after Yvonne nursed him.' Matron frowned. 'Hilda told me that Freddie didn't recover from his injuries. But at least he never knew what happened to Yvonne. I imagine that would have greatly upset him.'

'What *did* happen to her?' Olivia asked quickly. It seemed Hilda hadn't put this woman fully in the picture about her brother's death. Olivia wasn't about to fill in the gaps.

'Yvonne had broken up with her fiancé and decided to return to England but perished en route. The train taking her to Le Tréport came under fire. A very cruel twist of fate. I suppose it must have happened around the same time as Freddie died.'

Olivia remained quite still, wondering why she felt an odd sense of calm. She couldn't know for certain that Yvonne had been on her way home to tell Freddie she loved him.

Nevertheless, she followed Matron from the room privately convinced that was what had happened and praying that the two of them were reunited elsewhere.

Chapter Twenty-Six

'Eeh . . . you're a very pretty lass,' came a foxy Yorkshire voice.

'And you're a very cheeky fellow,' Olivia reprimanded, without losing her rhythm while scrubbing out a bed-side locker.

'Take no notice of 'im, Sister. He's got too much of what the cat licks its arse wiv,' a dry Cockney voice entered the conversation.

'Now listen, you two. First of all, don't call me "Sister" or I'll be for it. I'm not yet one of the proper nurses. I'm Miss Bone. And second, get your medicines down you or *you'll* be for it when Matron comes back. And me too, I shouldn't wonder,' Olivia added as an afterthought. One of the nursing sisters had told her to watch the Northern lad who was known as Yorkie. He'd been known to dispose of his detested castor oil in the foot bath when he thought nobody was looking.

The young Yorkshire sapper had a head wound and damaged feet. He had arrived on piggy back with a huge trench slipper covering a horrible mess of swollen purple flesh and pus-filled blisters. One foot had been worse than the other, and while Matron had applied her expertise to the worst wounds, she had allowed her probationer to bathe and dress the other foot. Olivia was grateful for her superior's faith in her. She'd been pleased with herself too. The young fellow, for all his brashness, had quivered and winced when his feet had been lowered into the foot bath. But when the job was done and the towels were laid out ready to dry him off he had sighed that it hadn't hurt him one bit to be patched up by her. Olivia had glowed all afternoon following this sincerely meant praise.

So in amongst carrying out her menial tasks, Olivia was slowly gaining the hospital experience and medical training that were so important if she were to become a real nurse. She dispensed the less potent jollops to keep the fellows' intestines moving. She shaved faces and even a calf too, to help facilitate the removal of a scrap of shrapnel. The fellow who'd had it dug from his leg now wore it as a badge of honour on the front of his bandage. He'd told Olivia he was taking it home for his missus to see.

It was breakfast-time in the camp hospital outside St Omer. The 'up patients' had gone to the dining hall, which was a fancy name for a marquee with trestle tables and chairs in it. The two patients confined to barracks had restricted diets and were in beds facing one another. As if in a race they grabbed their beakers, wearing expressions that might have led a person to believe they were being forced to take arsenic. In unison they tipped up cups, swallowed and smacked their lips as though having partaken of cognac.

'Wasn't so bad, was it?' Olivia wrung out a cloth soaked in Cresolis and wiped over the wooden packing cases that had been commandeered as linen stores.

'Worse 'n bad, that were,' the older patient grumbled.

'Need summat sugar-coated to take away the taste. A little kiss might do the trick.' Yorkie grinned and winked his unbandaged eye at her.

'Well, can't help you with that, matey,' Olivia returned briskly. 'Perhaps jam sandwiches will be round at teatime to sweeten you up.'

Cockney cackled a laugh at the blushing boy's expense. And Olivia went about her business, humming. She'd grown used to their flirting and teasing. It was all in good part with no offence given or taken. A wounded soldier seemed to prefer a joke to pity and would sometimes make light of quite serious injuries, accusing himself of making a meal of it to dodge Fritz. In turn the nurses ribbed him about swinging the lead, and about soon having him up on his feet and back on parade.

In fact, what most of the sisters wanted for their patients was exactly what the patients themselves longed for: a precious docket, pinned to their clothes by the doctor, that proclaimed them well enough to undertake the journey to England to recuperate properly. A Blighty one was viewed as a success all round.

'Miss Bone!' Matron poked her head through the tent flap. 'Incoming convoy.'

The warning had been unnecessary. Olivia's ears had already pricked up at the sound of increased activity outside. Then a bugle blast added to the noise and she rushed out to do what she could to assist in getting the new arrivals dealt with. The walking wounded with heads bandaged or arms in slings, or crutches aiding their weary progress, were already sliding themselves out of the ambulances that had drawn up. Stretcher bearers were hurrying to help those unable to make it into the hospital on their own.

The surgical and medical wards were in a collection of tents. As many as could be crammed into the field, had been. Any spare plot of ground on the periphery was taken up with chicken coops, or vegetable beds, or utility sheds. The huts housing offices and staff accommodation were ranged on the western boundary and carpenters were constantly at work increasing the number of dormitories. To maximise space some marquees were laced together at the top, and a tarpaulin tunnel ran between them. Each row of wards was known by a letter of the alphabet and each separate ward had a number. As they all looked so similar Olivia had at first got lost in the maze of canvas and rope but she'd got her bearings now.

Having darted to and fro outside, she quickly saw that there wasn't much she could do in the way of assisting the male orderlies who were already propping up the sick and wounded. Not wanting to get in the way, she went back inside and started turning down vacant beds so they were ready to receive a new occupant. In C4, her usual haunt, just three beds were spare. Olivia whipped along the tunnel to investigate the next wards in the line and find where extra spaces might be had.

'More malingerers from Loos, is it, Sister? Us lot's a sorry bunch, ain't we now?'

That dour comment greeted Olivia as she returned to C4, having counted at least eight extra berths along the line. And if beds here and there were closed up, possibly another few might be squeezed in too. If the extra equipment were to be had from the stores, of course.

Cockney had spoken in his customary self-mocking drawl. He was still seated at the ward table engaged in a sporadic game of solitaire with a pack of dog-eared cards.

He kept one jaundiced eye on the mud-encrusted Tommies filing in. The tent flap parted and a fellow on a stretcher with a crude box splint supporting his shattered leg was carried in by two orderlies.

'You could stand in fer the wicket with them timbers, chum.' Cockney nodded at the supports on the newcomer's leg.

'Nah. I'm first in ter bat, now I got me shin pads,' the wounded man retorted.

'Don't mind 'im. He's just pulling your leg!' Yorkie chortled his two penn'orth.

'Ain't sure if I want to stay in here with this bunch o' jokers, Sister.' The new patient gave Olivia a wink. 'Find us a better room, dear. Sea view'd be nice.'

'No sea view, I'm afraid. But you are going up the other end, in first class, away from the riff-raff.' Olivia pointed to a vacant bed she'd turned down many yards away.

'First class, eh? *À la carte* nose-bag, is it, Sister?'

'Of course!' she returned, pulling a semi-circle of chairs close to the paraffin stove so the fellow hobbling on a crutch and his pal cradling an arm in a sling could sit by the warmth. 'Lobster or steak for dinner . . . just take your pick.'

'Lobster or steak? What got served up yesterday looked like bleedin' stewed nag to me,' Cockney said, collecting up his cards. 'Glad I ain't allowed none.'

'It was casseroled rabbit and mashed potatoes and very nice it was too,' Olivia said. 'And if doctor says you can, you might get some dinner later.'

He pretended nonchalance but Olivia could see that Cockney was longing for a proper meal now he was recovering. He'd arrived with his back punctured by shrapnel but had told anybody who asked that he'd got what he deserved for running away. His comrades' version differed from that.

Cockney had deliberately turned his back to take the worst of the flying metal and shield a wounded rifleman lying on a stretcher at his feet.

In the short time Olivia had been at St Omer camp hospital she'd learned that none of the patients wanted to be praised for their bravery. It made them squirm to receive a compliment, though some had conducted themselves with astonishing valour. They didn't like to be reminded of it. Most of all they didn't like the other fellows in the ward to think they were swanking about it. Olivia imagined Joe would have been the same, had he survived to hear himself praised by the nurses tending his wounds. But he'd not got as far as an aid post alive, and the clutch of medals that he'd earned posthumously would never adorn his coat.

Matron strode forward and shot a nod at the fellows settling themselves down by the stove. 'Right, we need to get these muddy clothes off the new arrivals sharpish and get them washed. Steam bath for those who can manage to get there and blanket baths for the rest. I'll get the orderlies to lend a hand here.'

Olivia was waiting with the other nurses who'd clustered around to hear their superior's instructions.

'They need me in surgical as there's a young kilt with severe abdominal wounds going immediately into theatre.' Matron frowned. 'The ambulances are turning straight back. The drivers have warned us to be ready for another lot due in in a matter of hours. There are gas attack victims among them so set to. Allocate beds to the most needy and those who look likely to be back on active service soon can sit for now. Doctor will be round in due course and give his verdict. Bear in mind that we will without doubt need more capacity than we actually have.'

She turned to the group of regular nurses. 'Sister Bone must be utilised as much as possible, please, under supervision when necessary.'

Olivia was aware that this was the first time Matron had called her 'Sister'. The others were aware of it too. She could tell that not all of them were pleased by her promotion. But already her mind was running ahead ... to the areas in C5 and C6 where extra beds could be squeezed in. She voiced her thoughts, quickly and concisely, receiving a firm nod of approval, and a promise from Matron that an orderly would come and talk to her about shifting furniture.

'Best you collect up the clothing, Bone, quick as you can,' one of the unfriendly types ordered when Gladys Bennett had left. 'Or we'll all be crawling with lice.'

Olivia knew this was true. The casualties turned up caked in hard yellow dirt that had stiffened their field dressings. Some of the men were loath to have filthy bandages removed, thinking more harm than good would be done and scabs ripped apart. But a good soaking in warm water and Eusol and the rock-hard lint would eventually peel away and expose wounds that could be properly attended to. Sometimes maggots were already at work. But a lot of the parasites were carried in hair and clothing as well as gaping flesh.

The constant battle against infection and disease wasn't easily won, with little effective medication available to bathe bodies and sterilise equipment.

*

'Can I go home, Lieutenant? Please let me. I made a mistake.'

'I know, lad. And if I could, I would send you home. But I'm not able to do it.'

'But ... but ...' The trembling boy knuckled his nose free from snot, turning aside to conceal his tears as his fellow Tommies passed by. Even in such distress he feared being teased. 'But you're my officer and I lied and I shouldn't be here. So let me go back home, sir, please. Mother will be worried.'

Lucas took off his cap and thrust his fingers through his mud-matted hair. He felt like death warmed up and wasn't in the right frame of mind for this. He'd sunk a lot of rum last night while off duty, hoping to knock himself out. He still hadn't managed to sleep. In fact, he couldn't remember the last time he had done more than drowse for short periods of time. His head was thumping and his eyes felt hot and gritty with exhaustion. He cast a look up at a dirty dawn sky traced with star shells off to the east. Once the light was fully up the snipers would stop and the real business would begin.

The boy's keening was eating into Lucas and because he knew he was powerless to change things he grew annoyed with the lad and then with himself.

'There's no point turning on the waterworks,' he growled. 'That'll do you no good. It's your own bloody fault you're in this mess for lying to the recruiting sergeant in the first place. Now you need to accept you've messed up and start to grow up – very fast.' He grabbed the boy's shoulder and gave him a livening shake.

The boy hunched up his shoulders to his ears and started vigorously nodding his head in agreement. His helmet swung back on its strap revealing a stalk-like neck and a terrified white face covered in tears and snot.

Lucas shoved him down to a seated position in the funk hole, and squatted beside him. He shielded the boy's trembling form from view as more Tommies edged past. The timid lad had already been ribbed by some of his comrades. The men were on their way to the other end of the trench, to assemble there ready for the whistle sending them over the top. 'Listen, Carter . . . what's your name, lad?' Lucas enquired, forcing gentleness into his voice.

'Carter,' the boy whispered through palsied lips.

'Your first name . . . what's that?'

'Albert.'

Lucas dropped his head towards his knees. He'd taken a shine to this fair-haired lad from the start because he'd been reminded of Olivia's brother. The fact that his name as well as his looks were almost identical seemed a cruelty too far. 'Listen, Albert,' he croaked. 'If I could send you home, I would. But once you've signed up . . . '

'Ready, sir?'

Sergeant Dawson had come up behind Lucas to tell him they should join the others at the assembly point.

'Carry on, Sergeant. I'm on my way,' Lucas snapped over his shoulder.

The ginger-haired NCO stretched his thick neck to look at the boy, cowering behind their commanding officer's broad torso.

'Snivelling again, eh, Carter? That won't do yer no use, lad. Want to make yer mum proud, do you? Then fall in.'

'Yes . . . thank you, Dawson, I've got this,' Lucas said through gritted teeth, and didn't turn back to the boy until his sergeant had stalked off.

'Me mum don't know I've come, sir. She thinks I'm staying with me cousin and looking for work in Deptford. He took me down the High Street to join up. He's gone in the navy, has Bill . . . '

'You must write to her then.'

'But she'll be upset, sir.' Albert swallowed a noisy sob.

'Shall I keep him close to me, Lieutenant, when we go over?'

Lucas half-turned to see another young private hovering a yard away. He was older than Albert Carter, though not by much. But by Ypres standards he was almost a veteran, having been out here, for almost six months. Albert had only arrived three weeks ago and was too callow to be able to put a brave face on it as the others did. But it wasn't just children like this who knew what a dreadful error it had been to listen to pals' brash talk and recruiting sergeants' bullish encouragement. Self-inflicted injuries were being reported as men desperate to get back to their wives and families did whatever they could think of to try and make it happen.

'How old are you, Private Wicks?' Lucas asked.

Ricky blushed but said stoutly, 'Nineteen, sir.'

'What year were you born?'

Ricky flushed a deeper red. '1899,' he mumbled.

'So you're sixteen then.'

'And a half, sir,' Ricky confirmed, looking sheepish.

'And you, Carter? When were you born?' Lucas swung a glance at the blond boy, chin slumped on to his chest. Albert had pulled the tin hat back onto his crown but it swamped him, hanging down almost to his eyelashes. His shoulders beneath the khaki were narrow and bony.

'1901, sir,' Albert said. 'I'm fifteen come January.'

Lucas stared into space, wanting to find something profound to say. But there was nothing. No good reason he could think of why these two kids should run into machine-gun fire or stop bayonets. But they were in the army now and, if they refused to obey an order to go over the top, would be charged with cowardice and suffer the consequences.

'Right. When we go over, stay close to Wicks and I'll try and stay by the pair of you.' He yanked Carter up by the elbow and pushed him in front of him. As the two boys stumbled ahead over the duckboard, Lucas cursed every recruiting sergeant throughout England to eternal damnation and hellfire.

The Kitchener volunteers, plentiful at first, had steadily dwindled as dreadful reports of death and maiming got back from the Front. Women who should be wives and mothers in the prime of life were now bitter widows, dressed in black and old before their time. While on leave Lucas had become dejected to see how many of them there were. But youths wanting to act big in front of their pals could still be lured in with promises of regular pay and rations. Already there was talk that conscription would start now that recruiting sergeants were being sent out to harass men into joining up. But grown men were cannier than these kids.

'Can either of you run fast?' he called to them.

Albert turned about with a wondering expression on his narrow face. 'Shall we all run away then, Lieutenant?'

'Not unless you want to get shot for desertion,' Lucas retorted with a grim laugh. 'Runners are needed at times, to get messages to the ambulances that come forward and pick up casualties. Think you could do that?'

'I can run,' they chorused. They both knew they'd do anything rather than wait like this, shivering and with teeth chattering until the whistle shrieked in their ears and sent them scrambling up the ladders.

'Please God, I want to go home ... see me mum and me girl.' Ricky had closed his eyes and whispered a prayer. 'Got me letters here, sir.' He tapped his lieutenant's arm with one hand and his pocket with the other.

Lucas gave a nod. He knew. They all told him the same thing.

'You was the boss at Barratt's.' Ricky blurted out the first thing that came into his head, just to break the unbearable waiting. Not that it was completely quiet: somebody was playing a mouth organ somewhere in the trench. Ricky hated that mournful sound. If he could get hold of the thing he'd stamp it hard into the sucking mud.

Lucas looked at him in bemusement, wondering how he knew that.

'Me girl told me you used to be her sister's boss,' Ricky said through clattering teeth. In his head he was counting off the seconds. 'Maggie's me girl's name. Maggie Bone ... she writes to me, and promised she'll marry me when I get home ... '

The whistle sounded as Dawson emptied his lungs into it.

Lucas grasped Albert by the elbow, hoisting him up because he was too slight to make the fire step unaided.

*

'I'd like them both used as runners. Or if they could be transferred to the RAMC as hospital orderlies that would be even better.'

'Highly unusual request for active servicemen.' The colonel hardly bothered looking up from his desk ledger.

'They're not men, they're kids! I don't want them in the platoon. They're a hindrance. They can't properly handle a gun. They've not had enough training and the youngest especially is too nervous to be of use and should be kept back from the Front.'

'Best leave them where they are, y'know, Black. You'll be short otherwise. Every pair of hands that can handle a gun is of use ...'

'Did you hear what I just said?'

The colonel shot him a venomous look from under his brows, moustache twitching. 'Their records show they're nineteen and they've had their training, same as the rest.'

'They're children of fourteen and sixteen.'

'Not according to the records,' the colonel insisted, and snapped shut the book in front of him. 'If that's all, Lieutenant?' He sounded impatient.

Lucas knew this was a sensitive subject to raise with superiors. It was widely known that underage youngsters were serving but nobody dare say out loud that children were being accepted into the army and perishing on the Western Front. Nobody on the brigade staff wanted to put their head above the parapet either by speaking to the top brass.

'Well ... look, on the positive side,' the colonel drawled, all conciliation, 'if they are a bit below the limit now, they'll return home men before their time with real backbone. Make their families proud, that's the thing.' He stood up, indicating he'd heard enough and this interview was finished. He came round and gripped Lucas's shoulder. 'You're doing a fine job, Black. Heard you were mentioned in dispatches again. You run a good team. Brought them all through, didn't you? A promotion's there for the taking ...'

'I'd like them both sent home. Or transferred at the very least.' Lucas wrenched his shoulder free.

'For God's sake, man! They need toughening up, some of 'em. What are you so worried about?'

'That they'll end up fertilising Flanders fields before they're even old enough to shave.' Lucas knew he was wasting his breath. He subdued his loathing enough to salute before approaching the door.

'I will consult my superiors about your promotion,' the colonel called after him. 'Fine job you're doing, Lieutenant.'

'I'm not after promotion. I'm staying with my platoon. I've made that clear before.'

'Highly unusual ... man of your calibre,' the colonel muttered.

Lucas gave a nod, closed the door and said, 'Fuck you too.'

Chapter Twenty-Seven

'Rose!' Olivia flew across the frozen ground towards her friend. 'What are you doing here? Oh, it's lovely to see you! How did you know where I was?'

The friends embraced, their joyous laughter clouding the frosty air. Olivia had just finished her night shift and been slumped on her mattress, unlacing her boots, when an orderly had come to tell her that she had a visitor who'd arrived in an ambulance. She had wondered if Lucas had tracked her down. She'd written to him a few weeks ago, informing him that she was in France, but so far hadn't received a reply. She'd been fretting that if it were him, he'd have to have been injured to arrive in an ambulance.

'A few weeks back I met a friend of yours,' Rose explained. 'Hilda Weedon. She'd had a letter from you, giving this address. That's how I knew you were here. Anyway, I got sent this way to pick up supplies from the stores at Wimereux so I thought I'd make a detour to see you before heading back. I just bumped into two of the VADs that were shipped over with us.'

'I know who you mean. I travelled with them on the

train to St Omer then they got redirected. Oh, I can't believe you've seen Hilda! How is she? I'm so glad she received my letter. I've not had one back. Is she well? Is she still at Étaples? Or has *she* been posted to Wimereux as well?' Olivia rattled out questions, feeling her spirits soar at the idea that Hilda might be close enough for them to meet up on her day off. It would be wonderful to see a face that reminded her of home. She wanted to know Hilda's thoughts on the odd coincidence of Freddie and Yvonne passing away within days of one another.

'No surprise to me that your friend's not had time to write,' Rose told her. 'Hilda's up to her armpits, nursing at a casualty clearing station at Loos. Dodging shells all the time, they are, at the medical posts round there. I was sent to fetch some of the lads who weren't too badly injured and ferry them to the hospital train.' She paused for breath then ran on. 'They let me carry the ones who aren't classed serious and likely to peg out on me on the journey. Sometimes two of us would go in the motor but me partner's turned into a nervous wreck and come out in boils. Cor! She do look a sight, poor cow. All up here they are.' Rose patted at her throat, grimacing. 'She's been sent home and I don't reckon she'll be back.' She rattled on, 'So, as nobody else was spare, off I went on me own, and the clearing station where Hilda is ain't much more than a converted washhouse really and just a kilometre behind the line. She was saying they might have to pack up and move, they've been hit so often.'

Rose frowned and related, 'Hilda's been assisting an RAMC doctor to do operations on the poor souls that are too bad to shift. I asked her if they'd got enough equip-ment in that place and she said all they needed was a saw really. We did laugh . . . What else is there to do really?' she croaked, wiping her eyes free from tears that weren't all of mirth. 'Before I headed off with me patients on board, I gathered up all the stuff I had in the motor, even the stretchers and blankets, and give it to them. I knew I'd be in trouble when I got back to headquarters, but I didn't care. As far as me boss is concerned, I left me back door open while I was in the cabin filling in dockets, and the locals pinched everything.' Rose's voice had turned husky again. 'I thought the doctor might blub when I handed over the morphine. Weren't much of it either. Beg, borrow or steal it is in those places when they've got a rush on. They just can't keep up with it all.' Rose gulped and abruptly fell silent.

Olivia had listened to this open-mouthed. Finally she said, 'I don't know I'm born here, do I?' She glanced back at the forest of canvas lit with a faint pink blush from the wintry morning sun. All seemed to be quiet at present. They'd had a lull for a few days. But that wouldn't last. More convoys would be in, perhaps today, perhaps tomorrow. She'd imagined she'd seen the worst there was to see . . . suffering herself to witness it. But in reality she was one of the lucky ones. Enemy fire here was just distant noise and they felt secure in the knowledge there was little real threat to the hospital. 'I knew Hilda was a brick.' It seemed little enough praise but Olivia was lost for words.

'She's that all right. And she helped me give the motor a push that night when it got stuck in mud. The lads in the back tried to help, but what with one having a bullet go clean through his ankle and the other a busted wrist, they weren't much use. The fellow with the one good arm and two good feet sat steering and stamping on the clutch and accelerator while we girls and the doctor and hop-along put our backs out.' Rose flexed her spine. 'Still giving me gyp, it is. Then me lights went on the blink on the way back to the road. Pitch black, it was, and I didn't know where I was going or if I was likely to end up surrounded by "them blinkin' cabbage eaters", as the two lads in the back kept calling the Germans.' She snorted with laughter. 'Singing all the way to Arras, they was ... *Old soldiers never die, they just fade away.* I was joining in with 'em in the end though me mouth felt dry as carpet.

'Then, blow me down, a shell landed about thirty yards in front of the ambulance. Nearly wet meself, I can tell you. But I managed to keep the motor the right way up and swerved round the pothole. Thought me number was up, honest to God, I did, Livvie. The one good thing was I could finally see where I was going 'cos it landed on top of a poultry shed and started a fire.' She howled with laughter, starting her eyes watering again and making Olivia giggle too.

After a moment they quietened down and dried their eyes on handkerchiefs.

'Those lads I was moving that night, they kept me going, I reckon. At one point I thought I might just fold up. The only thing in me head was that if I got out of it alive, I'd scarper home the next day. But they just carried me along. "Stop the motor! Grub's up!" they was shouting when the chicken coop went up. But I put me foot down.'

The thought of roast chicken had brought with it memories of home for Olivia. Last time she'd eaten such a meal had been on Christmas Day with Alfie. And just a few weeks after that, on a perishing day in the New Year, Lucas had called and told her Joe was dead. Pulling herself out of her reverie she asked drolly, 'So you didn't even get a drumstick each?'

'Nah ... the birds was all long gone anyhow. Turns out the Germans had had them a while before when they passed through.'

'You're still here, so you didn't go home then?'

'Couldn't. One of the lads said I was a bonzer driver. He was an Australian. After that, couldn't chicken out, could I?' She smirked. 'Sorry ... had to get that one in.'

In the quiet that followed Rose's hysterical report, the two young women gazed at one another. In just over two months of being with Voluntary Aid Detachment on the Western Front they'd both lost fullness from their figures and gained new lines on their faces. But being fond friends, neither of them mentioned the other's decline.

Olivia knew that if anybody had tried to warn her of what she'd see and how it would affect her, she wouldn't have believed them. Lucas had told her she didn't know what she was getting into. But she didn't regret for one minute that she had come. In fact, she wished she'd turned up sooner. So she'd carry on joking with Rose, or her boys in their carpet slippers and baggy hospital pyjamas, as they mocked themselves and each other. What else was there to do but laugh or weep to release the agony of bottled up anger and despair, every time broken bodies were brought in or taken out covered in a sheet?

'You look well, y'know,' Olivia said gamely.

'So do you,' Rose came back with a grin. She grabbed her loose trousers. 'Could do with a bit more grub, but then I needed to lose a few pounds off me posterior.'

Olivia gave her a spontaneous hug. 'It's very good to see you, y'know.'

'How you getting on here then?' Rose looked about, taking out her cigarettes.

'Not offering me one?'

'Thought you didn't smoke.'

'Well, you were right about that. Didn't take me long to start once I got here.' Olivia took a cigarette and let her friend light it with a match. Her first cigarette had been taken on the day that she'd seen a gangrenous leg. She'd gone outside to breathe in some fresh air. One thing she hadn't been prepared for was the awful smell of dead flesh. One of the other off-duty nurses had been smoking by the washing lines and had offered her one. Olivia had gratefully taken it and puffed on it almost without it leaving her lips, not even wondering if she was doing it right. Now she got through a few fags a day and knew if she could get hold of more she'd smoke those too.

'Getting on all right here actually.' Olivia exhaled a plume of smoke. 'A Miss Gladys Bennett is our matron. She's a good sort. She's taught me a lot.'

'You mean the others are toffee-nosed.'

'A bit. Not all of them ... ' Olivia shrugged. 'Fair dos, anyhow. They know more about nursing than I do.' She looked at the motor her friend had arrived in. 'I've got the morning off. Fancy getting out into the countryside for an hour? Have you time before you head back?' She took another few swift drags on the cigarette then put the toe of her regulation boot on the butt.

"Course I've got time, that's why I'm here. I brought the motor hoping you'd have a few hours spare so I could teach you to drive. Said I would, didn't I?'

Olivia gawped at the ambulance. 'You're joking?'

'I'm not. I've been sent to collect medical supplies. They told me to come back later 'cos they've not yet done the stock check at Wimereux. Suits me.'

'Will you get in trouble for letting me at it?' Olivia nodded at the vehicle.

Rose shrugged. 'What they don't know won't hurt 'em. Bit like with the equipment going missing at Hilda's place. So, fancy it?'

'Not 'alf. Let's take a picnic.'

'Bit parky for that.' Rose rubbed her arms under her coat.

It would soon be December. The wards were chilly even with paraffin stoves chugging out fumes day and night. Olivia went to bed wearing layer upon layer of clothing. Still it was hard to keep warm and the chilblains at bay.

'I'll just get changed. Come along and I'll show you where I'm bunked and introduce you to some of me colleagues.' Olivia linked arms with her friend and steered her towards the nurses' quarters.

Chapter Twenty-Eight

Graves for the fallen British military were lined up in a newly extended section of the cemetery at Wimereux.

Olivia and Rose walked side by side, stopping at times then walking ahead of one another to stand in contemplation of a particular small wooden cross. Most bore names, a few did not. But beneath each neat mound lay a man who'd once had a family and hopes and dreams of a future.

The girls turned up their collars against the bitter air and thrust their icy fingers deep into coat pockets.

'Wonder how many of those fellows I've carried in the back of me van ended up here?' Rose murmured.

'I know some of our patients from St Omer are laid to rest here. The mothers often write, y'know, once they find out where their boys are. One woman came out to see her son when she knew it was hopeless. Well-to-do lady, she was. Very gracious and grateful for everything we did for him even though she never stopped crying.' Olivia remembered the young NCO and the pitiful state he'd been in with the lump of lead inside slowly poisoning him. She resumed talking through the lump in her throat. 'Of course, most mothers can't afford to come and visit even if they want to. But they beg for their sons' bodies to be taken home. They want somewhere to take flowers.'

'Yeah ... can't blame 'em for that.' Rose dug her nose deeper into her collar. Her eyes flitted over the simple burials. 'Not fair, is it, that they're all so far from the people who love 'em?'

'Perhaps they might come and see them, when it's all over.' Olivia stared down at the closest cross. It bore the name Private Richard Langdon. He'd served with the South Staffordshire Regiment and had died aged nineteen. 'They still might have grandkids one day, y'know. Those lucky ones that married young and had a family. My friend Lucas told me that some of the fallen don't look as though they've turned twenty yet have photos of their wives and a brood of little 'uns in their pockets.'

They wandered on, speculating out loud about how far the British cemetery plot would stretch by the time the war finally ended. And, please God, make that soon.

Olivia was pondering on something else as well. How many of the doctors and nurses, abundantly populating this area of northern France, would one day repose in Wimereux beneath smoothed foreign soil and a crude little cross? They'd be lonely, too, but for the colleagues, briefly known, who'd toiled and died alongside them.

Having meandered apart the two girls came together again at the exit. Before closing the gate Olivia hesitated then turned back and said, 'G'night, lads. Sleep tight.' In silence they descended towards the town and the ambulance parked at the bottom of the incline.

'Let's stretch our legs,' she had said while urging her friend to leave the vehicle a distance away from the cemetery at the bottom of the hill. She was glad they had battled against the icy breeze to reach the graveyard. It seemed fitting somehow to have made an effort to pay their respects.

Olivia's mind turned to Joe and his final resting place. A churchyard as yet unknown to her. She wondered if he was the only soldier there or whether other British casualties now lay beside him. She imagined they did ... wished it too. She didn't want him to be alone amongst strangers. Then she thought of Freddie. Poor sweet Freddie who lay in solitary confinement, in his own homeland. Had he perished here, in France, he would have rested shoulder to shoulder with his fallen comrades and been recognised as another war hero.

'Right. Time for a spot of lunch,' Olivia announced, shaking off her doldrums. 'There's a little baker's by the square. We could buy some croissants for our picnic in the van.'

'I do miss a nice doorstep of crusty English bread, spread with butter and jam,' Rose moaned. 'That's got to be the best thing ever when you're peckish.'

Olivia smacked her lips. 'I can still remember the taste of me nan's blackberry jam. I loved picking out all those little pips that stuck in your teeth. Nan had her own brambles out the back. Lovely Septembers, those were, gathering apples and blackberries and making pies and jam in her little kitchenette while me granddad sharpened her carving knives. He'd use the stone on the back step to do it. I never learned that trick, though he showed me plenty of times. Blunted 'em if anything, I did.'

By the time they got to the main street soft sleet had started to fall. They decided to have lunch in the cosy café rather than buy food to take and eat in the draughty ambulance. They ordered bread and cheese and coffee in stilted French that amused both them and the proprietress. Finding a table by the window, they settled down to watch the world go by. Their food was brought by the rotund *madame* who fussed with cutlery and flicked crumbs from the table with a checked cloth. Once she'd left them in peace they tucked in, remarking that it was better grub than they'd had at the Papillon. But, dour though the host there had been, they felt nostalgic about that first taste of Gallic hospitality on landing in France. Possibly their fondness came from remembering it as the lull before the storm. Once they'd finished their first course, and not wanting to leave just yet, they summoned back *madame* and ordered cream éclairs and more coffee.

'They certainly know how to make a cake,' Olivia said, once she was sure she'd scraped up every last trace of chocolate. When they'd finished their pastries they sat back in their chairs with groans of satisfaction. Turning their heads to stare out, they watched ice crystals begin meandering down the frosty pane as they thawed from the heat of the café. No words were spoken to express the enjoyment they'd gained from this unplanned outing, but both the young women wore serene smiles.

They'd recaptured the mood of a Saturday afternoon at home, spent with friends. And, just as at home, in a corner of their minds lurked the knowledge that soon it would be over and they'd be back to work. Far from dimming their enjoyment, the threat of tomorrow made today all the sweeter.

Having paid the bill, counting out coins fairly between them, they headed back down the road.

'Me eyes certainly are bigger than my belly when it comes

to the *fromages et gâteaux dans le café.*' Olivia made a fair attempt at the pronunciation, making Rose roll her eyes.

'Don't want to return to barracks just yet,' Olivia said as they strolled along. 'I'm not on shift until teatime. Shall we take a drive to Boulogne and watch the ships come in?' She dwelled nostalgically on the Boulonnais atmosphere, and although it was a miserable cold day felt a sudden yen to smell sea air again and see the fishermen going about their business.

Rose nodded eagerly. 'We could have a proper look at the shops. We didn't have much time before.' She opened the door of the ambulance then hesitated. 'There's not a lot of traffic – you could jump in the driver's seat.' She tutted at Olivia's uncertain expression. 'Got to start somewhere, Livvie. The road to Boulogne is as good a place as any, if you seriously want to learn to drive.'

It took Olivia a while to get the knack of changing gear but once they were on an open stretch it was just a case of keeping the right amount of pressure on the accelerator pedal – although her friend *had* quickly leaned over and assisted her in steering round a crater in the road when she'd nearly driven straight over it. The ambulance had been donated to the war effort by the Salvation Army, and was pretty new, Rose proudly explained, keeping her hand firmly on the wheel until Olivia regained control.

'Must keep the tyres in some sort of shape,' Rose added. 'They're in short supply.'

'Like everything else round here,' Olivia commented dryly. She kept squinting at the road. The sleet was persistent and the windscreen wipers seemed to work only when they felt like it. 'When you head back later, will you take a letter for Hilda and deliver it for me?'

"Course I will. I'll stop off at Loos soon as I can.'

'Must be nice, out on the open road.'

'Not if you've got a fellow groaning in the back and Fritz flies past and fancies a spot of target practice.' Rose grimaced and took a thorough look up at the sky through the spattered windscreen. The red cross painted on the vehicle was quite visible from the air. But not all German pilots saw ambulances as out of bounds.

'Have you managed to catch up with your dad or your brother since you've been here?' Olivia asked.

Rose sighed a negative. 'Mum wrote to tell me that Dad's regiment's on standby for the Dardanelles. Not going well out there, is it?'

Olivia knew that the Turks had the Allies on the run at Gallipoli and things looked bad.

'As for me brother ... Mum's not heard from him in a while. But it's just like him. Bloody selfish git, he is ... '

Olivia heard the tremor in her friend's voice and knew Rose was concerned about that long silence. But it was as well to look on the bright side; sometimes a party of men were cut off for weeks before they managed to rejoin their comrades and pick up post. Cockney at the hospital had regaled her with tales of having been stuck with just two fellows behind enemy lines for a fortnight before relief came. 'Was ready ter wave a white flag, they got on me wick so much,' he'd declared in his straight-faced way.

'How about you, Livvie? Heard from your lot back home yet?' Rose asked.

'Already got a drawerful of letters.' Olivia grinned. 'It's lovely to receive so much post. And parcels they've sent me! Alfie writes the most, love him. He tells me they're all doing fine and his leg's better.' She clucked her tongue in relief. 'He took a tumble just before I left. I worried that I shouldn't have left him in case he'd done himself a real mischief. The girls usually do a letter between them, then both sign it with kisses. They didn't have much to report other than everything was much the same as always. Knowing that was a blessing, I can tell you.' She smiled. 'They sent me a parcel of woollies when I said I had chilblains. The bed socks and gloves have helped stop me hands and feet feeling like blocks of ice at night.'

'Worst winter months are yet to come,' Rose warned.

'I know. Shouldn't grumble anyway,' Olivia chided herself. 'At least we *have* got beds even if they are rock hard.'

Rose mumbled agreement, peering through the windscreen for landmarks. 'Take that fork in the road and we're nearly there, Livvie.' She wagged a finger at a crossroads looming into view. 'If you pull over by that sign we'll swap places before we get to Boulogne. Don't want you driving straight off the end of the jetty.'

'Come off it! I reckon I'm a natural,' Olivia riposted.

'Right ... first you need to brake slowly, that's it, now get it into a lower gear, like I showed you. That's it,' Rose praised as the gears shrieked in protest but finally settled in. 'Now ... slowly ... foot harder on the brake ... and stop!'

The two girls shot forward on their seats as the ambulance came to an abrupt halt.

'Chrissake! Thought I was going through the windscreen, Livvie! When I said harder on the brake, I didn't mean just stamp!'

'I did all right for a first try at it,' the novice driver protested.

'Out you get then and swap over.' They raced around the

vehicle to change places, knocking the wet off themselves as they got back in, shivering.

'Wish I'd known you years ago, Livvie,' said Rose while smoothly working the column change and steering back onto the road. 'I reckon we'd have had some good larks together.'

'Still might ... when we get back,' Olivia said, and gave her friend a wink.

*

'Cor, ain't that pretty?' Rose cooed, admiring a crêpe de Chine blouse in a modiste's window.

'Pretty price an' all.' Olivia jerked a nod at a ticket that had 300 francs written on it.

'What's that in real money?'

'More than ten bob so it's too much.' Olivia cocked her head, assessing the little scrap of delicately embroidered material. It had exquisite pearl buttons and a nice fitted shape but the price seemed extortionate. In Chapel Street market she'd be able to pick up one just like it for under seven and six.

'Wish there were more days like this.' Rose sounded wistful as they walked on, arm-in-arm. The sleet had petered out and allowed them to do some window shopping without getting drenched.

'There will be.' Olivia sounded more confident than she felt. 'What did you do for work back home? I was a factory girl, making sweets.'

'Shop gel. Worked in a drapery. Didn't like it. Was bored all the time, serving old ladies with vests and bloomers. Dad said when he set up his own haulage firm he'd take me in with him and I could drive one of the motors. I fancied that.'

'Well, you are very good at it,' Olivia remarked fairly. 'I'm not surprised they let you join up as a driver.' She'd been thoroughly impressed by her friend's skill as Rose bowled them along, avoiding the worst bumps in the road with smooth steering and gear changes. 'I'm not going back to factory work,' Olivia added. 'I'll learn as much as I can here then get a job nursing, if I can ... ' Her voice faded and an amazed smile spread over her face. 'I don't believe it!' she burst out, turning to look at Rose excitedly. 'Am I dreaming or is that Hilda Weedon over there?'

'Bloody hell! It is!' Rose exclaimed.

Olivia dragged her friend on by the elbow, yelling out, 'Hilda! Wait up! Hilda!'

Hilda Weedon had been coming out of an office building. The girls knew it was used by the Red Cross because they'd been sent there after landing in France to find out about their postings.

Hilda glanced around, startled, on hearing their shouts. Her frown was soon transformed into a delighted grin and she rushed down the steps to meet them on the cobbles.

Olivia grabbed her in an embrace and they gleefully spun one another round on the spot.

'What are *you* doing here?' three voices gabbled in unison.

'Well, *we're* doing a spot of window shopping on our afternoon off,' Olivia informed her breathlessly. 'What about you?'

'I've just got my new posting. I'm leaving for Turkey in the next few weeks.'

'Me dad's off to the Dardanelles,' Rose piped up. 'Wish he wasn't. Don't like the sound of things over there.'

'Not much better here though, is it? Loos was lost at a

terrible cost.' Hilda sorrowfully shook her head. 'I wrote to you earlier in the week, Livvie, letting you know what I've been up to. Sorry it's taken me so long to reply to your letter. It's all been a bit hectic.'

'I've not received it yet, but don't worry about that,' Olivia replied flatly. 'Rose has told me all about what you've been up against in the clearing station. It must be dreadful, having men come in straight from the Front. By the time they get to us they've usually had their field dressings put on, and have settled down a bit from the shock of it.'

'It is tough,' Hilda said. 'But I volunteered to go when it all hotted up over that way, so no point boo-hooing about it now. I just bandage a few heads really.'

'You do not!' Rose snorted. 'That doctor told me he didn't know how he'd cope without you. And the two lads I had in the van were singing your praises ... along with a few other ditties.'

Hilda shrugged off the compliment.

'We need more people like you, Hilda,' Olivia said candidly. She had grown used to astonishingly brave people belittling their own efforts. The men she nursed did it, avoiding talking of any particularly valiant act with comments such as, 'Oh, it weren't nothing much. Any fellow would've done the same if he'd been there.' But she liked to let them know that she thought them admirable and felt privileged to have nursed them. Even if it had amounted to no more than shaving a bearded face or shearing off hair thick with nits.

'Got time to have a bite to eat?' Hilda enquired brightly, a blush still on her cheeks after her friends' words. 'I'd love to catch up and hear all your news.'

'Well, we've just stuffed ourselves to the gills at a café

at Wimereux. But I could murder a cup of tea … if we can find one.' Coffee was the preferred beverage in France. But some eateries catered *for le goût anglais*. Albeit with an accompanying sniff.

Once settled at a table in Le Café Bleu that had a splendid view of the harbour the girls ordered their drinks. Olivia and Rose found they had got room after all for a dish of *petits fours*.

'Where did your friend Cath get posted?' Hilda asked, spooning sugar into her tea.

'Oh, 'course, you don't know about Cath. She couldn't come after all. She got back with her fiancé and now they're married,' Olivia explained. 'She wrote and told me they had a quiet do at the register office then back to the local pub for a round of drinks and a few sandwiches. She was in the family way,' Olivia whispered and tapped her nose. 'But all's well that ends well.' She certainly hoped it would considering the bridegroom was still suffering from the effects of shellshock and didn't know he wasn't the child's father.

'At least she bagged her man,' Hilda said mournfully. 'The way it's going, there won't be any young bachelors left for us to marry when we get home.'

'We'll end up fighting over old widowers with bad breath,' Rose joked, biting into a marzipan apple.

'Or be spinster aunties, boring other people's kids with tales of what we did in the war.' Olivia had put on a crabby voice for the last bit.

And chuckle they did, though inwardly they howled at the terrible tragedy of so many young men never returning home, leaving the girls they'd grown up with heartbroken and bereft.

'I heard about Yvonne Fairley,' Olivia blurted out. 'What a thing to have happened!'

'I know. It's terribly sad,' Hilda sighed. 'Do you think she might've been going home to tell Freddie she'd fallen for him and had ended it with her fiancé?'

'That did cross my mind. We'll never know now.' Olivia gave Rose a potted account, not wanting her to feel left out. She implied Freddie's battle wounds had killed him. The quick glances that Hilda had shot her way during the recounting of the tale reinforced her suspicion that Freddie's sister was still sensitive about it. And who could blame her?

'I'll be spending Christmas in Turkey instead of the other way round.' Hilda quickly took up the conversation before Rose could ask any more questions.

'I've been promised leave. I'll be going home to have Christmas Day with the kids.' Olivia sounded pleased by the prospect. 'Matron sorted it out for me. I doubted at first we'd get along but she's a very good sort. She's a stickler for regulations but kind in her own way.'

'How are they all back home?' Hilda asked.

Olivia held up her hands with fingers crossed. 'Don't know why I worried so much about leaving the little darlings.'

'Does ... Lieutenant Black know that you're here?' An odd inflexion had entered Hilda's voice and she avoided meeting Olivia's eyes.

'I've written to him with my address. Not heard a peep back though.' Olivia felt something inside her tighten. She wanted to ask what the matter was but sensed that the question would be brushed aside and Hilda would prefer to open up when they were alone. 'Have you run into him on your travels? I worry about him. He's always in the thick of things. I hope he's all right.'

'About six weeks ago he brought some of his men into the casualty clearing station. It was just as the fighting at Loos flared up again. We didn't get much of a chance to say more than hello though.'

'Was he injured?' The knot of tension in Olivia's stomach tightened.

'He had some minor wounds, but nothing that seemed to affect him badly. I offered to take a look at them for him but he said there was no need.' Hilda offered round her pack of cigarettes. 'I remember that he made a joke about having the devil's own luck.' She paused. 'He asked after you. At the time I didn't know you'd arrived in France so couldn't tell him about that. I told him you were blooming when I last saw you in London and still thinking of volunteering.'

In the quiet that followed Olivia took several long drags on her newly lit cigarette.

'I should make a move and pick up those supplies, get them back to base or I'll be for it.' Rose grimaced and leaned her elbow on the table, cupping her chin in her hand.

'I ought to get back too,' Olivia said. 'I'm on duty at five and can't be late.' She never took liberties when relieving her colleagues. By the end of a shift a sister might be shattered mentally and physically if a convoy had turned up. And nobody knew when it might.

'You two finish your fags.' Rose pushed back her chair. 'I think I'll just scoot out and take another shufti at that blouse. We've got a Christmas dance coming up at RAMC headquarters and there's a rather nice corporal I've got me eye on. I've already checked him out and he's single.' She gave them a wave as she went out, calling, 'Won't be a mo' . . . I'll get you back on time, Livvie, don't fret.'

'I think Rose knew I wanted to have a quiet word with you.' Hilda sat back in her chair.

'She's a smashing friend. We met on the voyage over,' Olivia said. 'So ... what is it about Lucas you want to say?'

'I don't know if I *do* want to say anything. I'm not sure if telling you is the right thing to do, Livvie.' Hilda started taking frantic puffs on her cigarette.

'It wouldn't be right *not* to now you've worried the life out of me,' Olivia returned bluntly. 'Is he missing?'

'No, nothing like that,' Hilda quickly reassured her.

'Go on then, spit it out. Please don't tell me you've heard he's been captured and is a prisoner-of-war. I don't think I could stand that. And I know he couldn't either.'

'He's still with his platoon so far as I know, honestly.' Hilda bit her lip.

'You look like you don't know how to tell me he's in trouble.'

'*He's* not in trouble ... but his girlfriend is, if she's to be believed.' Hilda shook her head in mute apology for what she was about to reveal.

Olivia's mouth had dropped open. 'His *girlfriend*? What's she got to do with it? What d'you mean ... if she's to be believed? Have you met her and spoken to her?'

'I have met her and spoken to her. She's in France, Livvie. She followed him out here months ago. Her name's Caroline Venner and she's a VAD. She says she's pregnant and they're getting married.'

335

Chapter Twenty-Nine

Olivia found herself unable to speak. Hilda seemed to realise how shocked she was and went on to explain without
waiting to be questioned.

'I wasn't sure how things stood between the two of you,'
she started awkwardly. 'I didn't know whether to mention
it or not. I didn't want to hurt you. Lucas seemed to know
about you loving Joe. And you said he'd been your boss at
the factory and that you were friends. But I wasn't sure what
sort of friends you were.'

Hilda waited for a response of some sort but none was
forthcoming. The girl opposite her continued staring at her
fingers, curled on the edge of the table as though she might
overturn it at any moment.

'We never really had a chance to chat about boyfriends,'
Hilda sighed. 'I can tell now what he means to you. I wish
I'd kept my mouth shut.'

'No ... I'm glad you told me. We're just friends really,'
Olivia said huskily, flopping back into her chair. '"Master
and servant" he called us when I first knew him. It was the
day he gave me a job at Barratt's. It was meant to be a joke,

I know, but there was always that gap between us. He was posh and I was a factory girl. And that's it.' Olivia blinked tears from her eyes. All her thoughts about making him proud of her ... being his equal for strength of character ... seemed so much conceit on her part now. He'd never made a secret of the fact he had another woman, although he only reluctantly spoke of her. Olivia couldn't even blame him for leading her on with that kiss. She'd started it. She'd led *him* on.

Caroline Venner ... the name ran through Olivia's mind. She sounded elegant, as though she'd suit Lucas. She certainly sounded a more fitting match than Livvie Bone.

'What's she like?' Olivia asked. 'Is she pretty? How old is she?'

'She's a brunette ... willowy and polished rather than pretty. Can't hold a candle to you for looks,' Hilda said stoutly. 'Older than you, I'd say, by about five years.' She offered Olivia another cigarette, pocketing them when her friend declined with a shake of her head. 'Caroline's keen to get hitched, I reckon, before she gets any older.'

'Can't blame her. If it's the same girl he told me about a while ago, he's kept her waiting long enough.' Olivia's tone held a hint of bitterness. 'Well, good for her. I hope she makes him marry her, for the baby's sake.'

'Sorry to tell you like this, Livvie. If he's led you on a bit ... well, you certainly had a right to know. If it were me I'd want to, so I could give him a piece of my mind.'

'I'm glad I do know.' Olivia turned her fingers to clasp Hilda's hand, letting her know she'd no need to feel guilty. 'It's come as a shock and I feel like screaming about it, but I've no right to. He's never promised me anything. I'd let myself dream ... silly fantasies, that's all they were.'

She thought back. 'Joe liked him, and he knew that Lucas fancied me. Joe wrote in his last letter that if anything happened to him, he hoped Lucas would marry me.' She smiled wistfully. 'Joe was sweet like that ... he thought I needed protection even though I'd spent years looking out for myself and my family. He put silly ideas in my head.' She smothered a laugh with fingers pressed to her lips. 'No wonder Lucas hasn't been in touch. It's not an easy thing to bring up in conversation, is it, when somebody asks you how you are and what you've been up to? "Oh, well, actually I'm fine but my girlfriend's up the duff ..."'

Though she made light of it, Olivia was slowly starting to fume as she turned it all over in her mind. He *could've* told her things were now very serious with his girlfriend, just as a matter of courtesy. She might have kissed him first, but he'd bruised her lips with the intensity of his passion when kissing her back. If they were to meet now, outside this café, she knew she'd immediately recognise desire in his eyes when he looked at her. But men like Lucas Black, playboys with pots of money and good connections, wouldn't let something like a wife and child get in the way of them having their cake and eating it.

She'd thought the battles he'd been in had changed him ... making them more compatible. But she'd been wrong. They still inhabited different worlds. She couldn't blame him for believing she was up for a good time. She'd come on to him, not wanted that kiss to end, even though she knew he had somebody else. What was he to make of that? They'd talked about his girlfriend one day then Olivia had kissed him on the lips the next. Of course he'd read into it that she'd settle for second best.

Now her relationship with Lucas – even that teasing

innocent friendship they'd shared at first – was ashes. She felt bereft. But she'd always be grateful that he had given Joe a decent resting place. And she would find it one day, with or without him.

'If you bump into his girlfriend again, please don't mention me. I don't want her to think I've been chasing after her man. And if you see Lucas ... ' Olivia hesitated. 'Just tell him I'm fine and that I hope he is too. And that I understand he's too busy to write.'

'I wouldn't say a word to Caroline. She came to Étaples a few months before I arrived. She seemed quite reserved so I didn't really get to know her. I heard that she considered Lieutenant Black to be her boyfriend. She was proud of him.' Hilda chuckled. 'Who wouldn't be?'

'Me,' Olivia said sourly. So when he'd last been home on leave, and they'd gone to see Hilda, Caroline Venner had already followed him out to France? No wonder he'd avoided her questions about his girlfriend.

'Where's Rose got to? I should get back.' Olivia stood up, buttoning her coat. A glance through the window told her the sky was darkening again as if more bad weather was rolling in.

On cue Rose headed through the door, empty-handed. 'You're right. It's too much to pay for half a yard of material, pearl buttons or no pearl buttons. Ready for the off?'

They walked outside into the twilight, doing up their long, heavy coats. Hilda embraced both her friends and said to Olivia: 'You'll write to me once I give you my new posting?'

"Course. And I want some letters back!'

Rose and Hilda hugged too and similar promises were made before they headed off in different directions.

'Want to tell me about it?' Rose asked bluntly as they drove along the open road towards St Omer with the headlights picking out the road's rocky surface.

Olivia gave her a wry glance. 'Don't miss a trick, do you?'

'Nope.' Rose sent her a sideways glance. 'Man trouble, I'm guessing, concerning your special friend Lieutenant Black.'

'That's about the size of it.' Briefly Olivia recounted what she'd heard from Hilda.

'Are you ready to murder him?' Rose tutted in disbelief on seeing Olivia's shake of the head. 'Reckon you are. It's one less bloke to go round.'

'We'll all just have to settle for your old widowers with bad breath.' Olivia forced a giggle and discreetly thumbed tears from the corners of her eyes.

*

Gladys Bennett poked her head into the hut just as Olivia was crouching down to lace up her boots. She was making a meal of it because her fingers had turned stiff with cold. The sleet had recommenced falling and damp seemed to seep into her marrow.

'You're popular today, Sister Bone. You've another visitor.'

Olivia frowned, straightening up. She'd not been back from Boulogne an hour so didn't think it could be Rose again. And even if Hilda had thought of something else to tell her, it was a long way for her to have travelled. 'Did she give her name?'

'It's a Lieutenant Black ... and very handsome he is too. All the nurses who've spotted him are agog, and deeply envious.' The matron raised her eyebrows. 'I'd go and claim him, if I were you, before one of the others tries nabbing him.' She stepped into the hut as she noticed Olivia turning pale and sinking to sit on the edge of her camp bed. 'Is there a problem?'

'Not for me.' Olivia snapped herself to attention, jumping up. 'There might be for him though.' She yanked her starched cap into place on her fair hair. 'I'm due on the ward in about five minutes.'

'We haven't any major dramas going on, thank the Lord. I'll hold the fort for you in C4, if you're quick.'

Olivia didn't immediately answer because her thoughts were in turmoil. 'I've not much to say to him so I shouldn't be more than a few ticks.'

'Oh . . . sounds tricky,' the older woman remarked diplomatically. 'He's waiting in my office. I'll give you a quarter of an hour before making my presence known.'

'Thank you.'

Olivia headed off immediately, having decided that the only thing to do was get it over with. She would have liked some time to get straight in her mind how she felt about him, and what to say to him, now she knew what she did. But she'd been denied any breathing space at all.

Having dodged from tent to tent to keep dry, she arrived at the hut where Matron had a poky office. Various other small utility rooms were housed in it, stuffed with files and medical equipment. In the corridor Olivia hesitated, her chest heaving after her dash, breath misting the air. Her fingers quivered as she reached for the office door handle. And then her whole being followed suit, making her brace one hand against the wall to steady herself. It seemed so long since they'd seen one another and spoken . . . kissed.

She chased all such ideas out of her head and burst in.

'Hello, Lucas. How are you?' Her voice was cool, as she'd intended. But her heart was hammering as she looked at him. He had the power to make her marvel at his good looks every single time they met. She understood why her colleagues – more used to patched-together patients – felt like swooning over this fine specimen of manhood.

He was leaner and weather-beaten. But the rugged look suited him, made him seem less pampered, more danger-ous. A seasoned warrior.

She could see he'd sensed her frostiness. He looked thoughtful, subtly amused, as he always had when she'd stood up to him in the past.

Nurses gossiped and moved from place to place, telling their tales. She knew it wouldn't take him long to cotton on and saw the reluctant smile that tugged at his mouth the moment he did.

'I've just received your letter. I would have come sooner if I'd known you were here.'

That surprised her. But her green eyes, hard as stones, met his steadily. 'I sent it ages ago.'

'The platoon's been on the move. I only received it a couple of days ago.'

'Well ... not to worry,' Olivia dismissed this.

'I told you I didn't want you to come out here.'

'And I told you that I was determined to be useful. I'm very glad I came.'

'You can be a nurse in England. I want you to go home.'

Olivia snorted a laugh. 'Do you now! Well, I don't think you've got any right to tell *me* what to do. I understand why you didn't want me to come but I didn't follow you out here. I've no interest in spying on you to see who you're with or what you get up to, if that's what's bothering you.'

'It's not. Your safety bothers me. Do you read the papers? Do you know what happened to Edith Cavell?'

That took the wind out of her sails. Of course she'd heard about the nurse who'd been shot by the Germans for helping Allied soldiers escape from occupied territory. Olivia's colleagues had spoken of little else at the time of the cruel execution last month. But it hadn't been a deterrent to carrying on, it had been inspiring. Patriotism wasn't enough, and neither was Cavell's sacrifice. There were still men to be saved in her name. Her courage would never be forgotten.

Lucas discarded the cap he'd held in his hands, dropping it on the desk. 'You've changed ... grown harder,' he observed

'Once I thought you'd changed, become softer ... less arrogant. But I was wrong. You're still the same Lucas Black who thinks he always calls the tune. But I'm not your servant and I don't have to dance to it anymore.'

She could see he remembered that incident too when his subtly erotic description of them as master and servant had sent her scuttling from his office. He'd laughed then, and he did now. But in a different way. 'You've spoken to Hilda Weedon, I see.'

'Just this afternoon.'

He nodded, considering this. 'That's an odd coincidence. And bad timing on my part ... turning up when you're full of fury.'

'I'm not. There are far more important things to use my energy on than boiling up inside because of you.'

Lucas said sourly, 'I'd have to agree with you on that. But I'll explain anyway if you'll let me. I take it Hilda told you about a girl following me out here?'

'Don't be shy. You can use her name. Caroline Venner,

343

isn't it? If you want to worry about a nurse's safety in France, perhaps you should worry about hers and send *her* home as she's claiming to be your pregnant fiancée.'

'You don't know the full story . . . '

'I don't want to, thanks,' Olivia snapped. She made an effort to control herself. 'It's nice to see you, Lucas. I'm truly glad you're still safe. But I spent the afternoon with friends in Boulogne. Now I'm supposed to be on duty. So thanks for coming but I have to go on the ward . . . '

'How are your family? Are they coping without you?'

'They seem to be doing very well.'

'No more trouble from any direction? Herbie Hunter?'

'He's cleared off somewhere and good riddance. Nobody's seen him in a while.' Olivia remembered her father's cigarette case then. She hadn't thought of it lately. After all the ghastly things she'd encountered in this place, worrying about a jinxed piece of metal seemed laughable . . . inexcusable. Though she'd said she had to go . . . and she must . . . she didn't want to. She'd yearned to see Lucas since setting foot in France and couldn't stop yearning for him even knowing what she did. So she found something to talk about to prolong the agony of saying goodbye. She knew it had to be for the last time.

'Alfie told me he sold you our dad's pewter cigarette case.'

Lucas produced the thing from his breast pocket.

'I knew you'd keep it with you.'

'Lucky charm.' He idly tossed the case in his hand then held it out to her. 'Do you want it back? I only took it from your brother because he seemed obsessed with curses. He seemed frightened by it.'

'You should throw it away,' Olivia said huskily. 'It's true that it seemed like bad luck.'

'Not for me.' He rubbed his thumb over the dents on the box.

Olivia walked closer, squinting at the damage to the metal. 'What's happened to it?'

'That's a knife, and that's a bullet.' He flipped the cigarette case, showing her the marks where it had so far twice saved his life. He glanced at her upturned face. 'So either the devil is looking after his own or Tommy Bone is being kind to me at last.' He pocketed the case then lifted his hand to stroke his thumb over her cold, rosy cheek. 'I've missed you, Olivia. I thought I'd left you safe at home. I've been frantic to find time to come and see you from the moment I read your letter and discovered you were here.'

She stepped out of reach. 'You don't need to worry about me or make time to see me. Save all of that for the mother of your child.'

'It's not my child.'

'Oh, please, don't lie!' she cried in exasperation.

'I'm not.' There was no hint of anger or any attempt to persuade her in his answer. 'Nor is Caroline my girl-friend ... not in the way you see it, anyway.'

'What on earth does that mean?' Olivia choked.

'It means that things are complicated. Between me and her and my brother.' He smiled cynically. 'Did you think your lot were the only family with hatreds and jealousies tearing them apart?'

Olivia bit her lip, frowning. 'I know you don't get on with your mother and brother.' She paused, wondering what to believe. 'Is Caroline Venner the reason you fell out with your brother?'

'Partly.'

'Is he the baby's father then?'

345

'Only Caroline knows that. Possibly it's Henry's. I don't care either way. I know it's not mine. I'm not a fool and I'm not getting married. I understand enough about these things to be careful when I need to be.'

'I see,' she said quietly.

'I don't think you do, Olivia.' His hooded eyes travelled the length of her, from her serviceable boots to the fold of pristine linen she wore on her plainly styled fair hair. To him she looked ravishing, but then she always had, even as a factory girl with a sacking apron tied about her waist. 'You look very virginal,' was all he said.

She *was* dressed head to toe in white, almost like a novice nun. She hadn't yet received a blue nurse's set and pinafore and still wore a ward maid's outfit. She understood that the barbed remark was intended to let her know she'd not experience or sophistication enough to understand the complexities of carnal relationships. Unlike Caroline Venner, of course. If Olivia had taken up his offer and become his mistress when she was at home living with her dad, then no doubt she would know about the dark side of desire. But she didn't want that. The memory of Joe's sweet, clean love seemed preferable to a sordid affair with a man who played around with other women. She could see now that that was how it would've ended up with Lucas. For the first time Olivia envied her cousin Ruby, able to flit from man to man with not a trace of emotion. Olivia would've fallen hard for her first lover. Those feelings wouldn't have died if he'd married a girl like Caroline because in Olivia's mind love was meant to last. If that made her naive then she was glad she was. She was still young and, in time, might meet someone else like Joe and forget that once she'd been infatuated with her posh factory boss.

It was time to say goodbye before Matron turned up and things got awkward. But several times she'd noticed Lucas knuckle his side. This time when he did so he appeared to wince. 'Why do you keep doing that?'

'It's nothing ... just a scratch.'

'You're hurt?' Olivia stepped closer and saw a small bloodstain on the khaki jacket. 'Well, whatever it is you need a dressing on it.' She had learned from the other nurses to sound bossy when a man in uniform came to the hospital protesting nothing was wrong when clearly it was. 'You'd better let me take a look.'

She thought from his expression that he might refuse but he started unbuttoning his jacket. He slipped one muscular arm out of its shirt sleeve and turned sideways.

Olivia gazed at the swollen inflamed wound, trying to keep alarm from her voice when she said, 'How long have you had that? Is it a shrapnel injury?'

'Knife,' he mumbled.

'Knife? It's septic. Did you have it dressed immediately?'

Lucas shrugged back into his shirt. 'Sometimes that's not possible.'

'What are you doing?' Olivia began to stop him doing up his buttons but he caught hold of her wrists and wouldn't let go when she jerked back. 'It needs bathing, Lucas, with hydrogen peroxide. And it needs a clean dressing on it. It's septic, don't you understand?'

'It's too late now. I know it should've been stitched but I'll be fine as I am. I'm not feverish. It'll clear up eventually.'

'Why don't you want it looked at, you stupid man?' Olivia was angry with him, twisting her wrists free. She knew how easy it was for such wounds to worsen.

'Because I wasn't in France when it happened. And a

German didn't give it to me.' He seemed to regret letting that out and gestured brusquely at her to show he wouldn't comment further. 'It was healing quite well. It burst open again during a recent skirmish with Fritz. I would've had it dressed at the aid post but there were men in far greater need of attention than me.'

'Somebody in England attacked you with a knife?' Olivia demanded, sounding shocked.

'I've got one more day's furlough. Will you come out with me tomorrow?'

'Who stabbed you?' A sudden horrific thought occurred to her. 'Did your brother do it because he's jealous of you and Caroline?'

'He'd like to murder me. But no, he didn't, and I'm not going to explain it all right now. I'm around tomorrow. Will you come out for a drive so we can talk?'

'I'm sorry to interrupt, Sister Bone, but it's time for you to be on the ward.' Matron had given them fifteen minutes, as promised, and not a second longer.

'I'm just coming,' Olivia blurted, turning around to see her superior on the threshold.

'Very well.' The older woman swung a glance between the couple, sensing the tension in the atmosphere. 'I'll let you say goodbye but then I must have back my office, you know.' She closed the door behind her.

'What time shall I pick you up?'

Arrogant as ever, he'd taken it for granted she would meet him, Olivia realised. And how could she refuse? Though her bruised pride made her want to. She was desperate to know more about what had happened to him. She'd already worked out that the last time he had been in England was the night they'd kissed outside her door. He hadn't been injured then so it must have happened late that night or the following morning before he'd sailed. But there was a greater lure prompting her to say yes to his invitation. She'd have another opportunity to find out more about Caroline Venner, and why Lucas and his brother seemed to be fighting over her. He admitted that he'd fallen out with his brother over her, yet he also sounded quite indifferent to the fact that Caroline was carrying another man's baby. If indeed she was …

Olivia forced herself to concentrate on his injury, wondering if he'd returned to England again in the meantime to get it. She decided he hadn't. He would have gone to Islington to see her and found out from her family she was in France, not learned about it from a letter he'd received just days ago. Olivia concluded that his brother *had* attacked him, but pride … duty … whatever it was, forbade Lucas to talk about it. His family might have rifts driving them apart but, as he'd rightly said, so did her kin and scores of other people up and down the land. Lies were often born of resentful loyalties, as well she knew.

Lucas could tell she was finding it difficult to combat her pique and agree to meet him. He couldn't blame her for that. But he needed to explain, if he could ever find the right words. He inwardly ranted at himself for being a damnable fool. He'd been waiting for the perfect time to tell Livvie Bone he loved her and wanted to marry her. Or perhaps it had just been cowardice holding him back for so long. He still couldn't be certain that a dead man didn't have a tight grip on her heart, and he himself would be wasting his time baring his soul. He'd been protecting his ego and proceeding gently, and also allowing Caroline to persuade him he still needed her.

Now it was too late to backtrack; Olivia would think him a liar, whatever he said. She'd think she'd been right about him all along. Lucas Black was an arrogant toff, used to getting his own way. But not this time. He'd ridden rough-shod over his own heart this time ... but he'd grown used to being battered by sadness. And it was hard to believe losing in love could be more painful than shovelling up bits of boys to bury. But it seemed it was ...

'Are you on shift in the morning?' he asked hoarsely, rubbing the bridge of his nose to shield the brightness in his eyes.

'I start at five o'clock in the afternoon. I'll meet you in the lane at midday. I'll bring some antiseptic and a dressing to see to your wound.'

He approached her as though about to embrace her in thanks for seeing him, but instead brushed past and left her with a murmured goodbye.

Chapter Thirty

'You're in a dream, ain't yer, Sister?' Cockney said as Olivia removed the thermometer from his mouth, having taken his temperature for the second time in two minutes.

'Oh ... sorry ... miles away. Thinking of home,' she said on a sigh, filling in the obs sheet. 'I'm off at Christmas. Got ten whole days. Can't wait to see the family.'

'Me an' all,' Cockney said. 'Doctor come round this afternoon while you was off gallivantin' with your friends. I've got me Blighty pass.' He beamed and produced a ticket from his pyjama jacket. 'Gonna have a right old time of it in Shoreditch with the missus and the kids. Can't wait to see her face when she sees what I've brung her as a present.'

'What have you got her?' Olivia teased.

'Somefink naughty.' He winked. 'Ain't tellin' you no more than that. Nice little gel like you? Oh, no ... no.'

'If you've bought her a lacy scrap out of one of the draper's shops, it won't shock me.' She smiled as the grizzled man she'd seen every bare inch of while helping Matron blanket wash him on the evening he'd arrived, delirious with fever, blushed like a schoolgirl. 'Anyway, it's splendid news that you're going home.' She patted his arm in congratulation. 'And where's my admirer got to this evening?' She glanced over at Yorkie's empty bed.

'He's gone for a walk round the block. Now his feet's on the mend he won't stop using 'em in case they packs up on him again. Reckon they'll give him a dancing part in the Christmas concert coming up, don't you, Sister?' Cockney cackled. 'If he's still here, that is. He's hoping next time doctor comes round he'll get *his* ticket home.' He frowned. 'Anyhow, Dinkum's the one you gotta watch.' He wagged a finger. 'Proper keen on you, he is.'

Dinkum was a young Australian fellow. His real name was Johnnie Bell. He'd arrived a week ago with a party of fellow countrymen who'd been ambushed in a wood outside Ypres. They'd been brought in by a sympathetic farmer on his horse-drawn cart, sporting an assortment of wounds and spouting disparaging comments about the Boche's weasel tactics.

Johnnie's conversation was peppered with the term of approval 'dinkum' and it had stuck as a nickname. All the patients ended up being known by a moniker of some sort during their stay. The Aussie had a shock of auburn hair and a twanging accent, but in a strange way reminded Olivia of Joe despite looking and sounding nothing like him. Dinkum had made it clear from the off that he was soft on her. Olivia, as with all her lads, liked him back, but no better than the others.

Bantering with Yorkie was harmless fun, but with Dinkum it seemed different. She'd started cutting it out in case he again asked her to go to the theatre with him in Wimereux when he was well enough. She'd never knowingly lead him on.

'One of the other gels said you had a visitor earlier.' Cockney winked. 'A Lieutenant Black I heard it said.'

'Yes ... that's his name.' Olivia hadn't expected to hear it again so soon. Cockney was looking at her expectantly, so she explained in a throwaway fashion, 'He used to be my boss at the factory where I worked and came to say hello.'

'My pal Dawson from back home in Shoreditch, well, his commanding officer's Lieutenant Black. We was all billeted in town together a few month back. All the French gels flirted wiv the lieutenant.'

'Did they?' Olivia muttered. She gave Cockney an insouciant smile.

'Ain't heard from Copper in a while. That's what we called Dawson on account of his hair. The way I took the lieutenant, he don't seem a fellow given to popping over to say hello to casual acquaintances.' Cockney crossed his arms and gave an emphatic nod.

'And?' Olivia prompted when it seemed he wasn't about to say more. 'What is your verdict on him then?' She waited, feeling it was vital to have the opinion of this rough fellow who dictated his letters to his wife because he'd *never had no proper learnin'*, as he put it. He always thanked Olivia for writing down his hopes and his feelings and making sure they went in the post.

'That lieutenant's the finest officer what ever put two feet in shoes, is my pal's words.' Another nod followed this gruff announcement. 'Courage of a lion and looks after his men. Copper told me that, and he's straight as a die, so it's not tosh. Couldn't say that sorta fing about many of 'em wearin' pips.' He grinned at her. 'So your pa should give him the time of day if he comes a-callin' on yer.'

'Mum and Dad's passed on,' Olivia said, without any self-pity. 'Have to make up me own mind on everything.'

'Well, in that case, I'd give the lieutenant a recommendation . . . just in case you need one to say you'll take him.' He tilted his head to a foxy angle. 'Course, I'm told that gels fink he's good-looking too. But I don't see it meself.'

Olivia felt her cheeks growing warm at his teasing. Suppressing a chuckle, she moved on with a loud tut.

Though her feelings for Lucas were terribly mixed up she couldn't deny that hearing his character praised so highly pleased her. Knowing that Joe had been a hero to his pals had made her proud too. Plain words from plain folk who *really* knew what it was all about would always be worth ten reports written by educated people. After the guns fell silent no doubt these atrocious times would be picked over by politicians and academics who thought they had all the answers. And by then the Flanders mud would have silenced too many honest would-be narrators, who knew a different version of events.

*

The following morning Olivia had been excitedly getting ready to go out with Lucas when one of her room mates stuck her head round the door and burst out with, 'A convoy's coming in.'

The nurse followed it up with, 'Come on, draftie. It's all hands on deck. No time to be swanning off for lunch with a handsome man.'

The hum of motor engines could be discerned above the increasing din from outside. The sound of running feet and people calling out orders was then drowned out by a bugle burst. Quickly Olivia dropped her hairbrush, slipped out of her dressing gown, and started pulling on her uniform.

As the nurses hurried in the direction of the driveway Olivia noticed a saloon car was already parked there. In it was Lucas, smoking a cigarette. Either he was politely waiting until the appointed time before coming to find her or there was something he needed to think about that was making him hesitate before speaking to her.

'That's your Lieutenant Black, isn't it?'

Olivia turned to her colleague. 'Won't be a mo'. I'll just tell him leave's cancelled.' Not that she needed to. He would already have guessed. As she skipped between and over tent ropes he started to move the car away from the hospital entrance to allow maximum space for the stream of ambulances turning in.

Olivia chased after the vehicle and slipped onto the passenger seat with a breathless, 'I'm sorry, Lucas, but I'm back on duty, so can't come out ...'

'Don't be sorry,' he interrupted her. 'You told me yesterday you had more important things to bother about than me. And right on cue comes the proof.' He turned a bleak gaze on the sorry sights emerging from between the canvas flaps on the back of the ambulances. 'You were right about a lot of things. I wanted to speak to you about something important. Now isn't the time, though, I can see that.' He looked and sounded both relieved and disappointed by the delay. 'Anyway, there are matters I need to sort out. They've been left too long and it's best I get on with it. I wish things were different but I'm in a mess. I don't want you bothered by it. So I won't be back to see you for a while ...' He broke off and cursed as though regretting what he'd said.

'I understand,' Olivia replied hoarsely. He'd surprised

355

her by saying what he had. But she appreciated his honesty even though hurt and disappointed by it. They *did* need time apart to think things through without desire diluting reason. She could feel that familiar pull of attraction to him, even now when she should be rushing off to help her colleagues settle the sick and wounded. She sat still, wanting to savour these last few precious moments with him. And there was something she needed to know yet dreaded hearing.

'Before I go, tell me this. When we parted back in England you said you had something to say to me but the time wasn't right for making promises. Were you going to own up to being in love with Caroline, and wanting to propose to her? I know you said yesterday you won't marry her. Have you changed your mind because you're angry with her for cheating on you with your brother?'

'I don't love her.' Lucas sounded unemotional, his eyes fixed on the wounded men filing into the hospital. 'And she's not cheating on me. He's the one with a grievance.'

'Your brother? You mean, you're the guilty party?'

'Yes.'

Olivia waited for him to say more. When it became apparent he wasn't going to, she continued, 'One last thing. Did you want Caroline to go home when you found out she'd followed you here?'

'Does it matter?'

'Yes, it matters to me. Did you tell her to go back home, like you did me?' After a moment of silence she answered her own question. 'You didn't, did you? Because since she's been out here you've been sleeping with her, haven't you? You might not love her, but you are lovers . . .'

He swung his head and fixed her with his piercing blue

eyes. 'Yes, I've been sleeping with her. And God knows, it probably is the only time I do sleep. It's comfort, Olivia, and I need it.' He swore beneath his breath at her silence, as though it frustrated him. 'I never claimed to be celibate. When we met, you had Joe. You loved him and turned me down. What did you expect me to do? Join a monastery in case you decided to change your mind at some point?'

Olivia was taken aback by the harshness of his tone. 'No, I didn't think that. I knew you had a girlfriend ... or mistress, or whatever it is you class her as. You told me about her yourself. I merely imagined you might have had the decency to want to protect her once you found out she was pregnant, no matter whose baby she's carrying. But you're too self-centred to deny yourself, aren't you?'

'And you're not?' he mocked. 'You had me and your fiancé dangling on a string at the same time. You never did properly put me in my place after you got engaged, did you? Why was that? Was I too useful to you? As your boss and the giver of favours, you and your father both benefited from my pathetic obsession with you.'

'It ... it wasn't like that,' Olivia protested but her cheeks were flaming. She *had* used his interest in her to her family's advantage. It was what her father had wanted her to do. And keeping Tommy good-tempered and gentle had been her aim in life then, when they all lived together and he took out his fury on Alfie.

'Of course it was like that,' Lucas said dryly. 'And fool that I was, I was too lenient with you. I should have demanded favours in return. Taking you to bed would have made you grow up, if nothing else.'

Humiliated, Olivia made to slap him but his fingers encircled her wrist. 'You hit me once before when I told you some truths you didn't like. You won't do it again.' He carefully put her imprisoned hand down on her lap.

Olivia yanked herself free from his grip.

'That kiss you gave me – what was that for?' he drawled. 'Just to wind me up? Remind me that you've still got me pinned under your thumb?'

She tilted up her chin defiantly, aware of the hard glitter in his eyes. 'I know I shouldn't have . . . '

'Oh, you should have,' he growled. 'I've still got the taste of you in my mouth.' His hungry eyes moved over her face, rested on her full pink lips. 'You must be quite a novelty to the others,' he said abruptly. 'Factory girls are thin on the ground as VADs.'

'You think I'm not up to the job – not good enough? Just because I don't have a string of pearls and a cut-glass accent doesn't mean I'm any less useful here than your mistress,' she snapped.

'I meant, it's a costly business, packing in your job and kitting yourself out. That's all.'

Olivia felt chastened for having jumped down his throat when he'd made a valid point. 'I mortgaged Joe's house . . . my house,' she corrected herself. A smile softened her expression. 'I know he wouldn't mind that I've used the gift he gave me to allow me to come out here. I know he's proud of me.'

'He wouldn't object to anything you did,' Lucas said quietly. 'But perhaps that gift came with a poisonous sting in the tail.' He saw her frown and turned away. This wasn't the right time to bring out into the open the dreadful consequences of Joe Hunter's bequest. Two men she'd been fond of had been murdered because of Hunter Senior's jealousy and hatred after being disinherited. Three murders if you counted the killer's own death. But in Lucas's mind that had been self-defence. He didn't regret it. He'd do the same again to keep Olivia safe. He doubted he'd ever tell her. He knew she'd blame herself and then the guilt of knowing her father and Freddie Weedon had died because of her would eat up the sweetness in her character.

'Why do you sound so bitter about it?' she asked. 'You're surely not envious when you have a mansion of your own.'

Lucas choked back a laugh. 'No, I'm not bitter, Olivia. Not about your house anyway. But I do know from personal experience that unexpected windfalls can make families resentful.'

'My family have all benefited. I wouldn't have it otherwise. Joe knew I was close to the kids and would bring them to live with me.'

'You could do no wrong where he was concerned.'

'But you see me differently, don't you? I remember when you thought I was carrying Joe's baby. You were going to sack me. You told me a sweet factory was no place for a pregnant woman. And yet an Ypres battleground is, is it? What happened to that principled gentleman, I wonder?' she remarked acidly.

'I'm not a gentleman. I thought you knew that.'

'By birth you are. You might not like your family but they've kept you in clover. Perhaps you should at least try to live up to expectations, for your mother's sake.'

'By birth I'm Irish tinker stock. And my mother hates me for it.'

On the point of getting out of the car she hesitated and frowned at him over a shoulder. 'What?'

'Go on, you're needed,' he said roughly, nodding at the wards.

'What do you mean about Irish tinkers?'

'I told you I was adopted.'

'You said you'd no interest in finding out any more about your birth parents.' Olivia twisted fully back towards him.

'I changed my mind. I wanted to get things straight ... nothing hidden. But I know you'll just think me a liar whatever I say. You already do, don't you? Go on. For pity's sake, go. Take care of yourself, Olivia. I'd like you to write to me but if you don't want to ... I'll understand.'

She nodded, blinking back tears. He wasn't going to say anything more about it. He wanted her away from him. 'I'll just fetch some stuff for you to bathe your wound. I won't be a moment. Promise me you will use it regularly?'

He murmured agreement then closed his eyes, resting his forehead on the fist he'd propped against the steering wheel.

Olivia knew it was all over. Properly over. Whatever either of them said about writing, they wouldn't. A clean break was needed. Letters would make things worse.

She hurried to the store room and grabbed a bottle of Eusol and some lint and bandages then rushed back outside. But he'd gone. And she realised he must have really wanted to avoid speaking to her again. He'd driven over grass to get away because the ambulances were still blocking the drive.

*

'Hello, ducks. Remember me?' a voice croaked.

'Oh, I do, sir,' Olivia said, approaching the chairs encircling the paraffin stove in C4. Bertie Spencer – the war reporter she'd met on the boat with Rose – was sitting there, warming one of his hands by holding it close to the heater. The other was done up like a boxing glove, wound around many times with bandages, and she could tell from his badly inflamed eyes and rasping voice that he'd been gassed. As had many of the other incomers by the look of the poor souls. Some had their damaged eyes protected with dressings. Others were noisily struggling to breathe through fluid-filled lungs. All had raging thirsts and constantly gasped for drinks of water, which the orderlies and nurses hurried to fetch for them.

'The photographer didn't make it,' Bertie whispered, coughing up mucus into his handkerchief. 'Took us by surprise. Should've kept our gas masks with us but we were too busy setting up the bloody camera. First he wanted it here, then he wanted it there. Never heard that shell on its way. Too busy staggering about in the dark after the gas reached us. Blasted nuisance really.' He shook his head. 'He took some good snaps, that fellow.'

'Have you been out here all this time? Since I saw you last?' Olivia took his injured hand carefully in hers. It was helpful to distract patients with chatter while you dealt with their injuries. She'd barely recognised him. His neatly trimmed whiskers had grown into a bushy beard, matted with blood and foam. The dapper fellow he'd once been, who'd helped her combat her seasickness, was nowhere in evidence.

'Travelled back home twice, ducks, since I saw you. Wish now I hadn't made this trip. I wondered whether to, with Christmas just around the corner. My wife didn't want me to go. I got away by a fluke last time when the guest house at Poperinghe had its roof blasted to smithereens. Pushed my luck, you see.' When he'd regained his breath he asked,

'How have you been then, ducks? You look a sight for sore eyes . . . ' He attempted to chuckle at his black humour.

Olivia nodded and smiled to indicate she'd been fine. She knew this was, comparatively speaking, true. Her personal problems were nothing to what the soldiers and men like Bertie endured, day in, day out. Yet they all for the most part strove to stay chirpy. She knew that this man, in common with the others, would get a message home to tell his wife that he'd just encountered a spot of bother but it was nothing for her to fret about.

'Can't write a damn' thing now. Wish it had been my left hand caught it.' Bertie grimaced as the undone dressing began spiralling onto his lap.

'We'll have you back on your feet, Mr Spencer, and ambidextrous in no time.'

'That's a big word for a little girl,' he said with a twinkle in his tone.

'Be surprised what I've learned, sir, since I've been here,' she responded in the same vein. But it was harder to be cheery now. Far harder. Her hands were clumsier as she continued unwinding the filthy bandage, stained maroon with blood, from around Bertie's mangled fingers. She knew he was telling her again that he couldn't hold a pen or use a typewriter but the words were just a froth of noise in her ears.

Inside she was sobbing . . . wailing. For Bertie, for Joe, for Freddie and his lost love Yvonne. And for her father. She remembered suddenly her dad and her mum. That image of them, young and proud in their wedding finery, seemed to dance in front of her blurred vision. Then there was that other pain in her chest, put there by her love for Lucas. The thought of losing him was excruciating. She felt tempted to drop everything, to rush after him and beg him to open up to her. She wanted to know more about the feud with his brother and Lucas's relationship with Caroline. She'd believed him when he said he didn't love the woman he'd stolen from Henry Black. But his mistress still had a hold on him. If it *was* Lucas's child she was carrying, her claws would sink deeper into him. Irish tinker stock or not, Lucas would do his duty, as he'd been reared to do.

Yet Olivia believed he had fallen in love ... with her. She'd sensed he had loved her for a while but couldn't tell her. And it was more than just a lingering jealousy of Joe preventing him from doing so. There was a darkness in Lucas that seemed to go beyond the horrors of war or of knowing he'd sprung from lowly people. She imagined it was the guilt of betraying his brother with the woman they seemed to share that was affecting him so badly. But whatever it was, he didn't want to confide in her. So he'd avoid her and, without ever meaning to, they'd drift apart. And that was the most heart-rending thing of all.

Chapter Thirty-One

'Didn't think you'd get off lightly with a quiet little home-coming, did yer?' Matilda squeezed Olivia's hands in her own rough-skinned palms. 'Had to do you a party, love. Only fitting. Oh, welcome back, Livvie! We've all missed you, and we're all proud as punch of you.' She knuckled away tears.

'Missed you too, Matilda.' Olivia clung to her friend. She hadn't realised how much she'd needed this comforting hug from the sturdy person who'd been like a mother to her in recent years.

'Outsiders think the likes of us ain't got it in 'em to do what you've done. You've shown some backbone, gel. We're glad you're one of us, Livvie.'

Matilda Keiver turned her back on the bar in the Duke pub and raised her glass of Irish whiskey. 'Right . . . it might be Christmas Eve but there's a better reason to celebrate,' she bawled out into a room that rapidly fell quiet. 'Our plucky young Livvie's back home after nursing our men in France. And before she leaves here tonight, I want all of yers to stand her a drink.'

Olivia tugged on her sleeve. 'Bloody hell, Matilda. Can't drink all that lot,' she hissed. 'I'll be throwing up all Christmas and Boxing Day too, shouldn't wonder.'

'Shhh ... Don't matter if you're flat on yer back Christmas morning, love,' Matilda whispered as a chant of *For she's a jolly good fellow* started ringing out. 'Your Maggie an' Nancy can cook yer bird.' She winked. "Sides, if yer struggling to down 'em all, I'll help you out.'

'Start with that then, love,' Jack said, patting Olivia's shoulder with one hand and holding out a port and lemon in the other. 'Me wife's right,' he said in his gruff way. 'You're a credit to us, and I'm proud to say I know yer. It's good to have you back though. Even if it is just for the holiday.'

'Thanks, Mr Keiver.'

'Jack. You call me Jack. You're not a kid now, are you? You're a grown woman and a strong 'un at that.' He raised his tankard to clink against her glass, discreetly looking her over. She'd always been a shapely lass, and still was, but Jack could see that she was more slender. Her cheekbones were sharper too and her eyes shadowed, giving her a fragile beauty. He could see that being brave had taken its toll on this girl. 'How was it over there? Tell us the truth because I need to know.' He glanced at his wife, occupied talking to her sister. 'I'm enlisting in the New Year.'

Olivia swerved a glance past him to Matilda.

'She knows,' Jack said, reading her expression. 'Not sure it's fully sunk in though.' He sighed. 'I've got to do it. My little Lucy ain't growing up speaking German and that's final. We gotta stop 'em now in France or it won't be long before they're marching down our High Streets.'

'It's pretty grim,' Olivia admitted. 'So I'd say, don't go unless you have to. The greatest wish of all the men there

365

is to return safely to their families. I don't blame them.'

'Only right then that the likes of me relieve 'em so they can. They've done their bit. It's my turn now to do a shift.'

'Alfie's outside. He says, can he come in and stand with you?' Maggie had materialised at Olivia's side. She'd been allowed in the pub and had been sitting by the door drinking a glass of shandy.

Olivia had a feeling that Maggie was used to drinking stronger alcohol when out with her friends. But she was on her best behaviour tonight. They all were, so delighted were they to have their big sister back home for Christmas.

"Course he can come in,' Jack announced. 'Private party, this is. Your Nancy out there too, is she?' He waggled his fingers. 'Fetch 'em both in. I'll see it's all right with the landlord.'

'Nancy's at home. She's getting everything ready for tomorrow. I'm going back there soon to help her.' Maggie beamed at Olivia. 'We've got a surprise for you Christmas morning.'

Olivia put an arm round Maggie, drawing her close and kissing her forehead. 'And I've got surprises for all of you, too.' She'd spent hours looking round the shops in Boulogne while waiting to board the ship home and had bought them all Christmas presents, wrapping them in colourful paper to while away the time during the voyage.

'I'll go outside and fetch Alfie.' Olivia put down her drink and edged a path to the door. It took her a while as she graciously took compliments from Matilda's friends and neighbours en route. Alfie was sitting on the kerb with their cousin Mickey. Other kids were hanging about too, hoping their parents would remember to bring them that promised drink of pop.

As soon as her brother spotted her he jumped up and rushed to hug his Livvie as he had when a little boy, seeking solace after one of the beatings Tommy had inflicted.

When she'd walked through the front door yesterday, and even before she'd dropped her case in the hall, Alfie had bounded up to her, declaring that he wanted her to stay home now that she'd been to France. But Olivia couldn't promise anything of the sort. She knew she was going back. And would keep going back until there was no further need for her to do so.

Olivia ruffled his hair. She warmed his thin arms by rubbing them under his coat. It was a cold and misty night before Christmas. 'Come on ... you can come inside. Mr Keiver's said he'll speak to the landlord.' She beckoned to Mickey. 'You too. 'Spect you could do with a glass of pop, couldn't you?'

Mickey nodded eagerly.

'How's your mum doing?' Olivia continued, hugging her brother and dropping a kiss on his fair head every so often. She was glad to have some quiet time with him. She'd always been closer to him than to her sisters, having brought him up from a newborn. At that time her father could barely bring himself to look at his son. And nothing much had changed afterwards.

Matilda was kind to have arranged her welcome home celebration but Olivia knew she'd be glad to get home and sink into a chair there in the quiet. After months of frantic activity, physical and mental, she relished the idea of sitting for hours on end, doing nothing other than peacefully watching the flames dance in the parlour grate.

Mickey shrugged. 'Mum's all right, I suppose. Ruby got her a job at Barratt's. She's still moaning though.'

'Well, reckon we're all doing a bit of that.' Olivia smiled. 'And is Ruby still living in Wood Green?' She put an arm around Mickey's shoulders so she had a boy ... a brother ... to either side of her.

'Yeah, she's stopping there, so she said.' Mickey turned his face up to her, eyes popping with excitement. 'Guess what! That bloke Herbie Hunter who used to lodge with us ... he fell in a ditch one night and drowned.' Mickey screwed up his face in revulsion. 'We heard when he was pulled out he was all puffed up and rotted and couldn't even be recognised. He had his hip flask with his name by his side, though, so the police said it was him all right.'

'It's true, Livvie,' Alfie piped up. 'That's why nobody saw him again ... he ended up in Carbuncle Ditch.'

Mickey excitedly took up the story again, having noticed Olivia's utter amazement. 'A copper come to speak to me mum when they found out he'd lodged with us. They told us he was probably drunk when he fell in. The last night Mum saw him he'd gone to the pub and he always carried his whisky flask full up. Copper said it was empty.'

'Well, wasn't expecting *that* news,' Olivia finally said, having conquered her shock. With a sigh, she ushered the boys inside the pub.

'I didn't like him.' Mickey grimaced. 'He used to punch me mum when she asked him for his rent.'

'Me neither. He was weird,' Alfie agreed. 'So ain't bothered this time if Dad's cigarette case was to blame for him croaking. He did have it for a while.'

'The cigarette case isn't jinxed, Alfie. Lieutenant Black's got it with him and it saved his life. It stopped a bullet hitting him in the chest.'

Alfie grinned happily.

Olivia led the boys to the bar to buy their drinks. Despite all the merriment her thoughts remained rather solemn. She'd not liked Joe's father and wasn't sorry or surprised to hear he'd come to a wretched end. It seemed fitting, considering the dog's life he'd led his family. He'd been cruel, especially to his wife and her baby. Nevertheless it seemed that the roll call of the dead continued to mount even back home, and that thought was depressing.

*

The small graveyard seemed quite busy for a Christmas morning. But then the Bones were not the only ones wanting to visit their departed loved ones while, indoors, the annual feast roasted slowly in the oven.

On rising they had got dressed in their best clothes then donned aprons to begin the enjoyable task of trimming the plump chicken that was to take pride of place on the dinner table. As she'd watched them going quickly about things Olivia had felt proud of how capable her little family had become. Without needing to be told, Alfie had set about sweeping out the grates and setting the fires, bringing in coal and kindling to pile neatly on the hearth. He'd stoked up the kitchen range with Maggie keeping a watchful eye on the oven heat.

Maggie and Nancy had set the parlour table with cloth and cutlery then peeled vegetables and put the pudding on to boil, topping it up carefully with water when the plate beneath it rattled dryly. Olivia had been quite superfluous in the kitchen and it had felt odd, but pleasant to be told to go and sit down in the parlour because she was in the way.

'Can't wait for me dinner.' Alfie grinned, walking backwards along the cemetery path while talking to his sisters. 'Can I have the wishbone, Livvie?'

'I bags pulling it with you, 'cos I've got a special wish to make as well,' Maggie piped up.

'What about me?' Nancy said. 'There's things I want next year an' all, y'know.'

'We'll toss a coin for it.' Olivia smoothed matters over. They still found things to bicker about, she realised ruefully.

She glanced at a woman heading in their direction on the same path with three children holding hands beside her. None of the youngsters looked to be older than seven and they were as sombrely dressed, and as grave of countenance as their mother. Olivia tried to catch the woman's eye, to smile at her as they passed, but the widow kept her face lowered and ignored her quiet 'Merry Christmas'. The moment after the greeting had left her lips Olivia felt a fool for having made it.

Alfie had run ahead on the path again, carrying the bouquet they'd brought for their parents' grave. When they arrived at the right spot Olivia took the bunch from him and separated the stalks of holly and ivy and a few late Michaelmas daisies from the garden that had survived the frost. She handed them each some stems to put down.

'I miss Dad,' Nancy said as she crouched to arrange her posy.

'Me an' all,' Maggie sighed.

Olivia missed their father too. But she refused to wear rose-tinted spectacles about him. He had been a selfish and cruel man before his premature death. She wondered if any progress had been made in catching his killer. She realised she should ask her sisters if the police had been round with any news. But she didn't want to put a dampener on things, today of all days. Besides if they'd ever had anything important to report the girls would have written and told her.

She wondered if Sybil was thinking of Tommy at this special time. The grave had been bare so if the woman had visited the resting place of the man who'd fathered her children, she'd come empty-handed. Mickey had told them that he and his mum were spending Christmas with Ruby. Olivia knew she ought to make the effort to see her aunt before she returned to France early in the New Year. But Sybil had never exactly made her feel welcome.

'Shall we sing a carol?' Alfie suggested.

'Yeah, let's,' Nancy enthusiastically agreed. 'I reckon Mum an' Dad would like that.'

'You choose then.' Olivia said. After some arguing, they settled on 'Good King Wenceslas'.

They sang it quietly, without wishing to draw attention to themselves. But an old gentleman who had been tending a grave some yards away stopped what he was doing to join in. At the end he lifted his hat to them then carried on putting flowers in a pot. The widow, standing with her head bowed before a newly dug plot, didn't once lift her eyes or bestow a flicker of interest on the choir. 'I know you don't think it, but you *are* lucky. At least you got him back,' Olivia murmured. Then, with a last lingering look at the forlorn family, she turned to head back with the others.

To lighten the solemn mood that had settled over them she said, 'Bet Matilda's got a sore head this morning.'

'I reckon she was up with the lark,' Maggie giggled. 'Alice told me her mother can drink most men under the table and still be the first one out to work in the morning, collecting rents.'

'I'm glad she helped me out with all those port and lemons.' The barman had lined up at least a dozen that people had bought for her, but Matilda and her sister Fran had surreptitiously polished off two-thirds. Even so, Olivia had still risen with a throbbing brow.

After chucking out time at the Duke, the party had carried on at Matilda's place. Olivia had finally managed to escape home at one o'clock on Christmas morning, having joined in dancing the hokey-cokey up and down the street.

But the clean cold air had helped sharpen her up after too little sleep. She was glad they'd made this trip to Wood Green on Christmas morning. Like Alfie, she felt ready for her dinner now. She took his hand as they walked along, swinging it.

'Can we play charades after dinner?' he said.

'Don't see why not,' Olivia returned.

*

'Oh! It's really lovely, Livvie. Thank you.' Maggie had opened her present then jumped up from the table to hug her sister round the neck. Olivia had bought the blouse that she and Rose had thought too expensive. She'd gazed at it again in Boulogne and marched straight in and bartered for it. She'd got sixty francs knocked off and had felt pleased with herself. It was exactly what she would have done in Chapel Street market when intent on buying the kids nice Christmas presents she couldn't really afford.

So Nancy wouldn't feel left out of being treated as a grown up, Olivia had bought her some French perfume. At present, the girl was dreamily wafting the scent beneath her nostrils and humming to herself.

'Now yours, young man.' Olivia beckoned Alfie, still waiting patiently for his gift. She'd wanted to get him something to boost his awareness of being more independent so had bought him a leather wallet and had put a half-crown inside.

Alfie's heartfelt thank you prompted the girls to renew theirs too. Olivia was pleased she'd taken so long over choosing things for them.

'This is what we got for you. It seems a bit small and mean now.' Maggie had pulled open a drawer in the sideboard then held out a small rectangular package done up with red ribbon. 'We thought you could put it up in your bedroom over there at the hospital.'

Olivia pulled at the ribbon and carefully unfolded the tissue paper. Inside was a framed photograph of them all, taken in a studio. Her sisters were seated on a bench and behind them stood Alfie, looking every inch the budding heartbreaker with his slicked down fair hair and roguish smile.

'Wish we'd got you something else now . . . ' Maggie started.

'No, I couldn't have asked for anything better. I love it. Thank you.' Olivia put the precious photograph of her family to her lips, kissing the ebony frame. 'This will have pride of place on the cabinet next to my camp bed. Now I can look at you all every night before I go to sleep.'

'Can we have pudding now?' Alfie piped up.

'Guts!' Nancy tutted, but good-naturedly. 'I'm stuffed.'

'I'm sure you'll manage a small bit of plum duff,' Olivia ribbed. 'Come on then, let's get the table cleared and make some room.' She stood up, collecting plates that were empty but for gravy stains. They had thoroughly enjoyed their roast dinner but had carefully left enough chicken for Boxing Day.

Olivia put a match to the sherry-drenched pudding on its holly-bedecked plate.

They all watched, shining-eyed in the candlelight, as a magical blue flame shimmered around the aromatic sphere before dying away.

Nancy proceeded to spoon helpings into dishes and hand them round.

'Custard!' Maggie burst out and got up from the table to fetch the jug from the kitchen.

'Got the thrupenny bit!' Alfie crowed, taking the coin from between his teeth.

'You can't have the wishbone as well then,' Nancy said.

'Flick the coin, Alfie, and me and Nance'll call,' Maggie ordered.

As soon as the brass left Alfie's fingers Maggie shouted heads. It was tails and Nancy beamed.

'What about Livvie?' Alfie pointed out.

'Call, Livvie,' Maggie urged.

'Tails,' Olivia said.

'Tails, it is,' Alfie cheered. 'You get the wishbone, Livvie.' He eased it away from the chicken carcass.

'Best of three,' Olivia said, hoping Nancy would win in the end. She did, and Olivia made a show of disappointment. *Be careful what you wish for ... it might bring you no good,* her old nan used to say to her when she was little, to stop her wanting what she couldn't have.

A wish for Lucas to come back into her life would be sure to prove her nan's words wise.

After they'd cleared the dining table and carved the carcass clean for tomorrow's dinner, they put the chicken bones into a pan ready to make Boxing Day's gravy. The chores done, they made a pot of tea to take into the parlour.

'It looks lovely on you, Maggie.' Olivia settled comfortably back into the fireside chair. Maggie had come back downstairs wearing her new blouse while the other two took to their beds for a nap after their blowouts. Olivia was glad of this chance to have a private chat with her sister. Maggie was head of the household in her eldest sister's absence and they should have a discussion about the bills and budgeting and so on. And there was something else Olivia wanted to know.

'Have you heard from Harry?' She was hoping to hear the girl hadn't and that nor did she want to.

Maggie continued doing up the pearl buttons while shaking her head. 'He wrote to me a couple of times but I didn't answer. Ain't interested in having his letters, not since I found out he's been writing to fat Polly.'

'How did you find out?'

'From Ricky.' Maggie perched on the arm of Olivia's chair with a smile. 'Got something to tell you ... Ricky's asked me to marry him. I've said yes.'

'What! I didn't know you two were sweethearts.' Olivia took Maggie's hand in hers. She would have liked a bit of notice of that bombshell, but was determined to treat Maggie as her own person. Olivia still hadn't shaken off feeling guilty that her sister hadn't trusted her enough to tell her she was pregnant.

'Ricky's nice ... wish I'd taken more notice of him sooner. But it was always Harry fer me ... till I found out what he's *really* like.'

On the tip of Olivia's tongue was a reminder of how many times she'd tried to tell Maggie just that. Instead she hugged her sister, feeling thankful she had finally come to her senses. 'So have you and Ricky been writing to one another?'

'I send him letters all the time. He's in Lieutenant Black's platoon. Ricky said he's the best officer ever, and takes care of 'em all. Ricky said he's hoping to get transferred to be a stretcher bearer. Or a runner. He can sprint and they need people to fetch up the ambulances to the frontline.' Maggie fiddled with her pretty pearl buttons. 'Ricky's back home on leave in a few weeks. Can't wait to see him.'

'Are you getting engaged when he comes home?'

The girl nodded, looking bashful. 'He wants us to get married straight away. But I don't want to yet. We're too young and I ain't ending up like that poor cow over the cemetery with kids hanging on her skirts.'

Olivia was surprised that Maggie had even noticed the widow because she'd not said anything at the time. 'How about the others? Had any problems with them? Nancy in particular?'

'She's been good as gold. She knows if I so much as think she's been on a shoplifting spree again, I'll grass her up. She's learned her lesson, Livvie.'

Olivia was glad to hear it. The thought of Nancy bringing that sort of trouble home for Maggie to sort out had been on her mind at lot. She'd not wanted to interfere by saying anything to Nancy, going over Maggie's head. 'You do look lovely in that blouse,' Olivia said fondly. Maggie had matured. Her body was getting shapely and her bust contoured the bodice where once it would have hung off her flat chest.

'I'll take it off now before I spill something on it.' Maggie ran a loving hand over a crêpe de Chine sleeve, pink with pleasure at her sister's compliment. 'I'm not going to wear it again until Ricky comes home. I'll tell him it don't matter if he ain't got enough saved for a ring, 'cos I've got savings

376

of me own and don't mind buying it. I've seen one I like in Wood Green and put a deposit on it. Sapphire, it is ... '

'Sounds beautiful,' Olivia said, and watched her dreamy-eyed sister skip out of the room.

When she was alone Olivia rested her head against the chairback and watched the flames. She tried to concentrate on Joe, and her parents, but despite her efforts to remember the dead her mind wandered to the living. She wondered what Lucas was doing ... whether he'd managed to get home for Christmas. Or perhaps he hadn't wanted to see his family.

Still she wondered who he was spending Christmas with. And for the first time she pitied him. Once she'd baulked at the idea of him feeling sorry for her, living with a cruel father and with little in the way of material comforts. But there were many types of unhappiness within a home. For all his riches and privileges, he wasn't content.

She bucked herself up. She'd just spent one of the best Christmases ever. The best she could recall since her mother had died. And it wasn't over yet.

She went to the door and called up the stairs, 'Come on, you lot. Thought we were having a game of charades!'

Chapter Thirty-Two

Lucas watched as the two young privates ducked into the funk hole. It was a squash for a grown man to relax in the nook excavated in the trench wall, but they were small enough to squat together comfortably. Once settled they opened the Christmas present that they'd been sent courtesy of the Princess Mary Fund. They lifted the lids of their brass boxes, taking out things to examine before returning them to the tin. Wicks and Carter left the yellow packets of cigarettes on their laps. A moment later they'd torn them open and the eldest lad struck a tinder lighter obtained from his tin. They settled their backs against the mud wall, puffing away merrily.

Kids would have started on the chocolate. But childhood for them was finished. Lucas realised it was as well they'd not received a shaving set instead of cigarettes. They'd have wanted a swap on that. The two youngsters looked the happiest he'd seen them and he wished this moment could last, or be their last. Too soon the whistle would sound again, bringing fear and trembling. He'd feel it too, conscious as always that this time he might not correctly judge how to beat the guns.

The scent of tobacco wafted to his nostrils, making Lucas crave a smoke. He was in the officer's dugout, seated at a table strewn with identity tags and photographs and letters, all removed from corpses. It was Christmas Day and he couldn't stomach writing to women who didn't know they were widows, or gazing at pictures of smiling children who'd be crying by New Year. So he piled the things neatly then settled back in his chair and lit up. He thought of last Christmas Day, spent fraternising with the enemy on no-man's-land. The memory seemed dreamlike now ... talking German to an officer, exchanging cigarettes for candles with soldiers in grey uniform. All so polite to one another. Then later, before the light failed, both sides had set about the task of burying their fallen comrades, rotting on cratered soil.

Lucas flexed his fingers, recalling the jolt that had travelled up his arms as the shovel hit frozen ground. Joe Hunter and Freddie Weedon had been digging either side of him. Copper had been there too, swinging a pick. Sergeant Dawson was one of the few surviving members of the original platoon. This Christmas he was home on leave.

Lucas stretched out his legs, wincing as the movement caused the wound in his side to niggle at him. It was healing now. Caroline had been telling him since it split open to get it stitched. She didn't like blood on the sheets ... or on her skin. But he'd rarely taken notice of anything she said. And now he'd finished with her ... really finished with her ... he wouldn't have to listen to her complaints.

He'd got it looked at, to please Olivia. Which made no sense considering he'd no idea when he'd see her again. Or if she'd care that he'd taken her advice. But that was a stupid thought. He knew she would. Livvie Bone was beautifully honest and caring. And he loved her for it. He wondered what she was doing today and whether she was thinking of him.

Even when running, pistol in his hand, with watery guts and clumsy feet, he couldn't forget her. Sometimes he thought that the phantom in his mind was his lucky charm, not Tommy's pewter case, as roaring them on, he went first over the top.

Lucas stood up and went over to speak to the boys. 'At ease,' he said as they made to jump to attention. He handed over the chocolate that had been in his silver Christmas tin. 'Never got a taste for it,' he said truthfully. Working in a sweet factory had turned him off confectionery.

Ricky Wicks put down the lump of iced cake he'd been sawing into and accepted the gift with garbled thanks. He snapped the bar and gave half to Albert.

'Me mum sent a cake over,' Ricky explained. 'Do take a bit, sir.'

'Just a small slice, thanks.' Lucas accepted with a smile. He was never sent gifts. And only letters if they wanted something. No doubt they thought if he perished in the war they'd no longer need to ask for hand outs because riches would tumble into their laps. They'd get a surprise when they read his will. But he'd made sure to protect the people he cared about from their malice.

'We starting off the New Year as runners?' Carter asked, sucking on a square of chocolate. His clear trusting gaze was fixed on his officer.

'I've been told your transfers are in progress. When I get back from leave, I'll chase them up.'

'Thanks, sir,' Carter said.

'Have you written to your mother now?'

'Private Wicks done me a letter.' Albert jerked a nod at Ricky. 'He's good with words. We told her not to worry 'cos I'm fine an' dandy.'

'Well done. Just the thing mothers should hear from their sons. Merry Christmas,' Lucas said to them both and moved on. He climbed on the fire step and trained his binoculars on the opposite trench while chewing fruit cake. Mrs Wicks had done a good job. It was the best he'd tasted.

Again his thoughts turned to Olivia and he wondered what she was doing. And Alfie. He envied them their family life, unpleasant though he knew their lot had been when Tommy Bone was around. He had always wanted to have lavished on him that natural decency that flowed through Olivia and benefited everyone close to her. He wasn't giving up on being worthy of her love and loyalty. And returning it.

But not yet. He wanted to be honest with her. She'd never trust him again if he continued to conceal things from her. He wasn't the person she believed him to be. He wasn't absolutely sure himself yet where his roots lay. Or how sordid a tale might be unearthed about his father's affair with a gypsy woman.

He'd discovered that the man he'd taken to be his adopted father had sired him, although already married. His birth mother had come over with her Romany family on the boat from Ireland and they'd set up camp close to the Blacks' ancestral estates in Hampshire. From that coupling had sprung a tangled web of deceit, which was the reason why the woman who'd raised him, with the help of a succession of nannies, hated him. As did his imbecile half-brother who was bright enough to know he'd had his rightful place in the pecking order usurped.

Then there was the spectre of Herbert Hunter. Lucas's conscience didn't bother him on that account. But secrets and lies had a tendency to unravel. He never wanted Olivia to find out what the murdering wretch had told him before Lucas drowned him. Knowing who'd killed Olivia's father and Freddie Weedon was the greatest burden of all because nothing could be done now to change things. Hunter couldn't be brought to justice. Tommy's murder would remain unsolved and Freddie would remain branded a suicide.

If Olivia ever found out about Herbert Hunter's killing spree to get his hands on her house, every cherished memory she had of Joe would turn sour. The greatest puzzle was why that should bother Lucas when he had every reason to hate the man who still seemed to have a hold on Olivia's heart.

He focussed and leapt from the fire step just as he felt a breeze pass him by and saw sand dribble from the sack on the opposite wall. The shot had been almost noiseless. It hadn't disturbed anyone but him. He felt his chest thudding as adrenaline pumped through his veins. He gave a snort of relief, patting the bumpy pocket where his talisman was stored. Not that the pewter case would have received another dent. The sniper had aimed at his head.

'Merry fucking Christmas to you, too, you kraut bastard,' Lucas muttered, and finished his cake.

*

'Come to wish you a Happy New Year, Livvie. All right to come in?'

Olivia had opened the front door to see her aunt Sybil. Ruby and Mickey were behind her on the path.

Sybil held out a bottle of sherry as though it were an inducement to being allowed entry.

"Course you can come in,' Olivia said, conquering her surprise. As it was the season of goodwill she gave each of them a welcoming hug when they passed over the threshold.

On entering the parlour she could see that the only person pleased to see their visitors was Alfie. He and Mickey grinned at one another.

'Got me train set out on the landing. Fancy coming up?' Alfie said, already on his way to the door.

'Well, sit down,' Olivia invited as her sisters carried on playing a game of cards, mumbling greetings to the newcomers.

'Cup of tea anyone?' Olivia offered brightly.

'Wouldn't mind a glass of that sherry.' Sybil pointed at the bottle she'd moments ago handed over. 'You're partial to a sherry, ain't yer, Ruby?'

Her daughter answered with a vigorous nod that set the feathers on her fancy hat dancing.

Olivia glanced at her cousin. They'd parted frostily on the day the catfight with Cath had broken out in the factory forecourt. But it was New Year's Eve and Olivia thought bygones should be bygones. In the end it had all turned out as it should; Cath and Trevor were now husband and wife.

'I'll get some glasses,' Olivia said, opening the sideboard.

'So how's things at the factory?' She poured the sherry and gave Ruby hers with a smile.

'Bleedin' same as ever,' the girl replied then gulped at her drink. 'Short-staffed, we are, and it's getting worse as more of the married men jack it in to enlist.' She glanced at her mother. 'Mum's started there in packing with me.

Keeps a roof over yer head in the Bunk, eh, Mum?' Ruby rolled her eyes at Olivia to let her know Sybil hadn't gone willingly to work.

'How's Cath?' Olivia hoped to get a chance to see her friend before returning overseas. 'She wrote and told me she started at a biscuit factory after she quit Barratt's.'

'I heard she's gone off to stay with Trevor's gran down Kent way for Christmas and New Year. Not that Cath speaks to me after what went on.' Ruby gave a careless shrug. 'Weren't all my fault anyhow. Trevor was as much to blame. Water under the bridge now. Me an' Riley's happy enough. He's over in Ireland seeing his folks.' She polished off her sherry in a single swallow. 'Wouldn't mind another,' she said, smacking her lips and holding out her glass.

'And me,' Sybil said.

'Like Piccadilly Circus in here this evening, ain't it?' Maggie grumbled as the door knocker sounded again.

Olivia knew what her sister meant by that. She too had hoped for a quiet New Year, just the four of them, eating cake left over from Christmas and playing games until the clock struck twelve and they could all wish each other better times to come.

'I'll get it.' Nancy jumped up and went to the door.

'Oh, you've got company,' Jack Keiver said, hesitating on the threshold.

'It's nice to see you, Jack.' Olivia beckoned him in.

"Course I'll understand if you want to finish off this year indoors in peace and quiet. But Matilda sent me round, so I'd better ask anyway or I'll get me ear chewed off.' Jack chuckled. 'We usually have a knees-up round the piano on New Year's Eve and it's not unknown for a few drinks to be taken.' He winked. 'We'd be pleased to see you, if you fancy joining us. Everybody welcome, kids an' all. We've got a few hot sausage rolls in the oven . . . '

'Sounds very nice,' Sybil said, already on her feet and doing up coat buttons.

'It's nice of you to invite us, Jack, but . . . '

'I'd like to go,' Nancy quickly interrupted as she saw her aunt about to sit back down with a disappointed grimace.

'And me,' Maggie chipped in. 'I'd like to see Alice and wish her Happy New Year.' She made for the door with Nancy hot on her heels. 'I'm going upstairs to get ready.'

'Well, decision made.' Olivia smiled at Jack. 'Tell Matilda we'll walk round in a few minutes.'

'Take another small one then, shall we, while we're waiting for your sisters?' Sybil didn't wait for a refill from Olivia. She helped herself from the bottle on the sideboard.

When they were congregated in the hall, about to set off, Olivia hesitated, for some reason wanting to have a few moments on her own. Since she'd been home it had been a hectic round of catching up with everything and everyone. She'd not had an opportunity to be quiet and reflective in Joe's house. Her house . . . the wonderful gift that had provided her with a new life. She wanted to walk around alone as she had when she'd first moved in and it had still belonged to him. When he'd been alive and she prayed he'd come back to her.

'You lot carry on. I've just got to fetch a hanky.'

Alfie and Mickey had already run ahead and turned the corner. The girls too were on their way down the road, arm-in-arm. Their hair was neatly styled and traces of rouge darkened their mouths. Olivia had noticed her aunt's raised eyebrows and heard her sniff when the woman noticed her younger sisters coming down the stairs dolled up. They might still be young but Olivia reckoned they were women now and had earned their freedoms.

Sybil and Ruby were also walking ahead. Sybil had kept hold of the sherry bottle and suddenly her daughter relieved her of it. Ruby pulled the cork and took a swig, and the two women, already quite tipsy, started to roar with laughter as they took turns emptying the bottle.

Olivia closed the door on them. The rooms felt warm, inviting, and the embers dying in the parlour grate cast shifting shadows. She stood on the threshold then walked towards the mantelpiece, feeling the heat from the coal fire against her legs. She picked up the photograph of Joe, handsome in his uniform, and kissed his face before putting it down.

She'd not worn the silver locket she'd given him as a good luck charm. From the moment Lucas had returned it to her and told her Joe had died, it had stayed in a drawer. But that morning, on the cusp of a new year, she had re-read Joe's last letter, urging her to marry Lucas, and then taken the locket and fastened it about her neck. She put her fingers to the bump beneath her bodice, feeling its heart-shape.

She stooped and put another shovel of coal on the fire to keep the place warm for when they returned from Matilda's in a few hours' time. New flames flared, casting a golden glow on Joe's face.

'It's time for me to go now, Joe,' Olivia said softly. 'I know you don't mind. But I won't ever forget you and, as soon as I can, I'm gonna visit you in France and bring you flowers.'

Epilogue

Cemetery in Walthamstow, early-January 1916

It was cold and still snowing. The flakes were falling thicker than they had done an hour ago when the vicar had carried out a baptism then seen the family off into a white flurry. He pressed his hat down on his head, locked the church door behind him and set off. He was keen to get home before it settled and made the pathways treacherous. He hurried past the graveyard, barely glancing at the sombre grey stones. Something odd caught his eye and he slowed down then retraced his steps, frowning. He could understand the wall collapsing. It had been in danger of doing so for a good while. Every winter Jack Frost slid his fingers further into the mortar, loosening it. But the rubble had been cleared into a neat pile and there was no barrier now between the church-yard and the burials on unconsecrated ground alongside. Stranger still was the fact that somebody had made use of the fallen flint to mark the suicide's grave with a stone cross.

He knew this wasn't Freddie Weedon's sister's doing. Her neighbours had told him she was still abroad on nursing service, and she'd no other family who might have visited over the holiday. Perhaps a Good Samaritan had passed by and tidied things up.

The vicar frowned, brushing snow from his shoulders. He was in two minds whether to call a mason in tomorrow to rebuild the wall. But the church fund had been depleted after the stolen lead had been replaced on the roof. He wasn't sure he could meet another expense just yet. Besides, with the war dragging on, extra cemetery space was useful. The wall would probably have had to come down quite soon to make more room.

Hunching deeper into his coat, he hurried on towards the vicarage.

Wimereux Cemetery, mid-January 1916

Last time she'd come and climbed this hill she'd been with Rose. Today Olivia walked up to the cemetery alone. Rose had sent her a nice letter telling her she'd been granted leave until the end of the month but as soon as she got back to France they should get together and catch up with all their news. Olivia had also had a note from Hilda, sent from Turkey, telling her that she'd little to report. She'd had a dicky tummy all over Christmas and had spent the holiday in bed.

Olivia lifted the posy she carried, inhaling the delicate freshness of snowdrops. She had gathered them in the wood behind the hospital and put a few wisps of ivy in amongst the tiny flowers. She had a grave to visit. Bertie Spencer had died while she'd been at home with her family. Pneumonia brought on by the gas attack had done for him, Matron had told her, and he'd gone rapidly downhill. Though they'd barely known one another, Olivia had wanted to come and pay her last respects to Bertie. She'd liked him and had been tearful when told he hadn't made it.

She passed through the cemetery portal and walked along the path in the direction of the newest graves. She hesitated and peered down the serried rows. The cold January air was almost opaque but somebody was ahead of her and she'd recognise that tall broad frame anywhere.

'Lucas?' she called hesitantly.

He spun about immediately, frowning, then strode towards her.

'Olivia? What are you doing out on a day like this?' He drew her close, instinctively protecting her with his body from the icy white mist.

'Could ask you the same thing,' she said, smiling up at him. She felt joyous to see him so unexpectedly. Although it would have been nice if the meeting had taken place in more cheerful surroundings.

'Just brought these to put down.' She held up the flowers. 'A patient passed away while I was home on leave. I liked him very much.' She glanced at the new wooden crosses, so many added since last time she'd visited. 'He was a war reporter. I met him on the day I travelled out here, months ago. I was seasick and he helped me get over it. I felt fine on the voyage home.' She paused, feeling the weight of Lucas's stare on her. 'Did you manage to get leave for Christmas?'

'I went home just before New Year. Only had a week. It was enough,' he said dryly.

'How are your lot?' Olivia asked.

'No different.' He grunted a laugh. 'That's not quite true. I'm going to have a sister-in-law soon, and become an uncle.'

Olivia stiffened, wondering how to reply to this. She knew he was referring to his brother Henry and Caroline Venner getting married. The child was officially to be his brother's then. But she curbed her instinct to probe and said quietly, 'Are you pleased about that?'

'Very. I congratulated them on their engagement. I think they thought I was being sarcastic. I wasn't. I meant every word. I hope they'll be happy. Whether they will remains to be seen.'

'And you? Are you happy, Lucas?'

'I could be, quite easily.' He gazed at her mouth then lifted his eyes and gave that ironic half-smile of his. 'Time will tell.' He abruptly changed the subject. 'How was your Christmas?'

'Oh, lovely,' she exclaimed. 'The kids were all well, and adored their presents. And I ate and drank far too much. Matilda . . . ' She interrupted herself to say, 'Do you remember the Keivers?'

At his nod she continued, 'Well, they do love to have a party and it felt as though I danced my legs off and sang my lungs out twice in their front room. On Christmas Eve then again on New Year's Eve we all had rather a boozy time . . . ' She fell quiet, aware of his silence. 'Sorry, went on a bit, didn't I?'

'No, don't stop. I like to listen to you talk about it.'

'The only thing is, I would have liked to see my friend Cath. But she was away in Kent, so my cousin Ruby told me.' Olivia smiled. 'I hope it all goes well for her. Being as you were her old boss, I'll let you know when I find out if it's a boy or a girl, and that mother and baby are doing fine.' She showed him her crossed fingers. 'Other than that, I would have liked to visit Freddie's resting place. But time ran out. Hilda's just been posted to the Dardanelles so couldn't visit him herself. It would've been nice to have gone there for her and taken a Christmas posy. So I feel rather bad about that.'

'There's no need to feel bad. Somebody did go,' Lucas said.

'You?' Olivia beamed at him as he nodded.

'You can write and tell Freddie's sister that all's well in Walthamstow.'

'I will let Hilda know. I'm sure she'll be very pleased.'

They gazed at one another through the thick air. 'Why are you here, Lucas?' she asked suddenly. 'Are *you* visiting somebody in particular?'

He murmured an affirmative, thrusting his hands into his pockets. 'One of my lads got caught by sniper fire while I was on leave,' he said huskily. 'I was going to come and tell you about it. When the holiday was all done with and things back to normal.'

It took Olivia a while to cotton on. Recent conversations with Maggie played over in her mind. 'Who is it?' she whispered. Although she already knew.

Lucas took her hand and led her to the spot where he'd been standing when she'd happened upon him. 'Private Wicks was buried yesterday. He left a letter for your sister. It'll be sent on to her. He told me they were going to get married.'

Olivia's fingers had sprung up to cover her horrified gasp. From between her gloved hands she keened, 'Maggie said at Christmas that she'd accepted him. She thought they were too young to marry straight away. She was so looking forward to him coming home in a few weeks.'

Olivia thought of the French blouse that Maggie was saving to put on for Ricky, and the sapphire ring she had chosen for herself. Her heartbroken sister would probably never wear either. The ring would stay in the shop and the blouse in a drawer. Sobs threatened to stifle Olivia and she clasped her arms about Lucas's waist, seeking comfort from him in the way she always did. 'Oh, when will it ever end?'

'Not for a while yet, I'm afraid,' he said, tenderly smoothing back her hair with his fingers. 'The platoon's being moved. We go to Vimy next week. God knows what's about to happen there. More of the same, I expect.' He briefly fell silent. 'I'm so sorry, Olivia, that you found out about the lad like this. Will you tell your sister or leave it to go through official channels?'

'I'll write to her this evening,' she replied croakily. 'Oh, I wish I could be at home with her to comfort her.' She shook her head. 'They'll all be affected. Nancy and Alfie too.'

'I know . . . but they'll understand why you can't be there. They know you're thinking about them. Maggie will be all right, eventually.'

Olivia nodded, drying her eyes. He was right. Maggie was strong. They all were, and perhaps they had their father's harsh influence to thank for that. They'd survive and go on, just as the dry-eyed widow they'd seen with her children on Christmas Day would go on. She turned in Lucas's embrace so that her back rested against him for a moment. Breaking apart her snowdrop posy, she crouched down and put some stems on Private Richard Wicks's grave. She placed the others where a cross bore the name Bertram Spencer.

Walking back to Lucas, she said, 'You promised to show me where Joe is.'

'And I will.'

'When will that be, I wonder?' she murmured.

'Now? I've got the rest of the day off. We can be there by dusk. I'll get you back to the hospital by midnight.'

'Like Cinderella.' Olivia smiled. 'You would too, wouldn't you, Lucas?'

'Yes.'

'Thank you, you've never let me down, have you? If you promise something, you do it.'

'That won't change,' he said quietly. 'Even if something happens to me I'll watch over you. But some promises I can't make just yet.' He reached for her hands, drawing her closer. 'There are things I need to get straight in my head about myself and my parents ... my Romany mother in particular. I'm going to try and find her, accept that part of who I am. I don't want my problems to break us apart. What I feel for you is too precious to lose.'

'I know ... and I won't ask you for promises because what I feel for you is precious too.' She smiled. 'I'm glad you've decided to find your mum, Lucas. She'll be proud of you.'

'Are you proud of me, Livvie?'

'Of course I am ...' About to add that she loved him, something ... perhaps a memory of past jealousies, or the sorrow at the back of her mind over Maggie having lost Ricky, caused a lump in her throat and she turned aside with glistening eyes.

'Do you want to go to Joe?' he asked abruptly.

'I can't. I'm on shift at teatime. It doesn't matter for now anyway. I've promised him I'll take him flowers. There are so few to be had at this time of year.' She peered into the mist swirling over the graves. 'Will you write to me with your new posting, when you get there?'

'Yes.'

'I'll always write back.'

'I know you will, Livvie. Ready? I'll give you a lift to St Omer. I've parked just down the lane.'

With a last fleeting glance back at the graves, she took his arm and said, 'Come on then. We've both still got work to do.'

Keep reading for a sneak peek
at the next novel in the
Bittersweet Legacy series, *The Way Home*

Chapter One

Wood Green, North London, Summer 1916

'Mum would really appreciate you coming back from France especially for her funeral, you know.'

Olivia Bone knew nothing of the sort. It wasn't as though she and the deceased had got on. But as the woman had been her aunt, and also her father's dirty little secret, Olivia had felt that she owed Sybil Wright something. During his lifetime Tommy Bone had shown his lover little respect, and for that alone his eldest daughter believed there was a final debt to be paid.

Once their astonishing deceit had finally come to light, Olivia had thought she hated her father. That was before she joined the Voluntary Aid Detachment. As a junior nurse serving in a military hospital on the Western Front, she had seen things that had given her better reasons to rail at life's vile injustices.

Olivia's mother Aggie Bone had never known about her husband's cheating. She had died in her prime, giving birth to her only son. Thereafter, Tommy had carried on sneaking about with his wife's sister even though he was free to marry.

Now the adulterers were dead too, Olivia sincerely wished them both peace. Her mother had had the last laugh, after all. Aggie had been of a beautifully sunny disposition, popular with all. Her guilt-ridden husband had sunk into bitterness after she'd passed away and had eventually met with a violent end. As for Sybil, she might have managed to seduce her brother-in-law but she had never captured Tommy Bone's heart. He'd loved his wife until the day he was murdered.

Olivia's pensive mood was cut short by her cousin Ruby shaking a plate of fishpaste sandwiches beneath her nose. To be polite Olivia took one although the smell of bloater was making her feel queasy.

It was a stifling hot summer day and the windows and curtains had been closed in the small terraced house in Wood Green. The wake had been hastily arranged after Olivia had agreed to stump up the cost of a modest do. Ruby might have been the deceased's daughter but she'd baulked at the idea of laying out for a few plates of food to give her own mother a send-off. She had reminded her cousin Olivia – as she often resentfully did – that as the best off amongst them, she could afford to pay for things like funeral teas. Olivia knew she'd been fortunate to inherit her fiancé's house after he'd perished at Ypres. Nevertheless, she would far sooner have had her beloved Joe safe at home and was growing fed up of being put upon financially by family members.

Olivia was itching to leave the wake, or at least escape into the garden for a breath of air. After another ten minutes or so she and her brother and sisters would have stayed for a decent enough time and could catch the bus back to Islington where they all lived.

As Ruby wandered off to thrust the plate of sandwiches under other noses, Olivia's younger sister sidled up to her to hiss, 'Bleedin' stinks in here!' Maggie wrinkled her nose in distaste. 'Let's go home, Livvie.'

'In a little while.' She gave Maggie a sympathetic smile. 'Coming out the back for a breather?' she suggested, glancing about for somewhere to dispose of her half-eaten sandwich. She finally decided to take it with her and feed it to the sparrows in the garden.

'So what did the inquest make of your aunt's sudden passing, love?'

Before the girls had made it out of the parlour they were brought to a halt by a neighbour's question. Mrs Cook was clutching a cup and saucer in one hand and Olivia's elbow in the other. She inclined her head expectantly, hoping to hear some juicy gossip. All she got was a couple of neutral smiles, so she tried a different tack. 'Such a shock it was to hear what happened to the poor cow.' Ethel sucked her teeth. 'She looked right as rain just the week before when I bumped into her up the road . . . '

'It was her nerves made her giddy. Me mum suffered something chronic with 'em,' Ruby rudely butted in, making Ethel jut her chin defensively. 'She must've fainted and hit her head. Doctor said so.' Ruby pursed her lips as her next-door neighbour stalked off with an affronted sniff. 'Nosy old bag. Anybody asks what happened to me mum, just say she come over funny and fell off a chair while cleaning the pitcher rail.'

Olivia and Maggie exchanged a glance, murmuring agreement to the yarn. The family, and no doubt the neighbours too, knew that Sybil Wright had never bothered keeping anything clean, even herself. Their aunt had been a slattern and a drunkard; the parlour of her home held an unpleasant odour of ground-in dirt and stale alcohol. She'd had her accident after she'd been drinking. She *had* tumbled off a chair, fracturing her skull on the hearth. But it had happened while she'd been reaching for another bottle of gin, stashed on top of the wardrobe. The sisters understood that Ruby didn't want that broadcast. Neither did they. Family stuck together even if it meant bending the truth. Olivia pitied her young cousin Mickey; he had found his mother lying dead on the floor when he came in from school that day. The kitty kept in the jar on the shelf had been missing, but Sybil had been known to raid the rent money for booze. A full bottle of gin had been found smashed on the floor beside her. Ruby had bleakly joked that the sight of that going to waste would have given her mother a heart attack even had she survived the fall.

A pretty young woman had entered the parlour and was craning her neck to catch Ruby's eye. 'Connie Whitton's turned up after all. She told me she couldn't make it.' Ruby waved at the newcomer. 'Offer these around, will you, Livvie?' The sandwich plate was shoved at her cousin. 'They're already curling.' Ruby glanced at her neighbours, grouped together on the sofa. 'If you and Maggie could just lend a hand collecting up the used crockery and doing the washing up, that'd be a help.' Ruby sidled away to speak to her friend.

'Yes, sir, no, sir, three bloody bags full, sir,' Maggie muttered sourly, watching the two peroxide blondes nattering together.

'Come on, we did say we'd help out. Sooner it's done, the sooner we can head home.' Olivia passed the plate of sandwiches to her sister. 'Nancy can pitch in too.' She beckoned the youngest Bone girl with a jerk of her head. Nancy stopped staring morosely into her empty tea cup and got to her feet.

'Alfie's in the street kicking a ball up against the alley wall with Cousin Mickey,' she answered Olivia's question about their younger brother's whereabouts.

Alfie got on well with Mickey. The boys were both nearly ten years old and enjoyed a game of football. Just then Olivia's attention was diverted to a quiet commotion on the other side of the room. Ruby and Connie appeared to be bickering; a moment later they disappeared into the corridor as though to keep their differences private.

'You'll never guess what, Livvie?' Ruby had come up behind Olivia as she was flicking washing-up water off her fingers.

'What?' She turned about, drying her hands on a towel. She'd been expecting to hear something unfavourable after witnessing that scene but was nonetheless surprised to see her cousin's pallor. 'What is it?' she asked quickly. 'I saw you having words with Connie.'

'She's brought me dad with her. He turned up looking for us in the Bunk 'cos he thought we still lived there. He's waiting outside.'

Olivia was speechless. Edward Wright had disappeared a decade ago following a huge bust up when he discovered his wife and Tommy Bone were having an affair. Sybil and her kids had then moved into a slum in Islington known as the Bunk. 'Your *dad*?' Olivia exclaimed in an astonished squeak.

'He's outside by the gate. Ain't seen him in so long that I'd forgot I had one. Mickey was still in his pram when Dad run out on us. Perhaps I should just ignore him. 'S'pect he'll go away.' Ruby was keeping her voice low, shooting glances here and there to detect any eavesdroppers.

'Don't think he will.' Olivia gave a discreet nod of her head. But for Ruby giving her a clue to the stranger's identity, she would never have recognised the grey-haired individual who had just appeared in the doorway. She remembered her uncle Ed as a mild-mannered man with fair colouring; now he looked careworn and close to seventy. He wasn't that old. Her aunt had died at the age of fifty-one, just a couple of years younger than her ex-husband.

'Gawd's sake!' Ruby exclaimed under her breath. 'Why couldn't he wait outside? This'll start the old biddies off.' She looked flustered. 'What if he starts asking awkward questions about Mum and Tommy ... and us?'

'Well, you'd better go and say hello. He was Sybil's husband, after all. He must've found out about her funeral and come to pay his respects.'

'They never got divorced neither. Mum told me that. But we don't know him anymore ... '

'Reckon it's time to put that right,' Ed said gruffly. He'd come up unobserved behind Ruby, making her jump. 'It's been a long time, love. Too long. Wish now I'd mended bridges sooner instead of waiting until this sad day.'

'Too much water gone under this particular bridge.' Ruby wriggled her fingers free from his clasp. 'Mum could've done with some help while she was still alive. She might not have ended up in such a bleedin' state if we hadn't had to doss down in a slum.'

Ed flushed at the rebuff. 'You're still a lovely-lookin' lass,' he gamely persevered. 'How's little Mickey? Not so little now, I'll bet.'

'You've probably just walked straight past him in the

street. So that says it all really, don't it?' Ruby snapped. 'You don't know us and we've nothing to say to you. So go away and leave us alone.'

'Aw . . . don't be like that, love. When I heard about Sybil's accident I wept me heart out.' Ed shook his head. 'Not saying I didn't hate her at one time fer what she did to me, but I kept me distance and let her live her life as she wanted. Didn't interfere even though I've not been that far away.' He glanced at his eldest niece who'd been quietly listening to the exchange. 'How's your lot, Olivia? I heard that Tommy had passed on. Not going to be a hypocrite and say I was sorry. He and me wife between 'em ruined my life. Nobody deserves to go the way he did, though.' He paused. 'Ever find his murderer, did they?'

Olivia shook her head, giving her uncle a small smile. She respected his honesty and couldn't blame him for the way he felt. Only a saint would easily forgive and forget being made to look a fool by the people closest to him. In a way Olivia was glad her mother was no longer around and had been saved the humiliation this man had suffered.

'So where've you been then?' Ruby was incensed that they'd been struggling to keep a roof over their heads in the worst street in North London when this man could've pitched in and helped.

'I found a place over Edmonton way. I picked up with a widow and we're happy enough.'

'Oh, good fer you,' Ruby said sarcastically. 'So what's brought you back here then? Me mum didn't have two ha'pennies. If you've turned up hoping fer a pay-out as her next-of-kin, you can forget it.'

Olivia cautioned her cousin with a frown. Ruby was so

het up that she'd let her voice rise and hadn't noticed that her neighbours were taking an interest.

'Shut up now till we're on our own.' Ruby gave Ed a fierce glare. 'I'll get rid of this lot.' She made a pecking movement with fingers and thumb, mimicking gossips at work, then began grabbing cups and plates out of her neighbours' hands, receiving some indignant tuts. 'Thanks for coming, but I'm clearing up now.'

'We'll be off too and let you have a private talk,' Olivia said. Her sisters had returned from the backyard where they'd shared a crafty cigarette. They remained loitering by the door, uncertain what was going on but sensing a bad atmosphere. Olivia could remember her uncle but he was a stranger to Maggie and Nancy. They'd been toddlers when he disappeared, and her brother had been a new-born baby.

Once the parlour had emptied, but for family, Ruby blurted, 'I want you lot to stay.' She grabbed Olivia's arm. 'After all, I ain't *really* any more his daughter than you are. We both know Tommy Bone fathered the lot of us. And if Ed don't already know that, then it's time he did.'

For a long, embarrassing moment there was a leaden silence in the room. Then Ed laughed ... a shrill sound of disbelief. 'Who told you that nonsense?' He shook his head. 'Sounds like the sort of claptrap Sybil would come out with when she'd had a few. She liked to be the centre of attention. *I'm* yer dad, dear.'

'You're not. And neither is Mickey yours.'

''Course he is!' Ed looked to be getting narked now. 'The boy's got a bad foot. Wish he didn't, of course, but ... ' He shrugged. 'Me father's to blame fer that. He was afflicted 'n' all. He died quite young ... in the Boer War. He might've been a cripple but he didn't let it hold him back, God rest 'im.'

'You'd say anything, wouldn't yer, to get round me? Well, it won't work.' At first Ruby had been shocked, as they all had, when her mother had announced that Tommy Bone had fathered the lot of them. The girl had got used to the idea now, though, and liked being half-sisters with Tommy's daughters. She didn't want this man coming back into her life, stirring things up. Yet what he'd said about his father having a crippled foot was making her wonder. He'd not had time to make it up; it had come straight off the cuff.

Maggie and Nancy were rudely elbowed aside on the threshold as a broad-set, dark-haired fellow barged into the room. 'Who's dis now?' he slurred while swaying on his feet and glowering at Ed Wright. Riley McGoogan was Ruby's boyfriend. She'd banned him from her mother's funeral on two counts. Sybil couldn't abide him, and he used a wake ... or any gathering ... as an excuse for a booze-up. And when drunk, he was keen to pick a fight.

'Clear off and sober up. I told you to stay away.' Ruby turned her back on him.

'I stayed away, so I did, until I saw de old gels leavin' ...'

'Well, you're still too bleedin' early showin' yer face,' Ruby replied through gritted teeth. 'So piss off fer a bit longer.'

'If this fellow is upsetting you, dear, I'll get rid of him.' Ed was keen to show his protective, paternal side to win her over.

Riley was nice-looking, and when sober a fairly pleasant individual. But today he was neither of those things. His hair and clothes looked dirty and dishevelled as though he'd already been in a scrap. He looked to be spoiling for another as he turned a sneering look on Ed. 'No, I'll get rid of *you*.' He pointed a finger. 'Through that fookin' window!'

Olivia hastily steered her uncle towards the door. 'He's

Ruby's boyfriend,' she informed Ed in a murmur, escorting him into the corridor.

'We're off. We'll wait for you by the bus stop.' Maggie glanced nervously past them at the wild-eyed Irish fellow in the room beyond, swinging his arms about while arguing with Ruby.

'You'd best get going too, Uncle Ed. There's no reasoning with Riley when he's under the influence. Perhaps come back and see Ruby another time when things aren't so ... sensitive.' She gave him a sympathetic look.

'I didn't want nuthin' of Sybil's,' he protested. 'That ain't why I come. Tell Ruby that, will you? Just thought ... oh, it don't matter.' He sighed. 'Made a mistake coming today of all days. But I do want to make it up with me kids if I can. Sybil turned 'em against me. But now she's gone, there's a chance for us to muddle along.' He shook his head. 'They *are* my kids. Why me wife would tell such a wicked lie about it is beyond me.'

Olivia reckoned she knew why. It had been Sybil's greatest wish to get Tommy Bone to marry her. Perhaps she thought she'd hit upon a way to do it by telling him he'd fathered her kids. Tommy probably hadn't got a clue if he was responsible or not. All of them were blonde and had similar looks. Whatever the truth of it, Ruby had told her something earlier that she hadn't known. Ed Wright and Sybil had never divorced, so there could have been no legal union between her father and aunt. If Sybil had lied to Tommy about being divorced, perhaps she'd lied to him about other things too.

'What did Tommy say about it all?' Ed was like a dog with a bone, worrying at it. 'Did he claim he'd fathered 'em?'

'Dad would never talk about it,' she answered truthfully.

'They set up home together, so I heard. Tommy passed on not long after, didn't he?' Still Ed chipped away.

'They lived here, in our old house.' Olivia glanced back at her childhood home. Once upon a time the place had held happy recollections of when her mum had been alive, and the rooms had been bright and clean and full of love and hope. Those memories had withered now and for Olivia it was just like any other building in the street. Nothing special. Her home now … the place where she felt content … was in Islington. The property her soldier fiancé had left to her in his will.

'If I'd found out she'd been spreading such lies, I'd've been back sooner.' Ed sounded quite emotional. 'Made a laughing stock of me twice over. Cheating on me then telling everybody I couldn't father me own kids!'

'It wasn't like that.' Olivia patted his arm. 'None of us knew until quite recently. There was a big upheaval in the family when I met my fiancé and left home. It just came tumbling out then. Only us kids were told, though.' The scandal *had* leaked out more generally, in fact, but Olivia thought it best to play that down to save her uncle's feelings.

'So you're getting married, are you?' Ed managed a smile. 'He's a lucky man. You always was a lovely kid. Pretty as a pitcher. Just like yer mum.' He gave a rueful chuckle. 'I liked Aggie, y'know. Bet Tommy never knew that. But Sybil did. I told her it'd be a good thing if she could act a bit more like her sister. Your mum was a proper lady.'

'I still miss her something terrible,' Olivia said wistfully. 'But I'm not getting married. My fiancé died at Ypres.'

Ed gave her a clumsy hug. 'Dreadful the way the war's dragging on. I've volunteered part-time for the Home Front.

We've all got to show willing and I can fit it in between me work shifts.'

'I'm a VAD, serving in a French hospital . . . ' The rest of what Olivia had been about to say was drowned out. The argument that had been rumbling inside the house broke out in earnest. The sound of missiles being thrown could be heard. Riley burst out of the door and stomped off, swearing, having given Ed an evil-eyed stare on passing.

'He don't seem the sort any man would want his daughter involved with.' Ed grimaced. 'I know I've got no right to tell Ruby how to live her life though. She's a grown woman.' He glanced along the street to where his son was playing football. 'Glad to see the boy's not too down about losing his mother. Life goes on, don't it?' Ed sighed 'I'd best be off. You take care of yerself, Olivia.'

'You too.' Olivia looked at Mickey. He might seem as though he'd bucked up quickly but Ruby had told her he'd howled like a banshee for days after finding his mother dead. It must have been a dreadful scene for the poor lad to come home to. Yet when Sybil had been alive he'd had to be quite independent. His mother had been flaked out on her bed a good deal of the time, nursing her 'nerves' and her gin bottle. Olivia turned back to the house, knowing she should say goodbye to Ruby before escaping home to some peace and quiet.

Ed kept a careful distance behind Riley's lumbering figure. He came abreast of the boys playing football and stopped for a moment to watch them. He stepped off the kerb as though to talk to Mickey but then seemed to change his mind. He continued up the road and his son hobbled after the football his cousin had just booted past him. The crippled lad was oblivious to the fact that his father was close by, peering over his shoulder at him.

Ed was unaware that he, in turn, was being observed. The watchful man rolled himself a smoke while keeping a crafty eye out. But as the football bounced close to the hedge behind which he'd stationed himself, he pulled the brim of his cap low over his long, lank hair and quickly disappeared along the alley.

Do you love historical fiction?

Want the chance to hear news about your favourite authors (and the chance to win free books)?

Mary Balogh
Lenora Bell
Charlotte Betts
Jessica Blair
Frances Brody
Grace Burrowes
Gaelen Foley
Pamela Hart
Elizabeth Hoyt
Eloisa James
Lisa Kleypas
Stephanie Laurens
Sarah MacLean
Amanda Quick
Julia Quinn

Then visit the Piatkus website
www.piatkusentice.co.uk

And follow us on Facebook and Twitter
www.facebook.com/piatkusfiction | @piatkusentice

piatkus